100 Days From Home

anthony hartig

for

My mother and father for giving me life

My wife for teaching me how to live it

My daughter for giving it deeper meaning

100 Days From Home

CONTENTS

100 Days From Home
BOOK ONE
Hard Rain

FORWARD

You know who I am. I'm what you wake up to in the morning and often think about before you slip into your slumber at night. I am the story. I'm the scandals and the homicides; I'm the injustices to the poor and the vanities of the rich. I'm the rapist slinking into the night and the beaten victim huddled in the shadows. I'm the student riots, the jilted bride, and the kidnapped child.

The techs and the tradesmen read me on the way to work and on their coffee breaks. Diplomats read me over their breakfasts and the police check on me to see if I got the facts straight. Politicians seek to manipulate me for influence but are wary when I'm around because I find the dirt. I expose their secrets.

I'm the wet garbage that covers the homeless dead in the alley and the sparkle in the eyes of lovers embracing under the stars. I'm the sweaty-palm exchange between the corner crunch dust dealer and the young lawyer with a hand full of cash.

I make you gasp and laugh. I'm the corporate greed, the fallen priest staggering out of the strip club, and the celebrity's body found hanging in the hotel closet. I'm the shotgun found next to the housewife's body and the bleached bones exposed by the tide.

I make you think and I anger you; I frighten you but still you come to me for more because you think I also offer hope in these times of trouble. I bring you the war and the assasinations; the wonders of our universe, and the toil of deep space colonists and miners.

The military high command regards me suspicion--that I may tell too much, and the soldiers often hate me because I don't tell enough. But I'm there. I tell of the heroes and the cowards, the sacrifice and the glory.

I'm everything you love and everything you hate. I'm the night before and the morning after. You know who I am. I am the story.

DEFIANCE

Thick vines had slowly covered the rich soil through the years and crept up the walls of the concrete guard towers and bunkers. The tarmac for what was once the airfield was close to being completely obscured by a blanket of blue-green moss and the twisted roots of shrubs as the forest made its slow heavy advance into the fort. Most of the structures like the med-facility and mess hall had been disassembled, but the miles of razor wire and the electrified fence that stretched the perimeter remained silhouettes against the orange hue of twilight. It was just a matter of time before nature reclaimed everything that was hers and any trace of human occupation would vanish into the green landscape.

There was a time when this massive outpost supported the lives of thousands with its missile and gun emplacements and the air crackled with the tin voices of patrols calling in for fire support. The earth trembled with the salvos of outgoing rounds and the ground was always in motion. There were troops in full body armor that hustled awkwardly into gunships; great armored dragonflies that shot up into the wind and turned on a dime. Guard duty was posted for the night as soldiers took to the lines behind sandbags with mini-guns mounted on tripods. Whispering to each other in trembled voices, wide-eyed, and anxiously bitten lips as they stared out beyond the fenceline into the woods. Patrols floated through the forest like spirits back then, sweeping the ground in the shadows and setting up ambushes for the enemy that was doing the same to them.

Medevac's came and went with the wounded. Always the wounded, never a shortage of the suffering as the medtechs ran back and forth in the rain administering painkillers and screaming the word "Stat!" as they slipped through the mud from trooper to trooper. The body bags and their sorrowful contents that lay quietly in rows at the edge of the strip waiting for the next transport jet back to New Sierra. The dull patter of rain drumming down on them and forming puddles as soldiers walked by pretending not to see them. The troops believed the dead to be taboo and wanted nothing more than to avoid the black magic that took their lives from them.

That was a long time ago, now the remnants of the outpost stood darkly in the center of the tiny peeps and chirps of amphibians and insects. Memories drifting in and out of the mind with the images and voices of *the past. I could never forget about this place anyway, not a day passes when its vision doesn't needle its way into my thoughts. Triggered by some conversation with a colleague or some insignificant detail that I saw. It's always there and always will be. The Q will never leave me alone...*

Q 1

"Blood alone moves the wheels of history."

Benito Mussolini (1883-1945), 20th Century dictator

December 16, 2406

A heavy rain the night before I made planetfall had turned the ground into a grayish-red slush that made walking difficult. The mud was impossible and I seemed to sink deeper with every step. There was a chill in the air and I could see my breath as I struggled through the mire and light fog that covered the ground. I kept my gaze down and tried to look inconspicuous as I moved shoulder-to-shoulder through the loose groups of soldiers at the landing zone. They looked wasted and no one talked as I worked my way through the smell of body odor and spent exhaust fumes from the Dropships. The troops of 1st Division stood around and milled mindlessly in their ponchos and chain-smoked as they watched the Medics tend to the wounded. Even the wounded seemed too weary to do anything more than lie there and groan. They didn't scream and there was no hysterics; they were just too exhausted, too damaged, and too doped on painkillers. Wasted.

I eventually made my way to an area where a surreal silence seemed to hang frozen in the air as body bags covered in alien mud were loaded into gunships bound for New Sierra. There, a Chaplain holding a thrashed Bible quietly moved to each body giving last rites and making the sign of the cross over them. It was still drizzling, and I had just missed the largest battle in 1st Division's history, one that started as a skirmish when patrols clashed with tribal mercs and quickly escalated into a full-scale siege that ripped open the overcast skies covering the Pegasus Mountains.

Having just arrived to Q-781 late that afternoon, I had become self-conscious of my new body armor. No mileage to them, unlike the shredded gear the soldiers around me wore; caked in mud and grime, and I found it hard to make eye contact with any of them. Last night when I was still on the Normandy I was given these BDU's and armor by the Quarter Master and he shook his head as he slid them across the counter and said, "Good luck. It was nice knowing you when you still had balls." I smiled back not knowing what he meant and sheepishly took them back to my billet, and with no one around to see, I suited-up and looked at myself in the mirror. Striking poses and making warrior faces in an effort to look like a badass. Now in the presence of real troops, I felt embarrassed by my juvenile behavior, but it was my dirty little secret that only I would regret.

"There you are, Mr. Frye. I was wondering where you wandered off to." Sergeant Volman approached me as he removed his tactical helmet. "What a fucked-up place." He frowned as he took in the scene. The sergeant was with the Press Corps. and was assigned to be my "advisor" until I made it to the ground and hooked-up with my first unit, then I would be someone else's problem.

"I just talked to a Captain and he was able to point me toward the stand-down area for Recon. They're over here, follow me." He nodded as we began to walk through the soldiers again.

"This is your last chance, Mr. Frye," The sergeant said grimly, "you can still come back with me to the Normandy."

"I appreciate the offer Sergeant," I muttered, "but I've already come this far."

"I understand." The sergeant nodded. "Well, you'll be going to Defiance first. The guys I'm taking you to have been at the Q for a while. They'll take you as far as the fort. They're a Spec Ops team so your security clearances will allow you to tag along to a certain point, but I think you'll be on your own from there. Don't worry, you'll be in good hands tonight, Sir."

We stopped at a smaller clearing and I could see four men tightly gathered among the splintered trees and smoldering vegetation. "This is as far as I go, Mr. Frye." The sergeant said in a softer tone as he turned his gaze at the soldiers.

"Thanks for all your help, Sergeant."

"No problem, Sir, and good luck."

I shook his hand and turned to walk toward the team. I slowed my pace as I got closer and overheard a hulking soldier talking in an angry tone to the rest of the men. "Predators and prey, it's just a matter of how ya look at it. And the way I see it, tonight when we go into the forest, we'll be the wolves and I'm gonna get me some payback. Nobody fucks with Scarecrow and lives to tell about it."

They called him Genie (how he had gotten that nickname was a mystery, and no one's ever had the courage to ask him), he was 6'-8" of muscle-mass and unshaven attitude. A giant of a man with dark hair and a ruddy complexion and the most seasoned member in the Recon squad. I would later learn that soldiers like Genie are referred to as major nocturnal reptiles—a Recon phrase for cold-blooded killers whose sole existence in the war was to kill for pleasure. Everyone in his team seemed uptight when Genie was upset, and after losing a man during an ambush last week, he was upset. Everyone fidgeted quietly and took shelter in the shadows in his presence.

Genie turned to look at me and I swear he was scowling. "There something I can help you with?" He said in a deep raspy voice as he threw an irritated glare at me.

"Good afternoon," I replied, my tone projecting more confidence than I felt, "my name's Jacob Frye. I'm with The Metro." I set my duffle bag down and offered my hand to the giant. A few awkward seconds passed as he looked me over. I felt like squirming but held my ground.

"You're the newsie?" Genie squinted as he reached out and shook my hand.

"Yes Sir."

"Hmm, I was told to keep my eyes out for ya but I didn't think you'd show."

"Well as you can see I made it down in one piece." By then the three other soldiers had stood up and surrounded me. They were all carrying weapons that I'd never seen before, and I'll have to admit I was a bit unnerved being the center of attention.

"You made planetfall from the Normandy?" Genie grinned.

"This afternoon with a Medivac Wing."

"Did ya vomit all over yourself?" A young looking trooper asked, and the others smiled with mild amusement.

"No, I guess I got lucky."

"Lucky's the word all right. Cherry drops usually involve lots of puking." The soldier chuckled. "May be you'll make up for it later by shitting yourself…"

"You know," Genie interrupted, "the press never comes out to the field anymore to poke around like they used to. No offense, newsman, but it's been kinda nice not having media-pukes ditty-bopping in my war. Fuckers were getting to be a pain in my ass." Genie stated gruffly. "I kill someone and sure as shit there's a newsie taking pics and another taking notes for a story." He shook his head. "Anyway, keep your gear together, Frye," Genie pointed at the soldier that was asking me about my planetfall, "and just hang with Jackson for a few minutes. We'll be heading to Defiance as soon as our hog gets here." Genie shouldered his rifle and walked away.

I picked up my bag and Jackson waved me over to where he sat. He looked like he didn't have a care in the world as he leaned back on a smashed log with his weapon on his lap and his hands on the back of his head.

"He seems pissed." I whispered to the soldier.

"Don't mind Genie," he sighed, "he's only in a bad mood when he's awake."

"I think I'll just stay out of his way."

"Good idea."

After a few minutes I began to relax as I talked with this young man. As we chatted, I found out that he was a twenty-two-year-old kid with a touch of hero-worship for Genie.

"I'm sorry, man, that son-of-a-bitch is wired too tight, he's out of his fuckin' head in firefights, dude, takes too many chances." Jackson glanced over his shoulder at Genie and lowered his voice. "But I'll be goddamned if he ever gets hurt. It's like he's got a steel umbrella or something." Jackson was trying to grow a mustache and was failing miserably. You could tell from his eyes that he'd grown old before his time even though he'd only been with the squad for a year and a half. It was amazing how much a man could age just by being here. He'd lost a lot over the last year. Friends mostly, and his innocence. The war had taken his youth, but there was still a trace of naiveté in his countenance—the pout of a little boy gone astray and you couldn't help but wish that there would always be someone around to take care of him.

"Hey Jackson, you little shit heel," Genie grunted as he walked by, "I want your ass to be in full body armor when we go in tonight ya hear me? Last thing I need to do is stuff what's left of you in one of those fuckin' sandwich bags."

"Yeah, yeah, Genie," Jackson replied sheepishly, "no sweat, man, its mind over matter...if you don't mind, it don't matter."

"Don't fuck with me freshman, remember what that toe-popper did to Martin last week? I swear, when that mine went off under him he looked like four guys running in different directions at the same time. Wear your fucking armor tonight, and that's an order."

Jackson chuckled and stared into the treeline hoping Genie didn't see his tears in the rapidly fading light.

Scarecrow 3-6 was one of many five-man recon teams assigned to 22nd Bravo Company, 1st Division to gather intelligence on the enemy. Deep insertion phantoms that crawled beyond the lines of sanity just to lie motionless in the mud waiting for a chance to trophy souls. Genie scared me. He caught me looking at him once and I felt the sweat bead up on my face and I turned away as quick as I could hoping he wouldn't say anything. Not too long after that happened I locked eyes with him for a split second, and what I saw scared me even more. His eyes were hollow like he had nothing left to give, but they told the same story Jackson's eyes told: loss, grief, and a terrible sense of alienation. Then I noticed that he was smiling. A frightening maniac grin like he knew a dreadful secret that can only be learned by going the distance. A distance that I could never cross.

"Hey Chief," Petersen called out to Genie, "bird's on its way, man."

"'bout time, I don't feel like getting pissed on again." Genie said impatiently as he looked at the heavy clouds, "On your feet, men, moving!"

The thunderheads turned the sky into midnight and brought down a stinging rain that instantly soaked through the poncho and armor and chilled me to the bone. We moved to the edge of the clearing and took a knee. Genie pulled out a small strobe light and tossed it into the clearing where it began to flash rhythmically. Less than a minute later the gunship that would carry us from a secured LZ to some distant outpost touched down and sprayed the troops with the sour brine of earth and gravel from the down-blast of it's turbo-fan engines.

"Ok rich kids, let's get lucky and take some heads!" Genie screamed as we got up and ran hunched-over to the ship. "Hurry up! Get your asses in there!" Genie barked. "You too Frye, what're you waitin' for, a written invitation?" Genie grabbed my arm and shoved me into the hull of the Mark-IV where Jackson, Seer, and Petersen were already strapping into the webbing. The gunner took one look at me and told Genie that if I puked in his cabin he was going to pull my lower lip over my head and turn me into a cabbage. When he turned around I saw that he had written "BE NICE OR I'LL KILL YOU" on the back of his helmet. That kind of bitter humor was common here at the Q along with hard edged expressions like "WARGASM", "God Fears Me", "Born to Lose", or "Life of Pain" written on tactical helmets and body armor. Some wrote nicknames: "Sandman", "Death-Dealer", and "Kilroy" (rumor had it that "The Shadow" himself was running around with Delta Company with the "Night Stalker").

"Better hang on to your ass, Genie," the gunner yelled above the din of the engines, "this storm promises some serious chop! Yo, Jeebs, don't want these ladies to be late for the dance. Lift-off!" The pilot gave a thumbs-up from the cockpit as the engines put out a high-pitched whine and the ship lurched into the wind and shot above the forest leaving 1st Division behind in it's wake.

Oh yeah, high speed air-mobility, clipping tree tops and hugging the terrain. The gunship dipping and rising with the wind barreling outside the open hatch. Adrenalin overdose. Engulfed by fear and helplessness, yet an almost sexual craving for it to never end, for the rush to be as infinite as night. Untouchable and vulnerable. Invincible but at the complete mercy of the void and the elements of the storm. I was strapped between Seer

15

and Jackson, and looking out the rear hatch, hypnotized by the swirling rain caught in the vortex of the ship's turbo-fans when I heard a faint snore and noticed that Genie had fallen asleep.

Seer, a sniper that transferred from Division 15, elbowed me and winked, "Shit, he does that all the time, one time he fell asleep during a firefight. I know Genie comes across as an asshole sometimes, but don't worry, he's really a prick. Seriously, Frye, when it comes to combat, there's nobody else I would want taking point. Genie has the boonie-vodoo and even the Q can't put the dam-dam on him. He's not meant to die here. That's why Scarecrow squad is oh so fucking bad!"

"HOOAH!" Petersen added, "We're the baddest motherfuckin' werewolves this side of human space. When Scarecrow walks into a bar, the drinks are flowin' and the women are knowin'. You'll see for yourself when we get to Defiance."

Petersen and Seer were a mystery to me, both came from wealthy families. Old money from Earth and products of good breeding from a blue-blooded society. They were good people, but what inspired them to go through the brutal training of the Aggressor Forces and endure the hardships of battle on a hostile planet so far from home was beyond me. Somehow I suspected their reasons were based on bravado and not patriotism. They were experts at what they did. The elite. The most efficient killers the force had to give to the war. A fury of skill and cunning. Ghosts that would vanish into the landscape only to reappear behind you with a hand over your mouth and a knife to your throat whispering that it was your time to meet your god.

Like most soldiers on 781, the war made the brothers of Scarecrow 3-6 believers in superstition and omens; and the recent death of one of their comrades brought not just the sorrow of losing a close friend that they loved, but the primitive fear that death doesn't judge; both cruel and merciful, death will always be the ultimate predator on the battlefield.

The gunship banked a hard right and merged over a huge clearing in the dense forest where the lights and tall, electrified walls of Ft. Defiance loomed below. We circled the LZ that was filled with gunships and transports. The tarmac was congested with ground, munitions, and flight crews along with hundreds of troops filing in columns into dropships preparing for an operation in some forgotten latitude of 781. We touched down in a fenced off area next to some bunkers surrounded by razor wire, away from all the activity.

There were only two other gunships on the pad, a little larger and more heavily armed. Razorbacks. I stumbled out of the Mark IV, legs numb and equilibrium toasted from the turbulent ride. The sobering rain slowly bringing back my balance.

The gunner laughed and shook his head. "Damn, Genie, where the hell'd you find this clown?"

"He followed me home from the movies." Genie sneered as he adjusted his gear.

"Well, at least you didn't hoark-up in my ship!" the gunner replied lightly.

"Better be cool to 'im Jonesey, he's a journalist lookin' for a story."

"No shit? Who're you with newsie?"

"The Metro sent me out." I croaked and then threw up.

"The Metro! Folks back home want to know about the Q, huh? Well if you're gonna follow Scarecrow into the war, all I can say is good fuckin' luck, it was nice knowin' ya!"

"Fuck-off, Jonesey!" Genie barked.

"I love ya too, Genie, we'll see ya around." The gunner grinned.

Jackson, Seer, and Petersen took me to a bunker called "the Hilton" while Genie went into the Command Post for a debriefing. The bunker was dimly lit and had a terminal funk in the air, but it was warm and dry and a good enough place to shake off the cold. There were other troopers lounging around drinking and smoking, eating and trading stories when we walked in.

"Well I'll be goddamned! Look who's here, Scarecrow 3-6, larger than life and ten times uglier! Hiya Seer, how ya been?" She was a lean athletic brunette from Division 9 with a Reaper patch on her left shoulder.

"What's going on Lorrie?" Seer replied.

"Same-same, bro. God you look like hammered dog shit, what part of hell are you guys comin' from?"

"Sixty klicks north of the 13th Parallel with 22nd Bravo."

"Ouch, that's a rough neighborhood, there's some bad mojo out there."

"Yeah, tell me about it. Lost Martin last week."

"Shit. I'm sorry, Seer. Who's carrying the letter?"

"Jackson. He's takin' it pretty hard."

"I'll bet, poor kid, those two were tight. Come on bud," Lorrie put a comforting arm around Seer's shoulder, "have a drink with us. Hey Jackson, you toilet trained yet?"

"No, I nearly pissed myself when I saw you, Lorrie. How's the sweetheart of Division 9?" Jackson winked.

"Spreading fear and taking names, I really miss you boneheads!" Lorrie beamed as she lit a cigarette.

"You've always been a sight for sore eyes Sergeant," Petersen smiled and held out his arms, "come here and gimme a hug ya widow-maker!"

"HOOAH! For you my life, Petersen! Here's a kiss too. Who's the new guy?"

"That's Frye," Seer said with a nod, "he's with The Metro. Here to observe and write stories about us."

"How ya doin' Frye, been on many ops?" Lorrie held out her hand and delivered a shockingly firm handshake.

"Nope, just made planetfall today."

"And Command put you with Scarecrow?"

"Well, the main office requested coverage on the Aggressor Forces as well as the Infantry on 781, a special interest story."

"Jeez, did they break it off in your ass by sending you out here! I hope they're paying you well. Welcome to the Q."

"Actually, I volunteered for the assignment. And you'd be surprised how little it pays."

"Volunteered?" Lorrie gasped, "You're crazy newsie, no wonder you're with Genie's squad. Have a drink, you look like you could use one, you look like shit."

Sergeant Lorrie Isa and her squad had gotten to Ft. Defiance the night before and spent the day drinking at the Hilton awaiting orders for their next operation. She was a battle-hardened woman with steel blue eyes and finely chiseled features. Very attractive with a quick wit and unsurpassed intelligence. I knew from the way she confidently carried herself that she was deadly at warfare. The Reaper patch and stripes on her shoulders proved that as a soldier she was unparalleled. Sergeant Isa and Seer had a special bond since they not only went through boot camp together, but also endured the self-sacrifice it took to make it through the grueling training program as Aggressor Snipers.

"So check it out," Lorrie bragged as she leaned across the table, "we're sluggin' through swamp three klicks east of the Eadios River trackin' a group of tribal mercs two nights ago when Dean here hears a noise in the trees. I signal for an arrow formation and to prep to charge. I figured we're about to spring an ambush and we're gonna go through 'em before they can flank us. We're cocked and ready to rock when something bounces off of Pelzer's head. All of a sudden there's all this movement and howling around us and the infra-reds are going crazy. We open up and start slagging shit left and right. Fucking screaming coming from everywhere! We charge forward and run right into the mercs, then this big asshole steps in front of me, only he's so surprised by how cute I am he didn't know what to do; so I pump a few rounds into him before he has time to thank me!" Lorrie stood up and got more animated as she told the story.

"Meanwhile, Dean's going hand-to-hand with two guys," She continued, "so I pull out the spike and lobotomize one of 'em when I shove it into his ear from behind. We go belly down to the mud and start returning fire. Fuckin' branches and leaves and shit flyin' everywhere! Three minutes and we cease-fire, I crawl ahead to recon and give the all clear. We do a body count, and that's twelve confirmed for Dragon squad. We got 'em all! So we fall back to the trees to get a count from the first contact. We're thinkin' that we must have greased a platoon from the amount of screaming we heard. We look around and there's all these dead swamp apes and parts of 'em everywhere. I guess one of 'em hit Pelzer with a bogg-nut and we wiped them out when the sensors went off!"

The members of the two squads laughed so hard that Pelzer and Jackson fell off their stools and knocked the drinks off the table; all that did was bring a standing ovation from the other troops in the bunker.

"Damn it, I can't bring you guys anywhere!" Lorrie laughed as she jumped back.

Just then, the door opened and Genie walked in followed by the Brigade Commander.

"ON YOUR FEET!" Genie barked. The laughing stopped as everyone stood up and snapped to attention.

"At ease, people!" The Commander scanned the room. "I came by to deliver your orders. As of tomorrow night, the six Recon squads here will spearhead for the 15th Division. "The Big Red One" will join you in four days. This will be a joint effort with Fleet, and you and 1st Division will be authorized to call in air strikes to clear a path for the 15th. You will depart by gunship tomorrow at 2300 hours and insertion is at 0300 hours. Your destination is Uluwatu Valley in the southern hemisphere. Genie will brief you with the details. Good luck and good hunting. Recon! For you my life!"

"HOOAH Sir!" the troops bellowed in unison. And with that, the Commander turned and walked out into the rain.

"Well goddamn it," Genie sighed, "all patrols are cancelled tonight for everyone in this bunker, briefing is at 0500 at the C.P. tomorrow. I want everyone to bring your maps and GPS's. 'Till then, somebody get me a drink."

Q 2

December 17, 2406

I wasn't allowed to the briefing and it was just as well. 5am was just too early for my blood. From what Jackson told me, Genie wasn't too happy about being teamed-up with another Recon Unit since they were now a man short, but since it was Isa's squad, he was secretly pleased but wasn't about to admit it.

No one spoke as they checked their gear and ammunition. Some stripped their weapons for cleaning and recalibration, while others went over last minute checklists and area maps. They would be making their departure within the next thirty minutes and this moment of introspection seemed to be part of the ritual. Sergeant Isa sat alone with her thoughts as she honed a fine edge on her survival knife. To her right was a KC-26 Rifle and a belt of cychromium rounds, the Sniper's primary weapon. She also carried a Bolter Automatic: light, durable, and best of all, reliably deadly in firefights.

Genie just finished snapping the buckles on his body armor and checking his infra-red visor when he walked up behind me.

"Frye, we need to talk."

"Ok Lieutenant, what's on your mind?" I asked nervously.

"Step over here," Genie ushered me away from the others, "no point in the others hearing this. Listen, I know I can't stop you from going on this operation; you may not be making the drop with us, but I know you plan on going in with the 22nd at the end of the week. Look, you seem like a nice enough fella, I'd hate to see anything bad happen to you. I just want you to reconsider and wait 'till the 15th makes planetfall, may be even hold back at New Sierra a few weeks until Volengrad City is secured."

"I can't do that Lieutenant," I added stubbornly, "my people back home are counting on me to cover the war first-hand."

"Shit, newsman, you have no idea what you're getting into." Genie said angrily.

"Uluwatu Valley is one of the worst places here at the Q. It's crawling with tribal mercs and the 308th and 309th Mechanized Armored Division are lurking out there."

"I'll be alright Lieutenant," I tried to reassure him, "I can take care of myself, and I knew what I was getting into when I took this assignment."

"You think so, huh?" Genie frowned. "All right newsman, ya gotta go, then ya gotta go. If I had my way you'd be in New Sierra with the other pecker-neck reporters getting your stories from HQ. But get this, you little son-of-a-bitch," Genie growled as he grabbed my collar and leaned into me, "if you're gonna write about us, then write *about* us—you hear me? Tell it like it is, you tell them fuckers back home what it's like in this shitbox! You tell the truth as you see it and not the way Command tells you to see it, understand? You tell'em, you crazy little shit...tell'em about the Q!" Genie let me go and hissed as he stomped back into the squad bay.

"Okay you motherfuckers!" Genie yelled, "Get your shit squared-away and prepare to deploy for Objective Craven. T minus 10 minutes on the flightline. LET'S GET SOME TONIGHT! MOVE OUT!" Genie and the squad double-timed to the pad where two gunships primed their turbo-fans and their navigational lights cut through the night.

I watched from the doorway as they secured loads in the cabins and strapped in. The gunner from one of the ships looked over at me and smiled. It was Jonesey from last night. He gave me the finger and yelled, "Anything to get out of a job, eh newsman?" and the gunships lifted-off and vanished into the storm.

I stood in the empty bay listening to the rain and the wind howling through the compound like a banshee. Slowly, I gathered my personal items and put them back in my duffle bag. I strapped on my body armor, grabbed my pack, and headed out to the tarmac to catch a flight to New Sierra. On the way, I passed by "the Hilton", only tonight the lights were off and there was no laughter. I looked down at my muddy boots and kept walking; wondering if I would ever see Scarecrow and Dragon squads again.

It took me a damn near an hour to make arrangements for a seat on the next flight out of Defiance. At about 1:00 am, a large military transport jet taxied to a stop in the heavy rain, and we began boarding. I removed my poncho the moment I stepped inside and tried to shake off the cold. The mood in the cabin seemed almost festive as troopers going on leave to New Sierra goofed and called each other names. God they were a rowdy bunch. The kid seated next to me stared out the window and never spoke a word. Everybody cheered and applauded when we took off, and you could feel the tension loosen from the troops as we climbed away from Ft. Defiance.

I offered the kid a smoke to break the ice, but he just shook his head and looked back out the window.

"How long have you been at the Q?" I asked him.

He gave me a blank look; the weight of the world seemed to be on him.

He chuckled quietly and said, "Seems like my whole fucking life, mister. I guess I will have that smoke."

I lit it for him, and noticed that his hand trembled visibly as he took a drag and exhaled. He thanked me for the cigarette, turned his attention back to the window, and never uttered another word the rest of the flight.

Q 3

I checked in at the Weshaur Hotel about 3:00am. The lobby was filled with reporters, photojournalists, film crews, and television anchor people trying to book rooms for their extended assignments on 781. It was a madhouse as I plowed my way through the crowd to the elevators. I drew some funny looks being decked-out in full body armor and fatigues. I was cold, wet, and tired from the flight in, and my stomach growled from hunger. Every paper, magazine, and network had a representative here and I was curious to see if there was anyone I knew from back home.

Once I walked into my room, I threw my bags on the bed and unsnapped my body armor and tossed them onto the couch. I stretched as I stepped out onto the balcony for a smoke. The lights of New Sierra twinkled in the rain and the empty streets glossed in their reflection below. Half a block to the east was the legendary red light district of Emery Avenue. The one place in the city that never slowed down. Troops and businessmen mingled with pushers, pimps, and streetwalkers hoping to satisfy whatever fetish or vice they had.

"Hey John-eesh, what you need? Something for your head? Whatever brain-snack you want, I got...send you right into high orbit! No? How 'bout some push, man? I know this lady..."

"Step right on in gents, this club is top-notch! The hottest review you'll ever see in this star system. That's right, *the* Brandi West is dancing tonight. The hottest Serenian on Emery Avenue..."

"Hey sexy, you need a date? 40 Gelben will get you anything you want, I promise you'll walk away happy and smiling. I got a room over at the Plaza..."

It was all there on Emery, the bars, clubs, and parlors whose businesses boomed when the war broke out-bringing an endless and insatiable demand from military personnel as well as the locals. I flicked my smoke from the terrace and watched its journey to the puddles on the sidewalk five stories down. Yawning, I stripped and went to the bathroom for a hot shower; it would be a long day tomorrow. I needed to drop a line to the office to let them know that I made it to 781 safely, and there was a press conference at 11:00 that I planned to attend. The buzz I heard in the lobby as I checked in revealed that General Thomas Isley from Planetary Strike Force and Admiral Robert Jonas from Fleet would lead the conference and do a Q&A session on the upcoming battle for Volengrad City.

Volengrad, 781's industrial epicenter boasted a population of over thirty million citizens, most of them displaced during the war; was about to become the stage for one of the biggest campaigns in the Q's liberation from the grip of the Terekian quest for interstellar manifest destiny.

It was no secret to anybody that we would try to take the city back; it was just a question of when. It was also a matter of acceptable loss from a military and civilian standpoint. While there's never any guarantee of victory for any battle, to try to take what has become an enemy stronghold would be to pay an extremely high price with the lives of the men and women of our armed forces. That gamble never sat well in public opinion, especially on Earth and Syterra 12, but letting the Terekian Government get away with the murder of thousands of civilians in Volengrad was a harder pill to swallow.

Terekian propaganda termed the systematic assassination of Volengrad's government officials as well as the bombings downtown by terror agents during peak business hours (killing thousands) the "Cleansing of disease". The Alliance called it a terrorist act and promised the people of 781 justice. In the words of General Isley, "The Terekian tyranny has been found guilty of murder in the court of humanity, and the iron fist of the Alliance will seek retribution. The Coalition will atone!"

The eleventh hour has passed at Ft. Defiance; and the insertion of Aggressor Forces into Volengrad's southern border is the first strike of Isley's iron fist. But no amount of rhetoric will take the edge off the fear of the troopers being dropped into the cold darkness of Uluwatu Valley.

I toweled-off in the steamy bathroom and slipped on some comfortable clothes, I thought about another smoke as I walked over to the dresser, but decided against it. I smoked too much anyway. "What the hell did I get myself into?" was the last thought that crossed my mind as I nodded-off on top of the sheets.

December 18, 2406

I lay awake in the darkness for a half hour staring at the ceiling before I could muster the energy to get out of bed. I slept well, but was still tired. The rumble of my empty stomach reminded me that I hadn't eaten since making planetfall. I washed up and dressed and gathered my recorder and headed downstairs to grab a bite. It was only 8:30 and the lobby was already filling up with members of the mass media. Some sat around calmly and admired the exquisite art on the hotel walls, while others were frantically filing reports and photographs to their offices. I just finished calling in and was about to go to the hotel's coffee shop when I heard someone call my name.

"Oh my god, Jacob, I can't believe you're here!" It was Bob Stine, a reporter from the WCBR Express. He patted my shoulder as we shook hands, we had worked on the same stories in the past and had always been close friends. Sometimes we had the same sources and leads, and frequently ended up "on the spot" together as headlines broke. Bob was a modest man that never let ego get in the way of his work; his loyalty to ethical journalism was fierce, and I always held a great deal of respect for him. At 48 years old, he was in great physical shape, unlike myself—ten years younger and a pack and a half a day habit.

I remember my first assignment for The Metro. It involved the kidnapping of a young college girl who happened to be the daughter of the C.E.O. of the AeroTech Corporation. I saw Stine at the crime scene hounding the detectives for information. The authorities were always uptight when the press showed up, but Stine seemed to be welcomed by the police, in fact, the detective in charge spent time talking to him while the rest of us were rudely hustled away from the scene. I bumped into Stine the next day at the university the girl attended; I was hoping to scratch up some leads from her instructors when I ran into him in the hallway of the Engineering Department.

He recognized me from the day before and probably would have been leery of my presence, but he could tell I was raw and running on pure instinct. Perhaps that was enough for him, knowing that I posed no threat to his story, knowing that at one time he was in my shoes. Untested and inexperienced. Whatever it was for Stine, he took pity on me and actually shared information that he had culled from his sources. A generous but uncommon act in a cutthroat profession. From that moment on, we kept turning up at the same places as the case evolved over time. We became fast friends in our trade in spite of the fact that we worked for rival papers.

One evening, months into the story, one of my leads brought me to an abandoned apartment complex located in the inner city. The police were in the process of storming the building when I arrived. There was heavy gunfire from within the structure, and tear gas poured out of the windows as I watched from an alley. Within minutes the police reappeared with the kidnapped girl—shaking and in tears, but all right. That was when Stine showed up, he just missed the rescue, and knew I had the scoop as an eyewitness.

I don't know why I did it. I needed the story, but I let Stine have the collar; I figured that it was his network of informants that lead me there to begin with. In a way, as my career blossomed, I had come to consider Stine as a mentor. I always felt that he was watching over me as the years and stories went by. Eventually the job had taken us to different places of human space, and we lost touch for a while. Until this morning.

"So tell me Frye, when did you get to 781?" Stine inquired.

"Made planetfall two days ago with 1st Division's Medevac wing by the 13th Parallel."

"Oh jeez, Jake!" Stine laughed. "The Metro dropped you into "The Hump" on your first day? What the hell's wrong with them? Come on kiddo, let's get some breakfast."

We spent the time playing catch-up at the hotel café, and decided to hit the press conference together like old times. Stine had arrived at the Q six months earlier, but had never ventured beyond New Sierra for a closer look. He shook his head in disbelief after I told him what my assignment required me to do.

We ran across other people we knew in the lobby on the way out to the M.P.A.A.C. building by Emery Avenue. One of them was Tara MacIntyre, a very talented photojournalist that had been covering the war at the Q since the occupation. Her work had been splashed over every website and hardcopy magazine for years. Tara had more than her share of close calls in the field, but none of them were enough to stop her from grabbing her gear and hopping on the next gunship to join a patrol in the middle of nowhere; at least up until last year when things got really bad. Then she quit going out all together.

Tara hooked her left arm through my right and walked between Stine and me as we stepped out into the street. The storm had abated to a light drizzle, but the morning was still dark and frosty as the three of us walked out to the street.

"Mmm, I don't know Frye," Tara grimaced, "quite a few crews and journalists have gone out on some ops with the troops and gotten themselves killed. The ones that made it back swear they'll never go out again. I'm one of them. Does putting your ass on the line to cover the war mean that much to you?"

"Sure it does," I replied, "I want the truth, not M.P.A.A.C.'s version of it."

"Well my friend, bullshit is what you're going to get this morning, Isley's full of it." Stine chuckled. "I've been to a bunch of these press conferences here, and the only good thing about them is that they're on Emery Avenue. But the people back at the Express eat it up when the General makes a speech. He's an icon back home. Go figure."

"So what changed your mind about going out to the field, Tara?" I inquired.

"I was with Jill Forrester when she got killed." Tara sighed.

"Tara, I'm sorry. I didn't know…"

"It's okay, Frye. How could you know? Yeah, after Jill died it kinda changed things for me."

"Where did it happen?" Stine asked.

"Eighteen months ago at Cobbler's Pass. Mortars started coming in and tearing everything up and we were pinned down with 1st Division in what was left of a building. Jill and I had our backs against a wall that was falling apart faster than we were. Believe it or not, we were joking around with each other; talking about getting back to the city for a hot bath and a decent meal. Next thing I know her eyes closed and she slouched into me. I thought she fainted or something. I held her against me and shielded her face from falling debis. But when I looked at my hand, it was covered with blood. Jill's hair was soaked with it. Found out later a piece of shrapnel lodged itself in the back of her head."

"Jesus." Stine frowned.

"I still went out, though. A couple of months after Jill's death I was with the 1st again at Kon Lam Plains when a Sniper's round took the head off a soldier standing next to me. After that I said "Fuck this!" I don't need this shit, ya know?"

We filed into a lobby and the guards confirmed our press and security badges after we went through the detectors. From there we entered a large room where camera and lighting crews had set up along the sides; the center area was filled with folding chairs where we would be seated, and a platform with a podium dominated the front. Positioned behind the podium were two long tables draped in white linen with pitchers of iced water and crystal glasses in front of the empty seats for the speakers and their entourage. Soldiers with automatic weapons and ballistic vests watched suspiciously over the growing crowd as they walked up and down the aisles.

Tara smiled and punched me lightly on the shoulder. "Thanks for the company, guys. I'm going to sit up front to get some pics of Isley and Jonas. I think those two are hot!" Tara winked. "Let's hook-up for lunch after this, okay?"

"You got it, Tara." Stine beamed.

Surrounded by colleagues, the idle chatter and laughter turned into a low roar until General Isley and Admiral Jonas appeared on stage with their security teams followed by half a dozen men in dark suits. They talked quietly amongst themselves before taking their seats at the tables.

Isley was an imposing figure with countless campaign ribbons and medals on his uniform. He was in his late fifties, and with his gray crew cut and prominent jaw he seemed to personify the high command. No wonder Division chose him as their spokesman; he projected the image of heroism.

Admiral Jonas looked even tougher; he was older and seemed jaded by decades of service with Fleet. He glared at us as he surveyed the room and took his seat. His uniform had more decorations than the General's, and he was oblivious to anyone that found the thick smoke from his cigar offensive. There was an old story that the President of the Inter-Planetary Council asked him to put it out during a dinner with some diplomats, and the Admiral leaned over and whispered in her ear, dashed his ashes on the floor, and walked away chuckling—leaving the President blushing. Jonas was a bruiser of a man, and even his security team seemed scared of him.

A balding M.P.A.A.C. rep walked up to the podium and clicked on the microphone, "Good morning ladies and gentlemen. Thank you for taking the time to attend this symposium. As you all know this is a Level-4 Press Conference and M.P.A.A.C. media kits are in the lobby and will be given to you on your way out. I ask you to hold all questions until our speakers are done, and to present your inquiries in an orderly fashion when called upon by Admiral Jonas and General Isley." The suit paused to clear his throat, "Without further delay, it is my honor to present our first speaker, General Isley of the Planetary Strike Force."

General Isley stepped to the podium and launched into a long, boring speech concerning the supply logistics of Volengrad's up-coming invasion by the 1st Division followed by the 15th Division's landing force in the coming weeks. He was vague and yet was able to go into a detailed description about the Terekian Divisions suspected to be within Volengrad City limits. Isley had a talent for talking in circles, and it was exhausting to have so much military rhetoric thrown at me so early in the morning.

"Overall, I feel that Volengrad will be a swift and decisive victory over Terekian forces." The General said confidently. "I am confident that with the help of Fleet, we can minimalize the amount casualties and keep them within the boundaries of acceptable loss. The Alliance is technologically superior and better trained in warfare, and I believe The Coalition will relinquish the entire sector to us by late January. Questions from the press?"

A series of hands went up, and the flow of standard questions began to lull me into a stupor. I saw Tara sitting at the end of the third row and she just happened to turn around, look at me, roll her eyes, and subtly hold up her left hand in a loose fist and jerk it back and forth as an expression of her current thoughts of the conference. I had a hard time keeping a straight face.

"So this is their last stand?" A reporter asked the General.

"Doubtful. The Coalition still holds several quadrants in the Polaris and Medusa star systems. This is only their last stand in the Bakkus system before we push them out."

"Then why don't they surrender Volengrad?"

"It's their mentality," the General replied, "Terekians are a warrior race. Even when facing certain defeat they will not back down. To them it's not honorable."

"General, Sir." A woman raised her hand.

"Yes young lady." The General nodded.

She stood up and straightened the hem of her dress. "Jacqueline Rosenthal of the UPA. There are stories circulating about Aggressor Forces in Uluwatu Valley and that several high explosives have detonated within The Clover; have Special Operations units engaged the Coalition in firefights within Volengrad city limits?"

"I'm afraid I can neither confirm nor deny such stories, ma'am."

"In light of what happened to 1st Division during the Pegasus Campaign last week," Rosenthal continued, "do you honestly think we can take a stronghold like Volengrad in a matter of weeks?"

"Well," the General frowned, "Pegasus was a black-eye for both sides. While we did suffer from heavy losses, I consider that campaign an important strategic victory. The time has come to take Volengrad out of enemy hands and get the Coalition out of Bakkus once and for all. Next question please..."

She had drawn blood with that question and knew it from the General's evasiveness. "General," Rosenthal pressed on, "the K.I.A. and W.I.A. lists from Pegasus were staggering. Logistics reflects that the 1st Division suffered over a forty percent loss during that battle and most Companies are operating at half strength. Why are you sending the 1st into Volengrad?"

"Ms. Rosenthal," the General exhaled loudly, "the 1st is the most experienced Division here at the Q..."

"Not anymore." Someone behind me muttered quietly.

"...they will be reinforced with..."

"...fresh meat." The same voice chided.

"...additional troops drawn from other Divisions before they make the invasion."

A low murmur began to work through the crowd as press members talked among themselves.

"General Isley." A distinguished looking reporter with a gray beard and glasses stood up as if he were standing at attention.

"Settle down people. Go ahead, Sir." The General pointed and nodded his head in acknowledgement.

"Yes General, Gerald McMillan, New Chicago Times." McMillan was a retired Aggressor Forces Captain who followed the war closely from the beginning and his interests were more deeply rooted than most civilian journalists. "It's rumored that the Terekians have the 308th and 309th Armored Divisions in the outlying areas of Volengrad; they happen to be the largest Bopper Divisions the Coalition has, how are you prepared to deal with them?"

The General shifted uncomfortably at the podium. "I'm not at liberty to answer that question."

"To complement Ms. Rosenthal's first question, I've also heard from several reliable sources that the Alliance deployed A.F. operatives into the city over a month ago. Any truth to that?"

"I'm not at liberty to answer that question either."

"What about the rumors that the Coalition has nukes in Volengrad?" McMillan smirked, knowing that was a question that everyone wanted to ask.

"Speculation and rumor." Isley replied calmly. "The Terekian delegates at the Peace Talks assure us that no nuclear devices exist in Volengrad. The Coalition knows that Fleet in now in their galaxy with dreadnaughts on standby."

"Stand-by for what?" Rosenthal shot up and demanded.

"I'm afraid I'm not at liberty to answer that."

The crowd erupted with voices as reporters and journalist spat theories at one another.

"Order! Order please!" Isley shouted as he raised his hands as a gesture to bring the volume down.

"I hear that General Oss is actually in Volengrad," McMillan pushed, "is this true?"

"I can't answer that."

"General, are there any questions you can answer?" McMillan asked in an exasperated tone.

Isley looked grim as he clutched the podium. The soldier in him was showing, he looked unhinged by the series of questions and he was ready to strangle McMillan when Admiral Jonas stood up and moved forward.

"I'll take it from here General." The Admiral put his hand on Isley's shoulder and nodded as the General continued to glare at the crowd and returned to his seat at the table. "Good morning ladies and gentlemen." The Admiral grinned through a cloud of smoke. McMillan's disposition changed when the Admiral glared at him, and he quietly sank down into his seat. "As we speak, the F.S. Normandy along with four heavy cruisers have joined the 17th Fleet in orbit over 781. The Normandy is carrying the 9th and 64th Armored Wings. As you know, the 13th and the 16th Armored Wings have distinguished themselves over the skies of the Q over the years, and the 9th and the 64th will do the same over Volengrad City.

Photo recon has revealed missile and artillery batteries within city limits as well as heavy armor outside of Volengrad's perimeter. Our drones and Boppers will pave the way with the Armored Cav when our ground forces move on the city. Surgical airstrikes will aid in taking out Coalition Boppers before the 15th Division makes planetfall.

To answer your question about General Oss, if she is in Volengrad, we'll do our best to find her and take her down. We'd prefer to have her alive for the sake of Intelligence." The Admiral paused and sighed.

"Listen, Volengrad is a Coalition stronghold, and the Terekians are going make us pay dearly for every inch of it. This is going to be a knife fight and everyone's going to get bloody. One can always hope for a swift and uncontested victory, but I think the brutal reality is that if we are going to take Volengrad we are going to pay that price. You people came looking for a story, well you've found one. One of the byproducts of war has always been the loss of lives It's a senseless and ugly fact that we must accept. We have a tendency to refer to this loss as "casualties". Well I see nothing casual about dying. But what really bothers me is how we reduce the ultimate sacrifice of our troops to impersonal percentages and statistics." The Admiral softened and removed his cap.

"Most of you know that my daughter was shot down over the Tantalus Delta last year and was never found. As a father I will never understand why my child had to die, and I am bitter toward the Alliance and this goddamned war. As an Admiral of Fleet, I know that she, and thousands like her fought bravely, and gave themselves willingly to the cause of restoring freedom to the people of 781 and every territory occupied by the Coalition. We have all paid a heavy price. And nothing pains me more than making the decision to send more of our sons and daughters to their deaths. But we are soldiers. This is our job, this is what we do. The old saying "the end must justify the means" brings no comfort to me...it never has. Honestly, I believe we will have to destroy Volengrad to save it.

Let's stay focused on the fact that we're about to engage the Terekians for the last time here at Bakkus, and we're going to lose a lot of good people in this siege. It's our hope that taking Volengrad will force the Coalition to accept Alliance terms at the Peace Talks and we can put an end to the war when they realize they've lost Bakkus. Thank you for your time. I will take no questions."

Admiral Jonas and General Isley walked off the stage and left us sitting in silence. Stunned by the Admiral's candor, we sat quietly for a few minutes staring at each other before we got up and went back to the hotel.

Stine and I spent the rest of the day at the hotel bar touching base with friends and discussing the morning's conference.

"Nash" Yorita pulled a chair up to our table and mussed McMillan's hair as he sat down. "Jaysus Mac," Nash laughed, "you really got Isley worked into a twist this morning, man. You just became my new hero."

"You know me, Nash," McMillan smiled slyly, "anything for a laugh."

"Hey Nash..." Tara called excitedly.

"Hi Tara! What's going on, girlie?" Nash nodded.

"Read your last story, boy-san," Tara teased, "nice writing! We should team up for a project one day."

"Tara, that would be the shite!"

"Yes, that was an interesting piece Nash." Stine said over his steak. "Where'd you get the lead on that dealer selling Crunch Dust to officers?"

"I've got my ways."

"Uh-huh. You're gonna get subpoenaed by the Council."

"Well, if ya ask me," Nash winked, "some Council members are Crunch Freaks too."

"I doubt that," Tara interjected, "if they were, there wouldn't be so much indecision over policy."

"Doesn't matter, I'll plead "Servabo fidem"."

"That'll go over really well with them." Stine laughed.

Just about everybody planned to go barhopping at Emery Avenue tonight, but I wasn't in the mood. I planned on staying at New Sierra for one more night before heading back to Ft. Defiance where 22nd Bravo was staging for the invasion.

I sat at the table light-headed from drinking, and listened to McMillan telling Stine stories of when he served in the Aggressor Forces. McMillan planned on going with the 15th Division, and tried to talk me into going with him. He was going to make the insertion at Volengrad in a week, and I was going to make the drop into Uluwatu Valley in less than two days.

"Frye you're out of your mind!" McMillan laughed. "Uluwatu is a triple-canopy nightmare, and you don't have the training to survive in that kind of environment. Lots of booby-traps and poisonous snakes and shit. You won't last an hour. If you're not going to wait for me, at least wait 'til "The Big Red One" gets to the city. There's plenty of war to go around, Frye, don't be in such a hurry to get yourself killed."

"Yeah, I know what I'm doing, Mac," I said as I nursed my glass. "I'm going into this with my eyes open."

"What the hell, Frye?" Nash asked in a shocked tone, "This true? You're going to Volengrad?"

"Yeah. Oh not you too, Nash." I sighed and pointed accusingly at Tara, Stine, and Mac, "I've been catching shit from these three all morning."

"Have it your way Frye," McMillan said shaking his head, "I just hope you've prepared your mind for the unexpected. I've been in combat before," McMillan's voice got grave, "and I've seen things that you can't even begin to imagine. Things that can't be explained but just are. You're going to have to be able to accept things when they don't make any sense."

"Listen to yourselves," Stine cut in, "you're both crazy! I can't believe you two are actually going out there. You guys got some kind of death wish? Mac I can understand, he's always been a little bit off, but come on Frye, he's right, you don't have the training for this kind of shit! The Terekians don't care if you're a non-combatant. They're not going to spare you because you're a journalist. They'll see your body armor and take you for a trooper and kill your ass. Jesus Christ, guys, no story is worth getting killed for."

"Amen." Tara added as she half stood up and waved over a bartender from across the crowded room.

"Stine," I said angrily, "I'm going, and that's the end of it."

"Goddamn it Frye," Stine said, "you go and that's the end of you!"

"Hold on just a minute." McMillan protested. "You two need to stand down. Now Stine, shut up! Frye's a big boy now. He's not the kid you took under your wing over fifteen years ago. Shit Frye, I hope I see you in Volengrad. Man, I'm getting too old for this kind of shit."

The bartender that came to our table was actually the manager. He must have been in his late 70's, but still walked with a spring. It took him a couple of minutes to weave his way through the crowd. Everyone knew his name, and he knew everyone as well. He was gracious as people patted his back or shook his hand as he walked by. He smiled and nodded as he wrote down Tara's order. "Can I get you anything else, doll?"

"Naw, thank you, Eddie," Tara said warmly, "you're a sweetheart."

McMillan looked at him with an unfocused expression. "Hey, Eddie, who do I have to sleep with to get a drink around here?"

"Me." The bartender smiled jokingly.

McMillan got up, polished off his drink, and belched. "Well fuck it, then, I'm going out to Emery to get some push, you guys coming?"

December 20, 2406

I stood on the tarmac of Anderson Airport with roughly 250 troops just out of boot camp waiting for the transport jet to complete its taxi. Several sergeants ran back and forth screaming at the fresh recruits that would be replacements for 1st Division. Their language was colorful and they seemed to have an endless supply of creative names that they called the troopers.

"Jesus H. Christ, boy," A sergeant screamed into the face of a trooper, "I can't fucking believe a pencildick like you survived basic! You don't look like you've got enough hair on your ass to pack all that gear. What the fuck are you doing in my infantry shit-for-brains?"

"Sir, this trooper came to fight for the people of 781 and kick some Terekian ass, Sir!" The kid snapped with his eyes locked straight.

"Kick some Terekian ass, huh?" The sergeant glared.

"Sir, yes Sir!"

"Goddamn! I feel safer already knowing an asswipe like you is carrying a fucking weapon," The sergeant bellowed, "you look like the kind of maggot that would look good in high heels and a dress. How 'bout it, cupcake, you got a date for the prom yet?"

The trooper didn't know how to answer that one. He just stood at attention trying not to look scared.

"I'll take that as a fucking "No, Sir!"" The sergeant barked, and began pacing up and down the formation.

"Listen up, once we get to Defiance, you will be receiving your unit assignments. From there, you will be making your insertion into Uluwatu Valley by gunship. You are part of the first wave, which means the LZ the 9th Armored Wing clears for you will be hot. Reports show a high concentration of mercs in the area of operations. Those of you that make it will begin securing the LZ perimeter for the second wave. Resistance will be heavy but you'll have air support to take out any armor. Welcome to the fucking war! All right, transport's ready to board. Grab your shit, and let's rack 'em and pack 'em."

The whine of the engines faded into the background as I fell in line with the troops. We began to move across the tarmac towards the rear hatch of the transport where soldiers whose tour had ended were getting off the jet; they walked toward us in a long, ragged, unevenly spaced line. You could tell they had been through some shit; their armor was filthy, and their eyes were sunken with dark circles from lack of sleep. And with the exception of the exhaustion that made their shoulders droop, their unshaven faces carried blank expressions as they stared into the distance. The troops I was with couldn't bring themselves to look at them as we passed each other.

"Hey newsman!" The sergeant yelled as he jogged up to me. "If you plan on going in with 1st Platoon, you better take this." He slapped a small metal canister against my chest.

"Thanks, sergeant." I replied looking puzzled. "What is it?"

"It's a gas mask. The Trolls used chemical weapons on us during the last battle at Pegasus. Hope you live long enough to find your story, newsie. Good luck!" The sergeant slapped my shoulder and laughed as he ran up the ramp of the transport.

Q 4

The troops on the flight out of New Sierra to Ft. Defiance were unusually reserved, almost to the point of being completely withdrawn as they privately wrestled with their anxieties knowing their final destination. I went through the motions a thousand times in my head about what being in combat would be like. How would I act when the heat was on under fire, and God forbid, how would I react if I got wounded? Would I be brave and find that pool of courage to keep moving and do my job, perhaps even grab a weapon and fight if needed? Or scream and cry like a frightened, overwhelmed child lost in the shadows of fear? But like those seated around me, I was clueless, and that left me with an empty, quivering feeling in my gut that made me break a cold sweat.

In those moments of thought, death had become larger than life. Greedy and unstoppable. It had turned into a huge blackness in my mind; shapeless, cold and intangible. It stalked my thoughts and emotions and wringed the color out of them. It sat comfortably next to me like an old friend that came to visit and would not leave empty-handed. Death was a merchant that dealt with time, and I unconsciously bargained and pleaded with it to leave me be. In the end I knew. I knew that it would always have its way, but I hoped it would be merciful and take me quickly. Please don't make me suffer, please don't let me see you coming.

I snapped out of the daydream to the muffled murmur of isolated conversations in the cabin of the plane. For the most part, the flight was quiet as the troops tried to sleep or pretended they weren't afraid about going into battle. The tension thickened as we made our descent through the clouds into final approach to Defiance. The troops around me smiled at each other nervously and fidgeted with their gear as we made a bumpy touch down onto the tarmac and taxied to a stop. A sergeant walked down the aisle yelling at us to get it together and start filing out of the rear as the ramp lowered.

"Quit screwin' around and get on the line!" The sergeant screamed as a half chewed cigar dangled from his clenched teeth.

"The war'll be over by the time you get outside! Hurry the fuck up, we're wasting daylight! Jesus H. Butcherin' Christ! You people look scared, what is the hold up? GO! GO! GO! What, do ya want to live forever? Move it out!"

We trekked across the airfield as sergeants jogged along side ripping troopers new assholes for not moving fast enough. My only saving grace from being yelled at was the visible press and security I.D. badges hanging around my neck. A sergeant moved next to me and pointed to a group of buildings to my right. "That's you." He snapped. I broke formation and headed to the C.P. to confirm my attachment to 1st Platoon.

After going through an extensive security scan and frisking by two armed guards I was finally allowed into the C.P. I drew some uncomfortable stares from the officers and I felt like I had three heads as I was escourted into the command bunker. The nerve center of Ft. Defiance was filled with 1st Division's finest minds laboring over the logistics of a campaign that was building up to be the turning point of the war if Volengrad fell in the coming weeks.

"Sorry 'bout that reception," A Major smiled as he offered his hand, "you just can't be too careful around here." He said as he turned his attention to a holographic relief map. "I see you've got a Level 6 security clearance. You're the only civilian I've ever seen with one of those."

"I was subjected to an extensive background check, Major."

"I bet. Honestly, Mr. Frye, I was told to expect you, but I really didn't think you would show up for the party. Figured you would stay in New Sierra where it's nice and safe."

"You know, I've been hearing that a lot lately, Major," I said trying to regain my composure, "believe me, the thought of staying in New Sierra crossed my mind more than once on the flight over here."

"Tell me something, most of your people usually wait until the objective is secured before making an appearance. A lot of your kind have gotten killed over the last few years trying to cover this shitty war. It's gotten to the point where nobody from the media is willing to go out anymore, why are you doing this?"

"I'm still not sure about that myself, sir." I replied. "I think that if I'm going to write about the soldiers, then I better go out and meet them and see what they see to get an accurate picture of the war."

"Very commendable. In fact, I think you've got a lot of balls to do this. I hope you don't get 'em shot off while you're runnin' around out there." The Major said rubbing his chin. "If I were you, I'd put some more thought about going in with 1st Platoon. They are part of the first wave and it doesn't look too good for them. That LZ is going to be real hot. We'll be lucky if we take less than sixty percent casualties when we hit it."

"Well Major, I've heard a lot about Uluwatu Valley in the last few days; all of it bad, but I'm still up to going with your permission."

"Ok Frye, 1st Platoon's shacked in barracks 28C; but you better hurry, they deploy for Objective Craven in less than two hours. You'll want to get with Sergeant Parker. He'll get you squared away with what you'll need for the insertion. Good luck, Frye, and remember to keep your head down."

I shook hands with the Major and left the C.P. to look for the barracks. I watched at least thirty heavily armed Hunter-Killer teams of Mark-XII Razorback Gunships taking off into the overcast sky and head to Uluwatu as close air support. The compound was packed with troops being organized for the invasion; the 163rd Infantry would be spearheading as the first wave—the one I'd be going with in a matter of hours. I lit up a smoke hoping it would calm me down when a trooper came up from behind and startled me.

"Hey bro, can ya spare one of those?" He asked politely.

"Yeah sure, no problem. Maybe you can help me, can you tell me where I can find 1st Platoon?" I figured directions were a fair trade for a smoke.

"Yeah, just follow me, I'm heading over there now." He said with a boyish grin.

"I'm Corporal Warner, but everyone calls me Scat", he said holding out his hand, "1st Platoon's F.C.T.. You one of our replacements?"

"Afraid not, Scat, I'm Jake Frye," I said shaking his hand and holding up my badges, " I'm a reporter assigned to your platoon; I'm going to make the insertion into the valley with you guys."

"Whoa! No way dude! A reporter? Who're you with Mr. Frye?"

"The Metro. And please Scat, call me Jake."

"Oh, alright then. Jake. Boy, are you gonna blow everyone away when they find out who you are. Especially the Sergeant. Oh man, especially the Sergeant."

"Why do I have a feeling that this is not a good thing, Scat?"

"No, Pappy's cool as hell. He'll trip out on ya 'cause you're not one of the replacements he's expecting. Hey come on, ya gotta meet my bros inside!"

Scat couldn't have been more than 21 years old. He was a skinny, perky kid with blonde hair and glasses that he was constantly adjusting on his nose. He was the kind of person that always seemed happy and took a lot of kidding from the guys in the platoon. But you knew they were all fond of him. Especially the sergeant. Scat was like the little brother we all wish we had. At 5'-7" and 150 pounds soaking wet, you wondered how this kid humped around a com-link pack along with his gear and weapon. He seemed to have an internal engine that would drive him up hills and through the woods without getting tired.

"Hey fuckers, the Scat-man has returned!" Scat smiled ear-to-ear as we walked into the barracks. "And check out what I found wanderin' around: a reporter from The Metro!"

The troops of 1st Platoon looked at me curiously like a sideshow geek. Most of them sat on their bunks prepping their Bolter Automatics, stocking ammo, and checking their gear and armor when we interrupted them. We made our rounds as Scat awkwardly introduced me to the guys in his squad.

Pvt. James Willis, or "Willie" to his friends, came from a small farming colony on Syterra 12. Looking to get away from the small rural society where everyone knew everybody else's business, Willie joined the Planetary Strike Force two years ago to find a new life and found himself in the middle of a war wishing he would have stayed home to harvest crops with his family. He was a quiet, stocky young man of 24 years, and planned to marry his girl when he got out of the service. For now, she seemed to be the only thing that kept him going. Homesick and lonely like the rest of the troops, the dream of some day going home seemed distant and unattainable.

Willie sat on his bunk cleaning his assault rifle and squirreling away ammunition and grenades when he asked me why I was *really* here.

"Hell, I would imagine most guys would rather take HQ's word about how the war is going instead of layin' it on the line by coming out here." Willie said insightfully.

"I would have told them to kiss my hairy ass, if I was you. If my boss wanted a story about the war and told me I was going to the Q, I would've told him "You go. Get your own fuckin' story." I ain't goin' somewhere to have a Terekian cut my dick off and shove it in my mouth so you could have a headline for the morning paper." Willie said sharply. "Shit, newsman, they gotta be paying you some pretty hefty capital to take this assignment."

"Actually, I chose to be here, Willie." I said.

"Oh man," Willie chuckled, "looks like we've got something in common. I got "volunteered" to be here too!" We both snickered and shook our heads in agreement over our predicament.

"Yeah, sometimes a guy gets lucky; first Pegasus, and now Volengrad City." Willie said sarcastically. "I can do without this kind of luck."

"Why are you talking shit for Willie?" A tall dark haired trooper said as he tossed an oily rag aside. "You know you love this place, where else can you run around shooting people and get paid for it?"

It was Cpl. Stanley Lang. "Satch" as his squad called him.

"Shit Willie, sometimes you act like you're not enjoying your stay here. May be we should have room service bring you up something for your pussy."

"That depends, Satch," Willie glared.

"On what?"

"You buying?"

"Hell no!"

"Ah ya cheap son-of-a-bitch, why ya gotta be like that?"

Satch was from the sunny beaches of California, Earth. A run-in with the local police back home brought him to the armed forces.

"After they caught me stealing cars," Satch said smiling, "the judge gave me two choices: join up or lock up. I figured fuck it. I ain't doin' time in slam. Might as well make myself useful for a change. So here I am, the baddest of the bad. Doin' you good by doin' you in." He held up a Marlin/Fulcrum-38 Heavy automatic (known as the "38 MotherFucker" by the troops) with pride.

"Yeah one day when this war's over," Satch said patting the 38, "I'd like to bring this baby home with me and let the good judge know how much I appreciate what he did for me."

"Blow it out your ass, Satch, you're so full of shit it ain't funny." A soldier with "Moose" written on the breastplate of his body armor stood up. "Everyone knows the only reason you carry the MotherFucker is because you got a little dick."

"That's not what your mother said last week, Holloran." Satch said grinning, "You may not recognize her when you get home, I shaved her ass."

"Hey, fuck you!"

"Good come back, Moose. I hope you weren't up all night thinking of it."

"Actually I was up all night putting the meat to your sister."

"How was she?"

"It was like bangin' a stick in a garbage can."

We all started laughing as Satch and Moose punched each other on the shoulder playfully. It was their way of blowing off steam. When it came down to it, the jitters had put a bug up everyone's ass, and letting it show was taboo between the squad members.

22nd Bravo had taken thirty percent casualties in the battle for the Pegasus Bridge a number of weeks ago, and they were bitter over their loss of comrades. After regrouping at Defiance to lick their wounds and get replacements, Bravo Company was still undermanned and was about to be dropped into the biggest bloodbath of the war.

"Jesus, Satch, you think you can bring a few more belts of ammo with you?" "Doc" Powers said shaking his head as he inventoried his medi-packs for the third time.

"No sweat Doc, I don't plan on wasting any of it when we hit the LZ. I think six belts should get us by 'till the second wave arrives."

"I hope we don't have to wait too long for 'em," Doc said, "I mean I got a really bad feeling about this one, guys, those tribal mercs are worse than the Terekians. Bunch of fuckin' savages."

"Hey newsman," Moose said with a nod, "you gonna make this insertion without a weapon? I mean seeing that you're gonna be shot at, don't you want the chance to shoot them back? This is some heavy shit we're going into. You definitely need to be squared away before you go."

"He's right, Jake," Scat said leaning forward. "We need to get you a Bolter just in case. There's a good chance you're gonna need one."

"Ever fire a weapon before, newsman? Or is the only shooting you do with that camera?" Moose pointed.

"I used to hunt with my father when I was a kid, but it's been a while." I said somewhat embarrassed.

"Well, think of this as a hunting trip," Satch said as he held up his Bolter, "the only difference is that you can become the hunted if you're not careful. See this switch? This is the selector, you can fire single rounds in semi-auto, or fully auto depending on how many of 'em are comin' at you. Just remember, if you go to full auto, use short controlled bursts, it's more effective, and you don't waste ammo."

"Yeah, and you need to be careful where you're stepping," Scat added, "trip-wires or laser sensors could set off a booby-trap and put you in a world of hurt. I really hate it when they send peepers in on us, can't hide from them."

"What are peepers?" I asked.

"Airborne robotic cameras," Moose replied, "they're small and will buzz up to you and relay your position back to them. Then they pound your ass with artillery. Some peepers are infrared, so if you see one, shoot it and get the hell out of there. Chances are they saw you first and the copperheads are on their way."

"Nice to see you boys making the reporter feel at home." Sergeant Parker stood at the door with his arms crossed.

"Hey Pappy, how's it hangin'?" Moose said with a grin. "Um, just givin' the guy a few pointers before the game, coach."

"Sounds to me like you're trying to scare the shit out of him, Moose. You must be Frye." The sergeant held his hand up. "I'm Sgt. Parker, welcome to 1st Platoon. They told me at the C.P. that you were going to make the insertion with us." He looked at Satch as we shook hands. "Shit Satch, you think you got enough ammo for the MotherFucker? You plan on taking Volengrad by yourself?"

"Whatever it takes, Pappy." Satch said as he adjusted the belts on his shoulders.

"Well if that's the case, I guess the rest of us will just go home."

"Hey Pappy, you think we should get him a Bolter?" Scat said.

"Never happen, Scat-man, Frye's an observer," the sergeant turned to where I stood, "just make it a point to stay out of our way, Frye. If you get separated from the squad, you're on your own to make your way back. We're going to have too much shit going on to go looking for you."

Sgt. Parker was a burley 6'-2" and the oldest member of Bravo Company. He'd made the Planetary Strike Force his career, and at 43 years old with a wife and two kids back on Earth, the war could not end soon enough for him. After twenty years in the field, two wars, and the scars to prove it, he looked forward to a transfer back home and an easy desk job before he retired from the Force.

"Hey Pappy," another soldier yelled from the barracks entrance, "I brought you your replacements." A Lieutenant motioned with his head at the five recruits standing behind him. "Get inside men."

"Thanks L-T." Pappy directed his gaze to the troopers standing at attention.

"You guys got just enough time to find your bunks and drop off your personal shit." Pappy said firmly. "You two are going with Collins. He's in charge of 2nd Squad," Pappy pointed at the other soldiers, "and you two go with Torres in 4th Squad. That leaves you as my F.N.G." Pappy said glaring at the last trooper.

"What's your name kid?"

"Sir, Pvt. Tzuter, Sir!" The trooper said with a salute.

"At ease, Tzuter. Scat will get you set up with what you need and show you where your rack is. Dismissed."

"Sir, Yes Sir!" The recruit replied.

"Collins, Torres...your cherries are here; hurry the fuck up and get them squared away. You've got fifteen minutes." Pappy yelled as he walked to the end of the barracks, turned and bellowed, "1st Platoon, synchronize your watches and prepare to move out to the flightline in twenty minutes. We deploy at 01400 hours. This is it men, its time to earn our pay. Its show time!"

"Well Pappy, looks like we stepped into the shit again." The Lieutenant sighed.

"We sure did L-T. We sure did."

"Ok sergeant, we'll see you on the other side. Good luck."

"Good luck to you, sir."

It started raining again as we stood on the tarmac where over a hundred Hughes M12 troop carriers sat waiting in the deafening whine of their turbo-fans. Pappy and the rest of the sergeants ran back and forth ushering their squads into the slicks as the rain fell harder and reduced visibility to less than a hundred feet of gray haze.

"Ok Satch," Pappy yelled through the downpour and the ships engines, "the slick on the left is ours--#1170, get the squad secured and prepare for lift off, I'll be with you in a second!"

As I ran toward the transport with the squad, I noticed a rather curvy young lady wearing a very short skirt straddling a missile painted on the nose of the M12; there was a title in red letters proclaiming her as the "Daytona Bombshell". I strapped in at the back of the cabin behind the cockpit between Willie and Satch, when Pappy hopped inside and patted on the gunner's tactical helmet.

The pilot turned around and put his hand over his helmet mike, "Lift off in two minutes! We're going to have to fly over the storm, hopefully it lets up before we get over the LZ!" Then he looked at the gunner, "What's the status, Olson, are we good to go?"

"Let's get this bird off the ground!" The gunner yelled giving him a thumbs up.

I looked forward through the cockpit window and watched the ships two rows ahead of us take off into the high wind six at a time as the chatter on the radio with ground control droned in the background. The pilot and copilot flipped toggle switches and pushed buttons on the glowing instrument panel and overhead console as they checked for clearance with the Airboss.

The thrust of the engines from the row of slicks directly in front of us turned the falling rain into steam that fogged the cockpit canopy of our ship as they rose vertically off the strip and left us in their jet-wash.

"Raven-6, Whiskey Cell, Foxtrot-8, Defiance Control confirms green free and clear...verify Raven-6, over." The Airboss crackled over the radio intercom.

"Roger, Defiance Control. Raven-6, Whiskey Cell is green for take off." The pilot said mechanically into the headset.

"10-4, Raven-6, Whiskey Cell clear for take off. Good luck and stay out of harms way boys, Defiance Control out." A female voice replied.
The pitch of the engines turned into a scream, and the cabin vibrated slightly as we lifted off the tarmac and gained altitude into the dark gray skies.

My stomach knotted up as the M12 rocked and shook, and the world below disappeared through the clouds. We climbed at an alarming rate, and the g-forces pushed and pulled my insides in different directions. The turbulence was never going to end, and I felt the cold grip of fear on my throat and closed my eyes as my head swam in adrenaline and my guts tightened into a ball. Engulfed by the swirling storm, the cabin lights blinked on and off and jostled us between the hypnotic confusion of darkness and light.

Within those white-knuckled minutes that stretched an eternity, we broke through the thunderheads and were flying above the storm. The air was so calm when the slick leveled off into a steady formation with the other ships. I gazed out the rear hatch at the sight of sixty troop carriers flying in tight cells of ten with the afternoon sun peeking through the clouds behind them. I felt awed by its beauty. The rays of light contrasting with the thick grayish-black storm. The horizon stretched into a dark blue hue, and in the distance, the peaks of a mountain range capped with snow looked like islands surrounded by an ocean of clouds. The wind howled sharply passed the hatch sending a shiver down my spine as we flew full bore toward Uluwatu Valley.

"What do you think, newsman?" Willie asked as he leaned toward me.

"Hell of a view, Willie, I've never seen anything like it."

"Better enjoy it while you can, we'll be making the insertion in about two hours."

"Yep, in two hours we'll be making history!" Scat interjected.

"Yeah, if we live." Satch added.

"Hey new guy," Willie nodded at Tzuter, "you gonna be ok? You look like shit."

"Leave him alone, Willie," Moose said. "I don't remember you doing this good on your first op. Come to think of it, I think you threw up all over yourself the first time you rode a hog."

"That wasn't me, that was Scat!"

"Boo-shit! I thought you shit your pants on that ride, just ask Pappy."

"Yeah, that was you Willie." Pappy said rolling his eyes.

"Fuck all of you guys!"

"There it is, new guy"," Scat smiled. "don't mean nothin'."

"Hey new guy," Satch said, "What did you say your name was again?"

"Tzuter, sir, Donald C." The recruit responded.

"Well D.C.," Satch said with a grin, "What part of human space do you come from?"

"Hollywood, California, Earth, sir."

"Woo-hoo! Hollywood! Holly would if she could, but not with daddy home! I'm from San Diego. You stick close to me when we land kid, we'll get you through this in one piece."

"Thank you, sir, I appreciate it. I'm...I'm kind of scared right now." The kid replied.

"First of all," Satch said firmly, "You need to belay that "Sir" shit, you call me Satch. You're with 1st squad now. The hardest of the hard. We don't talk about being scared, we talk about being hungry. Right boys?"

"Yer fuckin' A right!" Willie exclaimed.

"There it is." Scat nodded.

"You understand what I'm telling you, kid?"

"Yes si...Satch." Tzuter said with his eyes cast down.

"Alright then, until we see what you're like under fire, do what you're told when you're told to do it. You get me, new guy? That goes for you too, newsman."

We passed the time with idle talk, and the members of the squad gave me and the recruit pointers on what to do "to keep your ass out of a sling" when we got to the valley.

"Remember to make sure you've got a tight seal on your face with the gas mask if they use chemical warheads on us." Satch said matter-of-factly.

"Don't take off your hood 'till someone gives you the all clear. Gas has a tendency to linger for at least an hour depending on the type they use."

"And never walk down a trail unless you know it's secured, it could be mined or booby-trapped." Willie added with a hard look. "And like Scat said earlier, keep your eyes open for peepers. Those little fuckers mean to do you some serious harm. If you see one, waste it and get out."

As the topic of conversation veered toward survival, the mood in the cabin grew more somber until nobody wanted to talk anymore. The last hour of the flight was spent in silent meditation as the squad checked their gear and weapons to distract themselves from thinking about what lay ahead.

Moose had nodded off and his head bobbed back and forth as he began to snore. Drool formed in the corner of his mouth and trickled down his chin onto his armor when Pappy gave him an elbow to the ribs.

"Damn it, Moose, that's disgusting." Pappy scolded.

"Huh? What? Huh?" Moose asked as his eyes flittered open.

"Wipe that shit off your face, that's fuckin' repulsive!" Pappy laughed.

Moose looked around the cabin in an unfocused daze, not realizing that we were having a good laugh at his expense. The gunner looked over at us and shook his head. "Fuckin' grunts." He said to himself as he adjusted his visor.

"Hey, check it out!" The pilot turned around with his hand over the mike of his headset, "I just heard on the open channel that the 9th Armored

Wing took out a Terekian armored column four clicks east of the section of forest they cleared for our LZ. Right now it sounds like there's an Aggressor squad pinned down by mercs, and they're requesting an air strike from the Ghostriders to take the heat off. The commander of the inbound squadron is Banshee-6. The trapped squad is Portland 1-5. Here, listen to this." The pilot put the channel on the intercom for us to hear.

"...getting our asses kicked, Ghostrider! We can't take much more of this! Shit! Shit! We can't hold 'em off! Where the hell are you Viperheads at?" A hysterical voice blared through the intercom speaker. We could hear the sharp staccato of gunfire and yelling in the background.

"Hang on Portland 1-5," another voice belonging to the squadron leader responded, "we'll be there in less than ten seconds."

"Hit the treeline! Hit the fuckin' treeline, Ghostrider! Oh shit! Here they come! Here they come!" The voice from the pinned squad screamed.

"Portland 1-5. Portland 1-5. Get your heads down. Banshee-6 is inbound. I have target lock on your grid. I've got a visual. I've got a visual. Holy shit! There's hundreds of 'em! Fox one...got 'em! Fox two...we have impact!" The squadron commander yelled triumphantly. "Banking right and coming 'round for another pass...let's light them up!"

"Ghostrider, you have a direct hit! Keep it comin', keep it comin'!" The voice on the ground begged.

"Roger, 1-5, stay down! Stay down!" The squadron leader ordered.

"Banshee-2 rolling in fangs out." Another voice cut in. "Fox one...we have impact in the grid. Fox two...eat slag, you son-of-a-bitches!"

"Oh fuck!" The voice from the ground force screamed. "We're being overrun! We're being overru..." There was a loud pop that made us jump as the radio went dead.

"Portland 1-5, what's your status, over?" There was no reply.

"Portland 1-5, this is Banshee-6, what's your status, over." Nothing.

"1-5, report your fucking status!"

"Turn that goddamn thing off!" Pappy yelled.

"Those poor fuckers." Satch said shaking his head.

"Damn! What the hell's down there waiting for us?" Willie asked wide-eyed.

"Hell, Willie. Hell." Pappy said under his breath.

"Ok men," the pilot yelled, "brace yourselves, we're ten minutes out from the LZ. We're going to make our descent and hit it at low level flight."

I looked out the cockpit window and watched the lead gunships break formation and peel through the clouds as our own ship went nose down at an angle into a steep dive. I clung onto the webbing with sweaty palms and took deep breaths when the slick dropped through the storm. The thunder around us clapped, and the gunship shook violently from the sound wave. We plummeted through the dark sky into a heavy downpour. The wind whistled from our increased velocity and I could see the other gunships behind us scatter into a wider pattern as we approached the landing zone.

The forest was a green blur that flashed into a blinding white from the lightning that cut furrows into the sky. Up ahead, Razorback gunships dropped smoke bombs on the LZ to conceal our insertion, and bombarded the treelines with plasmite rockets and titanium rain from their chain guns.

We decelerated over the smoky clearing as the pilot extended the landing gear and began lowering the ship.

"This is it!" Pappy yelled as he unbuckled himself. "Lock-n-load!"

We all unbuckled and held on. The landscape below came at us rapidly as the smoke covered the ship and filled the cabin with its acrid smell...sixty feet and closing...I coughed and tried to swallow, but my throat was cracked and dry with fear; my hands shook as I took short, shallow breaths...forty feet...the ground was scarred and pitted with craters from the air strike, and trees were scattered and smoldering in the upturned red-brown earth...twenty feet...glowing tracers from enemy fire emerged from the treeline and floated gracefully toward us and the other gunships. The gunner swiveled the chain gun and started returning fire into the trees...ten feet...the ship rattled loudly and lurched forward from the metallic impact of machine gun fire hitting the fuselage...

"We're taking heavy fire! I can't set her down!" The pilot screamed in a panicked voice. "You guys are gonna have to jump the rest of the way!"

"LET'S GO! LET'S GO!" Pappy yelled as he waved us out the door. I ran out the hatch and jumped, praying I wouldn't get shot in mid-air as tracers sliced through the downpour. All the breath was knocked out of me when I hit the ground and tumbled face down in foot deep mud. Stunned and suffocating, I snapped out of the shock of the fall and raised my head to look around. I could feel the heat of the gunship's engines on my back as it struggled to regain altitude through the chaos. I wiped the slick mud from my eyes and crawled behind a splintered tree trunk for cover, wishing desperately to be invisible.

Around me, troopers scrambled out of gunships. Teeth clenched in a rictus grin, and faces twisted with fear as they hit the deck seeking cover. Hunter-Killer Razorbacks hovered and darted across the trees strafing the forest with a steel curtain of suppressing fire that shredded the ground and vegetation into an ugly green slush that floated in the craters with the bodies of the enemy. The tribal mercenaries cowered in the shadows of the birds of prey as the pitched sound of Hawkeye plasma rockets and the sustained bursts of their guns chewed through flesh and bone.

The world turned black and red. Columns of smoke rose from craters like thick burnt fingers reaching out from the depths of earth to grasp the fallen bodies of soldiers and pull them into the cold ground. The muddy field seemed to boil with the mixture of blood, torn flesh, and splintered bone.

The sweet smell of burning carnage mingled with the spent odor of gunpowder and sulfur. It was the scent of war, and it sucked the air out of my lungs and made me dizzy from its morbid fragrance. I gagged and wretched; eyes watering and stomach cramped, my legs felt weakened as I huddled in the lumpy mud waiting to lose my mind.

The screams and cries of the wounded and dying filled the air. They called for their mothers. They called for their wives—they called, and only death answered.

Explosions from enemy mortars and rocket-propelled grenades rattled everything inside me and dulled my senses as the earth rose into the air and rained rocks, mud, and body-parts. The ground trembled with each impact and knocked soldiers off balance with the concussion. Engulfed by the cold embrace of fear, the constant pitch of machine gun fire highlighted the screams of pain and anger. Time compressed, and everything seemed to be in suspended animation.

The sharp pop of rounds ricocheting off the ground sent tiny steel splinters burning into my skin, and I could hear their hiss as they hit puddles of water behind me. Twenty yards to my left, a soldier lay in the mud facing up at the gray sky and driving rain; his legs shaking, and his head twitching uncontrollably as he vomited blood while he tried to stuff what was left of his torn intestines back into his body.

"Get off your asses and move forward!" Pappy screamed. "Concentrate fire on the treelines. LET'S GO!"

The soldiers of 22nd Bravo began crawling through the mud and over the bodies of their comrades as they painstakingly advanced toward the trees. Machine guns spit a steady stream of tracers at us from all directions and raked the ground, sending chunks of dirt flying into my eyes. I came across a trooper crawling at me aimlessly on all fours, groping, looking for something...

"Get down!" I yelled, "Get down before you get killed you idiot!"

"Oh god, I can't see! My eyes! I can't see!" He cried hysterically.

I crawled over, pulled him down into the mud, and dragged him behind a fallen tree. His face was completely missing, and all that remained was the bloody pulp of dirty tissue.

"MEDIC!" I screamed hoarsely. "MEDIC! Somebody help us!"

"Don't leave me! Please don't leave me! God, don't let me die!" He sobbed as he clutched at my sleeve.

"I'm not going anywhere, just calm down, just hang on for a second, buddy, help is on the way!" I tried to reassure him.

"MEDIC! We've got a man down! MEDIC!" I held his hand and cradled his head on my lap when the trauma kicked in and he started to convulse. An evil pink foam bubbled out from what used to be his mouth, and then he died in my arms.

"Shit!" I cussed to myself as I gently propped his head against the tree.

"I'm sorry kid, I tried," I said to him as I suppressed my tears. "I really tried..." I grabbed his Bolter Automatic and bandoliers, slung them over my shoulders, and began the long crawl forward through the mud. I got fifteen feet when I saw Willie kneeling behind a small mound shooting into the forest.

"Fuck you! You son-of-a-bitch!" Willie hollered as he fired. "Your mother has flat tits and hairy legs, ya fuckin' monkey dick cocksucker!" Willie ducked immediately as bullets ripped the ground open in front of him. I saw a mercenary dodging from tree to tree when Willie fired and punched a hole in his chest with his Bolter. The merc spun wildly from the impact and slammed against a tree trunk before he fell into the thick brush.

"Got cha!"

Ten feet to my right, Satch was crouched in a shallow hole with the Fulcrum-38 pouring fire into the trees. I made my way to him and slid into the muddy water.

"Git some! Git some you motherfuckers!" Satch screamed maniacally as he pulled the trigger.

"I see ya! Come on, Trolls! Come on in and git some!"

"Satch!" I yelled, "Where the hell are they?"

"Over there, between those two pines. There's a machine gun nest! There's at least a platoon sized element dug in there!"

I squinted through the rain and saw the silhouettes of mercenaries diving into shrubs and what had to be foxholes or trenches as Satch fired integrated aluminum rounds at them. I could hear their cries of anguish over the din of heavy fire as the 38 tore their bodies apart.

"Ok newsman," Satch said pointing at the trees, "I need your help on this one! I need you to take that Bolter and start firing into those trees over there. Remember how I told you how to use the selector? Set in on full auto. When I tell you to start firing, start pissing on 'em! I'm gonna make a run for those rocks over there and get in a little closer. That nest is wiping out too many of us! I'm gonna try to take it out. All right get ready!"

I held the Bolter up and sighted in between the trees where tracers lashed out and plowed through the field.

"Alright newsman, ready?"

I nodded as I tried to get my breathing under control, and put my finger around the trigger.

"Ready and...FIRE!" Satch jumped up and sprinted forward, firing the 38 as he ran toward the rock formation.

I fired into the shadows of the forest. If it moved or didn't look like it belonged there, I used the Bolter to erase it. All of a sudden a loud burst from an assault rifle went off next to my right ear. I looked over to see Pappy in the prone position in the mud next to me firing cover for Satch.

Scat fumbled with a fresh clip and slapped it into the chamber of his Bolter and began returning fire with Pappy.

"Keep shooting newsman!" Pappy yelled. "He's almost there!"

I focused on movement in the shadows and fired in short bursts. We kept shooting after Satch reached the rocks but the muzzle flash from our weapons had given away our position, and the machine gun started tearing up the ground around us. We tried to slide down into the crater, but it was too shallow. Steel splattered against the mud and buzzed over our heads.

"Shit! They've got us pinned!" Pappy barked.

"What about Satch?" Scat yelled, "He's cut off!"

"Damn it!" Pappy spit, "Gimme the radio Scat!

We were helpless. All we could do was lie flat in the puddle and try to make ourselves small.

"Rhino-6, Rhino-6 actual. Blastgate 1-1 requesting air support, over." Pappy yelled into the radio.

"Roger 1-1, Rhino-6 Hunter-Killer team is in route." A voice responded. "State grid lines for strike, over."

"10-4, Rhino-6." Pappy pulled out a small positioning device and started punching buttons.

The machine gun started zeroing in, and rounds began eating the ground in front of us. They snapped inches overhead like furious hornets with their terminal stings.

"In my playbook I read November, Foxtrot, Seven, Nine, Two, over." Pappy said as he flinched from the impact of a nearby explosion.

"Copy that 1-1," Rhino-6 replied, "November, Foxtrot, Seven, Nine, Two, over."

"10-4, Rhino!" Pappy bellowed. "Get these cheesedicks off my ass, Six! They've got us pinned down."

"Roger, Blastgate, we're rolling in on them now." The voice said reassuringly. "Lima Lima, 1-1. We are weapons hot."

Taking advantage of the gun's concentration on our position, Satch lobbed two thermite grenades into the nest. The explosion sent a fountain of earth and fire skyward, tearing the branches off trees and shredding limbs.

Razorbacks roared over us less than twenty feet from the ground bringing their wrath of mechanical thunder and technological horror. Trees were cut down and cauterized as their laser canons unharnessed their deadly pulse into the dense forest. The earth raged and burst before us as the woods were pounded, crushed, and torn to pieces. It rained clods of dirt and rocks. Stinging us as they fell from the darkened sky.

Pappy looked over the edge of the crater at the smoking woodline with the radio clutched in his hand.

"Stick around Rhino-6," Pappy said into the handset, "we're going in after them."

Pappy tapped on our tactical helmets. Stood up and looked around at the troops lying in the rain and blood.

"Come on you motherfuckers! GET UP AND GET SOME! CHARGE!"

The troops of Bravo Company got up from the slime of mud and human waste. Like a nightmare vision, they looked like the dead rising from the grave as they began their charge forward into the treelines. I stood up and started running. Screaming to the top of my lungs and firing the Bolter as I staggered and slipped on chunks of flesh and severed limbs that littered the field like a gruesome salad.

We became animals worked into frenzy for blood. Terror surged in my veins and the primal instinct of survival possessed me. Each time the lightning flashed, I glimpsed the frozen expressions of fear and madness on the faces of the soldiers around me. We want so desperately to live and will pay any price, but we must kill everything in our way. The punished earth was red and sticky with blood and entrails. It could no longer absorb the carnage that lay on her surface.

As we neared the treeline, the enemy mercs hopped out of their shallow trenches and retreated further into the thick woods. We overran their positions, kicking and stomping the bodies they left behind. The mercs that the troopers caught threw their weapons down and begged and babbled prayers before they were mercilessly beaten and stabbed. No prisoners would be taken.

We chased them deep into the woods, stumbling over roots and shrubs. When we got within range, they turned and began firing at our advance. I hit the ground immediately, but the trooper next to me caught a full burst of rounds in the chest and stomach. His body armor and torso exploded from the high velocity impact, splattering me with shredded sinew and shit.

Tracers and muzzle flashes lit up the darkness with their deadly strobe as we engaged in a close fire fight. Tree trunks were whittled to pieces as thousands of stray rounds from heavy automatic fire electrified the air. Rain rattled the leaves of the triple canopy over a hundred feet above us, and streamed down off branches everywhere in large fat drops.

The screams and cries became more unbearable. Their echoes in the forest magnified them and sent a shiver through me. I looked over at

Tzuter, the recruit that joined the squad less than four hours ago, his helmet was off and he held his hands up to his ears as he curled into a fetal position and trembled.

"Make them stop!" He cried in a high pitched voice as tears rolled down his cheeks. "Oh God, make them stop! Please make them stop! Make them stop! Make them stop!" He chanted as he rocked back and forth with his thumb in his mouth. He had been pushed too far and spiraled into insanity. His eyes were like fogged glass and I knew that he had lost himself.

The second wave hit the LZ, and hundreds of fresh soldiers stormed through the field into the treelines to reinforce our positions. Again the vicious clatter of machine guns dominated and barked like rabid dogs as they chewed up the forest floor.

I lay on my stomach as grenades exploded sharply through the branches and the earth heaved bodies into the air. I glimpsed at a fleeting shadow of something falling and heard a muffled thump on the moist ground cover as I watched the object bounce to a stop in front of me. I gasped as I came eye to eye with a severed head. Its mouth open in horror, hair greasy and matted, and the torn muscle knotted with arteries dangled sickly like the tentacles of a jellyfish. I screamed as I knocked it away and began throwing up.

Soldiers rushed past me as I dry heaved. The sound of automatic fire was dying down and being replaced by the shouts and screams of three battalions of 1st Division troopers charging into hand to hand combat with the mercenaries. There were quick flashes of silver as knives were drawn and sunk deep into flesh. Jawbones cracked as fists and rifle butts connected. Necks were snapped and the limp bodies of the enemy were cast aside. Throats were cut sending fountains of blood into the cold air as mercs fell to the ground gurgling for breath. The soldiers kicked, punched, and jabbed each other, it was like a vicious gang fight to the death.

Then out of nowhere, a mercenary came at me screaming and waving a sixteen-inch bayonet. His eyes gleamed, and his nostrils flared as he bared his teeth and growled. I stumbled backwards and lifted the Bolter and pulled the trigger as he prepared to carve me open. His head vanished in a red vapor as I emptied a clip into him. I turned around at the sound of footsteps behind me and found myself with a pair of hands around my throat. I was lifted off the ground as the merc shook and choked the breath out of me. I tried to claw at his eyes and face, but I was beginning to lose consciousness. I could hear the beat of my heart as my head throbbed from the lack of oxygen. The merc glared at me and screamed in his native tongue a stream of hatred and vengeance. Everything was turning black when he let go and an expression of surprise crossed his face. We both collapsed and I lay on the ground coughing hoarsely as I clutched my throat gasping for air. Moose helped me to my feet when I noticed Pappy wiping blood off his survival knife.

"Take it easy newsman!" Moose said as he held me up.

"You looked like you needed some help, Frye, you okay?" Pappy said calmly.

"Yeah, I'll live." I croaked.

"Well, it looks like we kicked their asses for now." Pappy nodded. "We just about wiped 'em all out. But a lot of 'em got away in the woods. We're gonna have to send out patrols."

I kneeled in the shadows of the trees with Satch, Moose, and Pappy trying to catch my breath. My face streaked with dirt and sweat, I trembled and coughed as I wiped the grit out of my eyes.

Willie and Scat had their hands full with Tzuter who had now slipped into an incoherent state. They tried to get him on his feet, but he remained curled up with his knees up to his chest. He mumbled quietly to himself, rocking back and fourth shaking his head.

"Come on buddy," Scat said gently to Tzuter, "you can't stay here, it's still too dangerous. We're gonna get you some help, okay? Come on, let's get you home."

"He's lost it Scat!" Willie said exasperated. "He ain't got his dogs on a leash anymore, he's fucking gone."

"Maybe we should get Doc. Maybe he can help him."

"Never happen, troop." Willie replied. "Can't put no bandage on his kind of wound."

"We need to get back to the LZ." Pappy said as he lit a cigar. "Make sure its secure and set up a perimeter. Satch, round up what's left of the platoon and have them meet at the clearing."

"Hey newsman," Satch smiled. "Thanks for covering for me back there, I owe you one."

"Yeah Frye," Pappy puffed, "you did good. Why don't you hang on to that Bolter for a while. Come on, let's go."

Exhausted but still on the high from battle, we made our way through the woods to the landing zone. The night had crept in and brought a stiff chill to the air and I was grateful the darkness concealed what we were stepping on.

We emerged from the treeline to the section of forest that had been cleared for our landing. Hundreds of soldiers had arrived and started the tasks of digging in, security, and cleaning up the landing zone. Flares illuminated the LZ and cast long eerie shadows across the landscape as gunships off-loaded more troops and equipment and took off. Not far above the treelines, Razorbacks stalked the night like hungry predators searching for their next meal. The battle for Volengrad City had just begun.

Q 5

The LZ was too muddy and filled with bodies and human debris to set up camp for the night. Even with heavy equipment and manpower, it will take days to sort through the dead and clear off the unidentifiable remains. We spent hours clearing an area in the woods and pitching small tents. Satch and Willie left a space open for me in their tent and somehow managed to scrounge up a sleeping bag for me from somewhere.

It was getting late. Satch and Willie napped, but I couldn't bring myself to unwind. So I got up and went back to the landing zone to wander and walk off the tension.

There were medics scrambling around treating the hundreds of wounded troopers, and loading them into the constant flow of medevacs that came and went. Doc Powers worked furiously with other medics trying to stop the bleeding of a chest wound on a soldier lying in the mud.

"Come on kid!" Doc said desperately as he applied pressure and bandages over the large hole in the trooper's chest. "Don't let go! Work with me and fight it! Fight for your life, man! You'll be on the next bird out of here, just hang on!"

"Doc." Another medic said sympathetically. "He's dead. There's nothing more we can do for him."

"No!" Doc cried. "We can save him! I ain't givin' up! Hit him again with morphine!"

"Doc, he's gone, man." The other medic said putting his hand on Power's shoulder. "We gotta try to help the others, come on."

"Oh shit." Doc sobbed as he kneeled in the mud next to the soldier, "Another one. I couldn't save him. I did everything and I couldn't save him."

"I know, Doc, I know. Get your head together, we've got work to do."

The toll of the wounded and the dead was devastating. So many will go home blinded, disfigured, and crippled. Many more died on the field that night before they could get flown out in time.

The mind went numb at the sight of hundreds of body bags lined up in the mud awaiting transport back to New Sierra. Thousands of hearts will be broken back home when the families and friends of these brave souls receive notice of their passing.

What an utter waste; the lives, the dreams and hopes, the youth and the innocence of these kids, fed into the fires of annihilation. For those that survive, painful memories will haunt their thoughts. For those that perished, perhaps their sacrifice will teach us that war is never a resolve. The lesson to be learned through the centuries of war's brutal legacy is that it is never worth it. Too much blood has been spilled, too many prayers unanswered, and too many tears have been shed. Humankind may never learn, and this will happen again.

Piercing shrieks and moans came from the larger tents that served as field hospitals as the wounded stacked up inside and surgeons began a long sleepless night of work. I saw a trooper come out of one of these tents, his tattered armor stained with blood. He sat down on the trunk of a fallen tree, lit a cigarette, and put his face in his hands and started crying. The loss of lives in the first wave was staggering, but for this young soldier, the loss of a buddy brought an immeasurable and demoralizing sorrow as he hugged himself and wept.

I overheard another sergeant telling Pappy earlier that when the war ended he was going to open a bar on Emery Avenue in New Sierra. Drinks would be free for the survivors of Uluwatu Valley. And if it got more than two deep at the bar he would know that someone was lying.

I rubbed my eyes and yawned. It was time to head back to the tent. It drizzled lightly, and the flares scattered in the LZ still burned bright and cast their chemical light against the treelines.

Several patrols walked single file into the woods and disappeared like apparitions. They were hunting parties with revenge on their minds. Some will return at dawn, and others will remain out there for days. Stalking, lurking, and waiting.

I shuffled back to camp and made my way back to where 1st Platoon had set up when I ran into Pappy and Lt. Reynolds.

"What are you doing up, Frye?" Pappy asked.

"Couldn't sleep, figured a walk would help." I said. "It didn't."

"Yeah, I know the feeling. But you really should get some rest. It's going to be a long day tomorrow if you still plan on coming with us. You can catch a gunship outta here tomorrow morning."

"No. I plan to stay a little longer if that's okay with you, sergeant. I'm on my way back to the tent now." I said.

"Tent? Which one? Who are you bunking with?"

"Willie and Satch."

"Shit." Pappy chuckled as he shook his head. "Don't you feel you've been through enough? Now you're going to bunk with those two clowns?"

"Frye," Lt. Reynolds smiled, "you'll never be asked to prove your courage again."

"I guess." I nodded. "Well, good night fellas."

I started back when Lt. Reynolds put his hand on my shoulder.

"Hey newsman, I wanted to thank you for your help." Reynolds smiled. "Pappy told me you covered for Satch during the assault, and even managed to get one confirmed kill today. I'm going to talk to someone up in brigade. You deserve something for your actions." He shook my hand and patted me on the back.

Then it dawned on me as I made my way back, I had killed another human being today. I had been so wrapped up in the day's events that I completely overlooked what I had done. My hands trembled, and my legs buckled at the thought.

"Whoa newsman! Go easy. How many times am I gonna have to pick you up today?" It was Moose. "You okay, man?"

"Yeah, yeah, I'll be alright." I said.

"Hey, what's wrong? Did you get hit and not tell anybody? You hurt Frye? I mean the way you were walking. Then you started to..."

"No, no, Moose really, I'll be okay. I think the day just caught up to me."

"Alright Frye, if you say so." Moose squinted. "It was that merc, wasn't it?"

"Huh?"

"You know, the guy you killed in the woods." Moose said insightfully. "You've never had to kill anybody before. And now that you have, it's starting to fuck with your head. That's it, isn't it Frye?"

I didn't know what to say, he was right. I stood there staring at him for knowing what I was thinking.

"Listen, I don't know if this will help you any," Moose said, "but you didn't have any choice. That fucker was going to shank you with that toad-sticker and you didn't let it happen. It was either you or him. That's what survival is about. That's what war is about. Kill or be killed. You get over what you did and drive on with your life, otherwise you're gonna end up like Tzuter. In a place with soft walls and high fences. You're all right newsman, you really are. And a hell of a shot too. You did better than most recruits. All I know is that if it ain't crawlin' up your leg, let it ride. I'll see ya in the morning at o'dark thirty."

I got back to the tent, peeled off my body armor in the dark, and crawled into the sleeping bag. I thought about what Moose said as I lay there listening to the dull patter of the rain. "...if it ain't crawlin' up your leg, let it ride." You're damn right, and I drifted off to sleep.

December 21, 2406

It was still dark, and it began raining hard again. I wondered if the sun ever came out in 781. Thunder rolled ominously on the horizon and the lightning flashed brightly in the morning sky. Willie and Satch sat up in the dull glow of a chemlight with their weapons disassembled. Cleaning the mud and grime off each part carefully.

Willie looked over at me when he noticed I was awake.

"I took the time to clean that Bolter for you earlier, Frye." Willie grinned as he occupied himself with his own weapon.

"There's a couple of packs of freeze-drieds in the corner." Satch pointed. "You need to eat to keep your strength up. We're marching out of here this morning."

"Where are we headed to?" I asked.

"An objective's been added." Satch said grimly.

"Well, Pappy says we're about twenty miles south of Volengrad right now. Highway 12 is six miles to the east." Willie replied. "About five miles north of us is the town of Merlock. It's occupied by Terekian forces, and we're going there to liberate the population. We're the fucking good guys, remember?"

"The only problem is that the mercs are gonna fuck with us along the way." Satch said as he began to reassemble the 38. "I heard that 2nd Battalion left for Merlock an hour ago, I guarantee they step into the shit before 0800."

"Hey Frye," Willie said, "remember what we were telling you about keeping your eyes open for trip wires and peepers and shit?"

"Yeah."

"Well now's a good time to keep all that in mind. Just stay close to one of us and keep your eyes and ears open, okay?"

"Hang back when we get to Merlock, newsman." Satch said. "The Terekians are a lot more organized than the mercs. Don't want you getting into a pinch."

"Here, take one of these, Frye." Willie handed me a small white pill.

"What is it?" I asked.

"It's called an "Afterburner", it's a stimulant. It'll give you the range for this sweep. It'll definitely cut the path for you. Go ahead and pop it."

I swallowed the pill and washed it down with some coffee from a small plastic bag.

"Fuck!" I said wiping off my chin.

"Yeah, that coffee does taste like shit." Willie laughed.

"The least you guys could've done was warn me!" I said feigning anger.

"We could've, but where's the fun in that?"

"Hey, you clowns better get your gear on and tear this tent down." Pappy said as he stuck his head through the flap. "We're gonna move out in fifteen minutes."

We hustled our things together and double-checked personal equipment before we stepped outside to pull up stakes. It was cold enough for me to see plumes of breath when I exhaled. The troops of 22nd Bravo huddled in a group waiting for the rest of 1st Battalion to assemble on the campground before we moved out.

"Son-of-a-bitch." Pappy cussed. "Waiting on Charlie Company again. I swear I've seen lawn ornaments move faster than them, fuck!"

"Watch this." Pappy winked at us. "Hey Reilly!" Pappy called to another sergeant. "What's the hold up with 4th Platoon? Your boys get their panties mixed up during a game of grab-ass last night?"

"Go piss up a rope, Pappy."

"Alright, knock it off you two." Lt. Reynolds intervened. "We've got a long day ahead of us without you guys fuckin' with each other. Sergeant Reilly, you're up front today. 4th Platoon walks point."

"You got it L-T." Reilly grinned and turn to his men. "Ok 4th Platoon, saddle-up. Lock and load!"

We fell into two long lines with eight to ten feet of space between troopers as we began to file into the woods.

"Spread out a little more!" Pappy yelled. "I want at least thirty feet between us and Reilly's platoon. No talking. Keep your eyes open. And shut the fuck up!"

The woods darkened around us, and the sound of twigs snapping and feet rustling through the layers of leaves blended with the rain's rhythmic patter on the canopy above. A chill started to work through my body armor and gloves, but it began to dissipate as we marched deeper into the forest.

I felt a small tingle in my fingertips and scalp as the pill I took began to take effect. Within minutes I could feel small waves surge through my body. I felt like I had an endless reserve of energy. I felt strong, and when I looked at the cold determination carved into the faces of the troops around me, I felt invincible. All my senses seemed dialed into the environment, connected, and sharpened razor-fine. I could see the veins in the leaves and hear the microscopic pulse within them. I tapped into nature and the spirits that walked the woods. I felt stealthy as I moved among the trees. The cloak of shadows that brought dread the day before had become intimate companions.

I looked at the Bolter in my hands and admired its balance. Its unforgiving bluish-black steel was my savior. Delivering me from death and at the same time becoming my rite of passage to walk with the warriors of Bravo Company.

We walked hours without a break. Every step we took was a calculated risk; waiting for somebody to hit a trip wire or break the beam of a laser sensor and trigger an explosion. Maybe we were walking into the kill zone of an ambush as the enemy patiently tracked our movement; waiting for the prime opportunity to kill as many of us as possible. Or maybe we've wandered into a sector that was laced with mines. Unaware of it until someone puts their foot on one and vanishes. Leaving the rest of us frozen in our tracks and afraid to move in any direction.

The strain of anticipation was maddening. Not knowing when it would come—if it would come or how. Perhaps this was the worst part of being in combat: the wait. Waiting for the enemy to strike at the jugular, the contact, when the world around you melted into pure fear. When instinct took over and your body plowed into the earth. Digging into it with your fingers and teeth and embracing the ground with your soul. Waiting for the deafening explosions of grenades or mortars landing next to you to stop as every bone in your body rattled; making you ache for hours with the throbbing pain deep in your head. Waiting for the gunships to come and pull you out of the deep serious as you watch your friends die of their wounds. Waiting for reinforcements to come as you desperately hold your position while ammunition quickly runs low. Waiting in the dark and watching the ungodly hallucinations of shadows as they transformed themselves into the enemy by the ancient light of the moon. Waiting for that letter from home when your mother and father tell you how much they worry about your safety when they read about the war in the morning paper. Waiting for the perfumed letter from your wife or girlfriend telling you how much they miss you, how much they love you, and how much they wish you were home. Waiting...always waiting...

There's never any slack cut for the infantry. Never any luxuries. They went without sleep, they went without food, they went without. Sure they griped and bellyached, but in the end, they always did their job. They were always up for the fight no matter how bad the odds against them were. They had a job to do, and they did what ever it took to do it.

We finally took a breather early in the afternoon, and I took swig after swig of water from my canteen to take the cotton out of my throat.

"Hey Frye, you better go easy on that or you'll cramp up." Willie ordered.

"I can't help it," I said, "I'm fucking dying of thirst!"

"He's right newsman," Pappy said, "drink too much and your gut's gonna knot up and you won't be able to keep up with us."

Pappy turned to the rest of the platoon that was scattered among the trees and shrubs.

"Ok listen up. Reilly just radioed and says that we're about a half a mile from Merlock right now. 2nd Battalion's moved in close to the town's southern border, and is waiting for us to get into position. We're gonna cut northwest from here and dig in on Merlock's western edge. 3rd Battalion's gonna hit 'em from the east. The 9th Armored Wing is on standby to scramble. They're gonna take out any artillery and heavy armor within the town's limits. Then we go in for the mop-up." Pappy sighed. "The only problem is that the Terekians probably know we're coming, they just don't know when to expect us..."

"Pappy look out!" Scat screamed as he jumped up and pointed at the trees behind the sergeant. "Peepers!"

We all hopped to our feet and saw four small gray spheres about eight inches in diameter hovering ten feet from the ground and darting through the trees. These flying sensors were a technological marvel. Equipped with tiny cameras and satellite linked positioning computers, they could be electronically guided from over twenty miles away. Anti-gravity cells in its power pack enabled it to operate in most atmospheric conditions; all packaged neatly in a titanium shell. The sight of one of these robotic sensors terrified foot soldiers because they meant certain death by relaying their positions back to the enemy; and to the veterans of 22nd Bravo, the presence of peepers meant that it was time to run.

"Oh shit!" Satch yelled as he raised the 38 and fired over everybody's heads.

The peepers exploded with a shower of sparks and smoke as they were riddled with automatic fire.

"Our cover's blown!" Pappy spit. "We need to get the hell out of here! Scat, give me the radio!"

"Red-6, Red-6 actual, this is Blastgate 1-1, you copy?" Pappy hollered into the handset.

"Yeah this is Six," Lt. Reynolds replied, "What the fuck is going on back there, Pappy?"

"Tell Reilly to get 4th Platoon the hell out of dodge now! We just wasted some peepers! They know where we are!"

"You've got it Pappy! Let's move! Try to make it to Merlock! Six clear!"

"Blastgate out!" Pappy shouted as he handed Scat the handset. "Alright, get your shit 1st Platoon! Let's move! Satch, take point!"

We scrambled through the woods carelessly. Over logs and through bushes, hoping we wouldn't trigger any traps or mines when we heard the shrill whistle of rounds overhead.

"Hit the deck!" Satch yelled, "We've got incoming!"

I dove to the ground and clenched my teeth as limbs cracked and snapped above us and shells hit the ground with a dull thump. White smoke billowed from the small craters in thick heavy clouds and began to creep and settle on the forest floor.

"GAS! GAS! GET YOUR HOODS ON! GAS!" Someone screamed.

I fumbled with the canister the sergeant gave me back in New Sierra and pulled out a hood with a built-in gas mask. I tore off my tactical helmet, slipped on the hood and started to panic after I put it on because I didn't know how to seal it to my face and armor.

"Pull down on the toggles!" Willie yelled as he pointed at my hood. "It's self-sealing!" He reached over and yanked on the toggles hanging from the front of the mask and I heard a small hiss as the hood and mask conformed to my face. The first few minutes would be the difference between life and death. If the hood and mask didn't have a tight seal, I will inhale the gas and fall to the ground writhing in pain as my lungs burned and my internal organs melted; coughing clots of blood while life slipped away with each convulsion.

"Get your helmet on, and let's get the fuck outta here!" Willie yelled.

The howl of chemical warheads crashing through the foliage made my hair stand on end, and their dull thump into the soft earth was like a fist to the stomach. The forest floor was knee deep with the greasy white vapor that settled heavily into the hollows in the ground. The sound of thousands of small woodland creatures filled the air with shrieks as they crawled and clawed desperately up trees for a breath of air before dying. They died horribly. Their little bodies twitching involuntarily as their insides turned to liquid.

We stumbled over roots and thick vines like blind men as we followed Satch through the dense pines and gas clouds. Up ahead, we could hear the members of 4th Platoon calling to each other as they rustled through the woods.

The lens of my mask fogged up from my breath as I pushed away branches that slapped against my chest and arms. The shelling had stopped, but the chemical vapor had spread through the woods like an angel of death. Silently floating between trees like a ghost on the haunt. It eddied around our legs and swirled in the clearings. The chemical cloud had become a white billowy carpet that covered everything and killed everything that it touched.

Suddenly, the forest was quiet. The chirp of insects had stopped. The rain had stopped. It was a long uncomfortable silence that needled its way to the nerves and turned your skin cold. Troopers always had stories that hinted at the supernatural, being on patrol deep in the rain forest when the buzzing of insects stopped, the birds quit chirping, and the croaks and peeps of reptiles and the chatter of small mammals all stopped simultaneously for no reason. Leaving an overwhelming silence that made the flesh crawl and left small bumps on the skin as a shiver ran up and down the spine.

We all stopped walking and stood absolutely still. I saw the others looking around, scanning their surroundings, weapons at the ready as safeties were clicked off. Sweat trickled down my face as I gripped the Bolter a little tighter and wiped the fog off the lens of my mask.

"God I hate this fuckin' place." Scat whispered.

"Shut up!" Pappy whispered back. "Something's way wrong here. Satch, what do you think?"

"I don't know Pappy, could be an ambush." Satch said warily.

Then it happened. For the first time since I made planet fall on 781, the sun came out. Thin bright rays slowly filtered through the canopy and reflected off the gas vapor, giving it a translucent quality as it ebbed on the floor. Its silvery beams broke through the leaves and branches above and cut through the dim forest like hundreds of scattered little spotlights.

Satch signaled an all clear with his hand, and we started walking briskly again, but the unshakeable feeling of being watched made us all skittish as we waded through the gas. We walked for an hour without incident and I noticed that the chemical fog was starting to thin out. I could see thousands of tiny bodies of the forest life that died from the gas littering the lush undergrowth.

We caught up with 4th Platoon and formed a line to sweep toward a clearing in the trees ahead. There were several trails that appeared through the brush, and judging from the condition of the churned mud, they were used frequently. The width and the depth of the furrows in the ground and crushed vegetation indicated heavy treaded vehicle traffic had passed through here recently.

"Can't say I like the looks of this." Pappy said as he examined the tracks.

"Sure looks like a lot of armor came through here." Reynolds replied.

"We better keep moving. We're getting close to Merlock."

"Look, over there!" Willie pointed at the clearing, "What the hell is that?"

Satch held up his right hand in a fist as a signal to stop, and we all crouched down into the white vapor. Pappy and Lt. Reynolds moved up to Satch's position, and the three of them disappeared into the gas as they crawled forward to the clearing.

"What the hell's going on up there?" Willie whispered.

"I don't know, but it looks like we found something." Scat answered.

Then the word came back for everyone to move toward the clearing. We gathered around huge ditches that were filled with the decomposing bodies of men, women, and children. They were common graves that contained the occupants of Merlock. They had been brutally slain and cast into holes in the forest and left exposed for the animals and the elements of nature.

The heavy rain over the last two weeks did terrible things to them. A light green mold had attached itself to their blackening wrinkled skin as they lay in their graves seeming to embrace each other for comfort and warmth. The expressions on their sunken faces was of anguish as if they still cried for help or begged for mercy in their final resting place. The naked bodies of the women and children settled any doubt that they were raped and brutalized before they were executed. The saddest part of this gruesome discovery were the children. Their poor broken bodies lay in unbelievably wicked positions like they had been crushed and thrown before being brought out here.

"Those motherfuckers are gonna pay for this!" Pappy growled.

"Your goddamned right they will." Reynolds trembled.

"It's fucking payback time!" Satch glared, "And I ain't sleeping 'til every Troll on this planet lies stinking in the earth."

"Okay, let's get it together," Lt. Reynolds said firmly, "22nd Bravo has a mission. Merlock's western border is just over that hill. Let's get in position and teach those cocksuckers some manners. Scat, get a hold of 2nd Battalion and tell them what we found. Relay the message requesting the 9th Armored Wing to level the town."

"You've got it L-T!" Scat nodded.

"Pappy, get the company up to the ridge of the hill and sit tight." Reynolds ordered, "We're gonna burn these son-of-a-bitches down!"

We moved out of the forest into the sunlight and removed our gas hoods. The cool late afternoon air brushed against my sweaty face as I inhaled deeply. We climbed the steep grassy hill in a running hunch as we leapfrogged for cover along the way. Any signs of fatigue or exhaustion in the troops was overpowered by anger and sheer hatred for the enemy. We ducked behind rocks and bushes, then crawled the last twenty feet to the top and lay on our stomachs in the prone position. I peeked down the other side of the hill and across a vast field at the town of Merlock.

A series of wide trenches eight feet deep connecting bunkers and machine gun nests lay behind three rows of razor wire that encircled the town's borders. Soldiers could be seen moving in them as they stockpiled munitions for the bunkers and reinforced their positions with extra sandbags. Parked every twenty feet along the trenches, dark green Taurus-17 tanks with reactive armor stood under camouflage nets with their 108mm plasma cannons sighted at the treelines. To the north, heavy armored personnel carriers lined up for a half-mile on the main road that lead into the town as two columns of troops marched through the guard gate into Merlock.

In several places within the town's main street, mobile surface-to-air missiles nestled between buildings as their crews fiddled with the guidance systems. Two gunships sat on pads on the roof of a four-story office building in the middle of town as their ground crews ratcheted napalm pods and high explosive incendiary bombs onto the winglets of the ships. A gentle breeze carried the sound of officers shouting commands to the troops that manned the trenches and spider holes. The peaceful rural town of Merlock was now a Terekian fortress in the state of alert.

"Jesus Christ," Pappy sighed as he looked through binoculars, "those fuckers are trussed. This place is an outpost for Volengrad."

"We're definitely going to need gunships on this one," Reynolds grimaced, "there's at least four Battalions down there, and it looks like we found elements of the 308th Armored Division."

"Shit, they've even got mobile SAMS stashed down there." Pappy frowned.

"Hey L-T," Scat whispered as he listened to the radio, "2nd Battalion says Razorbacks have been deployed. E.T.A. fifteen minutes."

There was a faint rumble from the west, and we turned our heads in that direction. We knew that the distant thunder on the horizon was not a storm, but an inbound flight of Nova-31 Rapiers from the 9th Armored Wing traveling at mach nine to deliver the apocalypse. I lowered my head in anticipation and clutched the ground and waited for the air strike.

Q 6

It was one of those M.P.A.A.C. tours of the Normandy three weeks ago led by an officer as we closed orbit on the Q, our little press group ended up in one of the staging areas where several squadrons of Nova-31s sat in a dark hanger in their silent vigil. I broke away and walked down the middle of the bay listening to my footsteps echoing off the walls as I looked at the Rapiers in the dim light. In a matter of hours the stillness would transform into the commotion of flight and munitions crews working furiously to ready the interceptors for another mission. The 31's were lined up in rows on each side of me as I passed them and when I got to the end, I stopped and walked down an aisle to examine one of the fighters a little closer.

I was amazed how large the jet was for a single seat fighter, its thick vertical rudders were nearly twenty-five feet tall and its streamlined fuselage was close to forty feet long. Its overall appearance was menacing from any standpoint, but up close its aerodynamic features displayed the perfect marriage between science and art. The 31's swept wings gleamed in the dim lighting as I ran my hand over one of the leading edges. I noticed almost sixty kills were painted as small outlines of jets under the cockpit. The pilot that flew this one was extremely good. An ace six times over by Fleet's standards and undoubtedly sporting the cocky attitude that most fighter-jockeys had: brash and arrogant.

"Beautiful specimen of aerospace engineering don't you think?" A voice asked from the dark.

"Sheesh, you scared the hell out of me!" I said as I caught my breath, "I didn't see you back there."

"Sorry about that. I didn't mean to startle you." A lean blonde woman stepped out from the shadows wearing a black flightsuit.

"Get bored with the tour?" She asked with a cold glare.

"Yes," I replied, "I think it's just a case of nerves, I'll be making planetfall in less than three weeks."

"Planetfall?" She squinted skeptically. "Oh you must be that reporter the crew's talking about." She said accusingly.

"There are bunch of reporters here, ma'am."

"True, but the fact that you're making planetfall into 781 without training tells me that you have a pretty high security rating. No civilian does this unless you have connections in high places or you're with the Agency. Besides, none of your fellow media-pukes are even leaving the Normandy."

She turned out to be Colonel Jillian Baker, the Commander of the 16th Armored Wing. I should have guessed by the squadron patch on her left shoulder of a black cat holding a comet. The notorious "Outcasts". She was the infamous "Sonic Angel" that the pilots of the Terekian Armada feared encountering in dogfights over the skies of the Q, and after realizing who I was talking to, I quit leaning on her Nova-31.

There was a rumor circulating in the Armored Wing divisions in Fleet that the Terekian government put a bounty on Col. Baker because she had shot down so many of their pilots that the rest of them were beginning to refuse to fly where the 16th was operating. With fifty-eight kills to her name, she was the stuff that folklore was based on. Apparantly Col. Baker was docked in the Normandy for a few days to brief the 9th and 64th Armored Wings about 781.

Col. Baker had an icy stare that made me uncomfortable as we talked. I couldn't put my finger on it then, but in retrospect, I know now that hard stare only comes from seeing too much combat. It's what every veteran called the "dead man's gaze"; that penetrating look into the great beyond that can only be earned by living on the brink day after day. When they've seen so much that they don't see anymore, and the colonel's eyes reflected the bitter coldness of a killer.

"Well one good thing about being in a 31 and engaging ground forces," Baker said casually, "unless you're going sub-sonic, you're moving so fast that if you get hit, you'll never feel a thing. Probably won't even see it coming. Can't really ask for anymore than that when you cash in. I don't have that luxury in high altitude air combat. Up there in the stratosphere or in deep space if you get nailed, you're better off dead." She said in a factual tone.

"I've seen what's left of pilots who've punched out in the stratosphere, the ejection capsule still wasn't enough to keep them from getting crispy during re-entry. Besides, the g-forces usually turn them into jelly before they sizzle. That's why every time I make a kill I try to do it cleanly and show a little mercy. I'll go for total disintegration and spare the Terekian the cook time even though they deserve to fry."

The colonel went on to describe the weapons capabilities and target acquisitioning systems on the 31 with zeal, and the effectiveness of certain weapons in zero gravity (multiply that devastation by a thousand in atmosphere) during high-speed engagements.

She was calculating and impersonal when discussing kill ratios and vector curves, and I began to get the impression that the colonel had long become the human integration of the Nova-31's weapons systems. Col. Baker had become one with the jet. The human element in the circuitry. The soul of the 31. She was the ghost in the machine. So in love with the technology that she stayed up late at night to sit in the dark with her Nova. It had become her soul mate. Her significant other.

Pilots usually develop an attachment to their fighters as they go through their baptism of fire, but the colonel seemed to have a symbiotic relationship with hers. The Nova seemed to be her reason to live, chasing the mythical gremlins at mach speeds as she plummeted into the battle for air superiority miles above the Q's surface. Flying the thin line of zero gravity in the never ending twilight hunt by radar for bandits. She lead her squadron into hostile air space mission after mission. Each patrol becoming more hair-raising than the last as she cheated the odds and increased the death toll of the Terekian pilots that flew the skies that belonged to the "Sonic Angel".

"This is my second tour over this rock." she frowned. "I've spent the better part of the last three years protecting M.S.R.'s and escorting troop carriers and haulers through them, but that was nothing compared to what I've seen over the Q and playing fighter support for dropships. But no matter what our mission is, we're always chasing demons."

"Chasing demons?"

"Every pilot fears something before a mission; incineration, disintegration, aerial and zero-grav combat, getting froggy during an engagement, and just not makin' it home. Your fears are your demons. We chase them across the skies and stars because at some point you have to face them, and it's best to face them on your terms and not theirs. Understand? Ground forces call us 'Ghostriders'. A nickname they derived from their belief that there's something in a pilot's nature that makes us not of this earth. That we're already dead. I could never figure out that boonie-voodoo shit those grunts always come up with."

While the infantry and aggressor forces fought for every square inch of real estate below, the skies of 781 belonged to Fleet, and Nova-31 pilots like Col. Baker had made a pact to kill anyone that threatened to take their sky away from them. I left her standing there in the dark with her arms crossed as she paced back and forth inspecting her aircraft. I could sense that her pride ran deep and I was just a brief intrusion in her world.

As we lay in the prone position looking down across a field at Merlock, every civil defense siren within town limits began to wail loudly, sending the Terekian soldiers into a mad scramble into their battle stations. The troops in the trenches and spider holes manned machine gun nests and cracked open ammo boxes while others propped themselves against the trench walls facing the treelines with their weapons ready. Tank crews climbed inside the Taurus-17's and shut hatches, while gunship engines started their high whine in preparation for take off as their ground crews did final checks on their munitions and ran off the roof with their heads covered.

The Terekian soldiers on the main road outside Merlock town limits broke formation and dashed toward the trees on the town's eastern border as the line of armored personnel carriers pulled off the road and began to scatter on the open fields. Their doors flew open as abandoning troops ran out to join the others in the shelter of the forest.

Scat broke the filters off a couple of cigarettes and stuck them into his ears as plugs and gave me that "here we go again" look as he clicked off the safety on his Bolter. Satch double-checked the charging clip on the 38, lowered the tinted visor on his tactical helmet and gave Pappy the thumbs up.

"Keep your heads down, and hold your fire 'till I give the word." Pappy barked, "The 9th'll put these sons-of-bitches in a world of hurt."

Two black dots appeared over the western treeline in the distance. Each time a tiny point of light noiselessly blipped from them, a section of Merlock exploded into an orange inferno. Sending shattered glass from store fronts into the air, and ripping streets open into a cratered landscape of rubble and exposed sewer and electrical lines. Sparks showered the wasted boulevards as electrical cables whipped uncontrollably like snakes, and fountains of raw sewage spewed in geysers onto the upturned sidewalks.

The 108's on the Terekian tanks recoiled as they bombarded the treelines but they were blown to pieces by the hailstorm of Genesis anti-tank missiles from the inbound 31's. Torn chunks of superheated armor from the burning tanks whistled through the late afternoon sky like meteors and skittered across the field. Everything was swallowed in a deafening roar that shook the ground like an earthquake.

Without warning, a tremendous white light flashed from the center of Merlock followed by a second of silence. The town below rumbled violently and erupted in fire as buildings exploded in fountains of steel, concrete, and dirt. Other structures blew apart from the nearby concussion sending clouds of dust and smoke into the air. Troops caught in ground zero were instantly vaporized as the light engulfed them. Other soldiers spontaneously combusted from the heat or perished in the impact of the "grid-buster" missile. My vision blurred when the heat from the explosion rolled over us in an invisible wave. The 9th Armored Wing had announced their arrival.

In the town below, the Terekians that survived the blast staggered through the piles of rubble in a daze like zombies. Many of them suffered from third degree burns and vomited pieces of burnt lung from neutron poisoning caused by the fall-out. Their skin bubbled and peeled from their hands and faces as they gasped for air and collapsed from exposure.

It began to rain. Fat drops the size of golf balls fell from the smoke filled sky in sheets. It had an unnatural grayish-black tint and felt greasy from the thick clouds of cinders and ash that floated heavily through the air. The rain was actually caused by the condensed moisture from the tower of heat and dust that rose thousands of feet above the town of Merlock.

A strong odor of burnt circuitry filled my lungs. The ionization of the air gave it an electric smell and left a bitter taste in my mouth that I couldn't wash out with water.

The shadow of technology loomed over the small town like a giant threatening to stomp it out of existence. The horrifying efficiency of the Alliance's war machine rumbled through the clouds in the sinister shape of Rapiers as they descended from the heavens into Uluwatu Valley. Once again death would be redefined and reinvented by science; from drawing board to battlefield, the only human variable in the equation is the subtraction of life in terms of whole numbers exponentially.

The birds of prey thundered at speeds that can only be rivaled by the force of nature. Like a giant hand sweeping over the forest, trees caught in the velocity bent from the blinding speed of the Rapier's final approach to their "kill box". Their launched missiles left no trace of their flight path as they traveled at sub-light speeds toward their targets.

The Terekian gunships hobbled into flight as the building they were on exploded beneath them. They peeled over Merlock and orbited the town's perimeter. Throttling furiously in an attempt to escape over the trees, but they were blown out of the sky by air-to-air missiles.

Within a fraction of a second, the two dots became Nova-31's with a thunderous blur of jet wash that cut twin paths through the trees as they flew low level at mach six. They were gone by the time their sonic boom flattened everything behind them. Debris and black smoke was sucked through the vortex left in their wake. My chest was pounded with the deep vibration of the sonic concussion that knocked the air out of me, and the Rapiers had disappeared into the sky as quickly as they came. Leaving me wondering if what I saw was real, or did I just imagine the fly-by.

Four more dots appeared on the thinning horizon like the horsemen of the apocalypse. As they closed the distance, what remained of downtown Merlock and its outlying suburbs was leveled flat by a steel rain of plasmite rockets. The town stood beneath a column of thick black smoke that billowed from its burning wreckage. Pounded and smashed flat mercilessly by the 31's, Merlock was completely destroyed. All that remained was the network of trenches and bunkers that surrounded the town with wire entanglements. The main road that was scarred with craters.

The Terekian troops crouched helplessly in their trenches while the world around them disintegrated into flame. Another flash of white heat appeared in the middle of the field followed by a second of silence before the ground was lifted and turned inside out. Bodies were thrown into the air hundreds of feet into the forest with fresh earth and rocks, pelting us with clods of dirt and lumps of flesh as the setting sun filtered through the thick smoke.

A number of Terekian troops tumbled out of their smashed trenches and tried to run for cover in the trees, but in their panic, ran into their own razor wire and screamed as they got tangled and cut; tripping over each other as they desperately tried to climb their way through. They were caught in the open when the 31's thundered over the woods snapping tree tops with the ear-splitting roar of their engines. The turbulence caused by the jet wash was like a hurricane that tossed wreckage from the demolished buildings cart wheeling for hundreds of feet. The trenches in the fields were bombarded with hundreds of anti-personnel mines from cluster bombs that sent thousands of steel fleshettes screaming through the air, ripping the earth to shreds and stripping flesh off the bodies of Coalition soldiers when the Rapiers dealt their final blow before vanishing into the clouds of twilight.

Six Razorbacks appeared over the treelines and began strafing the trenches and bunkers with their chain guns. Terekian troops screamed in agony as armor-piercing rounds blew them apart and trenches filled with carnage. The gunships began rocketing the eastern woodline where soldiers tried to seek cover, and trees were splintered and plowed down by the sustained bursts from their laser cannons.

Hundreds of muzzle flashes blinked in the woods when 3rd Battalion engaged the Terekian forces and pinned them in crossfire with the hovering gunships. We could hear the crescendo of Bolter fire, grenades, and screams of pain as the chaos in the forest evolved into the sheer madness of bloodletting when enemy troops were slaughtered in 3rd Battalion's ambush.

"Fucking fire!" Pappy yelled as he threw a thermite grenade, "Kill 'em all!"

We took aim and began pouring fire into the trenches. About sixty or seventy Terekians hopped up from their positions and charged at us through the wire, firing their weapons and throwing grenades in their suicidal advance. Several troops on our line were hit by enemy fire and tumbled backwards as RPG's blew them off the ridge. We threw grenades and cut them down with Bolters. Their bodies fell into the razor wire and bobbed up and down like puppets as their own comrades used them to bridge over the entanglements. My hair stood on end as they rushed toward us howling and screaming for our blood. Automatic fire and mortars ripped through our lines, and my ears rang brightly from a nearby explosion.

Beside me a trooper laid on his belly moaning, his skull had been split open by shrapnel and thick fluid and blood oozed from his head. I wiped his brain matter from my face and saw a man running on the splintered stubs of his legs as he carried the torn upper half of his comrade. He ran about ten feet when he was mowed down by enemy gunfire.

Around me troopers screamed and yelled obscenities as they returned fire or were wounded. The ground seemed to spin wildly and tremble as grenades and mortars exploded behind our lines. The earth constantly rained on us.

I looked over and saw a soldier sitting on the ground cradling his severed leg in his arms before his eyes rolled up white and he slumped back and died of shock and blood loss. Another pulled himself across the ground. Both of his legs were missing, and torn muscle and ligaments trailed behind him as he dragged himself to cover. I saw a trooper running for safety take a round in the head. His fractured skull exploded into a red wet cloud of blood on impact, while his body ran a few more yards spewing blood from the neck like a fountain before finally falling down. Another man had his lower jaw blown off, and he stumbled over me as he tried to find where it had landed.

Medics worked furiously trying to save lives and treating the wounded. They ran beyond the ridge to retrieve fallen soldiers who lay in the line of fire, risking life and limb in the effort to bring them back from a world of hurt. Many of them were killed in their attempts or were wounded as they became victims of the firefight.

Death stalked the battlefield like a hungry predator. A great beast with an insatiable appetite and unquenchable thirst for blood. Huge, unstoppable, and merciless, its great claws grasped lives in its iron grip as it consumed the bodies of men and tore their spirits to shreds.

I will never take life for granted after seeing so much of it wasted and torn from these brave souls. I've heard them scream in agony from their wounds and beg for one more chance. I've held a soldier in my arms and watched him take his last breath. I've heard them crying for the people they love as they suffered in the mud knowing they will never see them again. I've heard them pray and shared their fears. I've even taken a life and felt the shame of feeling no remorse for my actions, quietly trying to justify what I did was right and necessary for survival. I am frightened by what I have become and what I have witnessed.

But the war has changed them. Many have become bitter and callused. They find joy in the death of the enemy, and humor in their annihilation. How will they be when they return home? They made allowances for their deaths. The morbid thought that they would not survive the war; "If I get greased on this operation, make sure my mother gets this letter…" or "tell my wife and kids that their daddy was brave…" or that their best friend in the squad is passed a particular trophy or lucky charm if they are killed. I've seen half-assed "wills" hastily jotted on the backs of envelopes or soggy stationary while inflight to the drop zone or before making planetfall. But very few of them counted on actually living and making it home.

I recalled an encounter with a soldier at Ft. Defiance on my first night at the Q. We were getting loaded on alcohol in a bunker on the eve of his squad's insertion into Uluwatu, and he told me a story about the time he went home on leave last year. During a quiet dinner with his family, he asked his mother to "pass me the fucking biscuits and butter." Bringing stares, and an uncomfortable silence to the table. He said his parents were really upset when they found him hiding in the bushes in the neighbor's yard at three in the morning, half naked and sweating profusely. Mumbling something about a Terekian offensive at dawn. He claimed to have no memory of the incident.

His biggest complaint was the feeling of not fitting in anymore at home. He felt strange and distant from his family and friends. Even his girlfriend was scared of him, and the life that he left behind felt too small and restricted. And as odd as it may sound, he felt relieved to get back to the war where his buddies could understand him, and "people you knew you could trust" surrounded him.

Perhaps they were the saddest casualties of all, the ones that make it home physically but spiritually they still lived at the Q. So changed by the war that they became alienated from their own lives and strangers in their own homes. Left to deal with the guilt that came with killing and surviving. The psychological wounds that festered for years and sometimes never healed. They would spend their lives desperately seeking the answer to the question "Why me? Why did I survive when so many around me died?" And trying to sort through the broken pieces of the memories of who they once were, and the jaded image of who they have become.

Thousands of tracers poured from the treelines as three divisions engaged the Terekian forces in a set battle. The ground popped and crackled around us as enemy fire sent dirt and hot steel splinters flying. Rockets and mortars fell on us from the sky and we were stung by chunks of earth and rocks as the ground heaved from the barrage.

The Razorbacks circled the field like a pack of wolves, trying desperately to lay down a suppressing fire when two of them disintegrated in mid-air from direct hits by surface-to-air missiles. Another gunship had taken so much ground fire that it crashed into the trees and exploded into a ball of flames. Two crewmembers staggered out of the twisted fuselage, but were killed instantly by machine gun fire from a bunker. The three other Razorbacks broke engagement and hauled off over the trees and disappeared.

"What the fuck?" Satch said angrily. "Bunch of chickenshit motherfuckers! They left us, Pappy! They just up and left us!"

"Calm down Satch." Pappy replied, "They'll be back. They have to go and rearm. They spent all their munitions."

"Shit! We should call the 9th for another strike."

"That's a negative, Satch, intelligence wants POW's for interrogation. They want to know what's between here and Volengrad. Besides, we'll get gunship back-up, but for now we're on our own."

Torn bodies littered the fields that were slippery with entrails and blood. In every yard there lay a dead man, or what was once a human being. The air was thick with the smell of burning flesh and the sharp bitter odor of ionization. Night had come and darkness slowly cloaked the shattered landscape with a blanket of shadows that brought its chilling secrets of the unseen. Scattered fires burned in the fields and in the wreckage of Merlock, casting their eerie glow on the ground as embers popped and floated into the air.

The machine gun fire became sporadic and was highlighted by the occasional explosions of mortars and grenades. Miraculously, the Terekians had successfully held their ground. They lost thousands of men in the air strike and hundreds more in the bare-fisted battle, but there was still hundreds of them left to deal with, and they will fight to the last man standing before allowing themselves to be taken prisoner.

"Shit! Hold your fire!" Pappy yelled. "Save your ammo. I've got a feeling that they're gonna try to overrun us later tonight. We've got to hold this ridge." Pappy growled through clenched teeth. "Echo Company should be coming through the woods soon, but we need to dig in."

The night had settled in and the air was cool. The stars twinkled like distant gems as the dull glow of the moon of 781 filtered through the smoke. We lay on the ridge looking down at the trenches four hundred feet in front of us. We could almost feel the enemy staring back at our position.

Fog began to rise from the ground and fill the craters and hollows. A surreal, ghostly mist crept heavily through the forest and fields; long white streaks rolled slowly across the ground and spidery branches spread out like fingers. Growing thicker and cutting visibility to less than twenty feet. The fog covered the dead and wounded like a sheet and blocked out the pale moon, leaving us in total darkness. The gunfire and mortaring had stopped. We fidgeted in the mist. Waiting for the attack to come and listening to the hundreds of injured troopers lying out in no man's land. They sobbed and moaned from their wounds, and called for their mothers or cried out for help. Their voices seemed to come from another world, echoes from another dimension; distant, alien, and disembodied. Their cries sent a shiver down my spine.

The medics grew more frustrated by the hour. Almost every attempt they made to retrieve a soldier in the pitch-blackness caused by the heavy fog was turned back by machine gun fire, making it painfully obvious that the Terekians had infrared sensors. Hours passed, and the voices of the wounded grew hoarse and weakened to low groans and moans. They no longer cried out, but they whimpered and sobbed in the dark as we listened to our boys slowly dying off.

"Help me." Someone called weakly in the dark, "Oh God please, don't leave me out here. I can't move, please."

"Jesus Christ." Doc Powers grimaced, "That poor fucker's been out there all night, except now he sounds closer."

"Stand down, Doc," Pappy ordered as he put his hand on Doc's shoulder, "I'm not letting you go after him. The Terekians are probably using him for bait, hoping to draw us in."

"Shit Pappy, I've got to try something, he's dying."

"Please, somebody, help." The voice cried, "It hurts. I'm bleeding bad."

"Hang on, I'm coming after you!" Doc yelled.

"The fuck you are, Doc!" Pappy barked.

"The fuck I'm not! I think that's Moose out there, Pappy."

"Bullshit! It can't be."

"Oh no? When was the last time you saw him?"

"Shit! Shit!" Pappy cussed, "Moose! Sound off Moose, where the fuck are you?"

"Pappy?" The voice sobbed, "Pappy? Oh thank God! Pappy I'm hit bad, I think my legs are broken, and I can't move my arm."

"Shit!" Pappy whispered, "It's him."

"What do you want to do?" Doc asked.

"I'm gonna go get him."

"What! Pap, you can't! You've got to stay here with the squad. I'll get him."

"No. You stay here and wait, Doc, that's an order."

Before either of them settled their argument, Scat slipped over the ridgeline and began crawling toward where he thought Moose lay.

"Goddamn it Scat, get your ass back here!" Pappy yelled after him.

"No sweat, Pappy," He called back, "I don't want to live forever anyway."

He tried to grab his feet to pull him back, but Scat was already out of reach and began his journey down the hill.

"Scat, don't be an idiot, you'll get killed. Oh fuck it, hey Moose!" Pappy yelled. "Hang on, Scat's coming to get you!"

"Who?" Moose replied.

"Keep talking so he can find you."

Scat crawled over the stony ground, groping in the dark toward Moose's voice. His mumbling sounded like he was about twenty or thirty yards ahead. The earth felt wet and slippery, and a soft jelly oozed through his fingers as he pulled himself forward.

Meanwhile, my imagination went into overtime on what kind of gruesome mixture of fetid intestinal slime Scat crawled over. The strong coppery smell of blood permeated the air with the stench of shit and urine, and it stuck to the lining of my nose as I gasped for a clean breath.

After groping through the mud for ten minutes, Moose sounded like he was just in front of Scat. He reached out and felt his hand and grabbed hold of it and pulled.

"Moose, is that you?" Scat asked with a glimmer of hope.

"No, I'm over here."

"What the fuck!" Scat thought to himself. The hand he held had a bad weight to it—cool and lifeless. He reached out and felt the folds of cold rubbery skin and the moist stickiness of a mound of flesh—he didn't want to know what he put his hand into, but Moose was less than five feet ahead, so Scat crawled over it and continued to wade through the human soup.

"Moose, where are you?" Scat whispered.

"Right here."

He reached out again, hoping his luck improved. This time Scat was rewarded by the sound of Moose's sarcasm.

"Jesus Scat, if you're gonna touch me there like that, then there better be a ring involved."

They chuckled at his joke as Scat moved in next to him. It was pitch black, but he could feel Moose shivering from lying in the cold for hours.

"Hey Scatman, you are one crazy son-of-a-bitch. I think you pissed Pappy off back there."

"Fuck 'im in the fat part of his neck if he can't take a joke." Scat hissed. "How bad you hurt?"

"I think my legs are broken, and my left arm's pretty messed up too."

"If we can get you on your side, I can get under you and you can roll on top of my back. Hook your right arm around my neck, and I'll piggyback you back to the ridge. You up for it?"

"What the fuck, we can't dance."

"Alright, let's give it a try; let's get you on you side. Ready?"

Moose groaned as Scat rolled him onto his right side. "Motherfucker! Damn it Scat, I'm gonna get you for this!"

"Shut your pie hole, Moose, I didn't crawl all this way for the scenery." Scat said as he scooted underneath him into the muck. "Now roll yourself on to my back."

"AAARHH!" Moose screamed as he flopped over him. He put his arm around Scat's neck and began taking deep breaths in an effort to deal with the pain.

"Okay Moose, hang on, here we go." Scat strained under his weight. "Pappy, I've got him! We're on our way back!"

"Come on Scat, I know you can make it!" Pappy barked.

The crawl back was painfully slow. Scat was going back uphill, and Moose's added weight made him sink deeper into the mix of sucking mud and guts. His knees were skinned, and elbows raw; his whole body ached as he carried Moose through the darkness toward the sound of Pappy's voice. Scat crawled over several torn bodies. What felt like an opened ribcage jabbed into his stomach as he slithered over it and what certainly had to be the exposed lungs and other vital organs squished under their combined weight and made a sick bubbling noise. Scat felt like he was swimming in human debris and waste; the smell of shit was overwhelming and he stopped several times as he gagged and choked from the odor.

Moose and Scat breathed heavily as he punked him up to the ridge. He was tired and nauseated. Sweat poured over his face from the struggle and stung his eyes. Several pairs of hands grabbed Scats arms and pulled them over the crest of the hill into safety. Pappy, Doc, and Satch's faces were illuminated through the haze by a couple of small chemlights.

"Jesus Scat," Pappy scolded, "that was the stupidest thing I've seen anyone do in a long time. Thanks you crazy fucker!"

"Yeah, thanks Scatman." Moose croaked under his breath.

"Doc, how bad is he?" Pappy asked as he turned his attention on Moose.

"Well, Moose, you sorry piece of shit," Doc smiled, "you're gonna live, you've lost a lot of blood from the compound fracture in your left leg, but we'll get you fixed up. Looks like you're going home."

"You wouldn't bullshit me, would you Doc?"

"Naw, you're going to take some time to heal, and you'll probably have a limp the rest of your life, but you'll stay in one piece. Your arm's broken too. Pappy, we need to get him off this hill and get the medevacs down here for the rest of the wounded."

"Yeah I know, Doc," Pappy sighed, "dust-offs won't be in 'till first light, the only thing coming our way now are gunships to finish the job. Let's get Moose to the back with the other wounded. Echo Company is dug in at the treeline behind us. He should be safe there."

Scat sat quietly trying to wipe the filth off his body armor and face, but the more he wiped, the more it smeared on him. Sticky with blood, excrement, and god only knows what, he shook his head and looked up at the moon that peeked through the fog.

"Scat," Pappy's silhouette moved in the moonlight, "you did a very foolish and brave thing tonight. That's the kind of shit that gets people killed and earns them medals. What the hell am I going to do with you?"

"How 'bout making me a general?" Scat replied.

"You're a real work of art, you know it?" Pappy laughed.

Pappy's face was suddenly splattered with blood as Scat clutched his throat and began floundering on the ground gasping for air.

"Scat!" Satch screamed. "Oh shit! Scat's hit! DOC!"

Blood poured between Scat's fingers as he held his throat and beat the ground furiously with his legs. His eyes closed tightly and his mouth opened and closed trying to get air into his lungs. His glasses with cracked lens lay twisted on the ground beside him as he trembled and grimaced from the pain.

"Oh Jesus, kid, hold on!" Pappy cried as he removed Scat's helmet and cradled his head in his arms. "Let me see how bad you're hit!"

Pappy gently pulled Scat's hands away as Satch hit him in the leg with morphine. Scat's neck was torn to pieces and his windpipe was blown completely away. He had taken a round in the throat making it look like a pound of ground beef, and he was bleeding and choking to death as we helplessly watched.

"Shit Scat, you're a mess!" Pappy sobbed as he held Scat's hand. "Stay with me, buddy! It's not your time! Not now—not here!"

Scat stopped struggling as the morphine began to take hold, and his strained gasping became a soft gurgle.

"Pappy, he's not gonna make it." Satch whispered through the din of gunfire.

"Fuck you! Fuck you, Satch! He's gonna be okay!"

"Pappy..." Satch sighed.

Scat stopped twitching and died in Pappy's arms. His eyes and mouth were open, and his bloody face looked calm as he stared into the evening sky. Pappy hugged his limp body as tears tracked down his face.

"I'm so sorry little buddy." Pappy cried. "You're not hurting anymore. You're going home." He stroked Scat's hair and rocked back and forth crying. "You're going home..."

"Pappy, snap out of it!" Satch yelled. "We've got a job to do."

Pappy didn't hear anything around him as he held his dead friend.

"Pappy!" Satch gave the sergeant a hard slap to the face. "Come on troop! Drive on! Hellhounds on our trail—we got to go!"

The dull gleam left Pappy's eyes as he snapped back to his senses. He silently picked up the radio pack and strapped it on, then grabbed Scat's dog tags and reached down and picked up his buddy's eyeglasses and put them in his pocket.

The silence was shattered by the whine of gunship engines. Razorbacks flew out of nowhere and churned up the fog over the fields. This time twelve of them circled the area like hornets and bombarded the bunkers and trenches with cluster bombs and missiles. They weaved in and out of the fog and poured a steady stream of tracers down on the Terekians.

"Hit the deck!" Pappy screamed, "It's payback time!"

The ground raged and turned from the high explosives hitting the bunkers and splintering their steel structures. Chunks of shrapnel hurled through the air and fell among our lines as the earth trembled and heaved like an injured animal. Spouts of iron, dirt, and bodies were lifted skyward and slammed back to the ground with shattering impact. Incendiary bombs ignited trenches, trapping the soldiers inside to perish in the chemical fire, and secondary explosions tore the earth open when the enemy's ammunition bunkers caught on fire.

Chain guns from the ships chattered in their sustained bursts and depleted titanium rounds chewed holes through overhead covers made of steel. Terekians burned where they fell; and the fog glowed red and white as it reflected the flash of explosions and the blaze of the firebombs. The smell of gunpower filled my lungs as the ground rumbled deeply under me like some great creature was burrowing its way to the surface. I held my head down and clenched my teeth when plasmite rockets punched the landscape with craters.

Fleshettes from cluster bombs hummed and shrieked through the dark chill. The steel darts pinned and crucified the enemy to the walls of their trenches or stripped the meat off their bones, sending hunks of flesh and bone fragments spinning through the air. I looked down at the devastating firepower of the Razorbacks and the total destruction of the air strike and wondered how the Terekians crouched through that and survived the night.

Every square inch of Merlock and its surrounding areas was plowed and churned by gunfire and rockets. The aerial bombardment went on for an hour and a half, shaking and punishing the earth. The troops cheered and whistled wildly every time a missile or bomb took out a section of trench and sent the enemy scrambling into the open where they were plowed down by the chain guns. The thin outline of the horizon emerged in the distance; the beauty of its orange and purple hue was a stunning contrast to the horror of the night. The gunships stopped their assault and broke into pairs as they orbited the thrashed treelines seeking more targets.

We lay in the dim light watching the fog dissipate and the fires in the field leaping into the sky. The trenches burned and what was once the town of Merlock was now a huge desolate clearing in the Bellows Woods. Columns of smoke rose from the twisted wreckage and the ground lay smoldering and galvanized. The forest's treelines that bordered the town's perimeter were scorched and stripped clean of their foliage. They stood like broken skeletons reaching for the sky in the deep purple light of the coming dawn. I sighed in relief when 2nd Battalion emerged from the woods thirty minutes later and began to advance toward the devastation in a long sweeping formation. They carefully picked their way through the pieces of razor wire that lay strewn about the fields.

I looked at the troops that lay in the prone position across the ridgeline in the dim light. Haggard, torn, and filthy, they watched wordlessly through red-rimmed eyes as the fires below flickered in the aftermath. Some smoked, and others opened rations for breakfast, they knew that the worst was yet to come. Volengrad lay twenty miles to the north, and would not be taken as easily as Merlock. The battle there would be on Terekian terms and territory. 1st Division had been through the meat grinder over the years; every tough campaign the Alliance fought in the war, 1st Division was there to spearhead. Win or lose, they had seen the most death and drawn the most blood, and 22nd Bravo had always been the tip of the spear. The first in and the last out. They had earned the respect of Fleet as well as all the outfits in the Aggressor Forces.

I looked at the dirty tired faces of the soldiers, and I realized how young they really were. Boys with the eyes of old men. Instead of growing up, they grew old. Everything in between youth and maturity was the war. War became their surrogate mother that weaned them on death and loss, and nourished them with the blood of their enemies. I look at these young infantrymen and see a certain dignity and nobility. They have become rough, their language is coarse, and their humor becomes increasingly bitter as time passes, but that is because their lives are stripped of convention and luxury. Their nobility and compassion come from the way they live unselfishly and risk their lives to help each other. They share their food and they share their stories, and ultimately, they share their fears and sorrows. I look at these filthy men with dirt in their ears, and I feel like I have walked with kings. I put my head down and shut my eyes and passed out from exhaustion.

December 22, 2406

I woke up in a small tent, the corners of my eyes crusted with grime and my sense of direction turned upside down. I saw Willie sitting next to me. His helmet was off and his head was bandaged up. I had been out for three hours. I grimaced as I sat up, every part of my body was sore, and the muscles in my legs felt heavy like they were encased in lead.

"Hey look who finally decided to join the living." Willie beamed.

"Shit Frye, you gave us the scare a few hours ago," Satch grinned, "When you passed out, we thought you got hit by shrapnel. That shit was flying everywhere."

"Scat?" I asked through the cobwebs.

Willie just looked down sadly and shook his head. I could tell he was fighting back tears.

"What the hell happened to your head, Willie?"

"Almost got greased. Round grazed my temple and left a small groove. Its not as bad as it looks, its superficial."

"What happens now?"

"We're gonna stand down here a couple of days then get airlifted over to Highway 12. Should be a short hop by gunship. We're going right into Volengrad from there." Willie replied.

"So what happened with the Terekians?" I inquired. "They all dead?"

"All but four." Satch said grimly. "You should see the mess down there. That place is completely wasted."

I spent most of the morning cleaning up and snacking on rations. Not much of a meal, but a feast when you're starving, even the coffee tasted good. I couldn't believe how dirty my body armor was, caked with mud and stained with shit and blood. I was completely doused with grime. The worst thing about it was there was no place to shower. The best I could manage was a change of shirt, socks, and pants, and the sullen wish that it would start raining again to get most of the filth off my skin and armor.

We all smelled bad. Like the grave. We spent the last forty-eight hours being showered by shit, human debris, and every unimaginable thing repulsive to human beings. We marched through it, crawled in it, dug into it, and even tasted its bitter flavor. The smell of battle had woven itself into our clothes, and the pungent odor of stale blood, excrement, and heavy sweat followed us wherever we went.

Later that morning I stepped outside to go check out Merlock over the ridge. I strolled between the rows of tents set up in the forest as camp. Most of the troops sat outside to take in some fresh air as they went about the tasks of cleaning their weapons and restocking their ammunition before the next deployment on Christmas Eve. Apparently the supply ships had made their drops earlier that morning, and food and cigarettes were abundant. Freeze-dried rations were being passed out and squirreled away into packs along with containers of water and tobacco. A soldier can go without many necessities for days, but cigarettes, cigars, and chewing tobacco was a sacrifice he or she was not willing to make.

The closer I got to the edge of the woods, the thinner the foliage on the trees became. Branches lay broken on the ground in layers of leaves and pine needles, and thick sap trailed from the scars on their trunks. I felt a small drop of moisture land on my hand and wiped it off thinking it was water, but its stickiness caught my attention and I looked at the red smear between my fingers. I shot a look up into the trees and saw a body tangled in the branches as another drop dotted my cheek. I wiped it off and stepped out of the way of the next trickle. The trees were filled with bodies from the air strike. They had been blown clear out of Merlock and the impact sent them thousands of feet into the forest. The dead hung from the trees in twisted, broken positions like grotesque ornaments as insects swarmed over them in thick buzzing clouds. Bodies were strung up everywhere, and entrails dangled obscenely from branches, fat and moist, a nightmarish fruit for a bitter harvest glistened in the sunlight. I quickened my pace and tried not to look up as I made my way through the woods to the clearing.

The ground was chopped up and lumpy and the air was heavily laced with the smell of a slaughterhouse. Heavy tracked earth-moving equipment with huge plows crawled back and forth across the fields burying corpses in fresh trenches. The unofficial body count was somewhere over four thousand Terekians and rising. Razorbacks and medevacs came and went, dropping off reinforcements and dusting-off the wounded. The LZ was huge and tarmac was already being laid down to accommodate larger aircraft. The 17th Engineering Battalion had already started planning the construction of another base camp in the Bellows Woods on top of the now extinct town of Merlock.

I lit up a cigarette and walked along the ridgeline watching the activity. I was astonished by how much can be changed so quickly. Less than twelve hours ago Terekian forces occupied this area, now it was in the hands of the Alliance. Patrols would be sent out to secure a larger part of the sector, while a new perimeter is established for the new base. Miles of razor wire had been strung along the treelines, and specialists had already mined certain areas during the early morning hours. I flicked the cigarette butt aside and walked down the ridge for a closer look.

Newly arrived soldiers stood in formation down in the field next to the LZ. Their body armor was clean and untested, their uniforms underneath creased and starched, and their faces shaved and untainted by the crippling visions of battle.

I wondered about the human factor in the war; not just how the loss of lives could be counted and left open in a running total, but how the emotional loss remained unquantified through the decades; memories of sacrifices and stories that spanned for generations like the fading photographs of family members that hang on hallway walls or lay stacked in a forgotten album covered with dust awaiting rediscovery. Yes, we remember the fallen, and yes, we honor their memory, but we never really pay attention to the lesson that needs to be learned. That perhaps in their deaths, and somewhere in the halls of time when mourning becomes remembrance, their fading pictures will whisper to our collective conscience that we must never take life for granted.

I watched one gunship land in the field and splatter mud on a small group of troopers that were zipping up body bags, collecting dog tags, and taking the names of their dead comrades. They looked over as an attractive woman in a suit and a camera crew stumbled out onto the LZ. The visitors all vomited from the motion sickness moments after the ship departed, and the salty troops that were in the battle the night before just about fell down laughing.

The woman ignored the muddy soldiers and motioned her crew to start filming after she straightened out her outfit and brushed the hair out of her face.

"This is Mika Sheldon," she said with a serious tone as she clutched some papers in her left hand, "and behind me is the shattered remains of Merlock. After landing in the Bellows Woods two days ago and making contact with local mercenaries, 1st Division's invasion forces discovered the population of Merlock in mass graves not too far from this very site. Last night Alliance forces engaged the Terekians in a fierce ground battle that entailed armed propaganda that will ultimately lead to Volengrad City. The victory was reported by military officials to be swift and decisive, and Alliance casualties were minimal and well within acceptable loss."

The cameraman turned his aim at the freshly arrived troopers that began their march off the landing zone.

"As you can see from the condition of our brave boys," she said with pride, "they are already prepared for their next encounter with the Coalition in what will certainly be the turning point of the war..."

"Hey lady!" One of the troopers on KIA duty yelled. "Why don't you and them limp dicks come over here and film some of these minimal casualties we're sending home?"

"General Thomas Isley predicts that the Terekian occupation of Volengrad will fall in a matter of weeks as Alliance troops move into position in the next couple of days to begin the siege that will liberate Volengrad from the tyranny of the Terekian government..." Sheldon continued.

"Hey lady," the trooper yelled again off camera as he held up a dog tag, "you see this? This was Pvt. James Parrish, my buddy! And he was killed last night when an RPG landed next to him! He was twenty-six years old!" the soldier began to cry, "twenty-six! Or don't you give a damn?"

"In the up coming weeks," Mika Sheldon cast an irritated glance in the trooper's direction, "QSAR NEWS will bring you comprehensive coverage of the on going war on 781..."

"Why don't you tell them the truth back home?" the trooper sobbed, "they need to know that Jim Parrish is dead! Scott Soto is gone too! So is Reggie..."

"Come on, bro," another trooper put his arm around his friend's shoulder, "the world doesn't give a shit about us. We've got to get back to work."

"This is Mika Sheldon, in the killing fields of Merlock, QSAR NEWS, in Uluwatu Valley." Sheldon looked at the cameraman, "Okay Nate, that's a take."

"You sure you want to use that one Mika?" the cameraman asked.

"Yeah why not?" Sheldon replied casually, "We can always edit out that guy's ranting in the background." She gave the muddy troopers a scornful look, "Fucking animals..."

They were on the next gunship bound back for Ft. Defiance.

December 23, 2406

I woke up to a faint tremble of the ground. I sat up in the dark tent rubbing my eyes when I heard the distant roar of several explosions followed by more ground tremors.

"Sounds like the 9th and 64th are putting the hammer down in Volengrad." Willie said in the dark. "The fucking party's just getting started."

"Jesus Christ," I yawned, "sounds like the world's coming to an end."

"Air strikes, newsman, Fleet's clearing a path for us." Willie replied. "Grab your gear, let's head for the ridge and scope it out."

Willie took a flashlight and his Bolter and we started through the dark woods. The brisk air numbed my hands and the leaves rustled beneath us with every step. I could just make out the silhouette of trees and tents as we walked along. The sound of the air strike was a constant low rumbling in the background and the earth's vibration tickled my ears.

Once we topped the ridgeline, we looked toward the north and watched the bright flashes of exploding bombs and missiles flicker across the treetops where Volengrad sat less than twenty miles away. Tremendous explosions lit up the sky in the distance and the thunder of the impact rolled across the valley. Low storm clouds moved in from the east and reflected the fires from the strikes; red and orange mixed with the dark purple gloom of early morning as tracers ascended into the heavens in streams seeking to knock Nova-31's out of the sky.

The ground shook nonstop and the overcast sky slowly began to turn a brilliant red as the sun peeked over the horizon. Con-trails of surface-to-air missiles reached up from Volengrad through the clouds and bloomed into fireballs thousands of feet above the surface as several Rapiers disintegrated in midair.

It began to drizzle as the morning turned gray. The sound of turbo-fan engines cut through the air as lines of gunships inbound from Defiance filed in at treetop level from the south and landed in the fields below. They would be the ones to airlift us to Highway 12 tomorrow morning.

"Hell of a light show isn't it?" Willie nodded as he lit up a smoke.

"You think we'll be able to take the city back, Willie?"

"Yeah I suppose," he sighed as he exhaled a thick cloud of smoke, "but I think the General and that Mika bitch are wrong. Its gonna take more than weeks unless we use nukes, and I think we're gonna get our asses kicked pretty hard."

"I don't know Willie, the Alliance is going to throw everything into this one."

"Sure they will, but Volengrad's gonna be some hardcore door-to-door street fighting. This is going to take months, and a lot of us are gonna get killed doing it."

"We should get back to camp."

"Yeah, we need to get some chow. Pappy says 1st Platoon is goin' out on patrol this morning."

It was raining hard by the time we made it back to the campgrounds. The earth had turned into mud as we trudged to the tent, and the downpour had washed off the film of grime on my face and body armor. Pappy stood next to his tent with his arms crossed and a soggy cigar hanging from his lips.

"Well good morning ladies." Pappy glared, "I hope you can be ready to move out in twenty minutes, we're going for a little walk in the woods today."

Everyone assembled in the center of camp with light packs on under their ponchos and weapons locked and loaded. The rain pattered on the canopy overhead and streamed down branches and vines splashing into puddles below. The ground trembled with the rhythm of the aerial bombardment fifteen miles away, and the deep roar of high explosives sounded like the footsteps of a giant stomping through the dense woods. We cringed and put our hands over our ears when the air compressed a hundred feet above us into a sonic boom as Nova-31's passed overhead in full afterburner and rustled the triple canopy violently, the trees swayed in their wake as branches snapped and fell on top of us with a shower of leaves.

"Fuck, I hate it when they do that." Willie grumbled.

"Shit Willie," Satch grinned, "tell me you wouldn't do the same if you were in the cockpit of one of those."

"Damn right I would!" Willie said smiling, "you hogs would be sniffing my fart pipe if that was me."

"You're such an asshole, dude."

"Yeah, but you like me that way." Willie blew Satch a kiss.

Satch ventilated his backside and winked back.

"That smells tampered with."

"I think that knot on your head jarred a screw loose." Satch chuckled.

"Okay, listen up 1st Platoon," Pappy barked through the rain and distant rumble of explosions, "last night tiger scouts reported a band of mercs moving in the area. Probably gearing up for an assault on the camp tonight. We're going on a little hunt this morning to where the scouts saw them last. We'll be about half a click from here when we'll hook up with the reaction team that spotted the mercs. This is a search and destroy mission, if we make contact, our orders are to take them out. Satch, take point...let's move out."

We filed into the woods in a line. Twenty-three men. 1st Platoon had lost ten people in the last forty-eight hours and the strain was beginning to show on their faces. It was going on six o'clock when we hit the thick live curtain of the forest. Everything was circular and seemed to be growing from the top down rather than the bottom up. Millions of lush vines, some two or three inches thick, hung from trees and intertwined with one another and anchored themselves to roots that crawled across the ground. Thick tubular stalks of shrub-like plants shot up through the tangle six or eight feet into the air, their blue-green leaves catching drops of rain that trickled through the overhead cover.

The world was a dark wet cavern that smelled of rotting vegetation and fresh pine. The forest floor was soft and wrapped itself around my feet with every step; and always, the ground trembled as Volengrad suffered the wrath of Fleet's air power. The leaves that grew on the shorter plants were impossibly large; some reached four-foot diameters and displayed an awesome array of the different shades of green. The winding roots of the gigantic pines and other alien species of trees dominated the forest floor with their twisted network, but were concealed by ferns that covered the ground like a lush carpet. An infinite variety of mosses draped over branches and the deteriorating trunks of fallen trees.

We moved slowly for nearly an hour, constantly scanning the ground for trip wires and laser sensors. The muscles of my face began to ache from clenching my jaws too hard, and the back of my neck throbbed from muscle tension. I tightened my grip on the Bolter as we passed through a thick wall of moss. I was so preoccupied looking down that I didn't notice a huge snake wrapped around a limb above me until Doc tapped me on the shoulder and pointed up. This thing was a fucking monster. Its body was at least as thick as my torso, and its yellow unblinking eyes stared at me from its huge scaly head. Its long black tongue flicked in an out slowly as it tracked my movement, then it opened its mouth exposing thousands of sharp teeth and hissed at me.

"Jesus Christ!" I stammered as I raised my weapon.

"Hold your fire, Frye!" Doc yelped as he pulled my barrel down, "That son-of-a-bitch doesn't want you, it only eats birds."

"Bullshit! You don't get that big just eating birds!"

"Okay, it eats lots of birds. Besides, I think he likes you."

"This nature walk really sucks." I said catching my breath.

"Just stay cool Frye, you fire a burst and every merc within a mile from here's gonna know where we are. Just keep moving newsman."

The woods grew thicker and darker as we sloshed our way through the dense tangle. Every few minutes someone would get stuck in the mud, and it would take two other troopers to pull him free. Bolters could no longer be carried at port arms, but were slung behind our shoulders to keep from being knotted up in the vines. The soldiers pulled out their side arms and survival knives as they struggled through the thicket—hypnotized by the sound of their own heartbeats and bustling footfalls. The temperature dropped another ten degrees and every labored breath I took seemed to hang in a thick plume as I exhaled.

We broke through the tangle of vines and roots and found ourselves wading knee-deep in a stagnant pond, the agitated peeps, burps, and croaks of reptiles seemed to send a message to the rest of the wildlife in the forest that they were being invaded by uninvited guests. We brought our Bolters back to port as we crossed the pond on to its muddy banks. The patter of the rain grew louder and echoed above us like a waterfall in a canyon.

We slowly walked another thirty yards when Satch held up his arm as a signal to stop. We froze in mid-step and dropped into a crouch behind shrubs and bushes and tried to breathe quietly as we waited. Everyone's eyes darted across the trees, scanning for movement—waiting for the enemy to reveal themselves by initiating contact. The mad minute that lasted forever. When the world is torn apart by the eruption of a firefight and the slow motion illusion of hell breaking open gave you a teasing glimpse of death's savage character; when everything around you melted into chaos and spun itself upside down and you found yourself drowning in the flashflood of your own adrenaline. The anticipation was unnerving and squeezed fear into a funnel, drawing it out in long torturous strands of time. Making the wait worse than the contact.

Satch gave the signal to move up to his position and we got on our feet and tensely walked to where he was standing. There, hanging upside down from the trees, were twelve mercenaries, they had been skinned and gutted. Their penises had been cut off and stuffed into their mouths. Their eyes were carved out of their sockets and left in a small neat pile that teemed with insects, and their bowels lay in sticky heaps underneath where each of the bodies swayed. Tacked to a tree with a small hatchet was a note written in the local tribal dialect.

"Looks like the tiger scouts decided to take them out before we got here." Pappy said shaking his head.

"Hey Willie," Satch waved, "get your ass over here, need you to translate something."

"What the hell is it?" Willie asked with a puzzled look.

"Check out this note..."

"Whoa, don't touch it!" Willie held up his hands.

"Alright, alright. Do you know what it says, Willie?"

"ALIS UBERAL SARGETANIS UBETU DOMMINIS—DITANO TALEMAN BROHEIL" Willie read nervously.

"What the fuck does that mean?"

"That's Serenian. It means "Death lies waiting in the shadows—The Brotherhood of Night". My guess is that the scouts cut the eyes out to fuck with the mercs. Serenians believe that without their eyes, the dead won't be able to find their way into the afterlife, and they'll end up lost and wandering the earth forever."

"What about cutting them open and hacking off their dicks?"

"I guess they did that as an added bonus. It has a tendency to freak the mercs out a little more."

"Man, this is freaking me out right now. That's what I call some serious psy-war." Satch coughed.

"Fuckin' A." Willie glared, "Maybe we should get the fuck out of here. This kind of shit gives me the creeps."

"Yeah," Pappy nodded, "we better leave this shit alone. Them scouts went to a lot of trouble to leave their calling card. Come on, let's head out."

We turned back and crossed the pond and started through the curtain of vines. The eeriness of the forest made us jumpy and the thicket cutting visibility down to less than ten feet didn't help. We pushed our way through the sucking mud and struggled through hedges and shrubs that clawed at our armor and scratched at our faces. We came to a small clearing where the ferns grew waist-high and took a short break. I set my pack down and sat on a rotting log with Willie and Doc and took a few swigs of water from my canteen and passed it around.

I looked around the dim woods listening to the chirp and fiddling of insects and the pounding rain on the canopy above. Volumes of literature have been written over the last century about these woods in Uluwatu Valley. Poets romanticized their impenetrable loneliness and foreboding darkness, and writers fictionalized spirits and mysterious ghost towns that vanished after playing host to any unfortunate travelers that stumbled upon them during the night. The forest was spooky on its own without the enhancement of urban legends, but the fact that tribal mercenaries really crept around out here with every intent to do you harm was enough to keep you on that frosty edge for a long time. Setting up an ambush out here at night was insane, and the scouts and Aggressor squads that volunteered to do it night after night were the craziest of all. Stealthing through the undergrowth next to moving enemy columns and encampments and killing them silently one at a time under the cloak of darkness and dragging the bodies off to be found hours later by one of their own patrols, completely dismembered with the eyes missing. Spooky.

Even the most battle-hardened troopers of the infantry looked innocent compared to tiger scouts and the members of the Aggressor Forces. Especially the scouts. The scouts would walk into base camp in two man teams; faces streaked with camouflage paint, black floppy bush hats, and armed only with throwing spikes, knives, and piano wire, no body armor or tactical helmets or infrared goggles. They went on night patrols stripped free of technology and survived strictly on instinct and intelligence. The regular troopers always left a table clear for them in the mess tent and never spoke to them as they walked by. Spooky.

As we walked back through the camp's perimeter and reassembled in front of the CP, Lt. Reynolds stepped outside to talk to Pappy. The ground still rumbled from the distant explosions at Volengrad, and the rain clattered noisily through the trees above.

"How'd it go Pappy?" Reynolds asked.

"Pretty uneventful L-T, we didn't see shit."

"Just as well, you boys get some chow and rest up for tomorrow's drop onto Highway 12. We're going to hook up with the 8th Armored Division there and start shelling the city. Meet up at the fields at 0400 hours tomorrow by the gunships. We deploy at 0430 for the objective."

"Yes sir."

"I see you've hooked up with the scouts." Reynolds said dryly, "Why don't you show 'em where they can get some chow, Pappy, I'm sure they're hungry. They've been out in the woods for the last three days."

We all looked around and shot frantic glances at each other, and standing less than ten feet from our group were four tiger scouts. Faces blackened from the filth of the woods, they had shadowed us for over two hours in the forest and then slipped into camp within our ranks unnoticed. One of them tipped his boonie hat at us and grinned as he lit up a cigarette that he took off one of the dead mercs. Spooky.

Q7

"Night hath a thousand eyes."

John Lyly (1554-1606), English playwright

J.R. held a small mirror up to his face as he sat in the tent waiting for the sun to go down. He used his index finger to put the finishing touches of dark green chameleon paint across the bridge of his nose and left cheek over the black that he smeared on a few minutes earlier.

Thompson honed the edge of his ten-inch survival knife in the fading light, his throwing spikes sat in a neat line on his sleeping bag as he quietly focused on the task at hand and wondered if he should eat before going out on patrol tonight. His face was already painted up in green and black, and his woodland tiger suit bore no indication of rank or divisional patches.

"Hurry it up will ya J.R.," Thompson said as he secured his hunting knife into the sheath fastened to his leg, "the sun's goin' down and we need to get to the wire."

"Okay, okay." J.R. grumbled, "Lemme finish up my forehead."

"Jesus Christ, you're taking longer than my baby sister does. We're not going out for a night on the town ya know." Thompson said sarcastically as he gathered the throwing spikes up from the bedroll and put them into his wristbands.

"Okay I'm done." J.R. responded as he stood up and put on his bush hat.

"You got your knife and spikes?"

"You bet your ass," J.R. patted himself, "and I'm bringing this along tonight for a try." He held up three strands of piano wire that were two feet long with wooden handles tied to each end. A garrote.

They faced each other in the dim light and patted down each other's uniforms to make sure nothing jingled or would reflect light if the moon came out. Noise and light discipline. They would carry nothing out on the ambush but their hunting knives and throwing spikes that were matted in flat black paint. They weren't even allowed to wear their dog tags or carry a canteen of water or any web gear. They went out completely stripped clean of any firearms.

"Alright, looks like we're squared away and good to go, J.R."

"I hear Noble and King are goin' out tonight too."

"Yeah, we'll see 'em at the wire on the east end of the LZ."

"We better get goin' bro, it's getting dark."

"Alright," Thompson said as he took a deep breath, "it's time to creepy-crawl!"

They stepped out of the tent and began walking toward the smoking landing zone that 1st Division had secured just hours before. The lights from the flares cast a yellow glow on the landscape as Razorbacks and medevacs rumbled overhead in the evening sky.

When they got to the east end of the strip, they saw Noble and King standing next to the razor wire waiting. The perimeter guards lay in the prone position in shallow slit trenches behind sandbags with their Bolters propped up toward the treeline. The guards smoked and whispered among themselves and threw a few nervous glances at the two tiger scouts as Thompson and J.R. walked up to their two companions.

"Hey what's going on Thompson?" King grinned, "What the fuck took you guys so long?"

"Aw fuzz-nuts over here took forever getting his face painted." Thompson nodded at J.R.

"What the fuck, J.R., you got a hot date in the woods that we don't know about?"

"Let's leave your mother out of this, King." J.R. glared.

"Yeah, you leave my mother out of this," King smiled as he grabbed his crotch, "and I'll leave THIS out of *your* mother!"

"So what do we got going tonight?" Thompson asked.

"Last night Scarecrow and Dragon squads got into a firefight with a band of mercs, they figured about fifteen of them cocksuckers got away, probably still in the area." King said matter-of-factly, "We're gonna see if we can find them."

"All four of us going into the same area?"

"Yeah, northeast 136 to 225 degrees."

"Sounds good, let's get going."

The four scouts dropped to their bellies and crawled single file under the razor wire. The ground was still soft from the heavy rains as they pulled themselves across with their elbows. They zigzagged for fifty feet on their stomachs to avoid the mines that the engineers planted that afternoon, and scurried under trip wires that were randomly strung invisibly across the perimeter. When they passed the last string of anti-personnel mines a hundred meters beyond the razor wire, they crawled on all fours another sixty feet through the high grass into the dense ferns that covered the forest floor.

They crawled another hundred feet through the almost pitch black undergrowth, painstakingly plowing their way through the moist tangles before stopping to rest among the ferns. They leaned back-to-back against each other and took quiet breaths as they scanned the trees and listened to the sounds of the nocturnal life chirping and croaking at each other. It was almost impossible to see. The dark outlines of tree trunks towered over them like columns holding up the triple canopy of leaves and branches. A hundred feet above them, flocks of small exotic reptiles capable of flight fluttered noisily in the foliage and screeched at each other over territory. The tiny wings of insects hummed in their ears and assaulted their hands and faces as they crept over the earth toward a narrow trail that cut through the forest.

King leaned into Thompson's face and whispered almost inaudibly.

"We split up here, you and J.R. move up another fifty feet and me and Noble are going to the right another thirty feet from that trail. We'll wait them out from here."

"Okay," Thompson whispered back, "good hunting."

They spent the night listening to the chatter of automatic weapons as firefights erupted several miles away, and the occasional muffled explosions of grenades and mortars thumped in the distance. Their senses had sharpened to a state of hypersensitivity to all unusual noises, a twig snapping, the sound of footsteps, or the unusual silence that gripped the forest in a supernatural vacuum. They lay completely motionless in the soft moist groundcover listening and waiting. It began to rain rhythmically on the canopy overhead and the air brought a chilly bite as midnight approached.

The hours passed slowly, and the scout teams shivered in the dank tangles and listened to the rain cascading to the forest floor. Thunder rumbled overhead in the low clouds and the sky lit up brightly as lightning streaked across the horizon. A huge red and yellow spider the size of a man's hand danced across J.R.'s shoulder blades and made its way up the back of his neck and sat on his head fiddling with its legs.

"Psst! Don't move, J.R.." Thompson whispered lightly.

"What?"

"I said don't move. There's a red diamond spider on your head."

"Well get the fucker off me!" J.R. whispered back through clenched teeth.

"Easy now..." Thompson slowly pulled out a throwing spike from his wristband and threw it sideways at J.R. impaling the spider and sending it flying off his head into a tree.

"Jesus Christ!" J.R. exhaled quietly, "I thought I was a goner for a minute."

"So did I."

"Thanks, man."

"Hey I do my own stunts."

"What do you say we move out of here?"

"Let's go."

Around 4:00am, the high-pitched whine of turbo-fan engines sliced through the air above as a hunter-killer team of Razorbacks skimmed the treetops looking for targets. Their spotlights cut through the foliage as they hovered by--rustling the pines, firs and thick tree branches before disappearing into the void.

"Shit!" Thompson whispered. "How'd you like to have one of those come after you with guns blazing?"

"Fuck that! I'll take my chances with that spider."

"We should move up to the edge of the trail, it's gonna be light soon."

They lay on the moist layers of pine needles and rotting leaves beneath waist-high ferns watching the dense landscape slowly become visible as the dawn approached. The sound of the rain made it easier to move through the forest by masking their own movement, but it made their journey miserably cold. Not exactly a fair trade-off for the scouts.

Later that morning, the thick shrubs parted as the point element of 22nd Bravo Company followed by a platoon passed through the area where the scouts were hiding and almost put his foot onto J.R.'s back as a patrol hacked their way through the curtains of vines and moss toward the town of Merlock. The presence of the infantry didn't comfort them as they noisily passed by; the scouts sensed that the troopers in the company were on edge and likely to shoot first and ask questions later if they saw any movement, and they did not want to be the victims of friendly fire, so they chose to lay low and not let their presence be known.

"Think we should follow them?" J.R. whispered.

"No, we'll stay put 'til they're gone, then we'll move up the trail."

That afternoon, the storm had lifted and they concealed themselves in the hollows in the trunks of gigantic trees and waited for nightfall. They heard the faint mechanical whine of tiny engines through the trees and saw four peepers weaving through the air gracefully in the direction that the patrol had gone. Twenty minutes later, they heard automatic fire followed by the piercing whistle of incoming rounds. They listened to the woods being shelled two miles away and they knew that the patrol that nearly walked over them earlier had stepped into the shit.

"Poor dumb fuckers." J.R. said quietly to himself as he leaned back.

Thompson had melted into the shadows of the tree trunk, and brought his heart rate down by meditating and losing himself in quiet thought. The air was damp and musty but he felt safe, and he felt invisible. A small green lizard chirped and scurried in front of him in the dim hollow and he snatched it with his right hand and popped it into his mouth. It struggled for a second and he could feel its sharp tiny claws on his tongue before he crushed it in the back of his mouth and swallowed. He scolded himself for not eating before going out on the ambush.

Night came and the temperature dropped again. A thick fog began to rise from the ground and fill the woods with a ghostly presence. At least they were dry. They could hear the dull thud of explosions and the sustained bursts of Razorback chain guns chattering far away. Thompson and J.R. moved across the ground like apparitions. Always silent, and always blending into the darkness and mist. They settled between the trees and waited by a small trail.

Before long there was rustling in the shrubs and the sound of voices in a foreign tongue lingering in the dark. Thompson could make out the silhouettes of the mercs as they broke through the bushes and walked single file down the trail toward them. The mercs were careless and noisy and seemed to be relaxed as they made their way down the path.

Thompson and J.R. lay quietly on the ground and counted fourteen mercenaries as they passed them unknowingly, they were heading toward Merlock where the sound of a battle echoed through the valley. The two scouts tracked the mercs and caught up with them in a small clearing after an hour. The scouts split up and moved parallel with each other, hunched low in the thick ferns toward the band of unsuspecting tribesmen.

Then the last merc in line stopped to check his weapon, he chambered a round and glanced around the heavy trees to make sure his patrol was alone in the woods. J.R. popped out of the thick groundcover behind him and put his hand over the mercenary's mouth as he worked his knife into the man's throat and pushed out, severing the windpipe, muscles, and jugular. The merc went limp and J.R. let his body slide quietly to the ground. J.R. looked around the darkness at the shapes of trees and plant life and listened for more to come. He heard a sharp rustle in the shrubs and could barely make out the shape of another merc as he emerged through the hanging vines ten feet to his right. Suddenly, the merc stopped moving at him and disappeared into the ferns as Thompson pulled him down and drove a spike into his head through his lower jaw. J.R. smiled with relief before vanishing into the groundcover and moving toward Thompson and the hedgerows.

The scouts let the mercenaries move ahead to put some distance between them, and then began tracking the band through the woods. They tracked for three hours, following the trail of snapped twigs hanging from bushes, cigarette butts, and kinked vines, and caught them settling down for the night close to a stagnant pond. No matter how well trained troops were, they were always sloppy in the eyes of the scouts, especially when a large body of them moved through the dense forest. They always made noise, and they always left a clear trail if you knew what to look for. Hell, they may as well have driven a tank through the woods. The scouts dropped back into the thick vines and waited in silence as the mercs posted two men as guards while the rest of them slept.

At about midnight, Thompson watched one of the guards vanish into the undergrowth silently. The second guard went to investigate a few minutes later when J.R. appeared out of nowhere and looped the garrote around the merc's neck and tightened it, sending a thick stream of blood gushing out as the piano wire sliced clean through the fiber of muscle tissue into the third and fourth vertebrae in the neck. The merc's head tipped to the side lifelessly as J.R.'s garrote almost severed it completely off. Thompson suspected that King and Noble were in the area and had taken out the first guard, leaving the second for J.R. to kill.

The rest of the mercs snoozed peacefully, unaware that the scouts had crept into their camp with their knives drawn. Within a half hour, the throats of the last ten mercenaries were cut open and blood drained onto the forest floor, not a sound was made during the assassination, and the four scouts began the gruesome task of skinning the enemy and mutilating their bodies.

By dawn the bodies had been strung upside down in the trees and disemboweled, the eyes were carefully cut out and nestled in a small pile on the ground in front of the carnage. The whole scene was staged for the benefit of another enemy patrol to find with a small note pinned to a tree written in their language. The message was clear. The scouts were lurking in the woods and no one was safe.

Most of the time scouts will spare one merc from death and allow him to return to his village to tell what he had seen, spreading more fear among the local population and hopefully deterring them from going back into certain areas in the woods. But tonight they showed no mercy.

The four scouts fell back and hid in the thick tangles of the woods to wait for another patrol when 1st Platoon wandered through and discovered the slaughter. The troops milled around nervously under the watchful eye of the scout team, but had the good sense not to disturb what they were looking at. After a few tense moments, 1st Platoon headed back to camp and the scouts followed in the shadows.

Once they reached the camp's perimeter, they fell in line ten feet behind the platoon and followed them to the CP. They stood quietly by themselves and watched the troops goof on each other as their sergeant talked to an officer. Within minutes they had become the center of attention as the soldiers of 1st Platoon turned around in collective awe and noticed their presence among them for the first time. Thompson lit up a smoke and tipped his bush hat at them as a courtesy.

The scouts were filthy and covered with dried blood from the night's work. Thompson's belly growled audibly from hunger as he took a drag from his smoke and flicked the ashes on the ground. Pappy rubbed the back of his neck as he walked up to the team shaking his head and sporting an embarrassed grin.

"That yours or theirs?" Pappy asked as he pointed at the blood that glazed over Thompson's hands.

"Oh that's theirs, Sarge." Thompson smiled.

"We saw your little care package hanging in the woods."

"Yeah well, when you care enough to send the best…"

115

"Looks like you guys had a rough night."

"I've had better." Thompson exhaled a plume of smoke.

"Hungry?"

"I could eat."

"Come on then," Pappy motioned with his head, "let's get some chow."

"Lead the way sergeant."

The troops of 1st Platoon stepped aside silently and let the four scouts pass through the group and head toward the mess tent.

"How long have you been following us?" Pappy asked casually.

"About two and a half hours." King replied, "You fuckers almost stepped on us yesterday morning."

"Sorry about that, didn't know you were there."

"We know."

Pappy managed to get a quick look into King's eyes and saw the wet gleam of a savage animal trapped in a man's body looking back at him— restless, cold, and calculating. He picked up his pace as he led the scouts to the tent. Spooky...

MURPHY WAS A GRUNT

They were called grunts, it seemed like a derogatory term for the infantry, but it was one that they were proud of. The common foot soldier. It was a title stripped of glamour, but held the honor and glory.

They were rough and sometimes obnoxious with their humor, but they displayed a special brand of tenderness and compassion that they saved only for each other. The camaraderie derived from their shared experience of war brought them a bond that was sometimes closer than the ones they had with the families they left worlds away.

They went weeks without bathing and sometimes days without eating, they marched endless miles through triple canopy forests so thick that only the man directly in front and behind them was visible. They crawled in the mud and sometimes over their fallen comrades during firefights. They slept in the rain without comfort, fearing the shadows cast by an alien moon, and jumping at every small sound until the morning light dispelled their nightmares.

They were superstitious with their logic, and invested heavily in luck. If you were grazed in the head by a bullet, or a grenade landed next to you without going off, you were charmed, and would find other grunts huddled near you on the next patrol hoping that some of your luck would rub off on them.

Their language was colorful and laced with clichés. Often bitter from the loss of friends, and jaded from living on the edge day after day, only a grunt could find humor in a close call with death and laugh in the face of personal tragedy. Through the centuries the infantryman has kept the belief in "Murphy's Law" alive—"if anything can go wrong, it will." And even the members of the elite Aggressor Forces and the pilots of Fleet will grudgingly admit that Murphy was a grunt.

Q 8
"I piss titanium and crap victory!"

Lt. Fred Lasher (2379-2406), Gunship Crew Chief, 1st Div./34th HK Sqdrn.

The purple hour of dusk filled the overcast sky with its shade of loneliness and melancholy as the long shadows of the woods crept across the camp and slowly turned from gray to black. I stood outside the tent listening to the shrieks and chips of birds and the chatter of other wild life coming home to roost in the canopy above.

My thoughts wandered as I looked down at my tattered body armor and muddy boots. My hands were covered with tiny cuts and blisters, and my elbows were raw and scabbed. My body throbbed with a dull ache from being pushed beyond exhaustion, and my mind felt numb from experience. I had only been at 781 for a week and it already felt like a lifetime. I wondered how the troops, especially the seasoned veterans, could live like this day after day for years without falling apart or just falling down and dying from the fatigue.

I sat down and fished out a cigarette from my shirt pocket and took a long satisfying draw as I watched some troopers walking into the forest holding their weapons at port. I could hear the rumble of explosions coming from the north as Volengrad became the objective of Operation Archangel; Fleet's surgical air strikes that were slowly demolishing the industrial jewel of the Q.

I reflected upon how much I've seen and been through since making planetfall. I came to the Q under the guise that I had better be able to look at anything if I'm to cover the war in an objective manner, but nothing could have possibly prepared me for what I've witnessed, experienced, and even participated in. I wondered how I would begin to describe the paralyzing fear of rushing into a firefight to the editors back home, or the tremendous grief of these young men who watched their friends die in the heat of battle. How can my report possibly encompass the personal tragedies that have been imposed into the lives of so many people; how the death of one trooper cannot be measured in terms of impersonal statistics, but must take into account the emotional impact his buddies in the field feel when they retrieve his broken body, and the countless years of sorrow that his family and friends back home will live. How can I begin to objectively describe the bloodshed and the pain of the thousands wounded in battle, the ones who've sacrificed their eyes, their limbs, their innocence, and their dreams of going home in one piece?

It's impossible to be among these soldiers without getting involved in friendships. They've gone out of their way to protect me, given me shelter, shared their food, shared their stories and fears; I owe them, and I owe them big. I owe them the truth. Their story must be told to everyone back home. For as many reporters as there are in New Sierra covering the war, somehow the soldiers feel that it isn't being told.

They feel like they're being cheated. The real substance of what's been going on in 781 for the last five years is not making it. News crews are not showing or telling what really happened in most of the campaigns that were fought. Sure the public is informed by the mass media, but the media has just been regurgitating what M.P.A.A.C. has been spoon-feeding them since the conflict began. The saddest and most frustrating fact of the matter is that the members of the media unquestioningly accept what the fabulous M.P.A.A.C. tells them is the truth beyond the shadow of doubt.

Most reporters who come to the Q limit themselves within the boundaries of press conferences hosted by the military in New Sierra. Very few of them venture out to the field to take a first hand look for themselves. I can understand this. It's fucking dangerous out here. I've often thought about catching the next gunship out of here back to a warm hotel room and buying myself some company from Emery Avenue. I don't know why I've stayed when I can think of a million reasons to leave. Yeah sure, there was always the solid excuse for the justification of journalistic integrity and building a foundation of credibility based on first hand information, not to mention the secondary personal benefits with the angle that this was a fantastic opportunity for career advancement (if I lived through it), but what I think it really boils down to is self-respect and the respect of the troops around me. I can leave anytime I please and be done with this nightmare, but these soldiers that I've come to call friends can't. They're here 'till the bitter end. Not that my being here makes a difference or contribution to the daily effort of survival, but for some reason they think it does. They want me to get home alive to tell their story, and I owe them that.

Some reporters and photojournalists have requested a tour of the field via M.P.A.A.C., and a designated guide from the press corps will take them by gunship to secured firebases and outposts. A well-structured program of tours that somewhat guaranteed the safety of the civilian press. Once in a while a television crew will appear, but that usually happens after a particular sector is secured and the fighting is over. While the military has no jurisdiction of what and how the media reports stories (except for the more sensitive ops), the media has agreed with the Council to practice a certain amount of self-censorship of newsworthy materials, and closely monitoring how public opinion is shaped, thus the relationship between the mass media and the Military Press Advisory and Assistance Committee is born.

The Volengrad City press kit that M.P.A.A.C. handed out to all reporters is impressive, destined to be a collector's item really. Three packets containing beautiful glossy satellite photos from the 13th Parallel to the southern tip of the Tantalus Delta; outlining all the strategic Alliance and Coalition strongholds, a comprehensive history of the Terekian infrastructure, and digital video chips detailing descriptions of the various weapons platforms that the Alliance and the Coalition have invested in the war. Impressive alright, from an academic standpoint. My kit is gathering dust on top of my desk back in the main office of The Metro on Earth. As far as I'm concerned my editor can stuff it up his ass if he thinks I'm going to use any of it in my story when the time comes.

I think about the impersonal nature of my business and am sickened by the sterilization of all emotion from a story. How can I do that? How can I tell you about Scat's throat wound without recalling the sound of him struggling for his last breath and the look of release in his face as he died in Pappy's arms? How can I describe Tzuter's nervous breakdown during the first wave without seeing his tear-streaked face as he curled into a ball? How do I tell the story of the young trooper who carried his wounded buddy through crossfire to a med-tent just to watch him die on the table minutes later? These are the kind of stories that they don't want you to hear or read about. The real stories about the Q.

The irony of it all. There's enough information being circulated about the war on 781 to short circuit anybody's brain. From the declassified logistics of major campaigns to the personal profiles of all Terekian government and military officials. Whatever fact or tidbit of trivia concerning the war, it was there. The only problem was how accurate is the source? The best answer to that was to leave the soap and water journalism in New Sierra and dive head first into the shadows of Uluwatu Valley to rub elbows with the dirty-faced infantryman who humped through the bush wondering if he was going to live to see another day.

"How are our troops holding up, and how is the war effort going?" seems to be the most frequently asked question by the press and the folks back home. All I know now is that I'm not prepared to ask someone like General Isley this question. I don't think I could stomach any more of his sophistical dribble or self-righteous soliloquies. I would rather ask someone like Pappy or Willie who'll get straight to the point and tell me that their ass is ready to fall off from having it kicked by an artillery barrage. The truth? Oh it's still there, you just have to look a little harder. It's like an injured bird flopping helplessly on the ground. It has to be picked up and nursed back to health or it will die. It became the first casualty of the war, and like Admiral Jonas said, "...there's nothing casual about that."

I smoked in the dark and watched troops hanging around each other's tents shooting the shit. It would be an early night for all of us. Tomorrow we'll get our first look at the city that became the focal point of obsession in the minds of the high command.

I needed to get my gear in order. Since 1st Division's initial landing in the valley, I haven't taken one photograph. In fact, I haven't taken one snap since I've been planetside. I've got tons of information for my reports, but no pictures for back up.

I spent the rest of the evening in the tent talking with Willie and Satch watching them disassemble and clean their weapons. Willie sat down with me and patiently showed me how to break down a Bolter for a quick cleaning in the field. It was quite simple really. Whoever designed the weapon definitely had the soldier in mind. The heat shield on the barrel was an excellent idea, and even a novice like me could appreciate its ingenuity.

"One thing ya gotta keep in mind, Frye," Willie lectured, "is to clean your weapon every chance you get. Keeps the action smooth."

"Hey Frye," Satch interrupted, "I noticed you carrying that digital recorder everywhere, but I ain't seen you use it once."

"Yeah, you could say I've been a little preoccupied." I replied sheepishly.

"Trying to stay alive is a bitch isn't it?"

"It is around here."

"Hey, there are a couple of things you should remember when we get to Volengrad." Willie said as he slapped the stock back onto his Bolter. "First of all, never walk through the doorways of any abandoned buildings, and never pick up anything that looks out of place—could be booby trapped."

"And always remember that tanks and incoming fire have the right of way." Satch grinned.

"Try to stay close to the squad and make sure your armor is snapped tight," Willie continued, "shrapnel is gonna be flying everywhere."

"That and try not to look conspicuous, it draws fire." Satch said lightly, "and never draw fire, it irritates those around you. Remember, tracers work both ways; if the enemy is in range, so are you."

"Aw, will you shut the fuck up, Satch! I've got some good shit here for Frye, I'm trying to be serious for a minute!"

"Okay, okay," Satch laughed, "hey Frye, remember that friendly fire isn't, and suppressive fire won't."

"You always gotta get the last word in, don't you?"

"Hey what are the chances of finding those scouts and talking to them?" I asked naively.

Satch and Willie looked at each other and shook their heads knowingly.

"I don't think that would be a good idea, newsman." Satch grinned.

"Why not?"

"Well, those dudes usually keep to themselves, anyone who ain't a scout is an outsider. You don't want to get anywhere near them. They're fucking ghosts, man. Dangerous and scary as hell if you ask me. You saw them fuckers today. Shit, we didn't even know they were following us."

"You don't recommend me paying them a visit, then."

"Not unless you're thinking about taking a run at suicide."

"I'll take your word for it." I replied wryly.

"Anyway, check this out," Satch said as he cracked his knuckles, "when we get to Highway 12 tomorrow, we're gonna see Volengrad for the first time. The city's gonna be pretty chewed up from all the air strikes. What worries me is that we're going in with the 8th Armored Division after the bombardment. That means that the 9th and 64th Armored Wings probably didn't get all the artillery and missile batteries in the city."

"What are you trying to say Satch?" I asked.

"I'm saying that I think we're fucked. We're gonna have to blast our way into the city, and then it's gonna get nasty. At least the turret heads will back our asses up when we need them during the mop up."

"That's the truth." Willie smiled, "A grunt's best friend is a pissed-off tanker or a fully loaded Razorback."

"No shit, but I still think we're gonna take a beating on this op, at least 'til the 15th makes planetfall. Them fuckers got a bone to pick with the Terekians." Satch said sullenly.

"Yeah, ever since Trouvaughn." Willie frowned.

"Fucking Trouvaughn..." Satch nodded.

"What happened there?" I asked.

"You sure you want to know, newsman?"

Sometimes there are questions that shouldn't be asked, especially when the answer is more than you can stand to hear. Trouvaughn was a story of dread that still makes troops shudder when they hear the name, and give each other that hard luck look that said, "I'm glad I wasn't there."

123

Trouvaughn was a huge base camp that used to lie a few kilometers north of the 13th Parallel four years ago. Many divisions frequented the camp, and the artillery batteries in Trouvaughn supported troops on ops for miles whenever fire support was needed. But Trouvaughn was best known as the stand down and staging area for the 15th Division and the 175th Infantry.

The story that circulates among the Alliance troopers is one that's always whispered whenever it's brought up, but for the most part, nobody likes to talk about it. It's like opening up a wound that never quite healed and exposing it to infection.

Late one October night back in '02, Trouvaughn was taken by surprise with an air of arrogance and pure savagery by Coalition forces that left the military hierarchy of the Alliance reeling in disbelief when a massive Terekian air strike was launched that leveled the command center and wasted every gunship on the base camp's airstrip. Other targets such as missile and artillery batteries were also taken out in the initial strike leaving Trouvaughn defenses crippled against further air raids. The 25th Armored Division lost most of their heavy tanks during the strike, but Terekian forces mauled the remaining armor as the Alliance tried to defend the camp's perimeter.

Elements of the 15th and the 175th dug in and even tried several counter-attacks, but ground forces surrounded them as Terekian gunships flew in and tore them apart. The siege lasted for a week. Ammunition, food and water soon ran out, and the Alliance was cut off from supporting the trapped soldiers who were forced to endure nightly aerial barrages and daylight mortar and armor attacks.

The Nova-31 squadrons from Fleet were tied up in the sky in vicious dogfights with the Terekian Winged Armada, and our gunships and medevacs weren't able to get through the mobile SAMS that the Coalition set up in the sector. Flying a sortie over Trouvaughn was like trying to fly though an iron curtain, and during the week of the siege, Fleet lost over a hundred Rapiers to the Terekian Air Corps. Alliance gunships fell from the sky by the dozens in attempts to resupply the cut off troopers or aid them with close air support—it just wasn't happening.

During the week of October 16th, over three hundred gunships with their crews were lost to heavy ground fire. They say that hundreds of troopers died of their wounds that otherwise would have lived if the medevacs could have gotten through to dust them off.

Then the horror of horrors came. Thousands of tribal mercs and eight Terekian divisions backed up with heavy armor attacked the base camp with a blood swarming that even the Alliance never expected. Trouvaughn was overrun, and no survivors were taken.

This happened in the early years of the war, so the public or the mass media does not know about the fall of Trouvaughn. M.P.A.A.C. saw to that. But I'm sure if you dig through M.P.A.A.C. archives long enough, history will reveal itself in the form of a KIA roster that will go on for volumes. Not exactly the kind of story I wanted to hear before going to sleep, but one of many worth stashing in the mental files.

The rain started falling again, and the temperature dropped another ten or fifteen degrees. Thunder rolled across the sky and blended with the sound of air strikes at Volengrad.

I lay in the dark trying to fall asleep, but the constant tremors in the ground kept me awake along with the hollow thoughts of what waited for us at Highway 12 tomorrow.

"Hey Frye," Willie said in a small odd voice, "do you believe in luck?"

"What do you mean Willie?"

"I mean do you think luck just happens, or do you think it chooses you?"

"I'm not sure I follow you, Willie."

"What I'm trying to say is that I think luck chooses you." Willie said distantly. "Like when that round grazed my head, that same round killed the guy behind me. Left a four inch hole in his chest. A few weeks ago at Pegasus, a mortar landed next to that dude and never went off. Luck chose him that day, and then it ran out on him. I think when that round grazed me the other day and hit him," Willie's voice trembled, "his luck jumped out of him and into me. I swear, I felt it."

I didn't know what to say to Willie, and I felt an uncomfortable silence in the dark between us as we listened to the thunder rumbling through the clouds and the heavy rhythm of the rain on the canopy above.

"Sometimes I wonder how I made it this far," Willie sighed, "I've been through so many ops, I figure one day the odds are gonna catch up to me, and my luck's gonna run out. It's gonna jump."

"I don't know about that kind of shit Willie, it's too big for us to try to figure out. Fate, luck, whatever you want to call it, it's all beyond our control anyway." I said trying to comfort him.

"Oh man, this war gets old."

"No shit."

December 24, 2406

We stood in the downpour at the muddy LZ as the engines of the Mark-IV whined in unison with the other gunships. Their navigational lights blinked brightly over the choppy terrain and cut through the dark morning as we hopped on board and strapped into the webbing.

The gunner adjusted the mounting brackets, tested the tracks of the chain gun and double-checked the feed to make sure the suppressors were off for maximum grease.

"I piss titanium and crap victory!" the gunner smiled as he swiveled the gun back and forth. "High on War" was written on the back of his tactical helmet above a carefully drawn ace of spades. He was in full body armor; heavy leg and shin guards along with a Kevlar vest under his breastplates and abshields. Full gear for heavy action considering that gunners usually wore only the breastplate on normal missions. Seeing him decked in full armor only made us wonder what kind of mess to expect at the LZ near Highway 12.

The pilot turned around with a grim expression waiting for the crew chief to give the okay for lift-off.

"What's the status, Lasher?"

"We're good to go!" The gunner replied with a thumbs up gesture. "Let's get this hog airborne!"

"Roger that, chief!" the pilot looked around the cabin, "Here's the deal boys, the LZ is secured at Highway 12, but the 8th and the 25th are still taking heavy fire from the city. They're about two clicks from Volengrad limits and the Novas are still bombing the shit out of the Trolls. We're going in low for the insertion under smoke for cover. Once we hit the ground, you know the drill: assholes and elbows! ETA five minutes!"

"Let's get this show under way!" "High on War" yelled, "Lift-off!"

The gunship shot into the overcast sky vertically and the nose tipped down as we accelerated forward over the dense forest. The sky lit up in brilliant white flashes of lightning giving glimpses of the trees below and the sheets of falling rain. The wind outside the cabin howled by the open hatch where the gunner stood clutching the chain gun as he scanned the landscape rushing below us in a blur.

There were about eighty slicks that flew behind us in a scattered formation. Their navigation lights blipped in the heavy rain as they closed in on our position. Watching the gunships moving at such high speeds so close to the trees was terrifying and exhilarating. I shivered in awe of the power of traveling so fast toward a place so frightening. We pitched and banked with the wind and I could feel my heart in my throat as we clipped treetops in the weak light of dawn.

Pappy, Satch, Willie, and Doc sat quietly as they gazed out the hatch. They neither looked scared nor apprehensive, and that made me feel worse because I was. I could feel a coldness running through me as my guts tightened up and my hands began to sweat.

Thunder clapped loudly around us and I flinched at the tremendous sound wave as we merged over checkered fields of green that peeked through the thick smoke cover blowing in the breeze. The superstructure of Highway 12 appeared through the billows; a sixteen thousand mile masterpiece of concrete and steel. Its vastness stretching southeast into the woods as far as the eye could see, and northwest over rolling hills into the great city of Volengrad.

Highway 12 was over eight thousand feet wide and incorporated five sonic-monorail systems within its substructure. The rows of fantastic pillars that held up the highway like a suspension bridge were nearly fifteen stories tall and spaced every quarter mile the entire length of the intercontinental thoroughfare. Inside the H-12, the monorail ports and rest stops contained an assortment of cafes, restaurants, hotels, and specialty stores for tourists and long distance travelers. Self-contained mini-cities to accommodate any journey, but the glamorous neon lights of Highway 12 at the Volengrad Clover no longer burned brightly since the city's occupation. The superstructure was abandoned and blacked-out for a two hundred mile section southeast of the city, and the monorail service never came within five hundred miles. The ports and rest stops sat in the darkness gathering dust as a war raged around it like a storm.

Rumor had it that Aggressor sniper teams and recon squads had taken over the closed off section of the H-12 a week ago; ferreting-out Coalition Special Forces in a deadly duel over territory inside, and were now within city limits pinpointing Terekian armor and command centers for Archangel.

Highway 12 loomed majestically through the haze like a sleeping giant. A towering monument of engineering, breathtaking and bordering on the magical; like you couldn't bring yourself to believe such a structure existed until you saw it in front of you; and even then, you rubbed your eyes in disbelief as you craned to see how far beyond the horizon it stretched.

Below, through the breaks in the smoke, columns of tanks and hovercrafts under Razorback escort weaved over the hills and small streams toward Volengrad. Some tanks stopped abruptly in their tracks as they rolled over mines or were hit by artillery coming from the city, other tanks just vanished altogether leaving behind scattered debris and a smoldering hole in the ground to slowly fill with rainwater.

"This is it!" the gunner yelled as we descended into the smoke, the gunships around us disappearing into the thick cover as we made our final approach into the LZ.

The cabin trembled as the landing gear extended and locked into place. I looked down and saw the smoke swirling in tornados and the wet grass being blown flat from the down-blast of the turbo-fans as the ship decelerated for the landing.

The Mark-IV shook violently as we touched down, sending a thin cold spray of rain into the hull dousing our faces and ponchos. We stood up and filed out of the hatch onto the field.

"Bring 'em to their knees sergeant!" "High on War" screamed, "Git some!"

"HOOAH!" Pappy yelled, "You better believe it! Let's go men, time to regroup and take some heads!"

"High on War" gave Pappy a sharp salute as the gunship lurched forward and took off into the smoke toward Volengrad City.

Over two hundred gunships touched down within the first hour of dawn and unloaded hundreds of troopers as the smoke cleared in the LZ. My ears rang sharply from explosions coming from Volengrad as elements of the 8th and 25th Armored Divisions shelled their way closer to city limits.

The driving rain clattered on the ground as 1st Platoon assembled with the rest of the division behind several small hills in the grassy fields. Four miles to the north, the dark gray outline of Volengrad's skyline combed through the low storm clouds and columns of black smoke from three days of air strikes. The ground rumbled with each explosion as Terekian artillery smashed into the earth at the advancing Alliance tanks.

The earth around us was pocked with craters filled with water and ground mist. The ground vibrated harmonically with the barrage as columns of Centurion-9A tanks clad with reactive armor raced by in their mechanical clamor. Their engines screaming like jet exhausts as they rolled across the hills at sixty miles-per-hour. Their dark green and brown hulls and turrets cast ominous outlines in the haze as the iron behemoths rolled to their destination leaving deep ruts of mud in the soft ground.

A squadron of black reconnaissance drones flew overhead toward the city, their sleek fuselages blended with the dark gray sky as they left con-trails behind in their jet-wash. Within minutes they vanished into the concrete jungle of Volengrad's skyscrapers.

Clouds flickered brightly over the city from the shelling, and a thin layer of black and blue smoke hung low and heavy over the rooftops of smaller buildings. Hundreds of fires leapt in the distant shadows of Volengrad, their dull orange flames highlighting the silhouettes of the architecture that was under siege.

The rolling hills and meadows that lead to the great city slowly turned to fields of mud as columns of armor trekked across their beauty and scarred them with their tracks. Fountains of fire and dirt erupted into the sky, leaving huge craters upon the punished ground as the barrage drew closer to the landing zone.

"Bravo Company, listen up!" Lt. Reynolds hollered through the downpour. "The 8th and 25th Armored Cav. are getting slammed, but they've cut us a path to the city's southern border. They're being held off by the 309th Mechanized Armored Division with infantry support. Them Terekian fucksticks are dug-in! We need to get our asses over there and take out their legs ASAP! The 15th makes planetfall late tomorrow night and we'll rendezvous under the H-12 Volengrad Clover. Pappy, 1st Platoon leads the way. Let's get going!"

"Alright you crazy bastards, don't sing it, bring it!" Pappy bellowed through the numbing cold, "1st Platoon on me, the pride of "The Big Red One" is going downtown. We're gonna have to run for it. MOVE OUT!"

We jogged over the slippery ground in a strung-out line. Cover was sparse with the exception of scattered hedgerows and patches of high grass in the fields. My chest pounded with a dull pain after the first mile as I gasped for breath with every labored step; running up small hills and nearly stumbling down the other side. We were knocked forward into the ground several times by the sonic booms of Nova-31's as they continued to strafe Terekian missile batteries.

Lightning flashed in jagged streaks overhead followed by the loud crack of thunder. The rain stung my face and eyes and my sides throbbed from the run—wanting to cramp up and fold in half as I splashed through the puddles. I could feel the warm tingle of pain from my skinned knees sending a burning sensation up my legs. I wanted to stop, but I would be left behind if I fell, and I pushed on; head swimming in pain, and digging deep to ignore it, I had to keep going.

We were buffeted by the hot down blast of turbo-fans from low flying Razorbacks as they raced toward the gray silhouette of Volengrad's skyline. Their engines putting out a high whine and turning the rain into steam as they dipped and rose with the terrain in their ground-hugging flight.

An armored hovercraft with .30 cal. Plasma cannons zipped by with a shredded Jolly Roger flag fluttering wildly on one of its antennae. It was followed by twelve Centurion tanks moving at fifty or sixty miles per hour. The commander of the lead tank was propped in an open hatch on the turret with his fist in the air taking the full gale of rain in the face as they barreled past us kicking mud high into the air.

I could hear the muffled footsteps of the soldiers behind me rapidly catching up and passing by. Their unshaved faces streaked with mud and determination in a frozen scowl on their lips; their eyes in an unfocused stare, locked forward and engrossed in a vision of their destiny; dark, definitive, and waiting with an outstretched open hand to escort them in a journey of fear and pain. We ran, through the driving rain into the icy wind, through the open fields and over the hills through the high grass. Oblivious to the pain, ignoring the shrill whistles of incoming rounds and the constant tremors of the earth as it opened wide from the explosions, pushing ourselves further to the edge, beyond exhaustion, beyond sanity. One torturous step after another...we ran...

Q 9

"Fasten your seat-belts, it's going to be a bumpy night."

Bette Davis (1908-1989), 20th century American actress

I

As we neared the city, we picked up the pace and spread out in a sweeping formation, rushing forward and screaming as we charged closer. Centurions sat in a line behind a wide berm lined with hedgerows and high shrubs; their muddy hulls recoiled violently as their 104mm plasma cannons blazed, firing thermo-plasmite warheads into the city. The blast from their guns was a deafening roar as they plastered buildings with shells, sending bricks and steel high into the air. The ground shuddered with each salvo, and the thunder of their cannons echoed off the sides of the structures with a sharp slap of destruction. Smaller office buildings on the edge of the city had been reduced to smoking piles of rubble and shattered glass that littered the surface streets and alleys. Surrounding buildings were pocked and scarred from shells and bullets, and were partially blackened from fires that raged nearby.

Terekian gun emplacements fortified the city's southern border that was surrounded by razor wire, and their infantry was scattered across a long line of sandbags bombarding our advance with everything they had; RPGs and mortars howled and shrieked overhead with piercing whistles that made flesh crawl and nerves tighten. They pounded the earth as we ran through the onslaught of iron, fire, and lasers.

Red and green tracers sliced through the rain like small comets, and the air was electrified by enemy fire as rounds hummed and snapped by. The bark of automatic weapons ahead filled my ears as bullets tore into the ground in front of us. We dodged through the fire and fountains of dirt, jumping over small craters and the deep ruts in the chopped, upturned soil seeking cover behind the berms next to the tanks.

Shrapnel whizzed and zipped through the cold air from mortars and grenades erupting in the ground, and I could hear the sound of flesh tearing and bones snapping as the spinning fragments of razor-sharp steel knocked life and limb out of our troopers.

"TAKE COVER! TAKE COVER AND RETURN FIRE!" Pappy screamed as he threw himself into the mud.

The air sizzled with bullets ricocheting off the tanks with a sharp, hollow metallic ring—plowing the ground with a muffled hiss. Mud splattered in every direction as grenades exploded short of our lines and tossed pieces of iron and clumps of dirt into the overcast sky, raining rocks and hot steel splinters on us as we crouched in the mire from the concussion.

The whine of incoming rounds made my hair stand on end, and the earth shook as it was turned inside out from the impact. Fragments of steel screeched and droned through the air in dreadful symphony with screams of pain as wounded troopers rolled off the berm into puddles of mud below.

I reached around and opened a pocket in my pack with trembling hands and pulled out a small digital recorder and began recording the chaos that whirled around me like a mad circus. I could barely maintain a steady hand from the cold and fear that coiled itself around my body like a serpent. The earth shook heavily from a nearby explosion and sent me sliding down the berm into a crater filled with water.

I coughed hoarsely and gasped for air as I swallowed the thick grimy mixture of mud and rainwater when I noticed a headless torso floating next to me. I screamed in horror and flailed wildly to the edge of the hole and climbed out. I groped on all fours in the heavy rain, coughing and spitting as I searched frantically for the recorder that was blown out of my hand. I found it covered with sludge on the edge of the crater. It was still recording.

I clawed my way through the thick muck to the top of the berm and saw Satch lying in the prone position with the Fulcrum 38 propped on the edge of the bank firing a sustained burst at Terekians dug in behind a brick wall. The integrated aluminum rounds ate through the concrete and bricks, and I could see the high spray of blood over the top of the wall as tracers from the 38 flooded into their position and cut them to pieces.

I lay between two Centurions that stood twenty feet apart, the ground vibrated from their idling engines as their turrets transversed and pointed their cannons at a couple of .30 caliber Terekian mini-guns hidden between some low-story buildings pouring an uninterrupted stream of tracers at our troops. Bodies were ripped to shreds as their armor was riddled and flesh and bone filled the morning air. The tanks fired simultaneously and sent a volley of rounds slamming into the sandbags that protected the gun emplacements. Huge balls of fire and black smoke erupted from direct hits and pieces of concrete bounced across the streets as Coalition soldiers scattered into the shadows and hobbled in a daze before being cut down by Bolter fire.

I panned the recorder to the left to catch an Alliance tank killer on a narrow road behind a mound of upturned asphalt launching anti-tank missiles at a Terekian armored column moving down a wide boulevard. Thick clouds of white smoke filled the air as the missiles fired out of its pods with a high-pitched scream and blew holes in the Terekian armor four hundred meters away. Twisting their steel hulls in unbelievable jagged shapes on impact and blowing slag a hundred feet in the air. The shredded tanks stood burning on the boulevard; their hulls smashed, ripped, and blackened, and no signs of life ushered from the crews inside the wreckage.

Muzzle flashes blinked from machine gun nests surrounded by razor wire throughout the city's border that was now the frontline of battle. Rain fell and the wind-chill brought an uncontrollable shiver to my body. My fingers felt the needles and pins of going numb, and my teeth began to chatter.

I flinched at the sound of turbo-fans overhead when Razorback and Mark-IV gunships flew low, high-speed erratic patterns over our lines and showered us with thousands of spent casings from their chain guns as they fired on Terekian forces. They weaved through the air hammering titanium in sustained bursts—peppering the streets and buildings with countless rounds of suppressive fire. The sound of their guns and laser cannons was a dreadful mechanical bark from the sky that imprinted itself into the darkest levels of the subconscious. The high-pitched whine of a gunship's engines brought both comfort and fear. It was salvation and death; an angel of mercy and destruction, it was among all things to a foot soldier, a guardian.

The din of explosions and automatic fire echoed brightly through the hours of the gray morning. It surrounded me, it came from above and from the sides. It engulfed and possessed my senses like a relentless demon tearing my sanity to shreds. The constant dry chatter of the guns, the pop and sizzle of thousands of rounds slashing through the rain, the ear-splitting thunder of the ground raging from the mortars and grenades, the screams of the wounded and the bloodletting; the world became a crimson hell as blood and smoke mixed with liquid earth in spouts of mud and stone. The thick odor of gunpowder and the sour smell of death filled my lungs as the ground rumbled and shook violently.

Squinting, I turned my head away. Blinking from the bright daggers of laser fire that crossed and pulsed through the downpour, leaving their afterimage burned into my pupils like a brand. Horrific visions of the brutality of death and suffering were digitally imaged on the recorder as I watched the lasers cut limbs from bodies, or cauterize holes through the chests of soldiers. Bloodless wounds that left the flesh charred, gouged, and curled back exposing ripped muscle and tendons with a sickening stench that smoked and bubbled. A head wound from a laser rifle was one of the worst ways to die according to the troopers. Depending on the hit, your face or head is partly vaporized and you didn't die right away. Brain matter is liquefied and cooked as it oozes out of your head, leaving you kicking and screaming as everything goes black and you become the vegetable of your choice when your bowels let loose and you vomit helplessly until you choke and die of trauma.

The thunder. The constant stomp from the heavens as lightning spread through the gloomy clouds with its spidery fingers. The storm had become the backdrop for battle, as if nature herself cursed the actions of mankind. She brooded in the dark skies of apocalypse and protested our presence and how we punished her earth. How we scarred and defaced her beauty by conjuring the dogs of war and unleashed them to devour her sacred body. Her beloved earth. We punched holes in her with bombs and missiles, and littered her with the torn bodies of men. We painted her face with blood, and raped her with our fire, and now she stands above us weeping the cold tears of rain. She cries for our agony and tries to cleanse the blood we spill as we strangle her with our blind hate and ignorance. We do not realize that we are killing what we are trying to save. We have resurrected the ancient beast of war. A creature that sits upon a throne made of the bones of our fathers wearing a crown studded with eyes. It laughs at our self-destruction and glories in our slaughter. Beside it stands the sadistic whore called Fate that we honor with the spirit of the bayonet; before who's feet we sacrifice youth and virtue.

Faces of the dead, half covered with mud. Dull eyes open with a permanent gaze into the shadowy sky as they received benediction from the driving rain. Their twisted expressions of pain, shock, and surprise frozen and locked forever in memory. Some looked like they saw the horror coming and grimaced for the last time. Others looked calm, released from having to go on, and pleased that they didn't as they lay sinking into the cold ground; leaving behind their last moments and taking the hand of death to a place where suffering and grief are no more.

The wounded screamed as they dragged themselves across the mud, clutching the earth in their pain; eyes, limbs, and faces torn off by shrapnel, skin burnt by lasers, bellies ripped open by gunfire. They crawled and ran blindly across the tracers and pulsing blasters crying for help. They stumbled down the berms and fell into shell holes filled with grimy water. They were cut down by the dozens and lay in the mud moaning and shrieking from their injuries as the world heaved and surged around them. Some were buried alive by the falling earth—their hands grasped helplessly at the heavens as the mayhem entombed them in the sludge. Others lay drowning in the mud as the pandemonium of battle raged in a whirlwind of death and obliteration.

I glanced to my right through the haze of rain and smoke, a man sat propped against a rock. His body armor and pants had been blown off by the concussion of a grenade and shrapnel had ripped his penis and scrotum away. He sat staring in astonishment at the huge wound between his mangled legs—the blood and shredded tissue turning gray in the murky puddles as mud splattered on his shattered pelvis. He shook his head as he put a pistol to his temple and pulled the trigger.

Men in battle bargained with fate and made pacts with their gods. They prayed and pleaded through the chaos and destruction for the choice that isn't theirs to make; but one thing that is common in every prayer is the fear of "the wound of all wounds". The loss of manhood was the unspeakable nightmare that sat in the shadows of every infantryman's mind. The wound that was so horrid because it was usually survivable. Medical technology and reconstructive micro-surgery have made implants and artificials excellent, but it's nothing like having the real thing. The wound that made the toughest of men cringe at the thought and whimper at the reality. The one that made you want to drop to your knees with your arms extended to the sky and shamelessly beg, "You can take any part of me, but please, not THEM—if you do, then you better fucking kill me, you son-of-a-bitch."

I saw a soldier pulling himself across the ground as bullets chewed up everything around him. A medic ran over and dived to his side and used his own body to shield the injured trooper, the medic hit him on the shoulder with morphine, there was a brief flash of an explosion as dirt, rocks, and fire shot into the dark sky. They were both gone.

Troopers hit by blaster fire cringed as they cradled their arms and legs where smoking holes and lacerations sizzled from the laser wounds. One soldier lay in the mud calmly as two medics frantically applied ointments and salves to his smoldering body. His chest and stomach were pitted with cauterized holes from a laser grenade that went off next to him, and as he lay there, he knew he wasn't going to make it. Seventy percent of his body was burned and twenty percent of it was vaporized. The medics were about to hit him again with morphine for the pain and shock when the trooper looked up at them.

"S-Save it. Save it!" the soldier whispered, "I don't feel a fucking thing anymore. I seen guys get hit worse." He coughed up blood in a thick clot as a medic gently held the trooper's head up. The color had left the soldier's face and his skin had turned a sickly white in contrast to the blood that streamed down his chin.

"Oh shit. I'm all fucked-up, Doc." The soldier laughed.

"Hang on kid, we're gonna getcha outta here!" One of the medics replied.

"Is it night time already?" the soldier asked (his eyes were open and he was staring at the afternoon sky).

"Yeah, kid, it's night time."

"It don't hurt no more, Doc. I seen guys get hit worse." He said softly.

"Yeah kid, it's gonna be okay."

"I...Dad? Is that you?"

The medics looked at each other frowning, not knowing what to say.

"Yeah son, it's me." One of the medics said steadily as he leaned closer to the trooper.

"Good to be home, Dad," the soldier smiled, "good to be home..."

I've seen the war bring out the ugly and darkest side of the human psyche. The primitive savagery and cold-heartedness in behavior and spoken word. Atrocities that transcended the imagination and gave the backbone shiver that prickly sensation that shuddered the whole body and left your spirit damp, numb, and twisted. Even the midnight air couldn't match the empty chill I felt when I saw a young trooper dismember the body of an enemy soldier then bite the tongue out of the severed head as the rest of his squad stomped the corpse to a bloody pulp like some type of black ritual. It all happened in the war, and sometimes the things that occurred in the aftermath of battle were worse than the actual bloodbath itself. Some of the things you saw left you standing in quiet disbelief and shock. Grunts that kept pumping rounds into dead bodies just to see them twitch on the ground from the velocity. Sometimes when the enemy was hit, the troops would keep shooting just to see how long they could keep the body standing—a morbid game that kept the corpse weaving and staggering backwards and sideways in a wild slam dance of death as the impact of hundreds of rounds kept it on its feet until the body disintegrated. It seemed that even if you didn't participate in an action, you felt guilty witnessing it as if you had, and felt the burden of responsibility and shame even if you did nothing, especially if you did nothing to stop it.

But the war also brought out the noblest part of human character; the self-sacrifice and valor in the face of annihilation, the gallantry in moments of dying, and undisputed courage under fire as troopers gave their lives to save their friends or other soldiers they didn't even know. Thousands of these stories existed through the years of the war, and thousands of pacts were made between soldiers turned brothers during battle. Letters, photos, and addresses exchanged in the heat of the moment; each soldier promising the other to carry the mementos home to their buddy's loved ones if he didn't make it through the fight. Odd how in the midst of so much hate and destruction there can be compassion and strength in the smallest acts of kindness and friendship. The five soldiers that bought a bottle of cognac in New Sierra during leave and buried it in a field; the plan was that who ever survived the war was to go back to the field and recover the bottle and drink a toast to each of his fallen comrades. It seemed like a trivial and corny gesture when taken out of context, but to the five troopers who pledged their loyalty to each other, it meant everything. The very nature of the act a symbolic bond of friendship that even the war could not tear apart.

I guess that's how most of the soldiers kept their sanity and their ability to cope with so much loss. So many of them had such a fatalistic outlook on their own chances of survival that they never looked beyond the next day. They lived strictly for the moment. Embracing every increment of time like a precious gift that might be taken away, and nobody put as much thought into the breakdown of time like they did. Its measurement on a minute-by-minute and day-to-day basis, giving it a tangible quality, like a thin liquid that's impossible to contain. There is an old saying among the grunts, "Everyday above ground is a good day." And they never took it for granted. They joked about its cruel and almost laughable irony, how quickly time flew between operations and when they were on leave, but how it stretched into infinity in the "mad minutes" of a firefight or an artillery barrage. Time, no matter how much of it you thought you had on your hands, was always borrowed.

The nights were horrible out in the field. If you had any imagination at all, watching the sun disappear behind the horizon dropped your blood to the frosty level where movement was stiff and exaggerated, and revived the dusty childhood fear of lying in the dark wondering what was hiding under your bed or in the closet. Wanting to know, yet afraid to look for fear that there was something or someone really there waiting to grab and pull you under. It was unbelievable how many hues of black and gray the night had, and how deep they were as they swirled around you like a black mysterious tide that threatened to drown you in your own fear. No matter how many people were near you, you always felt alone because you knew they felt the same. Perhaps it was an innate fear passed on in our evolution to dread the dark. The unknown and the unseen that lurked and thrived in its dank womb. When the moon came out, it made it even worse. Its swollen presence casting its pale unnatural light from another dimension and making the shadows that reached across the landscape look more and more like the enemy crawling across the lines. It made you bite your nails in anticipation and put that hysterical quiver in your voice as you whispered a prayer, "Please God, fuck the boogieman and get me through this, and I'll never sleep again." After all, is it paranoid to think that people are out to kill you when people *are* out to kill you? Yeah, nothing like that delectable fear of the gloom that brought the sweats in the cold hours of darkness as the rain fell and sobered you to the fact that at some time—any given time, that boogieman was going to reach out and pull you under and drown you in that riptide of fear...he was coming, and there was nothing you could do about it but wait and pray for dawn...

Nightfall. I huddled in the mud next to the treads of a Centurion filming the mist slowly rising out of the ground, heavy and eerie in the moonlight, it thickened and began to fill the hollows and shell holes as it crept across the earth. The highrise buildings of Volengrad became silhouettes against a darker sky, slowly blending into the inky void and vanishing from sight as the cloak of darkness covered us; with the exception of hundreds of scattered fires that burned uncontrollably throughout the city, not a single light was on in any of the buildings or streets. Volengrad was blacked-out.

Automatic fire from the city was sparse, and the explosions from RPGs and mortars began to dwindle as the Terekians abandoned their positions and began to fall back in retreat. I could see the outlines of the huge piles of rubble and twisted steel girders from buildings destroyed during the bombardment. A light drizzle put a bite into the temperature that promised a long uncomfortable night in the mud.

"Jesus, it's cold!" Satch whispered as he rubbed his hands together.

"Yep, the hawk is definitely out tonight." Pappy whispered back, "L-T tells me that the tanks are gonna roll into the city around midnight, and we're going with them."

"Shit Pappy, we never get any slack."

"Yeah I know, but this is the only war we've got, Satch, so don't knock it. Intelligence reports that we've pushed the Coalition back to the center of the city, three days of air strikes and shelling from our armor weakened their defenses and put them in a world of hurt, but they're still full of piss. L-T figures after the first column goes down that street over there with the minesweepers, we can make a run for it. It's about fifty meters. Once we get into that boulevard, we can hole-up in one of them buildings and get some rest before we push toward the Clover in the morning."

"Fuckin'-A Pappy, ya think we got a chance?"

"We ain't got much of a choice," Pappy whispered, "but I think the odds are pretty good. Meet me at the bottom of the berm in thirty minutes, I'm gonna get the company together and get'em ready to move out."

"What do you think this one rates—about a four?"

"Yeah, it's about a four, closer to a five." Pappy smiled and tapped Satch's helmet before he moved away to gather the rest of the troops.

Hours crawled as we shivered in the mud and watched the mist. The moon occasionally peeked through the clouds and its silvery light filtered through the fog and highlighted the trees on the city's border, making their stripped, crooked branches look like bony fingers scratching at the sky. The ground fog eddied around the tanks and filled craters with its damp secrets. It drifted slowly over the roads like a lost apparition trapped in the void of time and space. Its loftiness was beautiful and peculiar, stirring the empty feelings of longing and alienation.

There were several vicious firefights across our lines, and the cough of machine gun fire rang fiercely in the dark as tracers from the city cut through the fog. I could just make out the outlines of the Centurion tanks on the berm as we assembled below them. Most of the tank crews had popped open hatches on the turrets and posted a man behind the .50 caliber Mini-guns mounted on top. Their grim silhouettes stirred in the haze against the shadow of the overcast night.

The strobe of muzzle-flashes in the distance gave away the enemy's position as they ripped our defenses with lead and steel, and the Centurion gunners retaliated when they pivoted and opened fire with the mini-guns. The guttural belch of the .50 calibers turned my stomach as a solid stream of fire flared vibrantly from their spinning barrels into the city and zeroed in on the machine gun nests until the muzzle-flashes stopped and the cries of the wounded started.

We could hear the injured Coalition soldiers moaning and crying out in the gloom as the fog crept into the city. Their own army had abandoned them and forced the hurt troopers that could still fight to hold their positions to buy time. They were given only one choice: victory or death; and as the hours waned, they faced being overrun and falling into the hands of their enemy. It was just a matter of time before we breached their defenses and began loosening the Terekian stranglehold on the jewel of the Q.

No matter what idiom people spoke, the language of suffering and demise needs no translation. A man screaming in pain as he lies dying in the mud is an image that all soldiers understand and grudgingly accept as the harsh sum of the equation: the dead grunt. The bottomline that's always in the red.

Their voices hung in the mist and their sobs and whimpers filled the darkness as the cold closed around them with its wintry fingers. Some prayed, others cried out what sounded like the names of their loved ones. Strange, exotic syllables filled with heartache, loneliness and desire that made us all homesick and realize that our sworn enemy was also human, and the hatred that consumed us made us blind to the stunning fact that the dying men in the mud was somebody's brother, father, and son.

I looked at the soldiers around me as they listened to the Terekians that perished in no man's land. We all crouched in silence. Tight-lipped and wide-eyed, wondering if there was anything left in our hearts like mercy, or if we had become the animals that we thought the Terekians were; it's always easier to kill the adversary when they have been reduced to something less than human, but how does one deal with it when you realize that the enemy is another person that is like yourself? That blood and pain, no matter how large the gap is in culture and language, are one and the same. The war has ruined us and made murderers of us all.

Then out of the darkness, barely within earshot from somewhere along our lines came the unexpected sound of a harmonica; small, distant notes filled with sadness that pierced the cries of the wounded and slowly brought a miraculous pause to the fighting that was already beginning to dwindle. The gunfire stopped. The flash of lasers died-off. The thump of mortars and grenades, and the blast of cannons all stopped. And both lines came to a hushed, spontaneous cease-fire as all the soldiers were hypnotized by the solitary music floating in the shadows.

After a minute, the scattered voices of the wounded Terekians unified into a low murmur, then a soft harmony started weakly across their perimeter and slowly built a momentum that spread through the lines...we began singing along with the harmonica until it was completely drowned-out by our voices. It was a folk song from Earth that became so popular with the troops that even the soldiers of the Terekian army had adopted it:

"I remember happy times,

I was yours and you were mine,

darkness came and you were gone,

hours passed until the dawn--

Empty feelings come and go,

trying not to let it show,

the freezing rain can't hide the tears,

you've gone away, but I'm still here--

Oh baby, I'm so lost and alone without you,

Oh won't you please take me back and save me,

when I'm cold and I'm scared and I'm troubled,

I just call out your name and I'm free..."

I've never heard that song sung with so much feeling and desperation. The sting of pure homesick hearts filled with the broken memory of a life so far removed from the war. A life when youth still held its innocence and the world was full of undiscovered wonder. When a young man's biggest fear was how to work up the courage to reach over and hold his girl's hand. We stood in the drizzle and mud singing together—half sobbing and sharing our loneliness and despair, and for that brief moment, we were human again, and when the song was done, it remained quiet for a few minutes.

Suddenly, the ground exploded in front of a tank behind a hedgerow, and we were showered with rocks and chunks of dirt, bringing an end to the cease-fire as automatic weapons cranked-up again across the lines.

"Fuck yoouu! Fuck yoouu, Terran scum...you die like piiigs!" a voice cried hoarsely in the dark.

"Shit. Listen to that!" Pappy said with a nod.

"Yeah, that Troll speaks pretty good English." Willie replied quietly.

"Must have gone to college."

"Fuck yoouu...I kill yoouu, madderfacker!" the voice screamed as another RPG blew a hole into the earth next to the Centurion.

"Kiss my hairy ass, you maggot-dick son-of-a-bitch!" the Centurion gunner screamed back as he opened fire with the .50 cal. in the direction of the Terekian soldier.

"You miiissed me, Terran piiig-shit! Yoouu shoot like blind ol' lady!" the Terekian laughed as he fired another misdirected RPG that fell short and pelted us with debris.

"Look who's talking' butt-munch!" the tanker hollered, "My sister throws 'em harder than that! And you guys need to find your own song!"

"Why? Are yoouu mad because we sing it better than yoouu?"

"Naw, we're mad 'cause you sang it so badly, so now I'm gonna blow your fuckin' head off!" the tanker bellowed as he squeezed-off a short burst.

"Yoouu shoot like yoouu sing, Terran bitch-face!"

"Aw hell, you couldn't carry a tune if it had handles on it!"

"Yoouu suck my balls, and your madder is a whore!" the Terekian screamed.

"At least I have a "madder", you incubated fungus!"

"Swine!"

"Cheesedick!"

"Piiig-shit!" the Terekian hollered as he fired several rounds that bounced off the tank's hull.

"Asshole!" the tanker retorted and sprayed the darkness with the .50 cal.

One tank commander paced between the Centurions inspecting the reactive armor on the hulls and scanning for damages on the treads. He ditty-bopped on the top of the berm in his jumpsuit and leather bomber jacket as rounds and laser fire popped and sizzled into the ground around him. Oblivious to any danger of incoming, he didn't even flinch when an RPG landed twenty feet from him and sent shrapnel humming through the air. He walked around without body armor like he knew that he wasn't going to die in a place like this. He was either a complete madman or a thrill seeker with a deathwish. The commander seemed to be above death, like it was an inconvenience that he didn't have time for; he was good, and he knew we were watching him, and knew we were digging him and how he didn't give a flying fuck. As he paraded on the ridge examining his track unit, I noticed that he wore a white scarf, and a pair of infrared binoculars hung from his neck swaying back and forth as he stomped through the mud puffing on a cigar.

He also had on a black cowboy hat that had a gold rope band with tassels hanging off one side, there was a pin of a skull with two crossed swords on the front of the hat—one of the most famous symbols of the ground forces. The Armored Cav. We were with the pros now, and he wanted us to know it. The commander put a lot of effort into his jive, and you could tell that he was serious about his job and how it got done. But he got really upset when he discovered the front track fender of his own tank had been blown apart during the afternoon barrage.

"Son-of-a-fucking bitch!" the commander cussed to no one in particular.

"What's wrong Captain?" the gunner on the turret asked, flinching as a couple of rounds ricocheted off the hull of the Centurion.

"Oh goddamn it!" the captain said disgustedly as he ran his hand over the torn fender, "We just had this fucking piece replaced last week...and look what they did to the paint! (He was referring to the shark's mouth design on the front of the hull). It's all fucked up! Goddamn it, those assholes are gonna pay for fucking up my tank!" the captain growled. "Hey Sherm!" the captain bellowed to the man on the turret.

"Yes Sir?"

"Tell Mac to fire-up this beast and call the rest of the units. We're going in NOW!"

The captain climbed up to the turret and reached for a headset as the Centurion's engines coughed black smoke and pitched to a whine as it rumbled to life.

"Echo 1-2, Echo 1-2, this is Sahara-6 actual, ya got your ears on?" the captain hollered into the mike.

"Echo 1-2 copies, go six." A voice cracked over the radio.

"Echo, I need the sweepers to hit that road west of our position to clear any mines. I'm moving on the objective, over."

"Roger Sahara-6, sweepers on the way."

"10-4 Echo, Six clear."

"Get some, Sahara-6. Echo clear."

Within minutes, eight minesweepers clanked over the road and shoulders side-by-side. Their huge hulls lumbered over the lane medians and heavy treads crushed the curbs to powder as they cut a path into the city with their sponson rollers and detonated several mines that sent asphalt chunks howling into the air. They began to draw fire as they pushed closer to the perimeter. Sparks from ricocheting bullets and blaster fire pinged off the minesweepers hulls harmlessly, but they took some direct hits from RPGs and ATMs, and the impact of the explosives began to take their toll on their massive treads. Their advance slowed until the Centurions moved in behind them and began shelling the Terekian positions with their 104mm cannons and plowing their way through the smoldering rubble. The deep prehistoric shadows of the minesweepers followed by the tanks looked like a great mechanical dragon breathing fire and grinding toward the city's border.

The recruits that joined 1st Platoon after Merlock was destroyed had gotten their baptism of fire this morning, but were still skittish from the paralyzing terror of combat. They had only been through one firefight, and that was just scant hours ago. They stood together in a small group as the platoon assembled behind the hedgerows. God they were young. So green that the veterans of 1st Platoon didn't even talk to them. Instead, they glared at the group of young men and shook their heads in disgust and pity as they walked by chuckling at their ignorance and rawness. I felt sorry for them. At least I had an idea of what to expect, these kids had no clue what was waiting for them as we prepared to move into Volengrad.

I eyed them carefully as they bunched together and fidgeted in the rain. In their eyes, all they had was each other to rely on. They knew that most of the old timers wouldn't take the time to learn their names yet alone show them the ropes until they've proven their worth in battle. Until then, all they had was the training they received at boot camp, everything else was "OJT". Trial and error, with very little margin for error. Lessons learned by watching those in the know: "Do as I do, and step where I step, and you *might* make it out of here alive." They had not developed an instinct for the sounds of incoming rounds, or how to tell the difference between mortars and the larger shells. The larger ordnance shrieked, whistled, piped, or howled. Smaller rounds whirred, buzzed, and screamed. Either way, you had to make a split decision to dive for cover or run like hell before it hit. A moment of hesitancy could mean the difference between life and death. If you were still standing after the first round hit, you deserved what you got. It seemed like bitter reasoning, but it was "the law of the jungle" as the troopers would say.

These kids still thought their body armor would protect them from shrapnel or blaster fire; and often, during a firefight, they would never stay low enough to avoid being hit. Some just stood there in a complete stupor watching the tracers snapping through the air until they were mowed down by machine gun fire. Others went the other way, they pulled cheap heroics like rushing machine gun nests or hanging on to grenades too long before they threw it. They always meant well, and most of them went on to become fine soldiers when they realized that the test for survival was pass or fail, and war didn't grade on a curve.

The replacements still had that astonished look of innocence in their eyes as they stood there trembling and biting their lips in anticipation. They flinched hard at the sound of every explosion—jaws clenched, and faces tightened with fear. I could see them jump when the machine guns barked in the distance. They have just been introduced to death and haven't grown to appreciate the cold friendship that he offered them. Death was still a huge shadow and ruthless thief of life. A horrid corpse in a black cloak that feasts on the souls of men, and the thought of an audience with him still made their palms clammy and their hearts thump. They have not accepted him for who he truly is: an angel of mercy that would deliver them from battle.

All these kids needed was time, combat would steel them against pain, and their instincts would be honed to a razors edge. Killing will become second nature, and their baptism of blood and fire will give them an insatiable appetite for destruction as they become members of that special fraternity. They will become salty and hard as survivors and never look back to the time when they were green and untested. They will learn to live their lives by the code of honor and put the brotherhood before anything, and eventually death will no longer be feared but embraced.

"Jesus Satch," Willie mumbled, "look at them sorry-ass mothers. They're just a bunch of kids."

"Man, I'm surprised that half of them even made it through the afternoon."

"Hey Torres," Willie nodded, "how many FNG's did ya get yesterday?"

"Three of 'em," Torres sighed, "but two got zapped this morning. They're goin' home via the KIA Travel Agency."

"At least they weren't here long enough to suffer." Satch frowned.

"Five minutes in this motherfucker is suffering enough don't you think?" Willie said cheerlessly.

"That ain't no shit..." Torres grinned.

"Torres!" Pappy yelled, "Get your squad together, you're gonna lead us in, just got a call from Sahara-6. They're in the city and there's light resistance. We gotta move, and I mean NOW!"

Lt. Reynolds stood in front of the group and cupped his hands around his mouth, "Listen up Bravo Company. Get your shit together. We're going in first. Charlie, Echo, and Foxtrot companies will be right behind us. Pappy, 1st Platoon leads. Torres, take point. Willie, keep the FNG's in the middle of the column. You're tending the sheep, Bo-peep, try to keep 'em alive. I want fifteen feet between men. We move single-file and I mean assholes and elbows, ladies. That's it. Let's saddle-up and lock an' load. We're gone in three minutes."

"Okay, all you fuckin' new guys," Willie bellowed, "gather 'round and take a knee."

Eighteen recruits surrounded Willie and Satch and crouched in the darkness as the rain began to fall harder.

"Listen up 'cause I'm only gonna tell ya this once," Willie glared, "there's a couple of things ya need to keep in mind when we get into Volengrad. First of all, keep your armor snapped tight. Once we get into it with the Terekians the frags are gonna be flyin' everywhere. What you guys went through today wasn't shit compared to what's waiting for us in the city."

"That, and always remember," Satch interrupted with a sly grin, "that tanks and incoming fire have the right of way..."

II

We jogged up to the broad, muddy shoulders of the street that the minesweepers and tanks had just plowed through and began running down the shattered lanes of the avenue that lead into the city. We tripped and jumped over craters, potholes, and chunks of concrete as the thunder roared overhead and lightning flickered across the heavy skies giving us fleeting glimpses of the dark highrise buildings that loomed closer with every step. The streets were littered with garbage, damaged cars, and bodies that were ripped to pieces during the barrage.

I could hear the heavy breathing of the soldiers running as I stared hypnotically at the shadows that lay ahead; I heard the panting, hysterical whisper of the trooper behind me rattling off the same line over and over again like a machine gun: "Hail Mary, full of grace...Hail Mary, full of grace..." never getting through the rest of the prayer as we ran through smoldering wreckage.

Hundreds of dead lay scattered on smashed sidewalks and upturned streets. Headless torsos twisted in gruesome positions and slung over bullet-riddled sandbags, bodies propped and crucified against blood-stained walls—some with weapons still in their hands; many lay sprawled on the ground staring blankly at the overcast sky with their mouths open and over-flowing with blood and rainwater.

Human debris was splattered over the surface of the streets like the sky rained death instead of water. Severed limbs tangled in shredded pieces of uniform and piles of flesh and sinew stretched across the wet pavement like jellyfish washed up by a killing tide from the red ocean of war. The rain fell and I kept thinking that the air would soon stink of rotting death.

I could see shredded razorwire entanglements against the smashed walls of buildings, and piles of rubble wrapped in webs of rebar strewn about like the skeletal remains of great beasts that died on the glossy asphalt. We crossed into Volengrad's limits.

The air was thick with the smell of sulfur, and gunpowder that mingled with the scent of wet blacktop and concrete. Conflicting thoughts of hollow fear mixed with the pleasant memory of spring in the city back home as the rain clattered lyrically on the boulevard and clouds of steam billowed out of manhole covers and rain gutters.

Wounded Coalition soldiers lay on the streets moaning and crying in pain as the fog engulfed them with its unearthly presence. They reached up at us begging for help as we ran by and grasped at our legs if we got within reach. We ignored them and kept running, trying not to kick or step on them along the way. We had no time for compassion or mercy. Our medics will eventually come to their aid after our own wounded are treated. Until then, they were in the hands of fate—if they lived, they would become P.O.W.'s, if they died, they will be buried in mass graves outside of city limits. Either way, we didn't care.

"Straight ahead, Torres!" Pappy pointed, "Let's get to that building over there and secure it!"

We could just make out the outline of a damaged three story building in the mist as we ran through the shadows. After sprinting forty yards, Torres held up his right hand in a fist as a signal to stop, and the ragged line of exhausted troopers came to a halt and crouched in the street while some scrambled for cover behind overturned cars that were still smoldering in the rain. We were less than twenty feet from the building's front entrance.

Torres signaled for the rest of the company to stay put while he and two others moved ahead to recon. I could see plumes of breath from the troops vanish into the midnight air as they anxiously watched the fire-team moving through the gray shadows with their safeties off and their Bolters held tensely at shoulder height.

"Careful J.J., watch your step…" Satch whispered to himself as he watched the three men creep to the foyer. "Slow and easy bro, check overhead…"

Torres leaned back against the wall of the building as he began to inch himself forward. The shattered glass and metal doors dangled on their creaking hinges before a darkened lobby, and from where I stood, I could just make out the shapes of couches, chairs, and tables sitting in the dimness of the cavernous atrium. Torres pulled out a thermite fragmentation grenade and did a silent count before he stepped forward into the entrance and lobbed it through the doors and jumped back behind the wall with the others. It detonated sharply with an orange and white burst of fire, sending glass through the air and a cloud of dust rolling out the entryway onto the street.

"MOVE! MOVE! MOVE!" Torres screamed as the three of them burst through the fractured lobby and began a room-by-room search for any enemy soldiers.

"1st and 3rd squad, that's our cue! The rest of you fuckers stay put 'til we give the all clear!" Pappy yelled, "Let's move in! By the numbers, watch for trip-wires and laser sensors. Go! Go!"

Twelve troopers got up and ran through the settling dust and smoke into the building while the rest of us sat shivering in the rain. I could hear the scuffle of their footsteps as they kicked open doors in a rampage and stumbled through the darkness and dusty haze of the first floor and began working their way to the stairwells.

"Jesus Christ!" Lt. Reynolds said under his breath, "I hate this waiting shit! I wish they'd just nuke this fucking city and call it good. Collins, where you at?"

"Over here L-T." Collins replied dryly. "What's up?"

"Get 2nd squad together, I need you in there to assist."

"That's affirmative, L-T. Hey Mac, get the boys to saddle up. We're going in."

Six more troopers stood up and flicked-off the safeties on their Bolters and scurried through the dark toward the building where Pappy and Torres' squads had already cleared the first floor and were headed up to the second level.

"Blastgate 1-1," Reynolds spoke lowly into a radio, "this is Red-6 actual, 2nd squad is in the house, I repeat, 2nd squad is in the house, over."

"10-4, Six," Pappy's voice crackled over the handset, "Blastgate copies, we're near the east stairwell getting ready to move up, L-T, so far so good. No rats in the kitchen. Over."

"Roger that, Pappy, we're comin' in, over."

"10-4. See ya inside. Blastgate clear."

"Six clear." Reynolds sighed and turned around. "Bravo Company, on your feet! Moving! Let's take the building!"

We ran through the rain single file; hunched over and frightened, I felt vulnerable as I listened to the sound of footsteps splashing in the puddles and the dull tink of ammunition belts as we darted through the shadows into the gray smoke that hung in the lobby.

"Spread out!" Reynolds yelled, "make double sure every room is clear. Every closet, every fucking door, check under every fucking desk. Take nothing for granted. Leave nothing unturned. DOUBLE TIME IT! MOVE! MOVE! MOVE!"

I hooked up with a four-man fire team from 3rd Platoon lead by a sergeant with "Wrath Child" written across the front of his tactical helmet, while the rest of the company scattered throughout the first floor and double-checked every room as a precaution. I turned on the digital recorder as we ran into a dark stairwell that lead to the second floor. One of the troopers lit a flare as we began our ascent, its white light hissed and popped with a shower of sparks as shadows danced madly across the walls.

We went through a fire exit into a pitch-black hallway where the musty air seemed thinner and colder. The illumination from the flare flickered like a torch in the gloom as we came to a shut door to our left. I could hear other fire teams rushing through rooms at the end of the hall in a frantic search—soldiers screaming "OT SOOK SHEATA!" ("Surrender or die!"), before kicking doors open and rushing in with the intent of killing on sight.

We gathered around the door with our backs to the wall when "Wrath Child" turned to his teammates.

"Okay, on three," he whispered to his team, "I'll kick the door open and you lead us in Russ!"

"Goddamn I hate this kinda shit!" a redheaded trooper whispered back.

"Yeah, this is about as much fun as a sucking chest wound." another trooper with "BORN TO LOSE" on his helmet responded.

"Knock it off you two," Wrath Child snapped, "your negative vibes are bringin' me down. Ready? On three...one...two..."

Everybody tensed up and held their Bolters up to chest and shoulder height. I inhaled deeply and held my breath.

"THREE!" Wrath Child kicked the door open and the other three soldiers jumped into the room and started pushing through the darkness.

"OT SOOK, MOTHERFUCKERS! OT SOOK SHEATA!"

"Get that flare over here McCall! We got another door!" Wrath Child bellowed.

"Here ya go Ash!" the redheaded kid said excitedly.

"QUIET!" the fire-team leader whispered, "I heard something moving in there!"

"Shit!" McCall said nervously, "I heard it too!"

"OT SOOK SHEATA!" Sergeant Ashford screamed and fired a short burst at the door's locked handle.

"Open that fucker up, Russ! I'm gonna blow away anything that moves." Ashford whispered.

"No shoot! No shoot!" a muffled voice cried from behind the door, "Seas sheata!"

"What the hell!" McCall sneered.

"Oh shit! Hey Russ, better run downstairs and get Chase in here, tell 'im we've got a live one." Ashford nodded. "And turn off that camera, newsman," Ashford glared at me, "you better step back. This could get ugly."

I shut the recorder down and slung the Bolter from my shoulder and clicked off the safety.

"Okay McCall, you ready, Logan?" Ashford asked the troopers quietly.

"Yeah, I suppose," a dark haired soldier sighed, "let's see who our mystery guest is. I'm good to go."

"Open the door." Ashford motioned as he silently mouthed the words.

McCall reached out and put his hand on the broken handle and slowly pulled the door open...

"No shoot!" a man's voice said weakly, "Seas sheata! Seas sheata!"

As the door swung open, the light of the flare flooded the inside of a small closet, and lying on the floor was a Terekian soldier in a tattered uniform with half of his head wrapped in blood-soaked bandages.

"Please, no shoot," the Terekian squinted up at us blindly, "help...seas sheata."

"Go easy Ash," McCall said cautiously as he kept a bead on the Terekian, "he's surrendering, but the Troll might be rigged."

"No, I don't think so," Ashford said reluctantly, "son-of-a-bitch looks pretty messed up."

"That don't mean shit, Ash. I say we waste this shitheel!"

"Negative, McCall. We wait 'til Chase gets here. I think Intelligence is gonna be real interested in him."

"Fuck that! I bet this cocksucker put the dam-dam on us when we landed this morning. Look at the patch on his uniform. He's fuckin' artillery!"

"Please, help..." the Terekian whimpered.

"Shut the fuck up before I shoot your dick off!" McCall screamed as he shook his Bolter at the wounded soldier making him cower and hold his hands up to his face.

"Stand down McCall, and that's a fucking order!" Ashford barked.

"Goddamn it, Ash, this fucker probably greased some of our bros!"

"Yeah maybe, but we're turning him over. He looks like an officer and he might be useful. So stand down and shut your pie hole."

"Hey Ash!" Russ panted as he reentered the room. "Chase is on his way up with a couple of engineers and a medic. He says not to move him, he might be rigged with explosives."

"Alright, we all sit tight and stay cool 'til Chase gets here. You hearing me McCall?"

"Yeah." The redheaded kid resigned with his weapon still locked on the Terekian.

"Logan?"

"Yeah I hear you, Ash."

"Light another flare, Russ, that Troll moves an inch, he dies." Ashford growled.

The fire-team kept their Bolters trained on the Coalition trooper that lay bleeding on the cold floor trembling in fear and pain. I looked at the Terekian and I felt sorry for him as he huddled against the closet wall shaking. "Jesus what am I doing here?" I thought to myself. The wounded trooper looked half blind and was scared out of his wits, but I couldn't help the mixed feelings of contempt and empathy that flowed darkly through me as I stared at the cringing enemy. This was the first Terekian I'd seen up close.

"Well, well, well, what do we have here?" a trooper asked as he walked into the room followed by three others.

"Hey Chase." Ash answered calmly without taking his eyes or Bolter off the wounded soldier. "Looks like we got ourselves a prisoner."

"Well that's just fucking outstanding. Let's step back and let these boys check him for wires."

The two engineers crouched down to the wounded Terekian and slowly ran sensors over him.

The seconds dragged slowly. "Looks like he's clean." One of the engineers declared softly, "But we need to pat him down for anything organic. Just keep your hands up where we can see 'em scumbag," the engineer leered at the injured soldier, "don't try anything stupid."

"I really don't think he understands you, Chuck." The other engineer said to his partner.

"Oh he understands me all right. Son-of-a-bitch knows he's in a world of shit."

"Okay, just be real careful."

They slowly patted the wounded man down, checking for wires and strings and emptying his pockets. The Terekian looked up at us with his hands on his bandaged head as the two engineers searched him.

"Please...help me..." the trooper grimaced as he was frisked.

"Just settle down big guy," one of the engineers glared, "we're almost done."

The Terekian groaned in pain and passed out when they flipped him over then dragged him out of the closet.

"Have at him Doc," Chase nodded to the medic, "get 'im ready to move. We'll take his ass downstairs and hold him until Intelligence gets here."

"Roger that." The medic answered dryly as he began his examination, "he's not too bad off, he's got a concussion and a couple of broken ribs, and his left leg's busted."

"Okay Doc," Chase squinted, "fix 'im up. Ash, you and Russ stay with Doc and help him get this dipstick down the stairs and tell Reynolds where we found him. McCall, Logan, get your asses out into the corridor. I want a word with you fuckers—NOW!" Chase said sharply.

I headed back down the stairs where the rest of the troops had regrouped in the lobby, I could see from the expressions on their haggard faces that the tension had begun to loosen its grip. Most of the troops lay sprawled on the floors using their packs as pillows as they settled in for a few hours of rest. The lucky ones managed to find comfort on the furniture that was not too badly damaged. The luckiest of all where the ones that found couches still in tact in the lobby to stretch out on. Ponchos had been cast-off and draped over tables, chairs and burned out lamps, but for the most part, they lay in wet torn heaps on the floor soaking the mud-stained carpet.

Chemlights and the tips of cigarettes glowed in the darkness. Tiny fires that seemed suspended in the air as soldiers took a few precious moments to smoke and pop open freeze-dried rations. Muffled conversations hung in the stiff cold air, and I could feel the lead weights of fatigue pressing down my shoulders.

My entire body throbbed with a dull ache and I realized that I've been getting by with only three hours of sleep a night. It wasn't even a real sleep, that was a true commodity here. It was more of a light half-conscious daze with your eyes closed and the mind still working, refusing to let its guard down. Sleeping but still aware of your surroundings and hearing everything going on around you. A half-coma induced by sheer physical exhaustion when the body demanded the rest to replenish its tapped reserves of adrenaline, but the mind's state of paranoia brought on by the fear of dying kept its functions working overtime...your eyes were closed, but you're still open for business, because when you closed your eyes here, you subconsciously feared that you would never open them again—one long sleep you'd never know. And when you woke up, you felt cheated, eyes feeling gritty like sandpaper inside the lids and encrusted with the bleak hours of half-life. You became a zombie deprived of the precious r.e.m.'s that your body needed, and instead of feeling refreshed, you felt more tired than ever before.

Outside, the rain had started to rattle down in sheets again and we were extremely grateful to have a roof over us for a change. Being dry on 781 was a luxury that we haven't had in days. It was now 2:30 in the morning. Christmas day at the Q.

III

I sat contently on the floor with my back against a wall and my knees drawn up to my chest. A cigarette burned loosely in my mouth as I debated with the thought of going on with the company or catching the next gunship back to Defiance at first light. I was so absorbed by fatigue that I didn't even hear Willie and Satch plop themselves next to me.

"Hey newsman," Satch grinned, "spare another one of them smokes? I lost my last pack during the run."

"Here take these," I insisted as I flipped him two unopened packs, "I've got two more."

"Thanks dude, I owe ya big time."

"Welcome to Volengrad City, Frye." Willie sighed.

"Gee, Thanks. I feel like a thousand miles of bad road." I smiled weakly as I exhaled a cloud of smoke.

"You look it." Satch nodded. "You know, I've seen a lot of shit since I've been here, and it seems that every campaign we go on now gets worse every time."

"How long have you been here Satch?" I yawned.

"Oh, let me see... ah, a little over two years now."

"Jesus. I've only been here ten days and it already feels like a lifetime."

"Yeah," Satch chuckled, "that's because it is a lifetime. I've lived a thousand of them by now, and I'm tired of this war."

"There it is." Willie smirked.

"How 'bout you Willie, how long you been on line?" I asked as I rubbed my eyes.

"I beat numb nuts over here by four months, I'm comin' up on two and a half years now."

"Man that's a long time."

"Forever."

"There comes a time in every grunt's life when you look back at everything you've been through and all the close calls you've had, and you start getting spooked by the smallest things." Satch sighed.

"You getting froggy, bro?" Willie asked in a concerned tone.

"Nah, I'm frosty. I'm just saying that some guys start to get zapped in the head after being in the shit too long, ya know?"

"Yeah I know," Willie said calmly, "I've been having this same dream for the last three months now. It's really weird."

"What's it about?"

"I don't know..."

"Come on dude, don't hold out on me if it's about getting laid." Satch laughed.

"Naw, it's not that good."

"Well? You gonna tell us?"

"Okay, but you two fuckers better not tell anyone."

"Hey come on bro," Satch said reassuringly, "you know I won't say shit, and Frye's one of us now. We're tight."

"Alright," Willie sighed as he stared at the floor. "It starts off at night and I'm in the woods with a patrol. Real thick forest, like the ones at Uluwatu. You know, the kind where it's so dense you can hardly see ten feet ahead of you. Anyway, we're moving through the shrubs and vines real slow. Watching our step, checking the ground in front for traps and listening to all the chirps and croaks and shit. For some reason I'm walking point, so I'm using my Bolter to push branches and undergrowth out of the way. I can feel the rest of the guys behind me, but I can't see them.

The moon's out and it's kind of a dark gray all around. I can see everything, but I'm more like feeling my way through the woods—almost like autopilot.

We come to this clearing and I see this dead merc face down in the ferns, so I cut through the bush and head toward him. I hear the rest of the squad moving in behind me as we close in on the body.

I'm checking all around, I'm scared shitless 'cuz I can sense that something's not right, like there's an ambush waiting or something, but I gotta go scope out the body. Don't know why, but I'm drawn to it. I get over the merc and I got my Bolter pointed at him when I reach down and flip the fucker over and see his face, and it's...it's..."

"It's what, Willie?" I leaned forward.

"It's me." Willie shivered. "I flip him over and I'm looking down at myself. I'm dead. I'm looking at my own dead body. My face is yellow and gray and all cut up. Fucking eyes staring back at me with worms teeming in a pink tangled ball in my mouth and shit."

"Man, that's way fucked up." Satch whispered hoarsely.

"No," Willie continued, "what's fucked is when I look up at the rest of the squad and see their faces. You see, they're all dead too, the skin on their faces and hands are all rotten and hanging and shit, and I can smell the death; and they all start laughing at me, then they raise their weapons and blow me away...I can feel the rounds going into my guts. Then I drop to my knees in front of my body that's lying on the ground, my corpse sits up and grabs me by the throat and starts coughing these fucking worms into my face. That's when I wake up."

"Shit." Satch said shaking his head. "That is one fucked up dream."

"And you have this dream every night?" I asked.

"No, not every night. Maybe once a week, but it's the same one I've had for months now."

"Fuck it Willie. Drive on." Satch grinned, "Don't mean nothin'."

"Goddamn, I hope not."

"At least you have dreams. They suck, but you have them." Satch said as he ran his fingers through his hair. "I haven't had a dream for two years now. At least nothing I can remember, and if they're anything like yours, I don't wanna remember them."

"One of these days," Willie said cheerlessly, "this war's gonna end, and I tell you what, there'll be nothing finer than goin' home. All's we gotta do is make it through this shit, and everything for the rest of our lives is gonna be gravy."

"There it is." Satch smiled. "What are you gonna do when you get home Willie?"

"First thing's first. I'm gonna take my girlfriend out to a steak dinner then bring her home and give her a white root-oil injection. I'm not getting out of bed for a week." Willie grinned. "Then I'll spend the rest of my days in the sunshine working the farm for my ol' man, helping him get the crops planted and harvested. Working the land and tending the animals. How 'bout you?"

"Maybe I'll come visit you sometime," Satch replied, "I've never been to Syterra before."

"Door's always open."

"When I get home," Satch gazed, "I'm gonna buy me a vintage '89 Aurora convertible. Machine gun blue with twelve under the hood. I can see me now, cruisin' down the gold coast with the top down and a hot babe with really big tits and a beer in her hand sitting next to me givin' me a fuckin' tongue bath."

"You know what I really miss about home," Willie said as he lit a cigarette, "is the trees and the way the leaves change colors in the fall. My father's land is really beautiful. The edge of his farm is bordered by the forest."

"I'll bet it's nice, but after everything we've been through in the woods out here, I don't think I'll ever look at the forest the same way again."

"No shit."

"First thing I'm gonna do when I get home is get drunk as a fuckin' monkey," Satch said, "then I'm gonna find the judge that sent me here and shoot 'im in the ass."

We all laughed and talked for another twenty minutes before I drifted off for some of that sleep. A flittering dreamless sleep where light and dark came together to form a haze of nothingness. A sleep that became a vacuum for r.e.m.'s and spent itself out in a false sense of rejuvenation.

Two hours later Willie was shaking me awake. I opened my eyes and could hear the dull tinkle of the rest of the troopers gathering their gear and shuffling in the dim room.

"Frye, wake up man." Willie whispered urgently. "We're moving out in ten minutes, get your shit together."

"Wha...?" I began to ask through the cobwebs in my head.

"No time for that shit now. We're moving out to the Volengrad Clover at the H-12 to secure it. The 15th is making planetfall tonight. Get your shit, we got to go."

I yawned and rubbed my eyes under the trance of exhaustion as I gathered my gear and snapped on my body armor in the dull glow of green chemlights. I could feel the stiff knots in my muscles as I stretched to get the blood flowing.

I looked around at the faces that surrounded me. Everyone looked like tired old men struggling to stay on their feet, like a ward of stroke victims fighting to keep their balance. Their eyes were locked in a hard concentration of vacant stares into another dimension, and their faces seemed carved in stone. Dead men walking.

I slung on my pack and checked my digital recorder and camera equipment; it was all in working order, and I privately marveled at the small miracle that any of it survived. I reached down and grabbed my Bolter, its cold indifferent steel seemed welded to my tattered glove as I slapped in a fresh clip and checked the safety. I looked up and noticed Pappy watching me gear up for the move.

"Jesus, newsman," Pappy smirked, "you look like you've had nine inch nails for breakfast. If you were any uglier, you'd look like one of us."

"I'll work on it."

"See that you do."

December 25, 2406

It was still dark when we filed out of the building. It had finally stopped raining and the streets shimmered under the glow of the setting moon as it peeked through the overcast sky.

Just thirty feet from the lobby entrance a Razorback gunship had landed during the night. It sat ominously in the shadows, a sleek mechanical bird of prey gleaming seductively in the mist, watching over us like a dark avenging angel waiting to rain its titanium rage on our foes. Scuttlebutt was that Intelligence officers had arrived in the gunship about an hour ago and were in the building firing questions at the captured Terekian. There was no doubt that Intelligence had doped up the Coalition warrior with psychotropic drugs and will bleed him for all he knew before he was deposited into the Barber Peninsula POW camp south of the Delta. Until then, the building will definitely be considered off limits.

We gathered in the cold and huddled in small groups trying to keep warm as we stared at the jagged shadows that slowly emerged from Volengrad's skyline.

"Alright 1st Platoon listen up," Pappy squinted in the darkness, "get your game faces on. We're getting close to the eleventh hour. Just got word from Brigade that the 5th and 9th Division have made planetfall on the west side of Volengrad about an hour ago."

We hooted, cheered, and cat-called Pappy with elation of the news of reinforcements. For as tired as we were, I could feel a boost in the troops' moral and a heightened sense of espirit de corps. We were worn down and salty, but we would drive on. The soldiers of 22nd Bravo of the "Bloody Red One" was ready to reassert their iron wills and grab the Terekians by their scrawny throats and turn them into believers.

Doc Powers sat on a curb with his face buried in his hands crying and shaking hysterically. "I'm so fucking happy..." he sobbed with relief.

"Okay settle down people!" Pappy bellowed. "The war ain't over yet. Command also confirmed that the 17th Airborne Sniper Battalion made

HALO insertions last night deep in the city. We've got less than ten hours to blast our way to the Clover before the 15th makes their drop tonight. After we rendezvous, all elements will converge downtown and sweep north. Feel the rush, troops, blood alone moves the wheels of history! Torres where you at?"

"YES SIR!"

"Your squad takes point. Lock and load! Let's move out!"

The dark shapes of skyscrapers towered overhead as we leapfrogged for cover down the wasted six-lane avenue. Ahead, the cough of automatic fire rang brightly in the morning air and hundreds of muzzle flashes dotted the gloom. The thud of grenades and the thunder of Centurion cannons echoed off the walls of the highrises that surrounded us like a giant cement canyon. Alpha and Hotel Companies had engaged the enemy four blocks away and the strobe of explosions lit up the heavens. Orange tracers stitched the gray alleyways and boulevards as we stumbled through piles of rubble from fallen structures.

The predawn sky was a blue-gray wash that shaded the buildings with its dull hue and gave everything a surreal blue tint in the thin mist that hovered over the streets. We moved through the shadows. Three hundred dark green phantoms armed and thirsty for blood weaving through the crushed lanes.

Mannequins wearing the latest high fashions lay on their sides in terminal rigor mortis in the shattered display windows of designer boutiques. Shrapnel had shredded their clothes as they stared at us blankly. They too have been killed. Satch stopped and reached into a window and slid his hand up the dress of a female dressmaker's dummy.

"Hey check it out," Satch chuckled playfully, "how many times have ya had the urge to do this?" Satch dribbled and rolled his eyes up with his tongue hanging out as he molested the genderless mannequin.

"You are one sick son-of-a-bitch, dude!" Willie laughed.

We moved on toward the east section of Volengrad where Highway 12 broke off into the Clover. The streets and sidewalks were covered with craters and piles of debris, broken glass and chunks of concrete littered every square inch of ground. Columns of smoke bloomed from the buildings around us like black roses of war. Fragile gray ashes floated through the air like snowflakes, and everything around us was engulfed in balls of orange flames as we moved into the bowels of the city. The atmosphere was heavy with smoke, and we choked and coughed as we ran through the clouds. The face of every building was pocked and scarred from air strikes and artillery barrages, and Terekian bodies were thrown everywhere from impact.

The dead lay scattered on the broken streets. Days have passed and the twisted bodies were grotesquely bloated from decomposition. They belched stiffly and hissed at us as we ran by; they were covered with soot and splotches of green mold, and the rain had done dreadful things to them. I gagged and wretched at the musky fragrance of corpse gas as they beckoned us from beyond.

Abandoned cars sat covered with a thick layer of gray dust along the curbs, their windows smashed and most of them riddled with bullet holes. Inside one automobile was a cadaver slouched behind the steering wheel. Its black wrinkled skin was drawn tightly over its skull and its jaw hung open in a permanent scream.

"Who is that Frye," Satch chuckled as he leered into the window, "someone you used to date?"

"As a matter of fact it was," I replied, "she still owes me money."

"You know," Satch reflected, "when you first got here, I figured you were just another poge. A total shitbird punching a career ticket, but you're okay newsman. I would go into battle with you any day. You've definitely got hair on your ass."

"Thanks, my parents gave it to me for graduation."

"We better get going."

We ran another block and turned a corner into the wall of an ongoing skirmish. The streets were filled with the chaos of automatic fire and screaming. The soldiers of Alpha Company were scattered behind doorways and overturned cars firing wildly down the darkened boulevard and shooting out the windows of the buildings that surrounded us.

"Over there!" someone screamed frantically, "I thought I saw a muzzle-flash at ten o'clock! Eighth floor of that building to the right. Nail 'em! Fucking nail 'em!"

Bolter fire rattled in sustained bursts as tracers cut into the dim morning and peppered the building's face with rounds.

"Cease fire! Cease fire!" a sergeant hollered. "Anybody see anything? Anyone see where the shots are coming from?"

A single shot in the distance echoed off the walls, and the sergeant clutched his throat and fell to the ground.

"Jesus Christ! MEDIC! MEDIC!" a soldier screamed as he sprinted across the pavement to his fallen comrade. He ran about thirty feet before another shot echoed and his chest erupted with a hard thump and sprayed the wet asphalt with soft lung and muscle tissue as he spun from the impact and hit the ground.

"Take cover goddamn it! COVER!" Torres yelled.

We hit the deck and tried to make ourselves as small and flat as possible. Satch crawled forward and propped himself behind the burnt shell of a car and began returning fire down the street.

"What the hell's going on here?" Reynolds asked as he crouched down with a trooper curled behind a small mound of rubble.

"Snipers, sir!" the soldier winced, "We was makin' our way down the street 'bout ten minutes ago. We was halfway through when they sprung the ambush. Snipers took out our point element then start pickin' us off as we scattered. They completely cut us in half. Goddamn, we are so fucked! Most of the company's pinned down up ahead."

"Calm down troop." Reynolds said coolly, "Who's your commanding officer and where's he at?"

"That would be you sir."

"What?"

"Our L-T was one of the first to get greased," the soldier pointed, "he's on the deck 'bout thirty yards up. Took a .50 cal. dum-dum right in the melon. We're definitely in a world of shit. Them snipers could be anywhere."

"Why didn't you radio for gunships?"

"FCT's wasted. They blew 'im in half and fucked up the radio."

"Shit!" Reynolds spit. "Pappy, get on the horn. Call Falcon Field and tell them we need gunsh..."

Another shot rang out and Lt. Reynolds' body slumped to the ground. His head was gone and one hundred eighty-seven pounds of fractured meat convulsed on the pavement as blood pulsed from his neck into a dark shiny pool.

"FUCK!" Pappy screamed as he lowered his head. "Falcon Command," he yelled into the handset, "this is Blastgate 1-1, do you copy?"

"Falcon copies," a voice crackled on the radio, "go ahead 1-1."

"Falcon," Pappy responded, "request immediate gunship support, we're pinned down by sniper fire. I repeat, pinned by snipers...honcho's down but need dust-off for wounded, over."

"Roger 1-1, gunships unavailable for immediate support. All birds committed to west end engagement with the 5th and 9th. Inbound hunter-killer cells from Defiance ETA one hour for Volengrad. Sorry Blastgate, no can do."

"Damn it Falcon, we're getting hammered!"

"One hour, 1-1. State coordinates, over."

"156/51 over."

"Roger, 156/51. Hang in there 1-1."

"Blastgate clear."

"Good luck, Falcon out."

"SHIT!" Pappy cussed.

"What's the word Pap?" Willie shouted.

"We're on our own." Pappy glared. "We either move forward and find a way to get Alpha Company out of the shit or leave 'em here and pull back and find another route to the Clover."

"What are we gonna do?"

"I say we go forward. Charlie, Echo, and Foxtrot companies need to pull back. Tell Collins and Torres we're gonna split up the company, I need six volunteers to stay with me. 2nd Platoon will take the FNG's with them, and I want the rest of the company to head out with Charlie and Foxtrot. They can move on our flank on the surface streets and get to the Clover. Let me call 'em now and tell'em to fall back."

"What bout the fucking snipers?"

"We take our chances and use ourselves as bait."

"Oh shit!" Willie grimaced, "I think I'm gonna hate this movie."

"Charlie Six, Charlie Six actual," Pappy belched into the handset. "this is Blastgate 1-1, you got a copy, over."

"This is Reilly, go ahead Pappy."

"Hey Tom, do me a favor," Pappy said coldly, "pass the word to Echo and Foxtrot to pull out of here. You guys need to haul ass too. Get to the Clover to rendezvous with the 15th. Take the rest of my company with you. Me and 1st Squad are gonna stay with Alpha and try to punch through from here."

"Pappy you're crazy. That's fuckin' suicide! Those snipers will kill all of you."

"We don't have a choice, we'll keep them distracted and you guys make your way to the LZ. We're wasting time, GO! We'll hook up at the Clover tonight."

"Pappy…"

"GET OUT OF HERE!" Pappy screamed into the radio, "We're wasting time!"

"Alright Pappy, good luck!"

"Luck's for amateurs. Get going, Tom."

"You always were an asshole. See you boys tonight."

"Blastgate clear." Pappy frowned.

"Charlie Six out."

Pappy put the radio away and ran across the street and dived behind an overturned car where two troopers from Alpha Company crouched.

"How many of your people are pinned down up ahead?" Pappy asked solemnly.

"About twenty or twenty-five of them, sergeant."

"How many of you are back here?"

"There's probably fifteen of us. Them snipers cut what was left of our outfit to pieces. We lost half the company yesterday morning during the barrage."

"Okay, here's what we're gonna do. We breakdown into eight man teams and start popping smoke for cover. When it gets thick enough, we move down the street most ricky-tick and by the numbers. Stay close to the buildings; keep moving, and pop smoke when we need to. With any luck we can regroup your entire company at that bank down there and make our way to the Clover."

"Sergeant, that's over a two hundred yard run." a trooper interrupted, "We'll get zapped for sure."

"We ain't got much of a choice, soldier!" Pappy barked, "We don't do this, the rest of your company's dead. Now get your men together and wait for my signal."

Pappy ran back across the street and ducked behind a shattered wall where the rest of us crouched in a line.

"Okay listen up!" Pappy bellowed, "Torres, Collins, I want you to take 2nd, 3rd, and 4th Platoons back the way we came and hook up with Charlie Company and get going toward the Clover. Take the FNG's with you."

"What the fuck, Pappy?" Collins protested.

"Do it! And that's a fucking order!" Pappy blared. "1st Platoon, I need six volunteers."

"This a suicide mission, Pappy?" Satch asked grimly.

"Yeah."

"Then you can count me in."

"Me too." Doc Powers nodded.

"You dickheads know you can't do without me." Willie grinned.

"I'm in." a dark haired kid named Lucas winked.

"I'll go with you." I said as I cleared my throat.

"Bullshit Frye, you fall back with Collins and Torres." Pappy ordered.

"Never happen, Pappy," I smirked, "I'm an observer remember? You can't stop me from going with you."

"You're out of your mind newsman. Anybody else?" Pappy looked around at the rest of the platoon.

"Pappy, I'm gonna stay with you." Collins demanded.

"Alright Jimmy," Pappy sighed, "I could definitely use you. Okay Torres, you're in charge of the company. Fall back and get the hell out of here."

"10-4 Pappy," Torres nodded, "see ya at the Clover."

"Alright men," Pappy said as he slapped a full clip into his Bolter, "get out all your smoke grenades and start launching them down the street, we need cover. We move out single file. Assholes and elbows on my mark. 1st Squad on me, Satch take point."

"You heard the man," Satch yelled, "we got a mission, let's get some!"

"Alpha Company," Pappy barked, "stay close and follow us. What's your name soldier?" Pappy asked a blonde kid.

"Morgan, sir."

"Okay Morgan, get your squad ready. Let's pop some smoke!"

It was a dreary sunrise made hazy by the fires caused by days of shelling, and the air smelled dank, burnt, and used. The dark blue sky seemed to tease us through the thin mist. A blue dome of heaven that smiled on us from above with the distant unattainable dream of peace and tranquility. Ahead, the separated members of Alpha Company were scattered throughout the street crouched behind cars and slabs of smashed concrete walls, frozen in their tracks and unable to move for fear of the unseen killers that stalked us with high-powered scopes.

We popped smoke grenades and tossed them down the street and watched them hiss as they billowed dark gray clouds. The stranded soldiers of Alpha Company took the cue and began throwing smoke around the area where they were pinned. Within minutes the entire boulevard was filled with thick gray smoke that concealed the sun as well as the buildings around us. Visibility was reduced to less than twenty feet. Hopefully the snipers in the area wouldn't be able to see us moving through the haze.

"Okay let's go!" Pappy motioned as Satch sprinted out ahead of the group. "Stay low and haul ass."

"Make like a bunny-fox!" Willie said as he gave me a slap on the back and gave me a thumbs up and a push.

I ran down the side of the street holding the Bolter at port. I strained my eyes through the smoke and could barely see the trooper running in front of me. I could hear the clink of equipment and footsteps of the other troopers of Alpha Company behind me.

My stomach tightened when the silence was shattered by the sharp sound of a gunshot that rang off the walls, and I threw myself down on the sidewalk and lay still.

"Pierce is hit!" someone screamed. "Somebody help me! MEDI..."

Another shot followed by the dull thud of a body hitting the pavement and the soft gurgle of life bleeding out of a young soldier's body.

"Don't stop!" Pappy screamed from behind, "Keep going!"

I jumped up and scrambled through the blinding haze; I could feel the flow of sheer terror surging through me like ice had been injected in my veins, my blood ran cold and I felt like jumping out of my skin. I could hear a hysterical tremble in my labored breathing and hear the frantic rhythm of my own heartbeat in my ears.

I stumbled over a body and hit the ground hard, knocking the wind out of me and leaving me sprawled on the curb in a daze.

"Come on!" a voice yelled in my ear as a pair of hands lifted me up to my feet and started pushing me along. "RUN! GODDAMN IT, RUN!" It was Morgan from Alpha Company.

We ran side by side for a few seconds before he pulled ahead and vanished into the smoke. I panted as I picked up the pace, and several other troopers passed me in a dead run. Everything around me was lost in a blur of fear and adrenaline as I ran by wasted cars and piles of bricks and cement. I passed by an overturned truck and glanced at a body curled on the street behind it before I realized that he was still alive. I stopped and grit my teeth knowing I should keep going, "Aw shit!" I cussed to myself as I turned around and ran back to the wreckage.

I bumped into several more soldiers on the way back that gave me frightened puzzled looks as they passed by, "Hey you're going the wrong way!" a trooper yelled.

"Just keep going," I snapped, "I forgot something!"

"It can't be that important!"He yelled back

"Oh yes it is!"

The trooper shook his head and disappeared into the fog. I got back to the truck and found a soldier huddled over his dead comrade; the trooper looked up at me with a tear-streaked face as he held his dead friend.

"This wasn't supposed to happen." The soldier sobbed. "Casey was younger than me. He was supposed to make it home and go to school and become a big shot—he told me so."

"You can't stay here bro," I said gently, "we need to get going before the smoke clears. Come on, dude, and get on your feet."

"I can't leave Casey. He's my bud."

"Well you can't damn well stay here. Get up! We'll come back for him later."

"NO!"

"Hey asshole!" I shouted as I reached down and backhanded the kid across the face, "HE'S DEAD, MAN! GET A GRIP! YOU'RE still alive, and we're gonna keep it that way!" I grabbed the soldier by the collar and pulled him to his feet, "Come on, we need to make tracks before the snipers kill our asses! Let's get out of here!" I let the kid go and shoved him hard down the street. We started running faster. Together, one step at a time.

"Pick'em up and put'em down, trooper!" I coaxed. "We've got a long way to go."

We made our way through the billows of smoke, and I could hear the mad running of the other members of Alpha Company as the pinned down soldiers got up from their hiding places and joined the ragged line of grunts running for their lives. I looked up and could see the shapes of buildings that towered over us starting to emerge through the smoke.

"Damn it!" Pappy cussed loudly, "everyone take cover and start popping more smoke, we're loosing our blanket!"

We ducked into doorways and behind what cover we could find along the avenue and threw smoke grenades up the street and waited for the clouds to fill the air. I stood in the entrance of a tobacco shop with the kid next to me. We pressed our backs hard against the wall and tried to catch our breath as the street cloaked in gray.

"Hey man," the kid said breathlessly, "thanks for what you did for me back there."

"Don't mention it." I replied hoarsely.

"If it weren't for you, I'd still be there. I'd probably be dead."

"Buy me a drink later, we ain't out of this yet."

"Hey look, the smoke's getting thick. Let's go!" the kid said as he stepped out from the doorway.

"WAIT! DON'T GO OUT THERE!" I shouted as I grabbed for him. But it was too late. Gunfire echoed from one of the buildings.

The young soldier looked at me with surprise, eyes wide with shock and the expression of somebody that woke up with a dead mouse stuffed in their mouth.

The poor kid looked down at the huge hole in his chest, then his eyes rolled white and he fell to the ground.

"Oh shit!" I trembled as I stepped further into the door with a hand over my mouth. "I'm getting too old for this kind of shit."

"MOVE! MOVE! MOVE!" Pappy's voice echoed through the street.

I jumped over the kid's crumpled body and started running like I was being chased by a swarm of bees. Never looking back...one step at a time...pick'em up and put'em down...my lungs felt like they were about to burst as I dodged the piles of debris and hopped over shell holes. Knowing that merciless predators with unblinking eyes were watching from above. Calculating our every move, patiently waiting for us to make the mistake of exposing ourselves through the smoke, even for a split second, it would be enough; when the last sound you heard was the sharp ring of gunfire before the world became silent.

"We're almost there!" Satch hollered.

"Alpha Company," Pappy shouted, "fall in and let's get the fuck out of here!"

"LET'S GO! LET'S GO!" several voices screamed in the haze, "MOVE IT OUT! MOVE! MOVE!"

"There it is! Hurry! Hurry! Get in the building! Hurry up!" Pappy ordered as we leaped up the wide marble steps that led to the entrance.

"Get your ass in there Frye!" Pappy bellowed as he pushed me into the lobby. "Hurry the hell up men, the smoke's starting to clear and we're out of smoke frags."

"We made it!" Willie laughed as he ran toward the steps, "We made it!"

A gunshot rang through the street.

"WILLIE!" Pappy screamed as he ushered the rest of Alpha Company through the door. "WILLIE!"

"Oh shit!" Willie groaned as he staggered and fell on the wet asphalt clutching his right leg, "I'm hit!"

"Hang on Willie!" Satch yelled as he pushed his way back through the group of troopers, "GET THE FUCK OUT OF THE WAY, ASSHOLES!" Satch hissed at the other soldiers, "I'm comin' for ya buddy!" Satch shouted as he got to the doorway.

"NO!" Willie shouted, "Stay back! Them fuckers can see through the smoke!"

"He's right Satch!" Pappy said through clenched teeth, "Those snipers have a bead on him."

"I ain't leavin' him out there to die!" Satch screamed into Pappy's face.

"Get your ass away from the door, Satch!" Pappy shouted as he pushed Satch back in.

"I'm goin' after him, Pappy!"

Another shot cracked through the haze.

"AAAHHH!" Willie screamed as he floundered on the street. His left leg had been severed below the knee leaving a jagged stump of bone as he pulled himself toward the steps.

"WILLIE!" Satch screamed maniacally as Pappy and Doc grabbed him and held him back. "LET ME GO YOU MISERABLE COCKSUCKERS! I SAID LET ME GO!"

A third shot sliced through the chill and found Willie.

"AAHH SHIT!" Willie screamed, as his right leg lay twisted and hanging by a thin thread of muscle behind him.

"Goddamn it! Let me go get him, Pappy! They're gonna pick 'im to pieces!"

"Stand down, Satch!" Pappy glared, "He's my friend too! I seen this shit happen before, that sniper's gonna make 'im suffer and try to draw us out there and kill us all!"

Members of Alpha Company propped tables against the windows and peered out at the surrounding buildings. "Anyone see where the fire's coming from?" Morgan frowned as he scanned the structures through his scope.

The sharp pop of another Terekian rifle sounded from a different direction...

"OOOHHH GOD!" Willie sobbed as he looked at the bloody stub at the end of his left arm where his hand used to be. "OH JESUS IT HURTS!"

"PAPPY..."

"I said stand down, Satch!"

"Oh shit, Pappy!" Doc sobbed hysterically, "He's gonna kill himself, look!"

Willie had taken out a grenade and was fumbling it with his right hand trying to pull out the pin.

"WILLIE, NO!" Satch screamed, "DON'T DO IT!"

Another gunshot overhead...

The grenade rolled harmlessly across the pavement as Willie lay on the ground staring in disbelief at the shredded bone and ligaments of his right forearm.

"Satch..." Willie cried through bloodshot eyes, "please..." he whimpered, "Please, Satch...it hurts..."

Satch had grown quiet as he stared across the doorway into the eyes of his best friend. Pappy and Doc Powers had let him go because they knew what had to be done. We all knew.

"Satch, please…" Willie cried. His grimy face streaked with the dirty worm trails of tears as he trembled on the street dying.

Satch grabbed my Bolter and calmly brought the weapon up to eye level and sighted-in his friend—his brother in the scope. His breathing was hard and steady as he concentrated on the final act of mercy. He could see Willie's puffy eyes looking back at him—begging…Satch's finger wrapped around the trigger and squeezed it back gently…smoothly…

Pvt. James "Willie" Willis

Beloved Son, Brave Warrior

KIA, Volengrad City, Q-781

Born September 3, 2383

Died December 25, 2406

Requiescat in pace

100 Days From Home
BOOK TWO
The Fall of
Because

FORWARD

There was a time in my life when I thought that things made sense. A time when I had the luxury of taking so much for granted. For me, it was all about waking to the realization that time was all borrowed. As I sat in the comfort of my living room reviewing digital images I took of the war, I realized how much I'd lost in such a short time. It took what seemed like a decade to gather the courage to dig up those discs for the fact that they would force me to confront feelings that I'd spent over a year avoiding. The layers of fear and despair seem without end as the faces and voices of friends that are no longer with us run across the screen and rekindle a story that is both fresh and centuries old.

Of course things have changed drastically since I was at Volengrad. My arrival was at a time when many reporters and journalists at the Q had decided to limit themselves to M.P.A.A.C. media packages and stay within the borders of New Sierra. Not to say that media reps had lost their passion for the story, but rather that too many journalists had lost their lives in the early part of the war trying to cover it, and the networks that sent reps in for a quick peek told them to stay indoors and they weren't about to argue over it.

Journalists like Gerald McMillan of the New Chicago Times, Bob Stine of the WCBR Express, Clara Martin of the Global Daily, Jacqueline Rosenthal of the UPA, freelance photographers like Larry Oha, Tara MacIntyre, and Grant Matthias are still putting everything on the line at 781. Correspondents the likes of Jill Forrester, John Mallory, Sakanashi "Nash" Yorita, Natasha Washington, and countless others who lost their lives to the conflict that turned our universe inside out makes me long for the ability to turn back the clock so I can see their faces again over a cup of coffee and a cheap danish. I miss them dearly and it hurts to look at old pictures of them.

The following pages are a collection of what I've seen and what I was told during candid interviews with the troops that I met. There are so many perspectives of the same battle, but these are the versions that I feel lucky enough to have lived to tell. The war itself has no storyline that can be followed or any type of character development that can be dramatized. These are events told by real soldiers in real time. To be fair to them, some names have been changed to protect their identities and families.

Hero is a title they would all deny. Their humility is astounding when you consider their bravery in that terrible place. Each suffered a private hell in loss and fear as they paid a price as they led us to victory. It is to them that I am forever indebted. They were my protectors, my teachers, and my angels.

I feel like my life was shattered by the experience, and a part of me is still running around the streets of Volengrad. It's only now that I can pick up the pieces and feel strong enough to move on. But memories are ghosts. No matter how far or how fast you run they will always haunt you. Embrace them and never forget. Salute.

Jacob Frye

VOLENGRAD

"Emerald City". There was nothing more memorable or spiritually moving than watching the sunset in its brilliance reflected off the mirrored highrises of downtown Volengrad. It would change the way you saw the radiance of twilight forever. It made you believe with a childlike wonder that the great city was built under divine guidance. But during the Terekian occupation, the jewel of the Q was a city caught in the crossfire of war and trapped by the onslaught of destruction. In the eyes of the Alliance's military hierarchy, its strategic value was immeasurable for the simple fact that it was the focal point of 781's industrial health.

To the soldiers that fought there, Emerald City held no architectural splendor or breathtaking beauty. They didn't view it the way the high command did, as a cornerstone victory that would change the tide of the war. For them, Volengrad was a concrete maze that held terror around every corner and death on every street. It was a haven for snipers and booby traps, a city of heartbreak and inconceivable fear.

The veterans of Volengrad never glorified or romanticized the campaign the way the media often did. For them, Volengrad was the city of lost hope and lost friends. For the survivors of Volengrad, the jewel of the Q was an unyielding nightmare that followed them home and haunted them with the memories of the comrades they left behind.It was a psychological wound that took the form of a recurring dream that nestled in their subconscious and tangled its dark visions in the cobwebs of anxiety.

The first impressions of Volengrad for me came from news coverage of the city's evacuation four years ago. I remember watching the panicked exodus of millions of civilians locking up Highway 12 as cars sat frozen in vapor lock for hundreds of miles, I remember the monorail stations packed and overflowing with citizens fleeing from the inevitable invasion.

I remember seeing heart-wrenching visions of children crying in the chaos as their parents carried them through the bustling crowds pushing through the streets. I remember the hundreds of dropships at the airport being mobbed by the frightened masses trying desperately to escape as Coalition forces moved closer to the city's borders. I remember the desolate streets filled with craters and piles of trash and rubble, and wind

181

blown paper sweeping across the dreary skyline. I remember the moldy carnage scattered on the smashed boulevards being eaten by the packs of hungry dogs that were abandoned by their owners and left to fend for themselves.

I remember the smiling dirty faces of the soldiers as they huddled for protection inside the wasted buildings eating freeze-dried rations and trading sea stories. I remember my friends that fought so hard as they struggled to come to terms with what was happening around them before they were killed. I remember...

Q 1

"My name is Death: the last best friend am I."
Robert Southey (1774-1843), English poet

Holly quietly stared at the Pershing 50 caliber sniper rifle in his hands as loose equipment in the jet's cabin rattled flatly in the overhead racks. Most snipers preferred the KC-26 Pulse Rifle because it was light, durable, and reliably accurate, but Holly favored the more temperamental Pershing for its range and penetration. The 50 cal. was considerably heavier, but its self-adjusting scope took the guesswork out of windage and elevation in the compensation for the range of the target. That technology combined with the armor-piercing integrated aluminum rounds that the weapon used made it virtually impossible for the enemy to find suitable cover. When used properly, he could blow a hole in anything up to a mile and a half away.

He never felt like talking before a drop because it always seemed pointless to pass the time with idle chatter. He tried it once before the last operation, but all that the bullshitting did was magnify the jitters for him. Since then, he preferred to keep to himself and spend the time in silent thought until they were over the jump zone.

He listened numbly to the background whine of the jet's engines and the muffled crackle of the tin voices from the radio in the cockpit. A red florescent bulb glowed dimly in the cabin as he looked around at the seven other snipers strapped in with him. That's four teams. There was a lot of talent and firepower on the plane tonight, and Holly contemplated how many snipers were being dropped into the city over the next three hours in support of Operation Uluwatu Prime. The entire 17th Battalion; five hundred snipers—two hundred and fifty teams spread throughout the city of Volengrad to bring their invisible wrath on the Terekians. Never in the history of the Alliance have so many special ops troopers been deployed to one area at the same time.

That's not what made this drop different in Holly's eyes, this insertion made him uncomfortable because it wasn't into Uluwatu Valley like the others. This was a HALO insertion into Volengrad City at night during a rainstorm...that, and he was operating under a black folder agenda that was far more ominous than the other snipers.

Holly glanced to his right and noticed Beach pressing a large pink wad of bubblegum to the side of the bulkhead with his thumb. Fucking Beach, always doing stupid little acts of rebellion like that when he thought nobody was watching, but he was a good soldier and an exceptional shot. They had been a sniper team for two years now, and Beach was a good partner. Meticulous and calculating, his sense of timing and his skills as a tracker were uncanny. At a lean 6'-2" he hardly resembled the stereotypical image of a sniper. Instead of being an unshaved introvert with a mean streak, Beach was clean cut, outgoing, and always looked sunburned...hence the nickname, but he was a good humored kid that took care of business with the cold professionalism of an assassin and he had definitely earned Holly's respect and trust over the years.

The small black jet shuddered as it hit some clear air turbulence and jostled its occupants for a few seconds.

"Sorry about that," the pilot grinned nervously as he turned to address the crew. "We're at seventy-three thousand right now, and we'll be climbing to eighty-six where we'll level off, when we hit the ceiling we should be two minutes from the jump zone. ETA eight minutes."

Holly and the rest of the snipers checked their TAC helmets and double-checked their weapons and equipment loads. Their faces were streaked black in disruptive patterns of grease paint making them look like cast members of a psychotic vaudeville, and their dark gray and black tiger-striped jumpsuits were stripped clean of rank except for one patch on the left shoulder...the Grim Reaper holding a KC-26 sniper rifle with the inscription "Sagittarius Diaboli"(Devil's Archer) in red letters underneath it.

Holly readjusted the Kirsten Automatic pistols strapped to his legs and tightened the granny leash on the flight pack when he glanced at his watch. 0100 hours, right on schedule. With a little luck, he and Beach would be on the ground by 0130 hours and could be set up well before dawn to provide overguard for the 15th when they made planetfall tonight at the Clover.

The pilot turned his head slightly still focusing on the glowing instrument panel, "Okay men, we'll be over the zone in two minutes. Depressurizing the cabin. Good hunting!" the door in the forward bulkhead of the cockpit slid shut and sealed, and they heard the slow hiss of the cabin starting to depressurize to the outside environment eighty-six thousand feet above the surface of 781. The temperature inside the plane fell drastically in a matter of seconds.

The snipers slid on their TAC helmets and unbuckled themselves from the webbing as the rear bay doors began opening with a mechanical whir letting in the freezing midnight air and the hard whine of the engines. The wind rushed by with a ghostly wail as they stared into the starry sky that surrounded the small jet.

Holly stood up and shuffled to the door where a small red light blinked rhythmically overhead. He braced himself in front of the opening with his back to the bitter gale, and faced the group of snipers, "Scared!" he barked loudly.

"HARDCORE!" the snipers shouted back.

"What are we!" Holly bellowed.

"AIRBORNE!"

"BLUE SKIES..."

"...BLACK DEATH!" The snipers replied in unison.

"STAND!"

The seven snipers jumped to their feet sharply and formed a tight line facing the great blackness of the sky.

"Sound off for equipment check!" Holly yelled above the sound of the rushing wind and engines.

"7—okay! 6—okay! 5—okay..." The snipers yelled in descending order as they checked the pack of the man standing in front of him.

"You have your assignments," Holly scowled, "get to your objectives and carry them out. I'll see you all at Defiance when this is over."

"HOOAH!" They shouted as they lowered the visors on their TAC helmets.

Holly watched the light above the door blip to a steady green accompanied by the piercing sound of a buzzer.

"SNIPER UP!" Holly yelled as he stepped aside from the door and looked into the womb of night.

"GO! GO! GO! GO!" he screamed as he waved each man out the door until he was the only one left in the cabin. He took a couple of steps back and inhaled deeply as he faced out at the giant shadow of space. He exhaled and sprinted forward and leaped through the doors into the void of infinity, leaving the noise of the jet's engines far behind.

He stretched out his arms and sprawled his legs in the hard arch position as he began the nine minute free-fall through the darkness. He looked up at the full moon hanging brightly in the northern sky casting its shimmering light across the thick storm clouds thousands of feet beneath him as the howling wind fluttered loudly against his jumpsuit. He was awed by the vast beauty of night and the sheer power of nature as he spun toward earth at a 130 knots.

Holly felt ageless as he sailed gracefully through the dark heavens like an ancient winged predator—untouchable and unseen, a shadow within a shadow. Shunning the earth for the dream of flight and experiencing the fragile balance of screaming terror and overwhelming tranquility. He checked his altimeter on the HUD of the helmet visor as he breathed deeply—seventy-three thousand, two hundred feet and falling...

He could feel his hands going numb, and he opened and closed his fingers to get the blood flowing. A thin white layer of frost began to form on the edges of the helmet visor, and he felt gravity pulling him faster to the ground. Holly shifted the position of his body and heard the dry crumple of a thin layer of ice loosen and break away from the fabric of his suit. He turned his head to get a visual bearing of the horizon and noticed the outline of another sniper silhouetted against the moon. It was Beach—sixty-four thousand, six hundred feet...

Up here, there was nothing but time, space, and acceleration, and his mind flashed like a high-speed picture show. Scenes from a distant life passed before his mind's eye in a spinning strobe of adrenaline; people, places, and scenarios crystallized in vivid memories that meant nothing to him now. All that mattered was the tremendous darkness that wrapped his soul with bone-chilling velocity. He felt a oneness with the icy wind that clutched his body as he fell through the winter sky—fifty-one thousand, four hundred feet...

He could see the multiple flashes of lightning in the cloud cover far below—distant, hypnotic, and violent. The dark gray clouds seemed frozen in a giant swirl that created the eye of the storm hundreds of miles to the north; deceivingly beautiful and strangely peaceful from above, but he knew they were plummeting head-first into the most fierce and unforgiving elements of nature—thirty-nine thousand, seven hundred feet...

Holly no longer felt the burden of the equipment and small oxygen pack strapped to his body, he felt weightless in spite of the 135-knot vertical air speed that hurled him toward the surface of the Q. He pulled his left arm tight to his chest and kept his right extended for stability. He could feel the hard resistance of the wind against him as he punched a small button mounted on a buckle on his chest with his left hand, and the straps for the oxygen pack unraveled and whipped free from his body—twenty-two thousand, three hundred feet...

The atmosphere was considerably warmer as he plunged closer to the clouds, and the moisture from the storm front made tiny beads of condensation trail erratically off his visor like he was running through a waterfall. Holly looked over and saw Beach in a hard arch forty feet in front of him before they punched into the clouds and disappeared—twelve thousand, four hundred feet...

Holly could feel microbursts of air currents slamming him around, and he fought to keep his body stable in the billowy gray soup. He couldn't tell if he was upside down or falling headfirst. Thunder rippled around him with a deafening sonic clap and the world flashed in brilliant white from lightning as he broke through the clouds into the darkness and heavy rain—eight thousand, five hundred feet...

He could hear and feel the cold rain pattering against his suit and helmet when he reached for the ripcord with his right hand and pulled—five thousand, five hundred feet...

Holly heard the dull pop of his pack blow open as his parachute slid out and began to bloom like a black canvas flower in the midnight air. He jerked hard as his body harness tightened around him and the chute opened and filled with air—two thousand, eight hundred feet...

He looked up to check for a proper deployment and healthy silk and insure the lines weren't twisted. Relieved, he listened to the dull patter of the rain hitting the black canvas as he reached up and grabbed the toggles to steer himself to the target—the roof of a sixty-story building. Holly could just make out the shapes of the highrises in the dark and the concrete ribbon of the Volengrad Clover at Highway 12 as he drifted swiftly through the city night.

The Head's-Up-Display in his helmet blipped his position with a soothing blue light and the target was highlighted in red—he was two thousand feet above the streets of Emerald City...

Holly banked right and headed for the buildings ahead of him. Three fourteen hundred foot skyscrapers loomed in the mist like glass giants threatening to swat him out of the air—the Aerodyne/Genesis Corporate Towers. "Jesus, this is going to be close." he mumbled to himself as he glided below the roofline of the concrete triplets—one thousand, three hundred feet...

He struggled with the turbulent updrafts that whiplashed between the structures and almost slammed into the side of Tower II as he weaved through the monuments of corporate enterprise. His stomach tightened as he turned the corner of Tower III and spotted the landing zone—the Volengrad-Sierra Chemical Research Building—nine hundred forty-three feet from street level...he was still four hundred feet away form the target, and the highrise was six hundred fifty feet tall.

"Shit!" Holly cussed to himself, "This is gonna be tight."

Holly raised his visor and felt the chill of the downpour brush against his face as he toggled down for a shallow glide path to the roof. He released the granny leash of the flight pack and let it trail eight feet below him as he prepared to land—fifty feet to the roof deck...he could see an abandoned heli-pad on the east end of the roof as he drifted down at 20-knots—thirty feet to the roof...Holly glanced up at the skyline around him to maintain his sense of perspective in the driving rain—fifteen feet...he pulled down hard on the toggles to break his vertical air speed and heard the flight pack skitter on the wet cement roof as his feet touched down and his parachute collapsed onto the deck.

Holly disengaged his risers and took a knee as he began rolling up the canvas in the darkness when a darker shadow floated down behind him in a silent landing—it was Beach. The two snipers yanked off their packs and began stuffing their chutes back into them.

"How was your flight Captain?" Beach asked as he jammed the canvas back into the pack.

"I want my money back," Holly replied humorlessly, "I think they lost my luggage and the in-flight movie sucked."

"Hey, you know what?" Beach squinted as he latched his pack, "It's fucking cold!"

"Thanks."

"I'm gonna take a look around and make sure all accesses to the roof are sealed off."

"You take the catwalk to the left, and I'll take the right. I'll meet you on the other side of the heli-pad." Holly replied.

"You got it boss."

"And Beach," Holly paused.

"Yeah?"

"Go ahead and rig any entrances you find with pyrogen frags. I want anybody that shows up uninvited singed beyond recognition."

"Roger that."

"Let's move."

Holly moved quickly up the steel grate stairs of the platform with a Kirsten Automatic drawn and held tightly with both hands in front of him. He sensed that finding any sentries on the roof would be highly unlikely in this kind of weather, but he had to be sure it was secured before they set up for the morning.

The rain came down hard and droned on the empty heli-pad in heavy sheets. It splashed on his face in fat cold drops that he found strangely refreshing as he moved down the catwalk. He gazed up at the Aerodyne/Genesis Corporate Towers that loomed another eighty stories above this building, and wondered how secure the three structures were of Terekians. He knew that the Aggressor Forces had infiltrated the city over a week ago, but he hoped with uncertainty that they were able to secure their objectives over the last few days—specifically the triple towers that made excellent vantage points for enemy snipers to nail them.

It never used to bother Holly before, but he noticed his attitude toward his own mortality changed after the last operation at the Pegasus Bridge. He remembered getting back to Defiance and the Major pulling him into the command bunker for the debriefing...

"So Capt. Holly," the Major stood up from behind his desk as they shook hands, "I understand you and Beach had quite a field-day with Bravo Company."

"We had our moments, Sir." Holly replied.

"I would say that's a huge understatement, Captain," the Major nodded as he sat back down, "you logged fifty-six confirmed in three days. What does that bring your total up to, son?"

"Five-thirty-eight."

"Five hundred and thirty-eight confirmed kills to date." The Major said solemnly as he lit a cigar and stared at Holly's kill sheets that were tucked in his personal file. "Jesus Holly, you're an extremely dangerous man. Do you realize that's a record?"

"I always wondered about that, Sir."

"Sit down, Captain," the Major motioned as he pulled out two glasses and a bottle from a drawer and began to fill them with bourbon. "I think you'll like this shit. It's two hundred fifty years old."

Holly was still in his muddy BDU's and he hadn't showered in days, but he was too tired and salty to care. He took the cushioned seat in front of the Major's desk and sighed as he sank into the chair a little further. The Major slid one of the glasses to him and offered Holly a cigar.

"Captain," the Major said calmly as he took a puff, "you've made quite a reputation for yourself, not just within the Aggressor Forces, but with the Terekians as well."

"Yes Sir, I've heard a few rumors."

"Listen, I don't know how quite to put this except to just come right out and level with you..." the Major said as he pulled out a piece of glossy paper and set it face down on his desk. "About a week ago a sniper team attached to a recon unit ambushed a Terekian patrol in the Bellows Woods in Uluwatu."

Holly took a sip from the glass and eyed the paper on the desk suspiciously.

"After our snipers killed everybody," the Major continued grimly, "the team searched the bodies to gather intelligence. As it turned out, one of their kills was a Terekian Special Forces operative. An assassin. They took this off of him..." the Major slid the glossy stock across the table to Holly, "go ahead, captain, take a look at it."

Holly set his drink down and reached for the paper and flipped it over. It was a photograph of him on the streets of New Sierra when he went on leave over a month ago. Holly picked up his glass and downed the contents as he studied the photograph in the dim light before placing it back on the major's desk.

"I look like shit in this picture." Holly said coldly.

"Captain, there's a bounty out for your head. It's obvious that your identity has been compromised," the Major leaned forward through the cigar smoke, "you're not the only sniper in battalion to have a price on your ass, but what caught our attention is the time and location this photo was taken. As you can see from the background of this snap, you've been shadowed. We don't know how long you've been tracked, but our network has uncovered evidence that this comes right from the top of the Terekian high command, which means every headhunter planetside will be clawing over each other for a chance to bring you down to collect the reward."

"Still a shitty picture of me."

"Let's get down to brass tacks, Captain, the Colonel and I have been talking, and we think it would be in your best interest to be pulled out of the field and transferred out of 781 as soon as possible. You know the rules."

There was an awkward silence between the two men as Holly frowned and stared intently at the picture.

"With all due respect Sir, I'd rather you didn't. I want to stay with my unit."

"Shit, Holly," the major said shaking his head, "there are enough hero's in this war. You've done more than your part, it's over for you, and now it's time to get your ass out."

"Negative Sir, in light of this photograph, I'd say this war's just begun for me. Besides, I don't think it's right to just up and run at the first sign of being targeted. I'd like to stay with my unit."

"Jesus, what the fuck am I going to do with you? Do you really feel that strongly about it, Captain?"

"Yes Sir, I do."

"Very well then," the Major sighed, "it's against my better judgment to let you stay, and the Colonel will enjoy chewing my ass to pieces. I *will* have hell to pay for sending out a short-timer..."

"Sir, permission to speak freely, Sir."

"Speak."

"Any idea who put a hit on me?"

The Major sighed and sat quietly for a moment. "Yes, Intelligence has a profile but you don't want to see it. You don't have the security rating."

"Off the record, Major, I think I have a right to know who contracted me."

The Major frowned and rubbed his forehead as if he felt a migraine coming on. He reached down and slowly opened a file drawer at the bottom of his desk and pulled out a stainless steel box with a built-in lock.

"I want your word that this conversation NEVER took place, you hear me Holly? You never saw a fucking thing, understand?" He glared as he flicked the combination on the lock of the box and pulled out a black folder that was a half-inch thick and placed it on the desktop.

"Yes Sir."

"Go ahead...open it."

Holly reached forward and placed his hand on the documents when the Major slammed his hand hard over his...

"What you're about to view has a Level One security rating—which YOU don't have, understand? This profile is NOT a hit." He glowered as he released Holly's hand.

Holly eyed the Major then opened the folder revealing a photograph of a high ranking Terekian National in full dress uniform. A very highly decorated soldier.

"This who I think it is, Major?" Holly asked with an astonished tone.

"General Rachel Oss."

"Fuck!"

"Nobody's been able to touch her. She's managed to stay a step ahead of every bounty hunter and assassin in the Q. Official stance is that she's hands-off. The Agency wants her alive. When the war ends they want to use her as a resource. Unofficially, she's far too dangerous to be allowed to live. As it is now, Captain, Oss has taken an interest in you," the Major paused, "she's nervous about 'The Sandman' rumors being passed through their ranks. To be blunt, Captain, Oss wants you dead."

"Major, I want this hit."

"She's NOT a hit, and if she were, I can't authorize that."

"Then don't." Holly whispered dryly.

A moment of silence passed between the two men as they faced each other.

"Get cleaned up and get some rest. You're going to Volengrad. Briefing is at the CP at 0400 hours tomorrow."

"Thank you Sir." Holly said firmly as he headed for the door.

"Captain..."

"Yes Sir."

"This is your last gig in the field," the Major glared through the cigar smoke as he noticed the black folder had disappeared from his desk and grinned, "after Volengrad, you're rotating off 781 for reassignment to Divisional HQ on Syterra 12. For you the war's over."

"Yes Sir." Holly replied.

"And Captain..." The Major added gravely.

"Yes Sir."

"Watch your back."

Holly strained his eyes to make out the shapes in the darkness as he moved over the grating of the skywalk when he thought he heard something shift around the corner of a small structure at the end of the landing platform. It was a noise that would have been comforting under different circumstances, but not tonight—maybe he was dramatizing and his imagination had been shifted into overdrive, but he thought he heard the very distinct metallic click of a round being chambered, and whether it was real or not, he knew it was meant for him.

Holly could see the glistening windows of the tiny building that had to be the signal center of the heli-pad. The lights were off and he hoped it was unoccupied as he couched low and made his way through the rain to the end of the walkway. He tensed up and quickened his pace as he took the steps down to the deck and slipped underneath the platform. He pressed himself against the cold steel supports and waited motionless in the gloom.

Lightning flickered vibrantly across the roof causing the exaggerated shadows of the pad to dance erratically on the deck. Holly could feel the chill of another presence close by, and everything seemed to funnel itself into a slow motion time warp as the sound of footsteps coming at him in the shadows echoed closer.

Another jagged flash of lightning streaked across the sky with a savage brilliance that lit up the roof and gave Holly a fleeting glimpse of the stocky silhouette of a Terekian soldier in front of him. Thunder roared as Holly stepped out from the shadows behind the guard and aimed the Kirsten Auto at the sentry's head and pulled the trigger.

Several muffled pops from the sound suppressor issued from Holly's pistol as the Terekian sentry jerked hard from the impact of three rounds entering the back of his head and peeled the top of his skull wide open sending blood in a fine spray into the downpour as the body fell to the ground with a dull thump.

Holly spun around and aimed the K-Auto at the hollow sound of boots running on the grating in his direction. He could see the hard shapes of three more Coalition troopers rushing toward him as he dropped to the prone position and opened fire with short bursts into the night. Their bodies spun wildly as if electrocuted from the impact of the rounds, and their arms flailed helplessly in the darkness before they fell to the platform.

Holly could hear the soft gurgle of one of the dying Terekians as he lay on the catwalk waiting for more sentries to come after him...then silence, not the kind of serene peace that soothed ragged nerves, but a tight peculiar silence that made him shiver as he lay in the rain anticipating the worse scenario. His instincts alarmed him with the empty feeling that something was desperately wrong, and he couldn't shake the pang to get up and run—instead, he rolled sideways off the walkway to the edge of the roof and doubled back the way he came.

"Beach, where the fuck are you?" He thought to himself coldly as he attached a retractable stock onto the K-Auto and ran up the stairs of the second catwalk. He moved swiftly and decisively forward through the misty darkness straining to see what lay ahead when he found Beach face down at the end of the skywalk. He kneeled next to his partner and reached down with his left hand and tried to find a pulse in Beach's neck. It was shallow, but he was still alive.

Holly rolled his friend over gently and Beach groaned as his eyes flittered open and looked up.

"I fucked up, captain." Beach whispered hoarsely.

"Save your breath," Holly replied quietly, "where you hit?"

"Oh shit, I'm gut-shot. Sliced right through my armor at point-blank." Beach coughed. "One of 'em was carrying a Falcon Silencer, and I walked right into the son-of-a-bitch."

"How many?"

"Four, I think they're Special Forces..."

"They're dead now."

"You need to secure the roof, Holly," Beach grimaced as he clutched his stomach, "get going, I can manage."

"We need to get you out of the rain. Think you can stand?"

"You don't ask for much, do you?"

"Come on troop, we're wasting time." Holly ordered as he hooked his arm under Beach's shoulders and helped him to his feet. They staggered down the stairs of the catwalk and ducked under the heli-pad.

"Alright," Holly whispered as he propped Beach against a steel column, "sit tight while I check out the signal center and secure the stairwell."

"Damn," Beach gasped, "I think I shit myself, captain."

"You'll be okay." Holly said reassuringly, but he knew Beach wouldn't make it. The strong odor of excrement was a sure sign of a lower abdominal wound, and Beach would die of poisoning if he didn't bleed out first.

"You better go, captain," Beach coughed, "you've got a mission to carry through."

"Hang in there, kid," Holly frowned, "I'll get you dusted-off first chance I get."

"Hurt them..." Beach nodded as he passed out.

"It's payback time, Beach," Holly whispered as he stood back up, "fuckin' payback."

Holly moved quietly through the shadows of the platform until he reached the signal building at the end of the skywalk. He stood with his back against the wall and the Kirsten Auto braced across his chest as he took a deep breath and lunged around the corner of the building ready to open fire...nothing. Nothing but the sound of gusting wind against the structure and the clatter of rain drops.

He paced cautiously on the deck toward the entrance of the tiny structure and crouched to avoid a window. The rain had abated to a light drizzle as he crept to the door that was left ajar and pushed it in. His eyes had finally adjusted themselves to the darkness, and Holly could see the communications console spread across the windows facing the landing pad. His first thought was to disable the control center before he realized that the equipment might come in handy later. He also noticed the temperature of the room was comfortably warmer and dry, he would have to bring Beach in here after he secured the next floor and rigged the pyrogen frags.

Holly moved cautiously through the room memorizing its layout when he found the entry that opened into the stairwell that would take him down to the next level. He pulled out a small sensor and ran it slowly up and down the length of the door to check for motion alarms and booby traps. It was clean. He put on his night vision glasses and slipped quietly into the pitch-black that lead to the next landing.

Holly clenched his teeth as he made his way down the stairs like a phantom. He was an element of the dark that descended invisibly through the layers of shadows. A modern day boogieman on the hunt, and the personification of the twitching fear that lurked under the thin crust of urban legend.

He pushed through the darkness as he exited the stairwell and entered a large room on the sixtieth floor; shattered bay windows let in a stiff midnight breeze and what little light the gray night offered, and flashes of lightning illuminated the gloom with its infrequent uneven glow. He could see the splintered outlines of overturned tables, desks, and couches. The walls were pitted with bullet holes, and a thin blue-gray layer of smoke lingered in the room, the air still smelled of gunpowder from a firefight, and about eighteen bodies lay motionless on the ground. Holly removed his glasses and crouched over a corpse to gather information on what might have happened, he was just about to reach down to pick up the weapon that lay next to the body when he felt the cold steel of a barrel press up against the back of his head...

"Uh-uh, Sees unden fuck shea tyre Sees wan dir."

("Uh-uh, I wouldn't fuck with that if I was you.") A voice whispered coldly from behind.

"I don't speak Serenian." Holly replied calmly through clenched teeth.

"Okay then," the voice answered, "then listen closely, 'cause I'm only gonna say this once. Set your weapons on the floor, and keep your hands where I can see them."

Holly sighed and blinked as he cautiously placed the Kirsten Auto on the deck and removed the second pistol from its holster.

"Shit, I can't believe I walked into this." Holly thought to himself as he pulled the Pershing 50 cal. off his shoulders and set it on the floor with the K-autos and remained crouching. He held his hands up and reprimanded himself for his stupidity.

"Very good," the voice whispered as the barrel eased off, "now stand up...easy now..."

Holly kept his hands up as he rose slowly to his feet and saw the silhouettes of four soldiers rise from behind the tables and desks. They kept their weapons trained on him as they stepped forward from the shadows.

"Okay, numb-nuts," the voice ordered, "make any sudden moves and your ass is toast, understand? Keep your hands up and turn around slowly. Hey Jackson, get some light over here."

"You've got it sergeant," One of the soldiers replied as he flicked on a flashlight and aimed it at Holly's face. "Shit! I think he's one of ours. Look at the patch on his arm, sergeant, he's a sniper."

"I'll be dipped in shit!" Another voice exclaimed, "So he is. Who are you, and who're you with?"

Holly squinted at the bright light and remained silent.

"Petersen, call Genie," the voice barked, "tell 'im we've got company. We need to get after the fuckers that ran up the roof!"

"They're wasted." Holly replied.

"All of them?" the trooper with the flashlight asked.

"Yeah, all of them." Holly squinted. "Who are you people?"

"Dragon 4-1," the voice answered and stepped out from the gloom, "I'm Sergeant Lorrie Isa, 9th Division. And you're?"

"Holly, 17th Sniper Battalion."

"Sorry about the reception, Holly," Isa said coldly as she eased her Bolter down and engaged the safety, "we're in the process of securing this building, and the last thing we expected is running into friendlies. Especially up here." Isa stated sharply as she looked at the patch on Holly's shoulder.

Holly lowered his hands and glanced at his weapons on the floor, "Do you mind, sergeant?"

"By all means." Isa replied. "When did you make your insertion?"

"HALO, 'bout an hour ago." Holly replied as he glimpsed at the Grim Reaper patch that was also on the sergeant's uniform.

"Airborne."

"Yeah."

"In this weather?"

"10-4."

"I didn't think that was possible."

"Sergeant," Holly glared as he gathered his weapons, "my partner's still up on deck and he's seriously wounded. I need to get him inside."

"Take us up there, we'll get 'im for you." Isa said grimly, "Jackson, call Genie and tell 'im the building's secure and to get his ass up here. The rest of you fuckers on me. Lead the way Holly."

The small group sprinted up the stairwell and through the signal center. A light fog had begun to settle on the roof as they made their way through the support structures of the landing pad to where Beach was lying on the deck in a pool of blood. They were too late. Beach's body sat propped against the steel column where Holly had left him. His eyes and mouth were half open and the expression of release and serenity was frozen on his face.

"Shit." Holly frowned as he kneeled next to his friend and gathered Beach's weapons and dog tags. "I'm gonna make those son-of-a-bitches pay for this."

"What was your partner's name, Holly?" Isa asked sadly as the other troopers gathered around them.

"Corporeal Lance Derry," Holly sighed, "we called him Beach."

"Let's get him inside."

"We need to hurry, I'm running out of time. I need to get set up before light, and I could use your help, sergeant."

"Roger that."

"Are you the only sniper in the squad?"

"No," Isa said dryly, "Seer's on his way up, he's from the 15th. He's attached to Scarecrow 3-6. Aggressor Recon."

"Outstanding, the more the merrier. My partner and I were assigned a two-fold mission. Provide overguard for the 15th and 163rd when they make planetfall tonight, and go after Terekian snipers until Volengrad is secured. I'm going to need you to help me cover this sector."

"Okay, what's your plan?"

"It's more like a change of plan, sergeant. A little improvising if you will." Holly nodded. "Our network believes that Coalition snipers will be operating in this area from several vantage points to harass the 15th when they get planetside."

"What do you want me and Seer to do?"

"I'd like you to stay on the roof as overguard while I go after the snipers. Basically watch my back when I go to the ground..."

"Hey Isa," a husky soldier in a tattered uniform interrupted as he loomed over the two snipers, "who's your new friend?" he was accompanied by three troopers that stood behind him.

"It's about fucking time, Genie." Isa said impatiently. "Thought you got lost on the way up."

"Who's this guy?" Genie grunted.

"Holly, 17th Sniper Battalion." The captain said softly as he cleared his throat.

"How the hell did you get up here?" Genie demanded. "Isa, I thought the building was sealed off! How'd he get by us?"

"I HALOed in."

"HALO! In this weather?"

"I wouldn't exactly say that I got by you," Holly replied, "the sergeant and her fire team ambushed me on the sixtieth floor."

"Who's the guy on the deck?" Genie nodded.

"My spotter." Holly answered.

"Shit," Genie spit as he looked at Holly suspiciously, "I have a feeling you didn't just drop in for the continental breakfast. I'm starting to sense a major SNAFU coming up. Now what?"

"Genie," Isa interjected, "Holly's going to need our help…"

Q 2

Sergeant Isa stared intently through the scope of her KC-26 Pulse Rifle that was propped on top of a parapet wall in the corner of the east side of the roof. She slowly scanned the streets six hundred feet below for movement as the sun peeked over the horizon with its orange glow.

A thin gunmetal blue mist floated between the skyscrapers several stories below like a filthy blanket shrouding the pocked architecture. The streets were littered with huge piles of rubble and smoldering debris from buildings that collapsed during the air strikes, and columns of thick black smoke plumed from the hundreds of fires that raged like a red and orange ocean throughout the city, giving the greasy air a gritty spent aroma that left an unpleasant coppery aftertaste in the back of your throat.

Isa shut her eyes hard and rubbed them hoping to break the crusty fatigue that set in from the sleepless nights of the siege during the week. She knew from experience that when the body was deprived of sleep for a prolonged period of time, the mind began to slip, and the already narrow margin for error in survival grew thinner with each passing hour. It's been four nights since she closed her eyes for rest, and in spite of the metabolism she built up over the years, she could feel the weight of exhaustion pressing down on her shoulders, and the numbing hypnotic trance of being "doped on the scope" as she traced the cratered landscape through the cross hairs.

Isa sighed as she surveyed the amount of damage on the streets and shattered storefronts. Automobiles were overturned or lay buried under thick slabs of concrete, and the charred, twisted hulls of Terekian and Alliance armor sat like blackened iron corpses on the wasted boulevards. Hundreds of bodies were strewn everywhere below, and she was grateful to be sixty stories above the smell of the massacre. She had never seen so much annihilation in her life. The apocalyptic vision of the smoldering metropolitan in the predawn light was staggering. Volengrad was in ruins.

Everything she looked at was filtered through smoke; the ragged outlines of damaged buildings, the Clover and Highway 12, and the hazy morning sunlight; giving the world an intensely surreal sensation, like some horrible daydream of standing on the edge of a desolate concrete valley overlooking hell. She shuddered and felt like doubling over as the hollow stitch of loss and misery floated through her dampened spirit, and she knew in her heart that Emerald City would fall, but it would be a costly victory.

Sergeant Isa winced as she watched large packs of dogs file cautiously through the alleys; sniffing, licking, and clawing through the dead. These canine packs were composed of diverse breeds that had been abandoned or separated from their owners years ago during the onslaught of the Terekian occupation. Being social animals, they formed hunting packs in an effort to adapt to what the war had done to their lives. As time passed, these creatures learned to thrive in the forgotten corners of the city and began to breed-out their domestic temperament in exchange for a feral disposition.

Through the years, the dogs had rediscovered and sharpened their hunting skills and refined their instincts. They had learned not to trust man and quickly grew wary of his presence, and they reacted with vicious cowardice at the sight of humans; baring their teeth and growling with their heads lowered as they slinked into the shadows. Knowing that it was humanity that abused them, mankind that bombed the shit out of them, then callously marveled at their nomadic natures as they wandered through the devastation scrounging for food.

They always appeared after firefights and barrages along with the flocks of huge featherless crows ("corpse birds" as the troops called them) and smaller airborne reptiles that descended from the dark skies in the aftermath of battle, squawking and screeching noisily as they rummaged through the scattered trash, and ghoulishly ravaged the dead for tender scraps.

Isa watched the dogs tear into the decomposing bodies with savage abandon. Their hunger dictated their behavior as they barked, growled, and fought each other for the best parts of rotting meat. She looked away with disgust when a large dog trailed off with a long strand of intestines from the shredded belly of a Terekian soldier and three other canines tore the rest of the carcass apart.

"Sergeant, over here." Seer waved as he looked over a parapet wall on the west side of the roof.

"What is it?" Isa replied as she snapped out of her daze.

"Looks like there's a fire fight down there." Seer said excitedly as he peered down at a smoke-filled street through binoculars.

"Shit, listen to that," Isa nodded, as the sound of gunfire echoed off the walls of the highrises, "sounds like a lot of lead being thrown around."

"Can't see a damn thing with that smoke cover." Seer frowned.

"Hey, I thought I just heard sniper-fire, listen..."

There was a distinct crack of a single shot fired.

"No doubt about it," Isa nodded, "that's a 134ATS rifle."

"Fuckin' Terekian Special Forces."

"Let's head down for a closer look. They're firing on somebody. Where's the radio? I wanna check in with Battalion."

"Looks like we're gonna get an early start on this op." Seer sighed as he handed Isa the handset.

"Rover-6, Rover-6 actual, this is Dragon 4-1, you got your ears on? Over." Isa spoke calmly into the mike.

"Rover copies, go ahead 4-1." A voice cracked indifferently over the radio.

"Rover, what's the sit.-rep on friendlies in our AO? Over."

"State coordinates 4-1, and we'll give you current stats." The voice replied.

"Rover, in the funny-pages I read 156/48 November-Whiskey, over."

"Roger, 156/48 November-Whiskey, stand by 4-1."

It seems inevitable that when time is crucial, the seconds lag on forever; and Isa and Seer fidgeted anxiously as they waited for an answer that they already knew.

"Dragon 4-1," the voice finally responded, "that's affirmative on the friendlies in your area, we have elements of the 1st Division that have entered Volengrad this morning in support of Operation Uluwatu Prime, over."

"10-4, Rover-6," Isa said dryly, "someone's taking fire in our sector, we're goin' in to lend a hand, over."

"Roger Dragon 4-1, just received word that elements of Bravo and Alpha Companies pinned by sniper fire in your AO and requesting gunship back-up. Assist Bravo and neutralize all soft targets. Don't lose sight of your primary objective, Rover-6 out."

"Dragon clear." Isa replied as she handed the radio back to Seer. "Let's see if we can shag-out some snipers. Those boys sound like they're in serious trouble."

"Wonder where Holly went?" Seer frowned as he rubbed the stubble on his chin.

"Don't worry about him," Isa replied, "I think he's more than capable of taking care of himself."

"What do you mean by that?"

"Geez Seer, didn't you recognize him?"

"Uh-uh, am I supposed to?" Seer squinted.

"Hhhmmm...you worry me sometimes, you know?" Isa chuckled softly as she shook her head. "Anyway, I couldn't place Holly's face at first, but I knew he looked familiar. Then it dawned on me when we helped him drag his partner out of the rain," Isa sighed as she gathered her gear and locked eyes with Seer, "Seer, you ever heard of the Sandman?"

"Shit, he's a fuckin' myth, Sarge. Scuttle-butt is that the Sandman is some kind of ghost. Besides, even if he really existed, nobody can possibly have a kill ratio that high...wait a second, you're not telling me that you think that Holly's..."

"The Sandman." Isa winked. "Come on, get your shit together. We're wasting time."

"You're fuckin' with me, right? How do you figure?"

"Remember that Terekian patrol we ambushed over a week ago in the valley?"

"Oh yeah, that was a hairy little firefight." Seer nodded.

"Well, after we wasted them, I was going through one of the bodies and found a photograph. It was a picture of Holly," Isa frowned, "the photo had some writing on the bottom. Eight million gelben for the Sandman. Dead."

"No shit?"

"Sent the photo back to Division, until that day, I didn't believe in him either."

"I'll be damned, that's creepy. The fucking Sandman."

"Let's get a move on."

The two snipers started down the long flight of stairs to the tenth floor, moving through the darkness boldly. Sinister entities on a savage haunt, intimate with the clammy touch of the shadows that shrouded them. Only the muffled patter of their boots and the small plumes of breath in the chill betrayed their presence as they jogged down the steps.

Stealth and surprise, the sniper's primary tools of warfare handed down for generations and cultured through the centuries. The hunters and the hunted...the soldiers that spent hours stalking the enemy or waiting concealed in the shadows for the opportunity to spring the trap—but how easily the roles were reversed in the deadly game of hide and seek, where timing, luck, and cruel fate were all elements in the contest of life and death. For them, the war was extremely personal. They saw the expressions of all their kills through high-powered scopes when they pulled the trigger and watched the single round tear through flesh and bone. Some snipers took the war to it's most intimate level—profiling and studying one person for weeks, even months. Learning his or her habits and routines, every detail of a person's life examined, dissected, and memorized just to set them up for the perfect "hit". When everything came down to the sweat-breaking moment of putting the crosshairs on the target and unleashing the fury of velocity on them. Those were a special breed of snipers; the hardened assassins that walked hand in hand with death.

"Sagittarius Diaboli". Perhaps the most respected and feared patch in the war among the Terekian Special Ops and the Alliance Aggressor Forces. Respected because of what the sniper candidates had to learn and endure during training; from honing their tracking skills and hand-to-hand combat (like the Scouts), to mastering the high-tech weapons of marksmanship. Feared by the enemy because snipers were quite demoralizing with their tactics of evasion and seemingly invisible nature when they struck panic with a single shot from nowhere. From everywhere. Sending entire columns of troops to the ground or scattering wildly for cover. Most troopers agree that one of the most frightening encounters in any battle is being pinned down by snipers. Hell, just the rumor of one in the area was enough. They didn't even have to do anything to put the fear out. Their presence was all it took to induce that horrible feeling of being watched and set your internal alarm ringing until it overheated and made the back of your neck flush with fearful agitation knowing that somebody was going to die.

"I hate them motherfuckers." A sergeant once told me, "They never come out and face-off. They always gotta be sneakin' around and pickin' us off one-by-one." He said in an exasperated tone. "About two weeks ago we was on a patrol, and we was movin' down this trail when our pointman takes a round in the face. Blew out the back of his head and the same round kept goin' and hit the guy behind him in the chest. Sprayed him everywhere. Anyway, some of us hit the deck, and some dove off to the side right into some fuckin' pungi sticks. Goddamn, them fuckers set us up and took almost half our squad out. They had us pinned and took their fuckin' time killin' us. By the time the gunships got there the snipers were gone. We took thirty percent casualties that day."

But you can bet your ass that even though the troops hated snipers, they always found comfort when *our own* traveled with them on an op. They felt like they had an extra edge when they were around, like snipers had some kind of special mojo. The primitive black magic boonie voodoo that snipers are believed to possess; the spirit of the grim reaper and agent of death. Ancient, mysterious, and undefeatable.

Soldiers always talked about fear in the oddest terms, defining it, denying it, and embracing it all at once. It all boiled down to what one soldier called "the pucker factor". Fear simplified and gauged on an imaginary scale of one through ten. The rating of "ten" being the highest and worst; "when you're so scared that your asshole involuntarily contracts and your whole body feels like shriveling up and disappearing into it." The kid explained to me with a knowing grin.

"But check this out, mister," the young trooper said as he lit a cigarette, "firefights have a pucker factor of five or six, unless there's a sniper, then it becomes a ten." The kid laughed and shook his head as he got up and walked away. Leaving me sitting there with a dry lump in my throat thinking that only a grunt could find humor in what he just said.

•••

Isa and Seer exited the stairwell and jogged down a corridor to the end of the west hallway. They came to double glass doors that opened into a large conference suite filled with beautiful wooden tables surrounded by leather chairs. Isa pulled out her K-Auto Pistol and shot out several bay windows as they weaved past the furniture to get into position.

"Hey Seer," Isa ordered, "we need to flip some of these tables onto their sides and get them by the windows for some cover. Come and give me a hand will ya?"

Within minutes the room was in shambles, and everything was rearranged into a small barricade against the windows facing the smoke filled boulevard. Isa and Seer kneeled on opposite sides of the room quietly peering down at the street below through the scopes of their rifles; they heard several shots echo off the walls of the surrounding highrises that were undoubtedly from high-powered weapons. Terekian snipers. Shots followed by the screams of pain as the enemy rounds found their targets.

"Shit! Those boys are getting hammered." Isa frowned as she tried to follow the sound of the gunshot. Isa looked at the windows of the building across from her as several more shots were fired and the screaming became a low whimper from the street. She turned her attention to the avenue below as the smoke cover began to thin, and could see a soldier lying in a shiny pool of blood at the bottom of some wide marble steps that lead to what looked like a bank building. He was still alive, but his legs had been shot off. He appeared to be talking to someone in the building when another shot rang out and the poor trooper began screaming again. This time his left hand was shot off. Isa watched the soldier lying on the pavement in helpless frustration, wishing she could run down there and pull him to safety when she heard the sound of Bolter fire below, and the soldier was still.

She began to tremble in anger as she scanned the buildings around her through the scope, and there, two stories above her in the opposite highrise, was the barrel of a rifle propped through a window. Isa could just see the top of the Terekian sniper's head through the pane as she drew a bead on him and squeezed the trigger...

Isa watched the top of the sniper's head spin off as blood, hair, and gray matter splattered through the room and his body flipped up and over from the impact of the round.

Unfortunately, her muzzle flash gave away her position and an enemy sniper in one of the highrises across the boulevard had spotted Isa and locked on his crosshairs. The Terekian had a clear shot and focused on the side of her head. He inhaled deeply then exhaled slowly to get his breathing under control. He could see Isa looking through her scope as she scanned the smashed terrain in front of her.

The Coalition sniper wrapped his index finger around the trigger of his 134 ATS rifle and took a slow shallow breath as he tightened his jaws and squinted. He smiled knowing that she would never know what hit her as he pulled the trigger...

Two shots fired a fraction of a second apart. The first shot came from Holly, who was kneeling by a window on an opposite wing three floors above Isa, the second was the Terekian's. Holly had scoped the sniper and put a round into his neck the moment the Terekian fired at Isa. The Coalition sniper dropped his rifle and clutched frantically at his torn throat as blood gushed out heavily...

Holly fired again at the sniper and watched his head disintegrate as the integrated aluminum round entered the Terekian's skull and exploded, leaving his body floundering on the floor next to his rifle...

•••

Isa was spun half way around as the bullet grazed her left cheek and split the skin wide open—she flew counter-clockwise and ended up on the floor on all fours groping for her weapon, blinded by her own blood.

"Lorrie!" Seer screamed as he dropped his KC-26 and ran to her aid, "Oh shit! Oh shit! Jesus Christ, don't die on me now sergeant!"

"Calm the fuck down, Seer," Isa coughed as she staggered to her feet, "it's just a flesh wound. The sorry son-of-a-bitch only grazed me."

"Shit that was close!"

"No kidding. Get me some bandages and tape me up."

"You're bleeding bad," Seer sobbed as he opened his small aid kit and began to bandage Isa's head. "I think you're gonna need stitches."

"I'll be damned if I let *you* sew me up," Isa chuckled, "nothing personal, bud, but I think you're kind of a butcher when it comes to first aid."

"You're a real gem, you know it?"

"Don't sweet talk me now, Seer, bandage me. Don't mummify me."

"Okay, okay, just hold still so I can finish."

"Now I want some payback on that snipe." Isa growled.

"I said hold still, and quit movin', you're gonna make the bleeding worse. Tell you what sarge," Seer nodded as he taped up the bandages, "you move down a couple of floors and cover me, I'm gonna make a run for that building across the street. We'll set up a crossfire over the boulevard."

"Alright, you get moving, I'll head down three floors. Go!"

Seer exited the building from the north side through a fire escape and ran down an alley, dodging and jumping over piles of rubbish and debris scattered on the black top.

He stopped before he reached the street and jumped over the remains of a stonewall on his right. He crouched with his back against the barrier for a moment to catch his breath and did a quick scan of the boulevard in front of him. The billow of gray clouds from smoke frags was beginning to thin out, but it was still soupy enough to make it across the street without being seen from above if he hurried.

Seer eyed a six-story building across the street through the haze. It had a lot of heavy damage on it's face from yesterday's artillery barrage, and all the windows were broken. It was a perfect place to hide with a good vantage point over the entire street. He kept his KC-26 rifle slung and disengaged the safety on his Bolter Auto as he wiped the beads of sweat from his brow. Seer blinked hard as he cast a worried gaze to the upper floors of the Volengrad-Sierra Research Building hoping that Isa was already in position. He felt the empty numbness of fear twist his gut like a hunger pang as he bit his lower lip and leaped forward and began running toward the structure.

Halfway across the avenue, Seer slipped on the entrails of a Terekian and fell on his side. He scrambled back on his feet and kept running— constantly glancing up at the building in front of him...

•••

Holly backed away from the window in a low crawl until he got to the heavy double-doors that opened into the hallway, he checked his gear again before he left the small office space and made his way down the corridor to a stairwell on the south end of the building that would lead down to the street. He felt the sharp rush of adrenaline pulse through his body like a tidal wave from the black storm of fear as he ran down the stairs. This was what he lived for; the hunt, the stalk, and the kill.

He alienated himself from his emotions, and only cold, hard predatory instinct drove him forth like a machine. The only thing that mattered now was the duel that would play itself out between snipers. When skill and cunning would override luck, and survival became a deadly game with absolute rules. Harsh, ruthless, and savage.

Holly stepped out of the staircase into a dim parking garage below street-level. The air was cool and dank as he padded quietly through the shadows and abandoned cars; he was about to cross a breezeway when he noticed a manhole cover in the corner by a guard shack. He jogged over to it and kneeled down over the grated iron vent. It was a storm drain, and he suspected that if he went down and followed the system, it would lead out to the street.

He reached down and curled his fingers around the grating and grunted as he lifted it up and slid it over. Holly saw the steel access ladder that lead into the dark tunnel below, and felt a small shiver work up his spine as he slipped on his night-vision glasses and lowered himself into the hole. It took some effort to maintain his balance as he hooked one leg through the rungs and reached up to pull the grate back into place, and he almost smashed a finger doing it. He felt overwhelmed by the musty fragrance of time and neglect as he descended into the gloom; the silence was an eerie hollowness that surrounded him as he scaled to the base of the ladder thirty feet below the street.

When he reached bottom, he turned around and drew his K-Auto and attached the retractable stock. Holly could see the small shapes of tiny rodents scurrying along the tunnel walls as they squeaked in agitation caused by his invasion. He could feel thousands of beady little eyes watching him as he started walking in the direction of the avenue...

•••

Isa leaned against a wall and readjusted the windage on her scope as she stared at the cratered street below. The smoke was starting to thin, and visibility was getting better as the morning sun rose above the horizon and took the edge off the chill in the air. Suddenly, she saw Seer dart across the boulevard, hopping over debris and bodies that littered the street. She watched him with clenched jaws as he slipped and fell, and then staggered to his feet, "Hustle, Seer," she whispered to herself as she held her breath, "haul ass!"

She felt the dull throb of pain as her wound burned on her face, she knew she was bleeding again and could feel the bandages get heavy as they moistened with blood. Fatigue was also beginning to set in again. Its burden a dept that would eventually have to be paid, and she fought to stay focused as she peered though the scope and watched Seer run into the doorway of the building across the street...

•••

213

Holly pushed though the darkness, surrounded only by the sound of his footsteps and the damp chill in the moldy air. God only knew what kind of life spawned in this subterranean world where time was both stretched and compressed. The silence roared. He was in one of the main branch lines of the drainage system that snaked its way under Emerald City in a labyrinth of gloomy tunnels that had sixty-foot ceilings in some sections. For as far below the street that he was, he was amazed to see some vandalism on the tunnel walls; weird drawings of the sun and strange characters or lettering painted or scratched into the blocks. Up ahead, he saw faint rays of light, and he quickened his pace toward what he hoped would bring him up to the street.

He reached the edge of the tunnel and stood beneath the soft beams of sunlight filtering through a grate above. In front of him was the central branch of the storm system. A massive cavern with a floor twenty feet lower than the level he was on, and Holly could see a tremendous river from weeks of rain running swiftly and noiselessly through the channel. He detached the stock from his K-Auto and holstered the weapon as he turned around and grabbed the first rung of the access ladder and began his ascent back to the world of light...

•••

Seer moved cautiously through the lobby of the building searching for a stairwell to take him to the upper floors. The reception area was in complete shambles from the impact of the recent air raids and artillery. Broken tables and furniture lay strewn on their sides under heaps of glass from the chandeliers that had fallen off the ceilings, and a thick layer of gray dust and ash covered everything. He paused when he reached the atrium where the elevators where. The mirrored walls where still in tact, and he was startled when he saw his own reflection. He didn't even recognize his own image and almost fired his weapon. Seer sighed in relief as he glanced at his grimy, unshaven face in the glass. It was tragic the way he aged so rapidly. He had the tired eyes of an old man.

He found the door that lead into the fire escape, and jogged up the stairs to secure the next level. It was a fairly small office building compared to the skyscrapers that loomed around it, but it had the luxurious suites typical for law firms established in Volengrad's business district. Seer could tell by the interior design that this particular firm had done well before the war. As he climbed the staircase to the sixth floor, he heard the sound of gunfire coming from above. He was not alone. Seer sprinted up the last flight and quietly opened the door into the hallway.

He kept his back against the wall as he made his way through the corridor. There were only ten rooms to search, and he kept his ears open for any sounds that would lead him to the shooter. Seer could feel the sharp tingle of fear at the base of his spine as he crept slowly down the hall. His senses were heightened by the rush of adrenaline that surged through him. He knew he was getting close as he paused in front of every closed door and listened for movement within the rooms.

Seer was halfway down the hall when he thought he heard something shift inside the office to his left. He took a deep breath as he stepped to the door and slowly pushed it open...

•••

Sergeant Isa leaned against the windowsill seven stories above the street and watched the smoke slowly dissipate in the morning light. The avenue was partially blanketed in the thin shadows of the highrises, but the landscape was still visible. She scoped the architecture around her and began to memorize the layout of the boulevard. Isa scanned the windows and rooftops of the lower structures for any movement—for any indication of the enemy. Terekian Special Forces soldiers were extremely well trained in urban warfare and the biggest mistake the Alliance's military hierarchy repeatedly made was underestimating their skills as warriors. But Isa knew better, she knew what they were capable of. She knew from experience that they were highly organized, well financed, and excellent fighters; unlike the tribal mercs that fought for the Coalition for money, the Terekian Infantry and Spec Ops fought for a cause. They believed in the politics of their growing empire, and she respected and feared them.

Isa panned the scope to the six-story building across from her. She checked each window facing the street when she saw something move in the fourth window on the sixth floor. She adjusted the focus and turned a small knob on the scope to enlarge the image. Isa saw a shadow in the room creeping toward the window. Then he appeared about three feet back from the window's ledge. A Terekian sniper wearing a black beret and a dark green uniform with black and gray stripes. Isa wrapped her finger around the trigger and waited for him to set up.

She could see him kneeling as he raised his rifle to eye level and began surveying the street below. Isa inhaled slowly and held her breath as she brought the crosshairs of the scope on the Terekian's forehead. Jesus he was young. Perhaps in his early twenties. Isa blinked, exhaled slowly, and pulled back on the trigger...

•••

Seer entered the office with light steps on the plush carpet. He held his Bolter up and made sure the selector switch was in full auto as he ducked into the shadows of the entryway. He took a step forward into a larger room when he spotted a Terekian on the floor snaking toward the window. He was holding a 134ATS sniper rifle. Seer set the Bolter down quietly against the wall and unsheathed his hunting knife. He would make this kill quietly.

He kept his back to the wall as he sidestepped forward, closer to the Coalition soldier; the Terekian got up on one knee and started scooping out the street when Seer made his move from behind.

Seer lunged forward silently and put his left hand over the Terekian's mouth as he shoved his hunting knife into the trooper's neck and pushed out—severing the man's windpipe and sending blood pulsing in a warm stream into the air. The Terekian went limp in his arms, and Seer eased the body down to the floor. He looked up out of the window when a shot rang out across the street...

•••

Isa almost pulled the trigger when she saw a hand wrap around the Coalition soldier's face and cover his mouth, then she saw a geyser of blood gush from his throat as a knife severed his arteries and his body wilted into Seer's arms.

She eased off the trigger and exhaled in relief knowing that she almost killed her partner when she saw another Terekian enter the room behind Seer. Isa squeezed the trigger and watched the trooper's chest explode from the impact of the round; his body was lifted off the floor and slammed into the wall behind him with a spray of blood and lung tissue...Seer spun around and hit the floor as the second Terekian's body peeled off the wall and slumped to the ground face-first.

The seconds droned on before Isa saw Seer pop up from the window and wave in her direction. He was unharmed and soaked in the enemy's blood, but unscathed. She watched him fall back into the shadows of the room and disappear...

•••

Holly grunted as he pushed up on the iron grate and was just able to move it enough to wiggle through. It was by sheer luck that he emerged onto the street three feet away from the burnt shell of a car that sat half cocked on a sidewalk curb. He crawled out of the hole and paused to look around his surroundings before he rolled under the smashed automobile. Holly lay still in the prone position under the twisted steel trying to get his bearings to find better cover and catch his breath. The smoke had diffused to a gray mist that filtered the sunlight, giving the air a soft haze that drifted over the boulevard like an apparition...

•••

Seer put his shoulder into the door that accessed the roof. Its hinges had rusted it shut, and he was forced to put some effort into breaking it open. He massaged and rubbed his shoulder after several attempts of throwing his full body weight into it. Seer grunted in pain as he hit it again and was rewarded when the entire door broke free of the jamb and slammed onto the roof deck.

He examined the area for suitable cover, and headed to the side that faced the avenue. There was a series of overhead steam pipes suspended on racks from the structural steel that was an ideal place for him to set up and hide without fear of being observed from the taller buildings around him.

He slipped into the shadows and got down on his stomach in the prone position as he propped his KC-26 on the edge of a very low parapet and took out his binoculars to eye the boulevard below. The minutes passed and the sunlight crept over the shadows of the streets and offered its warmth and revived misplaced thoughts of hope and peace. Seer sighed

217

and rubbed his weary eyes again and tried to hold back a yawn when he noticed a manhole cover on the street slowly being moved. He adjusted the binoculars and watched someone emerge from the storm drain system that ran beneath Emerald City.

He set the specs down and reached for the rifle and peered through the high-powered scope as the man showed himself—it was Holly.

"You fucking brilliant bastard." Seer whispered to himself with a smile as he watched Holly roll under a wrecked vehicle...

•••

Holly could feel the cold pavement through his uniform and jumpsuit, and his body shuddered involuntarily from the wintry morning air. He looked to his right and spotted the Volengrad-Sierra building eighty feet away, towering up to the heavens with the Aerodyne/Genesis Corporate Towers in the background. From the ground, the concrete and glass walls of Emerald City's skyline that surrounded him was incredibly breathtaking, and Holly felt his head spin as he craned to look at them. Simply beautiful, even scarred from the throes of war, Volengrad still sparkled like a rare jewel in the middle of Uluwatu Valley.

Holly inched himself forward to the edge of the wreckage and saw a large pile of rubble thirty feet away. The buildings around him looked clear for now, and he double-checked his equipment and prepared to sprint for a pocket in the debris...

He jerked back under the smashed automobile as gunfire echoed off the walls of the building and a bullet ricocheted off the pavement and sent concrete splinters humming through the air. He had been spotted, and now he was pinned helplessly under the watchful eyes of an enemy sniper...

•••

"Motherfucker!" Seer cussed silently as he got up and crouched on the roof of the building and looked through the scope of his KC-26 Pulse Rifle. He was still concealed in the shadows of mechanical equipment and overhead pipes, "Come on baby, come on out and play." He whispered to himself as he focused on the husk of a car below.

"I know you're down there cheesdick." Seer mumbled through clenched teeth as he zeroed his crosshairs on the vehicle, "You're gonna make me a rich fuckin' man, Holly..."

•••

Holly reached down and grabbed a smoke frag from his web-gear, pulled the pin and rolled it out in front of the vehicle. The thought of backtracking down the storm drain crossed his mind, but he couldn't bring himself to do it. He wanted to stay and find the Terekian shooting at him—he had to; his mission was to eliminate all hostiles. Running away wasn't one of his character traints, but getting pissed-off when someone was trying to shoot him was.

He unstrapped the Pershing 50 cal. Sniper Rifle from his shoulder and set it down on the pavement; it was too cumbersome to use in such a tight position without exposing himself. Holly would have to rely on his K-Auto and try to nail the sniper with open sight and controlled bursts.

He popped another smoke grenade and tossed it to his left a few feet; it hissed sharply as Holly watched the smoke billow and swirl into a huge gray cloud around him...

•••

"You slick son-of-a-bitch." Seer thought bitterly to himself as he watched the fog build around the sedan. "Come on and make your move, Sandman, ol' Seer's got something for you." He thought he saw a something move in the smoke next to the fading outline of the car and took a chance and fired.

The rounds glanced harmlessly off the twisted steel as the sound of Seer's rifle echoed through the street. He had missed Holly by a few inches, and the smoke had thickened a fifty-yard section of the boulevard making it impossible to see anything in that area. Seer strained his eyes for any sign of movement below...

•••

Isa stared hard though the scope at the building that Seer was in when she heard the sound of sniper fire. She recognized the weapon by sound.

219

A KC-26 Pulse Rifle...it had to be Seer firing on someone, but she couldn't see where he was. He also thought that the cloud of smoke that started to fill the air in the middle of the avenue was peculiar. Seer had somebody pinned down at street level, and she turned her attention to the smashed vehicle on the curb.

She adjusted her scope and zoomed in on the car. From her vantage point, Isa could just make out someone hiding beneath the shell of the car popping another smoke frag. It was Holly. Two more shots rang brightly from a through the avenue and Isa saw the sparks from the rounds ricochet off the burnt chassis of the automobile. Seer was shooting at Holly!

She frantically began surveying the windows of the law building for Seer. He had turned against the Alliance. He was now a freelance bounty hunter and traitor, and had to be brought down. Isa scanned the roof of the building and saw movement in the shadows. She blinked and rubbed her eyes to ease the strain. Then she spotted a silhouette among the shadows concealed in the tangle of pipes and mechanical equipment. Isa drew a bead on the shape and began taking slow steady breaths as she pulled back on the trigger...

...

Seer leaned forward and squinted hoping to get a glimpse of Holly through the thick smoke when he heard the shot ring out and echo through the streets. He flinched as the round pierced a steel pipe above him and high pressure steam billowed through the air with a loud hiss.

"Goddamn it!" He cussed loudly as he jumped back. "Motherfucker, you're gonna pay for that!"

"Think again dipshit!" A voice boomed from behind.

"What the..." Seer turned around and came face to face with Genie.

"You son-of-a-bitch!" Seer growled in a startled tone as he raised his rifle.

Genie was like lightning as he lunged forward and grabbed the weapon by the barrel, tugged it out of Seer's hands, and cast it aside. Seer reached for his knife when Genie drove his fist into his face and broke his nose. It felt like everything shifted into slow motion as Seer struggled to maintain his balance in a painful daze; he staggered backwards awkwardly and brought up his survival knife as blood flowed from his shattered nose.

He slashed wildly at Genie as the two men circled each other trying to anticipate the other's next move. Seer jumped forward in an effort to drive his knife into Genie's stomach, but Genie side stepped him and brought a blow down to the back of Seers neck that brought him to his knees onto the deck. Seer's knife went spinning out of his hands as he hit the ground and had the wind knocked out of him.

Genie reached down and grabbed Seer by the seat of his pants and uniform collar and hoisted him over his head and carried him to the edge of the roof...

"One thing in this world I can't stand is a traitor!" Genie grunted.

"Fuck you and anyone that looks like you, Genie!" Seer groaned.

"Taste your ass, motherfucker!" Genie growled as he heaved Seer off the roof,

"Enjoy your trip!"

Seer looked up at the sky as he fell weightlessly through the air...his last glimpse of life was Genie standing at the edge of the roof giving him the finger before everything went black...

Q 3

We stood in the musty dimness of the bank's lobby gazing at the crumpled remains of Willie's body outside as the hazy rays of morning light cut through the windows and announced the beginning of a new day. The troops milled nervously at our predicament of being pinned down in the building, but we were so grateful to be alive. I looked around at the tired faces that surrounded me, and couldn't help the feeling of being overjoyed by the fact that I was still here—scared shitless, but alive and kicking. Satch had become withdrawn as he leaned against a marble column and stared vacantly at the floor.

"Hey Pappy," Doc Powers whispered, "shouldn't one of us say somethin' to him?"

"No," Pappy replied quietly, "leave 'im be. Let 'im work it out." Pappy sighed as he looked through the door at Willie's broken body and lit a cigarette.

"Jesus, what the hell's going on out there?" One of the troopers from Alpha Company asked nervously as we listened to the sound of random sniper fire.

"It's a duel," Satch glared as he looked up with wet eyes, "ours against theirs. All we can do now is wait."

"Shit we can't just sit here and do nothing." Collins spouted angrily, "We need to find a way out and get to the Clover."

"Not with those snipers out there. I ain't going anywhere." Lucas snapped back.

"Stand down you two!" Pappy barked, "We've got enough problems and we can do without your bellyaching." Pappy glared. "Okay, listen up. Let's make sure this building's secure. Satch, I want someone posted at every entrance of this shithole. Everyone stay clear of the windows. Them snipers will see you before you see them."

"Hey Pappy…" Satch frowned.

"I know Satch," Pappy nodded, "we'll get 'im after this is over. I promise."

"I know," Satch sniffled, "I wanna write Willie's folks a letter. I—I think I owe him that, you know?"

"Yeah, I understand. Get some of these men posted on guard first, it'll give them something to do while I find out what the hell's goin' down out there."

"Roger that, Pap."

"And Satch..."

"Yeah?"

"Drive on, bro. It's what Willie would've wanted."

I sat down and removed my tactical helmet and inhaled deeply as I grabbed my canteen and took a swig of water. Some of the other troopers opened freeze-dried packets and took the opportunity to eat while we waited. I examined the scratches and dents on my grimy brain bucket, and felt an urge to take a marker and write "Why Me?" on it. Perhaps the most common question that grunts numbingly asked themselves when things went wrong or when times were especially bad. It seemed to encompass the irony and bitterness of their situation at the Q.

I looked at the silhouettes of the troopers in the sunlight as I lit up a smoke and took a drag. Everyone spent the last hour lost in their thoughts as we listened to the drama being played out above the streets. I could feel a great emptiness inside when I gazed out the entrance and thought about Willie. One minute he was here, a young man whose only dream was to make it home and be with his family and friends again; and then he was gone. I could still see him laughing as he punched Satch on the shoulder and teased him about being a hardened criminal and threatened to date his younger sister. It already seemed like a million years ago.

I feel like I've lived a thousand lifetimes since I left Earth. The misery and apprehension seems so far beyond words and experience; like I've been strangled by the war in a spiritual sense, and my soul has been cast aside into the inferno of ruin and alienation. I've realized how irreverent fate and circumstance are when it comes to friendships, because when the chips are down, the only way to make it through a war with your sanity intact is to draw strength from the camaraderie that develops between the men and women involved in the experience. It's through that intimate bond forged in the fires of combat that helps you deal with the fear, the anger, and the loneliness. Yet there is nothing more painful than the loss of a friend during battle; the incalculable grief that wraps itself around your psyche and turns your world upside down. Leaving you hollow so that you rattle inside when you sob.

I eyed Satch in the shadows as he composed a letter to Willie's parents, which would undoubtedly be a lie about how their son didn't suffer when he died. He will spare them the tragic reality and tell them only what they needed to know to give them closure. How Satch will deal with putting his best friend's life to an end will be a painful memory of sacrifice; haunting him like a sadistic apparition. A specter of guilt with the icy revelation of remorse and agony. I watched him for a few minutes and I could see his hands tremble every time he paused in thought, and I turned away shamefully not wanting to share his burden or feel the chilling tide of sorrow rise within me. I knew that if I stopped to grieve or lingered with my thoughts I would crack.

Pappy keyed the handset calmly as he placed his rifle down and rubbed his forehead. I could see the exhaustion ringed in dark circles around his eyes as he took a deep breath and sighed.

"Rover-6, Rover-6 actual, this is Blastgate 1-1, you copy? Over." Pappy coughed.

"This is Six," a tinny voice echoed through the lobby, "go ahead 1-1."

"Six, we're pinned by sniper fire and Falcon can't get gunship support, request fire mission, over." Pappy said tensely.

"That's a negative, 1-1, fire mission denied," the voice crackled, "too many friendlies in your area. Switch to channel 3.5, Aggressor squads are in your AO with sniper teams. I repeat, go to 3.5 and coordinate with Scarecrow and Dragon squads, over."

"Roger, Six," Pappy grinned for the first time in days, "we have elements of Alpha Company with us, and we're gonna try to punch our way to the Clover if we can get out of this fucking building. Over."

"10-4, Blastgate, roll out the red carpet for the 15th. Six clear."

"Blastgate clear." Pappy said as he changed frequencies on the radio.

"What are you smiling about, Pappy?" Collins asked.

"If what I'm thinking is true," Pappy said in a low tone, "then we may just make it out of here alive."

"What do you mean?"

"Huh? Oh never mind, Collins, just tell the men to stay alert and stay clear of the windows.

Pappy walked away from the group into the shadows as he held up the handset and cued it again, "Scarecrow 3-6, this is Blastgate 1-1, copy. Over?"

Nothing but the white sound of static.

"Scarecrow 3-6, this is Blastgate 1-1, do you copy. Over?"

Again, nothing.

"Shit! Dragon 4-1, this is Blastgate 1-1, copy. Over?"

Nothing.

"Damn it," Pappy spit, "they ain't out there!"

"Hey Pappy!" Doc Powers motioned.

"Yeah what?" Pappy glared.

"Get your ass over here..."

"What's goin' on, Doc?"

"Listen..."

"I don't here anything." Pappy sighed as he crouched next to Doc.

"Yeah...the sniper fire stopped. It's been quiet for the last ten minutes."

"I'll be damned."

Everyone in the room quit stirring and tensed up in the silence as we all moved toward the main entry way. There was the indiscriminate glow of cigarettes in the dim room, and I could hear the sound of my heartbeat pulsing in my ears as we strained at the stillness in the air.

I noticed my palms had moistened with sweat as I tightened my grip on the Bolter and looked at the soldiers around me. They were all locked in a hypnotic stare out the windows into the ravaged streets and the huge shadows cast by the buildings that surrounded us.

"Pappy." Doc whispered as he raised his Bolter and peered through the scope.

"Yeah?"

"I think I see something moving out there."

"Where, Doc?" Pappy whispered tensely.

"Up about fifty meters," Doc pointed, "ten o'clock. Right next to that car on the sidewalk. Something moved. I fucking swear I seen something move!"

"I don't see anything…"

There was a metallic "clink" of a round being chambered that echoed through the dark lobby behind us and we froze in our positions, knowing that we were no longer alone in the building, and that who ever had sneaked into the structure had caught us off guard. We were fucked, and we knew it. My jaws tightened as I prepared for a close quarter firefight that I probably wouldn't survive…

Pappy shifted his gaze to the rest of us and gave a small nod as a signal to wait for him to make the first move. Everyone side-eyed each other as we readied to spin around and start the mayhem of another mad-minute. One that would leave most, if not all of us dead…

"Everyone stay calm," a voice boomed from the shadows, "I know what you're planning to do, and believe me, it won't work. We've got your asses covered from every angle."

"Identify yourselves." Pappy said calmly as he kept his eyes locked straight ahead.

"Pappy, is that you?" the voice asked in a lighter tone.

"Genie?" Pappy snapped back.

"Yeah!"

"Oh fuck me!" Pappy laughed in relief as he lowered his rifle and turned around. "You scared the shit out of us."

Genie stepped out of the shadows grinning along with Jackson and Petersen.

"We scared you?" Genie smiled, "Have you seen yourself lately?"

We all lowered our Bolters and looked at the three troopers walking toward us. Pappy and Genie walked up to each other, shook hands and embraced.

"I thought you said you had us covered from all angles?"

"I'm full of shit." Genie grinned.

"Yeah you are."

"Actually you are covered. Hey Isa, it's okay! Get the rest of your men in here!"

"Man, am I glad to see you guys." Satch sighed.

"Hey Satch!" Jackson chimed.

"Hey Jackson!" Satch smiled brightly as he hugged his friend.

"Well isn't this touching," Isa smirked, "we homesteading Genie? Or do you and Pappy want to get a room and spare us from watching this horrid display of male bonding?"

Everyone laughed and stepped toward each other shaking hands, slapping each other on the back, and hugging. Doc began fawning over Isa's wound, giving her painkillers, sewing her up, and changing the dressing.

"You're gonna have a scar, sergeant." Doc frowned, "But a plastic surgeon can make that go away."

"Nah," Isa replied quietly, "I earned it, and it's a keeper."

I glanced around the room and noticed Isa staring at me as Doc quietly wrapped gauze around her head. Her piercing blue eyes shined brightly though the expression of weariness on her face.

"You look familiar, soldier." Isa grinned as she nodded at me.

"Hold still sergeant." Doc demanded softly as he finished the dressing.

"Where have I seen you before?" she squinted, "Have you always been with the 22nd? Or did you just transfer?"

"Actually, sergeant," I sighed and rubbed the stubble on my chin, "we met at Defiance a few weeks ago before your deployment to Uluwatu. It's me, Frye, the newsie from The Metro."

"Good God." She chuckled loudly shaking her head, "fancy meeting you here."

"Yeah, small world isn't it?" I smiled.

"You getting that story that you came for newsman?"

I nodded and looked down at the floor, thankful the room was dim and hoping that she couldn't see how worn out I must have looked. How chewed over I felt. But she knew. Even through the shadows I could tell that she sensed it.

I reached into my pocket, pulled out a cigarette and fumbled for my lighter.

"Can you spare one of those, newsman?" Isa smiled.

"Yeah sure." I said quietly as I handed her one and lit my own. She leaned forward into my lighter, cupped her hands around the flame and inhaled deeply. I noticed how grimy her hands were through her tattered gloves; they looked blistered and held their share of tiny cuts.

Isa took a step back and exhaled as she eyed me over.

"Jesus, newsman, you look like shit."

"You said I looked like shit back at Defiance."

"Well you did." Isa grinned. "And you *still* look like shit."

"Thanks."

"You actually made the landing with the first wave?"

"Yeah, fond memories of the insertion. I don't think I've ever been so scared in my life."

"I can't believe you survived, Frye." Isa beamed shaking her head.

"Neither can I."

"Well then," Isa nodded as she opened her canteen and raised it in a gesture of a toast, "here's to the only thing that matters newsman. Here's to going home."

Pappy and Genie stood in the middle of the room talking as the rest of us cracked open freeze-drieds and shared them with the Aggressor troopers.

"Where's L-T?" Genie asked, already knowing the answer.

"No." Pappy shook his head and stared blankly at the floor frowning. "Seer?"

"Long story there, bud, I'll save it for ya over a drink when we get back to Defiance."

"Hey Pappy," Satch said grimly, "sorry to interrupt, is it safe out there? I want to get Willie."

"Yeah, Satch," Pappy nodded, "let's go get 'im."

Dark gray clouds loomed in the distance promising another rainstorm by nightfall. The dull thud of explosions echoed through the alleys along with the faint tat-tat of automatic fire. Skirmishes erupted throughout Volengrad as infantry and armored divisions engaged the Terekians in the western sector of the great city.

Heaviness filled the air as we quietly stepped outside the bank and watched Pappy, Satch, and Doc unfold an extra poncho, pick up Willie's torn body, and carry him back up the steps into the building. There was a lonely, high-pitched cry overhead. I looked up into the bright afternoon sky and saw a hawk floating gracefully in the wind, circling and looking down on us. So far away, like a fading dream melting into the cast of blurred memories. I exhaled a tired breath and looked at the piles of rubble and twisted steel strewn about the shattered streets, and the rising smoke from the smoldering fires. I sighed and walked back into the building with the others as the sound of thunder rumbled from the horizon.

Q 4

I

Two battalions from the 249th (Devil Dogs) were crammed into two Echo Class Dropships at 1100 hours on Christmas day. By 1130 hours, they made their departure from the F.S. Dorsey and began their mach six entry into the eastern hemisphere of 781. Inbound for Volengrad, the ride was at best uncomfortable for the occupants as the ships flew in loose formation with four Novas from the 16th Armored Wing.

The troops sat quietly inside the cabins. They were exhausted from the transport from Syterra, and most of them slept. Some wrote letters home and some passed the time with idle chatter. It had been an uneventful journey and the troops were grateful for the down time. The crew of the Dorsey probably sighed in collective relief now that the 249th had departed. Transporting four hundred war dogs and their trainers into a battle zone was never an easy task. It was a lot of mouths to feed on a DSA.

Stilman ran his hand across Sukie's thick brown fur as he thought about what lay ahead in the landing zone. They had done many insertions under fire, but for some reason that he couldn't put his finger on, this one felt wrong. He had an unshakeable feeling about this mission that kept gnawing at him. There was a finality to it that seemed to carry a heavy weight.

"Volengrad." He whispered to himself. The very name made him want to cringe inside.

He had seen the body bags and wounded piling up in the hangers and corridors back on the Dorsey as they maintained a steady orbit around the Q. What a fiasco; med-techs scrambling through the halls in blood-soaked scrubs, the smell of iodine, shit, and alcohol, and the overpowering aroma of blood—thick and coppery as troopers howled in pain from burns, shrapnel lacerations, multiple gunshot wounds, and severed limbs. He felt a shiver run up his spine.

"Get a grip on yourself," Stilman thought as he stared at the back of the seat in front of him, "stay focused!" He reached into an inside pocket of his Kevlar vest and took out a small pink dog collar with petite gemstones sewn into it. It was worn, faded, and the buckle was tarnished, but it made him smile with comforting memories of Sukie's puppyhood as he turned it slowly in his hands and thought of better days in Academy.

Sukie lay quietly next to him with her head down on the grated floor. Her green eyes darted around the cabin. Always alert, and always on a vigil, she never let her guard down. Typical of dogs and their handlers, she and Stilman had been a team since her birth. This created a bond between them that would last a lifetime. If anything happened to the handler during combat and he or she was not able to return to active duty, the dog was either reassigned to the Sentry Division or retired and rehabilitated into mainstream society.

Over all, Sukie was a beautiful specimen in spite of her clipped tail from the last campaign. She was large for a female Winthrop Wolf-Sheppard. At one hundred and seventy-eight pounds, she was a menacing 4'-4'' to her shoulders when she stood up.

Dogs like Sukie were products of the Winthrop Corporation's Biogenetic Engineering Division that specialized in the design of canines. She was physically faster and stronger than other domestic breeds. Her sense of smell, sight, and hearing were far more superior, and her capacity for cognition seemed limitless; enough to alarm the researchers that bred her species that they may have overcompensated for her intelligence. There are three classifications of dogs bred in the Winthrop labs. Class C dogs were designed for law enforcement services such as drug, contraband, and bomb detection as well as tracking. Class B were canines trained in search and rescue operations and life safety. Class A dogs were military dogs trained in combat, tracking, SAR, and everything Class B and C canines specialized in. All of Winthrop's creations carried a tiny implant in their bodies for identification and tracking.

The ship lurched forward, startling everyone, and a few groans from soldiers waking up murmured throughout the compartment. Suddenly the air cracked to life as a voice came over the intercom. It was Commander Noboru.

"Get your gear prepped people," his harsh voice squawked over the speakers, "make sure your dog's harnesses are snug, their armor is tight, and you're getting a reading on their tags. We'll be touching down in T minus eight minutes. Let's get our watches in sync and double check your body armor. It's now 1552 hours. Intel reports an abundance of snipers in our AO. We'll be hitting an LZ in north-central Volengrad and sweeping south toward the H-12..."

Stilman patted over Sukie's body armor before checking his own. Sukie raised her head and looked at Stilman trustingly as she let out a small bark and licked his face.

"Alpha, Delta, Foxtrot, and Whiskey Companies will be landing with us in the same area," Noboru continued, "stay alert, keep your teammate quiet and your eyes open for booby traps..."

Stilman began snapping the buckles on his Kevlar breastplate and going over the ammunition clips in his bandoliers for this Bolter and side arms.

"...if you find any mines or sensor triggered devices, call it in ASAP and we'll get EOD in to defuse it. Do *not* make any attempts to dismantle the mechanism..."

Sukie's ears perked straight up, she was getting restless and wanted to stretch out her legs.

"Easy, girl," Stilman said calmly as he stoked Sukie's head. "we'll be on the ground soon."

She looked at him and whined quietly, then set her head back down on the grating.

"...keep in mind that this operation is a search and destroy," Noboru bellowed, "and that means no prisoners. All the commands you give your dogs are to terminate with extreme prejudice. If you encounter any friendlies in need of assistance, stay with them and radio in your coordinates. Okay, troops, lock and load. We're two minutes from the LZ."

The sounds of clips slapping home into Bolters and rounds being chambered resounded through the fuselage. The ship trembled as its landing skids lowered and the cabin depressurized. Outside, the Nova-31's had broken formation as the dropships decelerated in their final approach into Volengrad's skyline. Overhead, aerial drones weaved through the skyscrapers gathering data and taking images of the streets and structures in a methodical search for Terekian armor or gun emplacements.

The ship's engines pitched to an ear splitting whine as it came to a hover two hundred feet above a major boulevard and released a cluster of smoke bombs for cover as they rapidly descended to the ground. The door gunners in full body armor stood behind their .50 caliber mini-guns as the rear cargo ramp began to lower, letting in the burnt smell of the air and filling the cabin with smoke as they touched down onto the street.

"Welcome to Emerald City!" Noboru shouted. "We got a reason! LET'S MOVE IT OUT! BY THE NUMBERS! GO! GO GO!"

Stilman unbuckled himself and looked at Sukie. "Let's go." He said calmly, and Sukie jumped to her feet and shook herself off. They filed out on to the smoke filled street in a jog then spread out quickly to clear the landing zone. The heat from the ship's jet exhausts felt good to Stilman as he took a deep breath and Sukie pulled him forward. He looked to his right and saw the faint outline of the other dropship and its blinking navigation lights in the thick haze as he moved down the shattered sidewalk.

"Everyone take cover," Noboru ordered, "they're about to lift off."

Sukie veered to her left and lead Stilman behind the twisted husk of a truck. He crouched and took the safety off his Bolter as he leaned against the blackened panels of the vehicle. He squinted hard at the intensity of the jet blasts as smoke swirled around the intakes and loose trash and debris tumbled past them.

"Jesus this place is thrashed." Stilman thought to himself as he watched the ships disappear and listened to the sound of their fading engines. Sukie stood up and began guiding him down the street. He held the leash tightly, but there was still eight feet of slack that he cut for his partner. He could see the other handlers and dogs silently making their way in different directions through the haze.

She sniffed at the ground with her ears pointing forward as she pulled Stilman through the piles of rubble and smashed automobiles, sorting through the thousands of scents that permeated the wet pavement and stale breeze. Her senses led her through the avenue like radar, knowing which odor to ignore and which to dial in on. The smell of gunpowder filled the air along with that impossible gray dust that settled on everything. The rattle of automatic fire and the thump of explosions echoed in the distance, and the ground shuddered constantly from blast waves.

"This place is too quiet." Stilman thought as he gazed at the buildings that towered around them.

She led Stilman past a huge crater in the street left by the bombings, it was half filled with grimy rainwater and a bloated corpse bobbed grotesquely in the center. Broken glass, spent shell casings, and rubbish littered the boulevard and every building bore the pockmarks of heavy fighting. Dead Coalition and Alliance soldiers were scattered on the avenue. Neither army had returned to claim them and they lay forgotten in the elements.

They turned to the right and hopped over a stack of bullet-riddled sandbags that surrounded a Terekian 20mm auto-cannon that had been blown apart and moved quietly through a long narrow alley that emptied into a smaller street. Stilman unhitched the leash, whispered the hunt command into Sukie's ear, and let her push forward on her own. He flicked the selector on his Bolter onto full auto and began wading through the scattered trash on the ground, watching every step he took as he kept an eye on his teammate sniffing through the shadows.

They were halfway down the surface street when Sukie stopped in front of a doorway and quietly bared her fangs. Her ears flattened as she took cautious steps toward the dingy entrance, paused briefly to examine the foyer for tripwires and sensors, and then slinked into the gloomy structure.

Stilman stepped to the side of the door and brought his Bolter up to port. He took a deep breath, lowered his infrared visor, and ducked through the dim threshold. He could hear his heart pounding as he crept behind an overturned table and scanned the dusty room for a thermal image. He watched Sukie's red and orange body heat radiating where her body armor didn't cover her. She circled around some stacked crates and disappeared behind a dilapidated display counter. Suddenly, there was the shuffling of footsteps in the corner as boxes and crates were knocked over—Sukie's vicious growls filled the thick air as a desperate struggle stirred a cloud of dust…

"OH MY GOD!" someone screamed in terror, "GET THIS MONSTER OFF ME! OH G-GOD DON'T LET IT KILL ME!"

"OT SOOK!" Stilman yelled as he jumped up and fired a short burst into the air, the room lit up from the bright muzzle flashes as the rounds ricocheted off the walls and ceiling, "OT SOOK SHEATA, MOTHERFUCKER!" Stilman bellowed as he worked his way through the shadows and cobwebs.

She had pinned a man on his back and her massive jaws clamped down on his throat as she let out a low snarl and began drooling on him. The man lay frozen in fear with his hands above his head and his lips trembled as he strained to make out the shape of Stilman looming over him with his weapon pointed at his head…

"Ot Sook, fuckhead! Your ass belongs to us now!"

"Oh God don't let it kill me!" the man whimpered. Sukie clamped down harder on his neck and gave him a quick shake and a savage growl to let him know who was in charge.

"AAAHH! OH SHIT! PL…PLEASE—PLEASE MERCY!" The man gasped.

"You speak English well, shitpicker!" Stilman said with surprise.

"I'm—I'm not Terekian…" the man replied, "I'm from here…I'm—I'm a resident…please…"

Stilman lifted his visor and clicked on the flashlight mounted on his Bolter. He noticed the man's face was smeared with grime as he squinted up at the beam and tears ran down his face. He was probably in this late fifties judging from his thick gray beard, but it was hard to tell in the poor light. He was heavy set, and wore layers of filthy rags under what used to be a formal dining jacket. He also had on cloth gloves with the fingers cut off and Stilman could see the black dirt caked under his fingernails. The man's body odor was musty and it was painfully obvious that he hadn't bathed in a long time.

"Sukie," Stilman said calmly, "stand down."

Sukie released the man's throat but stood over him with her head inches from his face, staring him down with her gleaming emerald eyes waiting for the command to terminate. Her hot breath steamed into the man and made him flinch as she kept a guttural tone rumbling in her throat.

"Who—who are you?" the man asked tensely as he tried not to look into Sukie's glare.

"I'm with the Alliance." Stilman replied. "Now what's more important is who are you, and what are you doing here?"

"Oh thank God!" the man sighed and closed his eyes. "Thank God for ya, son."

"I asked you a question..."

"Turk." The man answered. "Turk...I—I can't remember my last name. It's—it's been so long...so long ya know."

"What are you doing in the city?" Stilman demanded.

"I just came up to get some air and see if there was anything I could find that they left behind that we could use. Maybe some food or water or guns," he stammered nervously, "there's always fighting going on now. Always at night, but they leave. And when they do, they leave stuff. Sometimes it explodes, sometimes if you go through the bodies you can find food."

"What do you mean "we"?" Stilman asked suspiciously as he kept his Bolter trained in the stranger's head.

"I was about to look around, then all this booming all around me and there was all this smoke. Then you came with the others so I ran in here to hide, I thought you were them. Terekians!"

"Okay, old man. Calm down, you hear me? It's gonna be alright." Stilman lowered his rifle and sighed.

"Oh I know...you're Alliance, sonny!" Turk smiled weakly.

"Let 'im go, Sukie." Stilman said grimly, "Get up old-timer." Stilman ordered and took a step back. "You've got some explaining to do. You said you were a resident?"

"Yes. I've lived here all my life. I'm one hundred percent Volengradian. Shame what happened to the governor years ago when his car blew up. I don't think it's supposed to do that when you start it."

"So there's others here with you?"

"Yes, yes there are."

"How come you didn't evacuate the city when you had the chance?"

"It's a long story, son, and this is our home. We're not going anywhere." Turk frowned.

"Where are the others?"

"Down."

"What? Down where?"

"Hiding."

"Listen, Turk, where are your friends? I promise we won't harm them."

"Oh I know," Turk smiled warmly, exposing yellowed teeth. "You're Alliance..." He reached out and started shaking Stilman's hand vigorously. "You're Alliance!" He whispered and began to cry.

•••

"Ghost-6, Ghost-6, actual," Stilman spoke into his headset, "Ghost-6, this is Horseman 1-2 do you copy?"

"Six copies," Noboru answered back, "go ahead 1-2."

"Six, I've found a survivor in sector three, possibly more in the immediate area. 156/34, over."

"Roger, 156/34, we're on our way, hold the prisoner."

"He's not a prisoner, Commander, he's a resident."

"What?"

"I'll explain it to you when you get here, 1-2 out."

"That's a huge dog." Turk said apprehensively as he reached out to pet Sukie. "I don't think I've ever seen one this big before..."

Sukie barked and bared her fangs and Turk withdrew his hand quickly.

"I guess he doesn't like to be petted by strangers, huh?"

"Down girl." Stilman commanded, "It's okay girl, stand down."

"My apologies, I mean *she* doesn't like to be petted by strangers."

"So you'll take us to get the others?"

"I'm not supposed to but I guess I have no choice."

"No you don't, our Command is unaware that there are any people other than the Terekians left in Volengrad."

"We'll see, son," Turk said with his eyes cast down, "like I said, this is our home and we don't want to leave."

"How many of you are there"

"Oh there's a lot of us...thousands."

"THOUSANDS? How do you hide thousands of people?"

"It's not easy," Turk chuckled quietly, "we move our camps around often. We never stay in one place for more than a couple of weeks. But that depends, ya see, there's been all this fighting lately, you can feel the ground shaking, hard. And it's loud, we can even hear the explosions from where we're at."

"What's going on here, Stilman?" Noboru asked from the doorway as his dog began barking at Turk. Six handlers stood behind him in the alley with their weapons ready and their dogs had entered the room and lurked in the shadows unnoticed as they surrounded the homeless man.

"Commander," Stilman reported, "we found this man hiding in the building when we cornered him He's a friendly, sir. A refugee."

"No shit," Noboru glared as he lowered his rifle, "talk to me old man."

Turk straightened up his posture and gave Noboru a salute with his right hand as he tried his best to stand at attention. The other troopers looked at him with amusement.

"Sir," Turk said politely, "I was just telling this splendid young soldier about why he shouldn't kill me with that monster dog."

Sukie barked loudly and Turk flinched hard.

"I've lived in Volengrad all my life, sir," Turk continued, "born and raised here actually, but when the Terekians came, a lot of us couldn't get out of the city. Believe me, we tried, but we were turned away at the monorail stations and jet ports because of—well, because of our appearance being homeless. So we did what we had to do to survive. It was just a matter of time when they took over the city. By then we made it a point to vanish from sight. It was the only way we knew."

Noboru removed his tactical helmet and ran his fingers through his crew cut and sighed. He looked Turk over silently as he fished for a cigarette and lit it.

"Jesus Christ," Noboru squinted, "you're a transient?"

"We actually prefer to be called "Freemen", sir." Turk replied shyly.

"You're telling me that all the homeless people of this city got left behind?" Noboru gasped. "Shit!"

"No sir," Turk interrupted, "most of them left the city with the rest of the population. Walked out, really. Some of us just chose to stay behind. We have no place to go or anyplace we would rather be."

"How the hell did you slip by the Terekian army all these years?" the Commander asked in an exasperated tone.

"We umm...managed, sir."

"You "managed"?"

"We went underground into the city's storm and sewer systems. We have camps down there and we keep moving. We come up at night and see what we can steal from the Terekians and loot what we can for supplies from the stores. Of course since the occupation, the Terekians have looted everything. Slim pickin's now, sir, ya know?"

"Shit. We need to round all of you up and get you evac'ed out of here ASAP." Noboru turned to the soldier standing to his right, "Franco get a hold of HQ. Tell'em we've got civilians in the zone. Let'em know I'll assess the situation and get back to them about how many troopships we're gonna need to get these people evacuated."

"Roger that sir." The soldier with a radio pack replied as he stepped outside the building.

"Okay old man," Noboru exhaled deeply, "take us to your people." Noboru turned to the other soldiers, "Sims, Stilman, and Morey, on me. Yarns, Knight—you stay here with Franco. Lead the way, Pops."

The old man took the four soldiers into a small utility room in the same building. The windows were shattered and allowed the waning afternoon light to outline the dusty office furniture and shelves. He scooted behind a metal rack containing cardboard boxes and felt around the tile panels on the floor. One panel was subtly out of place; he gave it a quick nudge and three feet to the right a small hatch in the floor slid open exposing an access ladder that descended into a very dimly lit tunnel below. The dogs began barking and pacing around the entrance...

"Sukie, heel!" Stilman ordered, and she immediately settled down.

"This is it gentlemen." Turk announced quietly. "Follow me." He lowered himself into the hole and started his climb down.

"Morey," Noboru said lowly, "you and Sims stay here with the dogs, Stilman, let's go." The Commander slung his Bolter around his left shoulder and followed Turk down.

They climbed down the opening twenty feet and found themselves in a tunnel. It was thinly lit every ten to fifteen feet with green chemlites, and was twelve feet from floor to ceiling. With the exception of the sound of trickling water, there was a dank eeriness in the silence of the cavern.

"These service drains run under almost every building in the city." Turk whispered. "We're going below them into the main system. We're only in one of the capillaries right now. Come on."

II

"Jesus, newsman," Genie grinned, "you actually look like someone worth talking to now."

"Tell ya what, Genie," Pappy cut in, "when this is all over, I'm planning to buy this man a drink when we get back to Defiance."

"Hey we need to get a move on, Pap. Looks like we got some rain coming in again." Satch said as he peered out the door.

"Doesn't this place ever dry out?" Pappy sighed and turned to the rest of the troops gearing up. "Ok 1st squad and Alpha Company, we're moving."

"Here's how it's gonna work, Pappy," Genie ordered, "Isa is going to move ahead of your point-element till we get to the Clover, then she's gonna go high and find a spot somewhere overlooking the AO to provide overwatch. The rest of us will move with your team down the street. We've got inbound Hunter-Killers from Defiance that should be able to provide air support by the time the 15th makes planetfall tonight."

"I heard the 249th is already in the city," Pappy added, "but I don't know exactly where they're at right now. We're all supposed to rally at the Clover by nightfall."

"That's it Pap," Satch grimaced as he shifted his pack and nodded at the rest of the soldiers, "we're ready to go. I got some of Willies things for his folks."

"Collins take point," Pappy bellowed, "Satch, hold thirty feet behind him."

"Jackson," Genie pointed, "you're behind Satch, Petersen, you follow."

"Alpha Company," Pappy ordered, "two columns. One on me, the other to our right flank. Morgan take fifteen of your men for our flank. Keep your spacing wide and stay half a block behind us."

"I'm outta here, men." Isa said solemnly, "See ya on the other side." And slipped out onto the street.

"MOVING!" Genie yelled as he led the way out.

The sky had darkened as the storm rolled over the city and the wind began to pick up and bring a hard chill in the air. I could smell the rain coming. We walked briskly down the boulevard with our weapons held at port. The buildings loomed round us menacingly with their dull lifelessness as we made our way to the rally point eight blocks to the south. I couldn't shake the feeling that we were being watched the whole time.

I was skittish and becoming a "luck freak" as troopers would say; constantly looking for omens or signs that would give some kind of meaning to things that I saw or heard. Clues sent from the beyond. A divine tip-off if I was going to live or die. Everyone eventually went through the trip, forecasting their own death or survival before a battle, hoping in some vain way that they could touch and turn the odds by thinking about them hard enough, then searching for those subtle signs in their physical environment (like the way a chemlite glowed or patterns in the clouds) that could be mistranslated into something they could trick themselves into believing that everything was going to be alright, even though it was unrelated to anything as large as destiny. What is, is what is; choices in reality that aren't yours to make. Choices out of reach and already made for you. Smack it and move on. The only choice you had was how willing you were to accept the unknown.

It didn't matter if you had a family waiting for you back home, or you were the biggest guy in your squad, you were young and had dreams, or that you carried a lucky charm in your pocket; you just learned to live with it. Not knowing to the point of not caring if it happens to you or not. Sooner or later you learned to live for the moment because it was all you had. The past and the people you knew were all ancient history, what counted was the here and now. And the future? Well, you secretly hoped it was waiting for you...but it is what it is...

The long shadows of twilight crept over the pavement and engulfed the streets with its inky fingers. Above us a thin blue layer of mist from the fires floated like a ghost, and the smell of burnt air filled the lungs with a gritty feeling. From the ground came a deep tremor from the distant air strikes on the west side of the city. A low cloud cover had settled overhead and the threat of rain became real as it began to sprinkle. Tiny drops dotted the sidewalks in their random pattern, then large fat drops splattered the cement and asphalt.

We moved wordlessly in a ragged line in the downpour; miserable and tired, yet afraid and alert. Peeked on the adrenaline that wouldn't let us rest, the fear that pushed us forward and numbed the mind. Smashed storefronts, wasted vehicles, piles of rubble, spent ammo casings, and the smell of gunpowder and the rotting wet dead assaulted the senses as we took heavy steps in the dark. My stomach twisted with anxiety and my muscles tensed to the point of cramping as I listened to the drone of the rain. I wanted so badly to find some corner to run to and just be left alone. To curl up and pretend that this was all a bad dream, and that I would wake up and be astonished about how frighteningly real it all was.

We made it six blocks when it happened. One of the troopers from Alpha Company on our right flank tripped a sensor-detonated mine and vanished in a blast of black smoke and savage white light. We hit the deck as the sound wave of the explosion rolled over us and crawled for what cover we could find as pieces of blacktop pelted us and debris skittered across the ground.

Suddenly, machine gun fire erupted from the windows and rooftops of the buildings around us. Hundreds of muzzle flashes blinked from the shadows and red tracers slashed through the rain as bullets tore into the streets and kicked splinters in every direction.

"AMBUSH! AMBUSH!" Genie yelled as he ducked into the entrance of a store.

"Red 2-7, Red 2-7!" Pappy screamed into the radio. "Copy 2-7?"

Rounds popped and ricocheted off the ground as we scrambled. We could hear the men from Alpha screaming as they tried to move forward in our direction. I rolled behind a car and peered though it's broken window at the buildings across from me. Automatic fire echoed through the boulevard and I saw soldiers dart into the shadows looking for safety.

"Someone pop smoke, goddamn it!" Morgan shouted.

"We're out of smoke frags!" Collins yelled.

Satch dove out of the darkness and landed next to me. He leaned against the car and propped his 38 on the trunk and fired short bursts into a window on the third floor of a building opposite us.

"They got us pinned!" He screamed.

The flash of another explosion ripped into the night from an alley and its concussion knocked us both flat. This time we saw a figure emerge from the smoke and stagger into the middle of the street. Doc ran toward the man but was turned back when bullets ripped open the ground in front of him. The man limped awkwardly at us like he was drunk, smoke floated off his smoldering uniform as he drew closer. His arms had been blown off and his intestines trailed behind him and tangled themselves around his legs before he fell face first into a puddle.

Muzzle flashes blipped in the dark with the jagged clatter of gunfire as bullets riddled the street and hissed through the downpour. The night split open with the eruption of orange and white flashes as explosions from grenades and RPG's lifted sections of the street and turned them over in the air. We could hear the shouts of enemy soldiers from above us as they fired down into our scattered positions. They had us trapped and knew it, and would undoubtedly take advantage of our confusion and kill us all off.

"Red 2-7, Blastgate 1-1 is pinned!" Pappy screamed into his handset over the din of the firefight.

"Roger 1-1," A voice squawked, "We're falling back on your position, we can hear the fire!"

"Make your approach from the northwest, Reilly," Pappy flinched as a round popped on the wall behind him, "and have Torres bring the rest of Bravo from the north east."

"10-4, Pappy! Sit tight," Reilly replied in a hurried tone, "we're going to try to flank them from both sides and get you out of there!"

"This is getting bad!" Pappy gasped. "I can't tell you how many are out there. We tripped an ambush and they're all around us."

"On our way, Pappy! Just hang on!"

"Watch your step back here, Reilly, they've got the place mined..."

An RPG detonated and Pappy suddenly jerked his head back as if jolted by electricity, and was thrown against the wall. Blood trickled down from his helmet and his radio lay in pieces on the ground in front of him with his Bolter.

"PAPPY!" Satch screamed as he crawled over to where Pappy lay. He gently slid his hand behind Pappy's head and lifted it up slowly. "OH SHIT! DOC! PAPPY'S HIT!"

III

Turk grabbed a small lantern stashed in a crevasse and turned it on. It was getting increasingly darker as they walked further down the tunnel. Thousands of small rodents watched from the cracks in the walls and squeaked menacingly as the ones caught in the open scurried across the floor over their boots. Every twenty or thirty feet there were symbols carved on the walls like angelic script, and they became more frequent as they walked further into the bowels of the storm system.

"Jesus, look at all the shit on the walls. I can't believe there's vandalism, even way down here." Stilman observed.

"Gangs." Noboru replied quietly.

"No, Freemen did all this." Turk smiled as he pushed forward. "It's the way we communicate with other bands. It's a code we invented. We have to let each other know where our camps are and where they can come and be safe."

"I'll be damned." Stilman squinted.

"I'm tellin' ya son," Turk's voice echoed, "before the war chased everyone away, most people never saw us anyway. Sure some folks would stop and give us money or somethin', but for the most part we get ignored like we're invisible. People tend to forget that we're people too. Many of the Freemen were regular ol' folks before they got down on their luck, lost everythin' like their jobs and homes—families even. They end up on the streets of Emerald City wanderin' and beggin' for money or food."

"Is that what happened to you, Turk?" Stilman asked.

Turk stopped and sighed. He turned around with the lantern held to his face with a small, embarrassed smile. For the first time Stilman really looked at Turk, *really* looked at him, and noticed a quiet gentleness in his eyes. A look of experience and an understanding of the world.

"Yeah, that's what happened to me a long time ago." Turk grinned, "I've been on the streets for over twenty-five years, and I really don't care to go back to the life I had before. Sometimes it's dangerous on the streets, ya know? Can't let your guard down. Especially at night. Sometimes there's gangs that used to come after us for no reason. They'd come to our camps and beat some of us up. They don't take anything, they'd just come and beat you down bad and laugh about it. Usually kids that come and do that" Turk said sadly. "The police don't care. Nobody does. I lost some good friends that way. Beat up so bad you couldn't even recognize them. We took them to the hospital but they died anyway."

Noboru and Stilman frowned at each other and listened to Turk as they continued into the void, going further and deeper underground. The air was dank and twenty degrees cooler, and they listened to the sound of their own footsteps echoing off the massive walls of the tunnel as they made their way through the gloom. The soft light from the lantern made their shadows dance gracefully as the sound of hundreds of wings fluttered unseen above them and high-pitched squeaks bounced off the walls.

"When the Terekians landed and started moving to surround the city," Turk reminisced solemnly, "there was nothing but panic everywhere. I mean to get the entire city evacuated, Jesus, I ain't never seen such chaos, ya know?" Turk shook his head and sighed. "After the women and children where taken out of here it became a real mess. Every man for himself. We tried to board the dropships the Alliance had at the jet ports, but they could tell we were street people and turned us away, can you believe it? They just pushed us away from the ramps at gunpoint like we were shit. Same thing happened at the monorail stations..." Turk frowned. "Move along, maggot! Citizens first!" they would say, then give us a shove."

Stilman and Noboru looked at each other again shamefully, knowing that the old man was telling the truth.

"Ah, no big deal though, ya kinda get used to bein' kicked around, but sometimes I think it's better to be ignored, ya know? So a lot of Freemen took off walkin' outta here, makin' the hike toward Volstok."

"Volstok?" Noboru interrupted. "But that's almost five hundred kilometers from Volengrad."

"Yeah, well, what are ya gonna do, ya know?" Turk replied. "Anyway, the rest of us decided to stay behind. There's no way we were gonna stay up on the streets with Terekians walkin' around, so we went down in here."

"You mean to tell me that in all these years, the Terekians never thought to come down to these tunnels and check for stragglers?" Stilman asked in an astonished tone.

"He-he, oh they've been down here," Turk winked, "but they never came down too far to explore. Especially as far down as we are right now. We built false walls and panels over entrances and hatches that lead down deep. The patrols they send down here walk right over or past all the ways to get through. Even their motion and infrared detectors can't find us."

"I can't believe you've remained undetected by Coalition forces for as long as you have."

"Like I said, sir," Turk grinned slyly at Noboru, "we manage."

The trio continued into a larger tunnel where they heard the buzzing of insects humming from a cavern up ahead.

"What is that noise?" Stilman squinted.

"Specter wasps." Turk whispered.

"Wasps?"

"There's a certain wasp that dwells in the darkness. We call 'em Specter wasps. They usually have five or six scouts around their nests. They're very aggressive. When the scouts are disturbed, the entire nest will attack. We use 'em to block some entrances and tunnels by placing nests on the walls or ground. Some of our Freemen learned how to handle the wasps without getting stung. The wasps recognize their scent and don't bother them."

"That's ingenious," Noboru gasped, "a natural alarm system."

"Yes," Turk grinned, "it's always been enough to turn enemy patrols away. Some of their soldiers have been stung to death and they had to send more people down here to get 'em back. After awhile their patrols quit coming down beyond the first level of tunnels. They must figure that if they can't get through then nobody can."

Stilman gazed at the swarm flying erratically overhead as they moved into the cavern.

"Don't worry, young man," Turk said cheerfully, "they won't sting you, they know my scent. Just don't make any sudden movements and don't run."

Noboru and Stilman inhaled quietly as wasps hovered around them with the deep drone of their wings.

"How poisonous are they?"

"Depending on your size, usually three or four stings will paralyze or kill you."

"These things are huge." Stilman gawked.

"Almost there." Turk said dryly. "So we learned to stay clear out of sight over the years. The only time we came up top was at night to scrounge around for food and drink. Sometimes we'd get lucky, but the Terekians looted everything in sight when they took over. But they're a careless lot, ya know? After a while, their guards at night got too relaxed. Sometimes sleep when they're not supposed to, giving us a chance to steal from them. Anything we could get our hands on; food, water, and weapons."

"Weapons?" Noboru snapped.

"Oh yeah, Commander, weapons. Guns, explosives, you name it. Even got some of their uniforms. Hey, we're here!"

They emerged on grated iron platform with rails above a huge cavern where they saw hundreds of tents and lean-to's set up along two wide concrete banks. A tremendous river of rainwater forty feet wide divided the camps as it ran swiftly and silently down the center. The warm orange glow of small campfires was spread throughout the encampment where people milled around and cooked, and the echo of voices laughing and fragments of conversations drifted up twenty feet to where they stood. The view was both shocking and inviting.

"Jesus…" Noboru said breathlessly as he took in the scene that lay before him.

"Come on," Turk smiled, "follow me."

He led them down a narrow, winding stairway that brought them to the first bank. They wandered quietly through the campsite. Conversations between people turned to silence as the trio passed by, and the two soldiers found themselves feeling uncomfortable as its occupants looked them over with quiet contempt in their eyes. Stilman noticed that they were being followed by a small group of men wearing shredded clothes before he realized that they were surrounded.

"That's far enough." One of the men said in a graveled tone as he stepped in front of the trio. He was younger than Turk, probably in his late forties with a stocky build and a long scraggly black beard. He was wearing an old worn-out trench coat with oil stains. "Let my friend go." He demanded as he opened his coat, lifted up a Terekian SKG Assault Rifle and pointed it at Noboru. Stilman made the motion to raise his Bolter but was greeted by the sound of weapons being pulled out of coats and jackets by the men that surrounded them.

"Set your gun down, mister," the man ordered, "there's no way you can win this."

"They're with the Alliance." Turk replied, "It's okay, they're here to help us."

"Bullshit!" the younger man barked, "Nobody helps us! Especially assholes the likes of them. They're almost as bad as the Terekians!"

"Calm down Jinx," Turk motioned with his hands, "all of you just calm down. These gentlemen are okay, I wouldn't have brought them here if I thought otherwise. We're gonna need their help anyway. We can't stay down here forever ya know."

"Step away from 'em Turk, I don't trust any uniform!"

"Easy Jinx, I said they're with me. Now quit pointing those guns at us. It's gonna be okay."

The group of Freemen looked at each other with uncertainty, then looked at the bearded man for guidance. The young man glared coldly at Noboru and Stilman for a few seconds then glanced at Turk with his teeth clenched.

"Shit!" Jinx exclaimed disgustedly. "Give me one reason why I shouldn't blow this guy's head off! How do we know they're not Terekians in Alliance uniforms?" He raised the automatic rifle to Noboru's head and pressed the barrel between the Commander's eyes.

"Because I saw them land! NOW PUT YOUR GUNS DOWN!" Turk bellowed. Jinx sneered at him and flicked the safety off the weapon.

Noboru stood calmly with the rifle pressed against his forehead and his arms to his side. He noticed a small blue tattoo of a series of numbers and tiny symbols on the back of Jinx's right hand.

"I give you my word as an officer of the Alliance Strike Force that we will not harm you or your people." Noboru volunteered firmly.

"What good does that do me? Your word means nothing here, and your uniform brings no comfort to us." Jinx growled.

"Then I give you my word as a fellow P.O.W. from the Shealan Deathcamps." Noboru replied coldly.

"What?" Jinx asked pensively as his eyes widened, the statement physically shook him, "Say again?"

"That tattoo on your hand," Noboru sighed, "Shealan, May 2384 to January '86, I was there for the uprising and overrun. I was in "G" Camp. C.B.9."

Jinx squinted as pulled his rifle away from Noboru's head. "Show me."

Noboru slowly removed the leather glove from his right hand and revealed a similar tattoo. Jinx reached down and grabbed the Commander's hand for a closer look.

"Those were some rough times back then. I was in "D" Camp. C.B.2." Jinx said somberly as he examined the tattoo on the commander's hand.

"I'm just happy to be alive." Noboru whispered.

"Me too."

"Jinx," the Commander continued, "the only way you could have ended up in Shealan must mean that you must have served the Alliance at one time…"

"Yeah, I'm former Aggressor Recon." Jinx replied as he looked around the group of men. Turk nodded at him reassuringly and motioned for him to lower his weapon.

"Okay," Jinx frowned, "if you're vouching for them Turk…" he said reluctantly, then shot an icy stare at Noboru and Stilman, "but you fuckers better be for real." Jinx gave the group a signal. The Freemen slowly lowered their weapons but still eyed Noboru and Stilman suspiciously. Jinx looked to some ledges along the cavern walls thirty feet above the camp. "It's okay," he yelled, "they're Alliance."

Noboru turned and looked up to where Jinx was casting his gaze, and was taken aback by the fact that they were completely surrounded by fifty or sixty others hiding in the shadows aiming Terekian weapons at them.

"How many people are down here?" Noboru asked trying not to show his surprise.

"This camp alone there's probably three hundred of us." Jinx replied dryly.

"Citywide, there's four major clans." Turk added.

"Is there a way you can contact the other camps?"

"Only by messenger on foot. Could take days." Turk replied.

"Shit," Noboru cursed, "I wanted to get all of you out of the city in the next couple of hours, but it doesn't look like it's going to happen. I just don't want any of you to get caught up in crossfire."

"What do you want to do, Commander?" Stilman asked apprehensively as he looked around and watched more Freemen gathering around them.

"Turk," Noboru said firmly, "we're not going to be able to evacuate you in time. For your own protection I'm going to have to insist that you and the rest of the Freemen remain down here until we can get some ships to take all of you out of Volengrad. But we need your help in finding the other camps. If you could get word to them and have them meet here for staging it would be greatly appreciated. I'll allocate some of my men to help you out."

"Will do, Commander." Turk nodded. "Jinx, can you get our runners together? We need to send them out to let the others know to meet here."

"Alright, Turk." Jinx smiled weakly. He turned to Noboru and held out his hand. "I'm sorry about your reception, Commander," he said as they shook hands, "it's just..."

"I understand." Noboru finished. "Believe me, I understand."

Jinx shook his head meekly as he placed his weapon back in his coat and turned to the other men.

"We've got work to do." Jinx said to the others. "Let's go."

"You'll have to excuse Jinx," Turk frowned as he spoke to the two troopers, "he's a good man. Couldn't run this clan without his help. He's taught us a lot about survival down here and how to use and care for weapons. I never knew he was a soldier at one time, although it explains a lot about him."

The Commander looked over the shadows cast by the campfires blankly and reminisced of the last war he fought in twenty years ago. It was too much for him now, and he felt his age weigh heavily on his spirit. He had made his mind up a long time ago. This war would be his last if he survived it. He'd seen and been through too much and he was tired of the suffering and the personal sacrifice.

Noboru ran his fingers over the tattoo on his hand before putting his glove back on. He watched Jinx disappear into the camp as he thought darkly about his past and his involvement in the Bio War of Shealan and the deathcamps. His days as a P.O.W. haunted him with horrible drug induced memories of torture and despair, just fragments of visions and feelings that made no sense, fleeting pictures of faces and sounds, but he remembered the darkness of his concrete cell clearly. The damp chill of the air, and the cries of other prisoners echoing down the halls as they were beaten. He had outlived his own fate a thousand times and no longer wanted to tempt it further.

He understood men like Jinx and why they isolated themselves from the world, but he knew better than to pity him. He knew that he just wanted to be left alone and not asked any questions. That everything in life was small in light of his experiences, and that everyday was just another struggle to maintain an even keel in an otherwise apathetic world.

"Can you have someone lead us back to the street now, Turk?" Noboru asked calmly as he sobered out of his daydream, "We've also got a lot of work to do."

IV

"PAPPY!" Doc screamed as he ran to where Pappy lay.

"Shit, Doc," Satch whimpered, "ya gotta save him!"

They both flinched as a grenade went off a few yards from them and scattered rubble on the pavement.

"Help me get his helmet off, Satch!" Doc Powers yelled through the din of gunfire as he cradled Pappy's head.

"His head's bleeding!" Satch cried.

"Open my medi-pack and hand me some gauze—quickly!"

Satch rifled furiously through Doc's pack. The ground heaved violently in the rain and the night closed in around us.

Pappy opened his eyes and began to grimace from the pain.

"Pappy!" Doc smiled, "Pappy, can you hear me?"

Satch and I huddled over Pappy in an effort to keep the rain off his face. Pappy just looked up at us and took shallow breaths as he tried to regain his senses.

"He's gonna be okay." Doc said reassuringly as he wiped the blood off the side of Pappy's head. "He's in shock from the concussion. His eardrums may be damaged."

"Well we need to get him the fuck out of here!" Satch demanded as he ducked a stream of red tracers humming overhead. "We gotta get 'im some place safe!"

Pappy tried to say something but couldn't get the words out. His hands trembled as he tried to grab for Satch's sleeve.

"Relax buddy." Satch said as he leaned into Pappy, "We're gonna getcha out of here."

"T-take…" Pappy whispered.

"Don't try to talk. Save your strength, goddamn it!" Satch barked.

"Take First Platoon…" Pappy coughed, "…and get to the Clover."

Suddenly a silhouette emerged from the flash of explosions and stumbled our way. I could see him dodging bullets as they splattered in the puddles and ricocheted off the street sending chunks of asphalt into the air in fountains. The figure turned to his left and let out a short burst of automatic fire as he ran. The muzzle flash from his weapon was a brilliant white light that flared from the barrel as he dove into our position. It was Genie.

"Cocksucker!" Genie spit as he took a deep breath and wiped the rain from his face, "Almost died of lead poison!"

"Hey Genie!" Satch said through clenched teeth. "You're just in time to help us get Pap out of this shithole!"

"What?" Genie said excitedly when he looked over at Pappy. "What the fuck, Pappy? I leave you alone for five minutes and come back to find you lying down on the job? You're fired!"

"Yeah good help is hard to find nowadays, ain't it?" Doc flinched.

"How bad is he?" Genie gasped.

"He's fucked up from the concussion of a frag." Doc frowned, "I don't think he can hear anything. I think his equilibrium is totally screwed up."

"Leave me..." Pappy croaked as he made an effort to reach his Bolter.

"I think the war's over for ya, Pappy." Genie winked. "Tell ya what," Genie yelled through the downpour as he turned to us, "you guys move on ahead, I'll carry Pappy into that building over there."

"Always playin' the hero, aren't cha?" Satch said mockingly.

"Hey Satch..." Genie replied.

"Yeah?"

"Open your butt, I gotta piss!"

"You son-of-a-bitch!"

"Cover me you bums." Genie smiled as he grabbed his Bolter and threw Pappy over his shoulder and darted through the rain and smoke...

Q 5

"Through me is the way to the sorrowful city.

Through me is the way to eternal suffering.

Through me is the way to join the lost people...

Abandon all hope, you who enter!"

Inscription at the entrance to Hell

Dante Alighieri (1265-1321), *Divina Commedia* "Inferno"

I

Holly lay prone in the shadows on the edge of the roof of an eight-story office building overlooking the boulevards and alleys that surrounded the Volengrad Clover Interchange. The weather was awful, but it was nothing new to work under extreme conditions of rain and high wind. The sinister outline of the H-12 superstructure rose from the ground before him like a great monster that stretched far into the darkness and mist.

He could hear the firefights throughout Emerald City and saw thousands of tracers cutting into the night. He shifted uncomfortably as he peered through the scope and tried not to think about the chill that ran through his body. Holly was exhausted but his senses felt oddly refined and sharpened from adrenaline. He felt in tune with his environment and the elements that it offered, and his instincts played host to the night.

Somewhere out in this vast concrete jungle was General Oss. The only thing that aerial recon had to offer were possible structures of where her command center could be located by the triangulation of EMF and C&C transmissions. Beyond that, the most Holly could hope for was that he was within a hundred kilometer radius of her. His primary mission brought him to south Volengrad, but now he felt alone. Holly had another agenda, a personal matter of singling out the General and killing her. Not for the Alliance, but for himself. She had put the fear in him with a contract, and he knew that with someone like her alive he would never be able to quit looking over his shoulder for the rest of his life. The price would probably always be on his head even after her death, but he wanted the satisfaction of knowing that she was dead and that he was the one that killed her.

His instincts were telling him that Oss would need an egress from the city when the time came. He didn't believe that she would allow herself to be taken prisoner, and the odds of finding her were extremely narrow, but Holly was going to try.

With Alliance forces closing in from three sides and pushing to the center of Emerald City, and the 15th making planetfall on the southern sector, he concluded that Oss would try to punch through at the Clover to escape. She had to be near the Interchange.

Holly wiped the rain from his eyes and continued his scan of the streets and buildings around him. The wind howled and the chill factor was almost unbearable as he fought to keep his teeth from chattering. He needed desperately to disassociate himself from his physical body. To leave it behind while he focused on the mission. He needed to be able to concentrate on the task that he was trained to do. To phase out personal discomfort and funnel his instincts into that tiny space that revolved around the trigger of the Pershing .50 Caliber Rifle and its scope. To compress time into frozen reality where the only thing that would matter was the world in the crosshairs. When everything around him ceased to exist except for velocity and his target.

Holly could see the flicker of a muzzle flash coming from a window on the tenth story of a building two hundred thirty meters from his position. He sighted in his scope and tapped the infrared button on the mounting bracket as he zeroed in on the image of a human figure concealed behind the sill. He wrapped his index finger around the trigger and inhaled gently as he got his breathing under control. He could see the outline of the Terekian sniper clearly through the downpour as he squeezed back on the trigger...the rifle bumped hard against his shoulder from the recoil of the shot, and he watched through the scope grimly as the soldier jerked backwards from the impact of the round and a cloud of blood sprayed in the air as his weapon fell out the window onto the street below...

•••

Genie panted heavily as he ran with Pappy over his right shoulder. Rounds buzzed overhead and snapped around them as they made their way across the street to a ragged structure. A savage blue light erupted from a laser grenade as it detonated on the sidewalk thirty feet from them and sent bright daggers of particle-lite spinning through the darkness. Genie ducked as he kicked open the door and carried Pappy into the building. He stumbled awkwardly in the shadows looking for a place to set him down when a round shattered a bay window sending a spray of glass through the room and ricocheted off a wall.

"Shit that was close!" Genie grimaced as he set Pappy down on the ground.

Pappy looked up gratefully as he reached for his Bolter on the floor next to him.

"YOU'LL BE SAFE HERE, LAY LOW AND SIT TIGHT," Genie shouted unconsciously, "WE'LL COME BACK FOR YOU FIRST CHANCE WE GET!"

Pappy grabbed Genie's sleeve and looked up at him grimly, "Get my boys to the Clover. Help Satch get them through this until the 15th arrives."

Genie pulled out his canteen and popped off the cap. He handed it to Pappy as he looked out the shattered window into the rain. Pappy reached into his tattered flak jacket and pulled out an envelope that was folded into a small square.

"Take this." Pappy said quietly as he pressed the envelope into Genie's hand.

"Pappy..." Genie frowned.

"Take it, goddamn it!" Pappy ordered. "Just in case something happens, you know what to do with it."

Genie put the letter into his pocket and put his hand on Pappy's shoulder, "I promise," he nodded, "we'll be back for you, Pappy. I gotta come back," Genie winked, "you still owe me thirty gelben."

Pappy smiled even though he didn't hear a word that Genie said, and he leaned against the wall and sighed, "Get going."

Genie stood up and slapped a fresh clip into his Bolter. He gave Pappy a thumbs-up as he slipped out the door into the downpour...

...

Stilman and Sukie pushed through the darkness along a chipped-up sidewalk. They headed south in the direction of the Volengrad Clover and could hear a skirmish a few blocks ahead of them being highlighted by sniper fire in the distance. It was considerably colder and he could see the plumes of breath from Sukie's mouth as she trotted cautiously in front of him.

Suddenly, Sukie stopped dead in her tracks with her ears flat against her head as she began to snarl. Stilman moved up along side of her and kneeled behind the husk of a burned up truck as he raised his Bolter and began to scan the street. Sukie whipped around abruptly and knocked him flat to the pavement and took off running in the direction of where they just came as a burst of automatic fire rattled from a doorway twenty meters ahead and sent rounds sparking off the wreckage where Stilman was crouching.

Stilman caught his breath as he turned himself over and crawled forward looking for the muzzle flash through the rain. Sukie had vanished into the jagged shadows of the street, and all he could see was the dark blue outlines of the buildings and debris around him as they melted into the gloom.

Thunder rolled ominously overhead as thin streaks of lightning cut furrows through the black sky and lit the boulevard with a surreal brightness that gave broken glimpses of the glossy cityscape. The sharp bite of machine guns rattled through the avenue along with the thump of multiple explosions ripping through concrete.

Stilman heard a bark from the darkness followed by screaming. He looked up the street and heard Sukie's growl when he saw three figures run out of an alley onto the smashed lane. He kneeled up and let out a burst of automatic fire and watched two of them hit the ground hard and scatter their weapons into the puddles of water. The third man had seen his muzzle flash and drew a quick bead on his position and began returning fire.

The rounds snapped by him and punched holes into the panels of the vehicle as he rolled under the truck for cover. The Terekian charged in his direction and sprayed a clip at the steel husk sending orange-white sparks flying with the metallic pings of impact. Suddenly, a huge shadow appeared from the mist and knocked the Terekian to the curb. Stilman watched in terror as Sukie tossed the soldier through the street in an almost playful fashion. The silhouette of the flailing limbs and helpless screams of the man were drowned-out by savage growls and gurgles of a predator caught up in the ecstasy of the kill. The soldier's body went limp as she bore down on the trooper's neck and tore his throat open with one savage bite and twist of her massive head. He heard the wet snap of cartilage and could almost feel the life squeezed through Sukie's jaws.

He put two fingers into his mouth and let out a piercing whistle. Sukie stopped her attack and looked in his direction attentively. Stilman sighed in relief as he stood up and walked toward her. He could see the blood-matted fur on her head shimmering in the downpour as he crouched next to her and looked down at the mangled corpse sprawled on the pavement. Her glimmering eyes embraced him warmly in the purple murk of the storm as she rubbed up against him affectionately and licked his face. Stilman wrapped his left arm round her body and stroked her gently as she leaned on him and sat down submissively.

"Good job, girl." He said quietly as he grimaced at the torn body. "Let's get the hell out of here..."

•••

Turk rummaged quietly through his belongings and put what he thought he needed in a small rucksack. Every now and then he stopped packing and watched the flames of the campfire dance hypnotically in the soft darkness of the tunnel.

"Turk," Jinx said stoutly, "just bring water and dried food. Maybe some clean rags if you got'em. We have to travel light and carry ammo for our weapons."

"Jesus, Jinx," Turk replied gravely as he looked upward where the rumbling vibrations of explosions going off at street level worked their way down through the tunnels and echoed through the cavern, "ya can really hear'em going at it up there."

"You don't have to do this Turk." Jinx said as he cast a worried gaze at the old man. "You can stay here where it's safe and wait on us to come back. The Alliance will be coming here to look for us."

"No, it's my duty as a citizen, as a Freeman to fight and win our city back from them. I'm in this for the long haul."

"Very well then," Jinx nodded, "here take these," he reached out and handed Turk an ammunition belt filled with rounds and a survival knife in a sheath, "you're gonna need'em. I'm gonna round up the rest of the men. We have to move fast and get to the surface."

"Aren't we gonna wait for the Commander to send some of this men down?"

"No time for that. If we're gonna do this we have to act now."

"Alright, Jinx." Turk sighed. "Let's make it happen."

The two men walked to the center of the camp and stood quietly for a moment. They looked longingly at their friends and watched tents being taken down and fires being put out and felt the sentiment of loss slowly shading their emotions.

Jinx stepped forward and cleared his throat...

"Freemen!" He shouted as he looked around the encampment. The rest of the men stopped what they were doing and began to gather in a loose group.

"Freemen!" Jinx bellowed. "Let's take a minute and think about this...you're all here now by choice, but I want you to *really* think about what we're about to do." Jinx looked grimly into the eyes of the men that surrounded him. "For years we've hidden from the world and kept to ourselves. We cowered in the shadow of the Terekians that walk the streets that used to be ours. Tonight it all changes. Tonight we take back what's ours. Tonight we take a stand. We're the last citizens of Emerald City, and we're about to go up against the largest ground force the Coalition ever put down into a capital. The only way we're going to do this effectively is by the cut and run tactics. We're gonna have to out-snipe and out-smart them." Jinx cast his gaze to the ground and sighed, "I'll understand if any of you want to back out. Now's the time to do it, and I wouldn't blame you if you did. What we're about to do is suicide, and I can't ask any of you to make that kind of sacrifice. I'll be honest with you, the odds aren't good, and most of us probably won't see the morning light. There's too many of them up there and they're better trained and better armed than we are. What we're about to do is madness..."

"Fuck it Jinx," one of the men in the crowd yelled, "if you don't stand for something, you'll go for anything! I go where you go!"

"Yeah, Freemen forever!" Another shouted as he raised his weapon.

The crowd began cheering and whistling enthusiastically to show their solidarity. They raised their rifles and fists in the air and hollered loudly as they tightened up their circle around Turk and Jinx.

"...madness..." Jinx repeated quietly to himself. "I just want you to know," Jinx continued as the mob quieted down, "that no matter what happens, I've never been prouder than I am now. You are my family. My brothers. It has been an honor knowing you, and will be a privilege fighting next to you. Whether or not Emerald City falls, know in your hearts that the Freemen took up arms and fought for her bravely and honorably which is more than any citizen could be asked to do..." He stepped forward and offered his hand to one of the Freemen who shook it firmly then embraced him. "God help us all." Jinx muttered as another Freeman stepped forth and hugged him.

"OKAY YOU CRAZY SONS-OF-BITCHES!" Turk bawled hoarsely as he glared at the crowd and chambered a round into his rifle, "LET'S KICK SOME FUCKIN' ASS! FREEMEN FOREVER!"

The crowd roared wildly and raised their fists in the air again in anger and determination. Their unified voices bounced off the walls of the cavern and echoed through the tunnels, filling the darkness with their chant: "FREEMEN! FREEMEN! FREEMEN..."

•••

I huddled behind the doorway of a ruined storefront and watched hundreds of red and green tracers sizzle through the rain. I flinched at the sound of automatic fire ripping through the night as thousands of rounds buzzed through the streets and pocked walls with piercing ricochets that sent plaster and concrete chips flying. A dark blue mist hovered ominously over the boulevard as I peered from the entrance and shivered from the cold. I could feel the fear coiled tightly in my chest ready to unwind and spring through my heart. I wanted to run but couldn't move. My legs felt like lead was wrapped around them.

Sharp thumps of grenades erupted across the street and the ground trembled violently and heaved up into the blackness as chunks of asphalt rained heavily onto the road and scattered like a thousand spiders. I could see the wounded crawling through the midst of chaos and bodies lay everywhere. Lightning danced fiercely through the low clouds followed by rolls of thunder that took me in the gut. It was hard to distinguish between the thunder and the bursts of explosions. Havoc was flash-frozen in time but caught in a giant swirl of adrenaline that fused me to my environment and took me out of my body to swim in a river of annihilation.

The dry staccato of machine gun fire shrouded my senses in a crisp blanket of pain and dread. The ground was raked and plowed-over by their rattle and eternal chatter.

I watched men running hunched-over through the jagged shapes of fallen buildings; the smoldering piles of concrete and twisted steel rising from the ground like massive tombstones. The city shook and the world rose in a gigantic shadow of smoke and darkness.

"Get goin'!" Someone screamed. I felt a hand grasp my sleeve and tug. "Frye! FRYE!" I snapped out of my daze and found myself face-to-face with Doc Powers. "Goddamn it Frye!" He yelled. "Keep moving! Standing still will get'cha killed! GO!" He gave me a shove out the door and we ran through the avenue as rounds cracked inches above our heads. Automatic fire blinked from windows and rooftops across the street as the whir of bullets lashed into the ground ahead of us.

We staggered as a tremendous explosion lit up the building that we just left behind and scattered glass and steel onto the boulevard. Splinters of concrete pelted us as an RPG detonated to our right and the concussion knocked us to the curb. I pulled myself forward and hid behind a pile of rubble when I saw Doc lying face down on the sidewalk ten feet in front of me. He was unconscious. The rain came down in blinding sheets and the wind had picked up into a stiff icy gust. I jumped up, ran a few steps, then dove next to him. Rounds splattered the puddles around me as I grabbed Doc by his collar and dragged him back behind the rubble and collapsed.

"DOC!" I screamed as I wiped the rain from my eyes and patted his cheek. "Doc!" His eyes opened in a haze of faint recognition as he looked at me bewildered.

"What hap..."

"RPG!"

"How bad...am I?"

I looked him over quickly, "You ain't bleeding!" He exhaled in relief and sat up and took a deep breath. "Think you can get up and run?" I asked as I handed him his Bolter.

"Yeah, I'm okay." He grimaced as he got up into a crouch and checked his gear and medi-packs.

"Frye, we need to move forward and hook up with the others!"

"You sure you're okay?"

"Yeah! We need to bounce!"

We peeked over the mound and scanned the avenue for cover as RPG's piped through the gloom. Highrises loomed ominously through smoke. Ghostly outlines against fires and the flickers of explosions. The ground seemed to boil as tracers swept across the fallen bodies and tore the dead to pieces. We saw four wounded troopers trying to crawl for cover. They clutched at the pavement as they dragged themselves through the street and the raking fire.

"Jesus," Doc squinted, "wounded! I need your help, Frye. We need to go get'em!"

I gave Doc a look of pure astonishment that told him that I thought he was insane.

"Frye listen to me. See that alley over there?" He pointed to a narrow passageway between two structures that had been badly smashed from a bombardment. The alley was partially blocked-off by a mound of debris eight feet high. "I need your help carrying the wounded over there."

"Doc we're gonna get our asses killed doing this!" I hissed.

"Yeah? So what's your fucking point?"

I blinked at him wordlessly as I checked my Bolter and flipped the selector switch to full auto and grit my teeth into a scowl. "You cocksucker! I'm gonna get you for this!"

"Follow me..." Doc got up and shot into a hunkered sprint down the street.

"FUCK!" I spit as I got up and ran after him.

We hopped over small craters still smoking from the grenades that created them and scurried around chunks of cement with twisted rebar jutting out of them like spikes. We got to the first soldier who looked up at us with surprise as we got down next to him. Doc opened a medi-pack and cracked open a small plastic vile with a needle on it and handed it to me.

"Hit'im in the arm with that Frye!" He instructed as he pulled out another vile and cracked it open.

"Wha...?" I croaked.

"HIT 'IM!"

I jabbed it into the trooper's right arm and squeezed the tiny tube empty. The soldier looked up at me calmly and panted as he bit his lower lip and clutched my sleeve.

"Thanks doc!" He murmured softly as he looked at me gratefully.

"Oh I'm not a Medi..."

"Where's it got you troop?" Doc interrupted as he plunged the other needle into the wounded man's arm. Doc gave me a tight-lipped glare that quietly conveyed a simple message: "SHUT-THE-FUCK-UP!"

"My left leg is fucked, doc!"

Doc and I threw ourselves over the soldier as a grenade went off thirty feet away and sprayed gravel on top of us.

"Lemme take a look at that leg, kid." Doc said calmly as he pulled out his survival knife and began to cut away the trooper's blood-soaked BDU's and exposed his wound to the chill of the night. The kid grimaced hard as he grabbed my hand and shut his eyes tightly. He had an eight-inch gash on his thigh that went straight to the bone, and he was bleeding badly. Doc worked quickly as he tore the soldier's pant leg into thin strips and tied them around his leg by the groin area just above the wound then pinched the split flesh together.

"Frye," Doc said in a steady voice, "get the wide bandages out of my backpack and some cotton wadding. You're gonna have to wrap 'im up while I keep his wound closed."

I fumbled for the cotton and tore open the plastic they came in and handed them to Doc as I unraveled a roll of bandages. Doc grabbed the cotton and wiped the oozing blood off the laceration while he kept the gash closed with his left hand.

"More cotton, Frye. More cotton!" He snapped urgently as he pinched the split flesh and skin together.

"Doc, am I gone die? I can't feel my leg no more."

"No, you ain't gonna die, son." Powers said as he pressed the cotton wads down. "I ain't gonna lie to you, kid, it's right to the fuckin' bone, but missed your artery, some ligaments are torn. Wrap 'im up Frye. But you'll live to tell your kids about it."

"What about my...will I still be able to..."

"Yeah, it's okay." Doc winked, and the soldier sighed in relief.

I began wrapping the bandage over the bloody rain-soaked cotton frantically.

"Nice and tight, Frye, nice and tight." He instructed. "Atta-boy!" He nodded as he took the roll from me and finished the dressing.

"We're gonna get'cha out of here into some cover, kid. But ya gotta work with us, okay?" Doc said reassuringly.

"Okay." The soldier coughed as he looked at both of us.

"Let's get'im on his feet, Frye."

We each hooked one of his arms around our shoulders and started running toward the alleyway. The young man grimaced in pain as we ran, and hopped on his good leg in an effort to help us.

We were halfway to the alley when an ear-splitting burst of automatic fire went off next to us making us flinch and stagger. It was Satch.

"I got ya covered!" Satch bellowed as he leaped over a crater and sprayed the second story of a building behind us with the 38. "Haul ass, goddamn it!" He screamed as he fired from the hip in short bursts that flared IAR's through brick and concrete walls.

We ducked into the alley behind the pile of debris with the wounded trooper and set him down against a wall.

"Stay here and don't move kid!" He ordered. "We're gonna get the others!"

"God am I glad to see you, Satch!" I said breathlessly.

"Ain't over yet, Frye." Doc said as he readjusted his gear. "Satch, we need cover fire. There's three more out there."

"No sweat, Doc." Satch sneered. "I got your asses...now git!"

"Ready Frye?"

"Yeah!"

"On me—LET'S GO!" Doc barked as he dashed into the open in a low run. I jumped up and followed as Satch propped his weapon on top of the pile of bricks and steel and began to fire into the windows across the street.

Forty feet out lay another trooper against the twisted chassis of a car; we could see rounds popping around the injured soldier as we drew closer. He huddled against his cover as bullets pinged noisily off the husk and shredded the sidewalk next to him. We ducked behind a small mound of rubble fifteen feet away.

"Shit! We'll never get to him!" Doc shrieked. "They got'im pinned!"

"There, on the roof of that building." I pointed and raised my Bolter and aimed.

"Don't take the shot, Frye." Doc snapped. "Your muzzle flash will give us up."

I could barely see the outlines of four Terekians behind a parapet wall. Their heads just peered over enough where they could see the soldier behind the car, but they had to stand up to shoot at him.

"I can get them, Doc!" I half-whispered through clenched teeth as I squeezed on the trigger of my rifle. "Just a matter of timing..." I thought to myself...

"Frye!"

At that moment, two of the Terekians stood up to shoot at the soldier and I fired a sustained burst. I watched them spin backwards and tumble in slow motion. The other two stood up and pointed their weapons at me when an RPG whistled in and blew them off the roof in a three-story somersault into the night.

"Christ, Frye!" Doc gawked. "Where the hell did you learn to shoot like that?"

"You otta see me on the dance floor."

"Shiiiit!"

We ran to the injured man and crouched next to him as Doc rifled through one of his medi-packs and cracked open another vile and handed it to me.

"Where ya hit, soldier?" Doc asked the kid as he prepped another vile and looked him over to assess the extent of his injuries. The soldier's armor was half torn off, and his uniform was covered with street sludge.

The wounded man grimaced and closed his eyes as he let his Bolter fall to the ground.

"I can't move my legs, doc!" He gasped.

"Shit! Can you feel them, or are they numb?"

"Oh I can feel them alright!" The trooper said tearfully as he looked down. "Fucking RPG blew a hole into this pile of shit I was hiding behind and sent me flying. Don't remember much after that."

"I just need to make sure that we can move you. I can't take that chance if you have a spinal injury." Doc injected his arm with amorphenacycline and the trooper immediately slipped into a half-nodded state of euphoria as his eyes glassed over and his body slumped.

"We're gonna have to carry him Frye. But he's gonna be dead weight in the condition he's in."

"Here Doc," I said as I handed him my Bolter, "take this and watch my back."

I leaned down and slung the soldier over my shoulders and felt the pain of a thousand needles in my back as I stood up with a grunt.

"Let's go!" I croaked painfully and began to run. The wounded man groaned as he bounced with every step I took.

I could see Satch firing above our heads as we neared the alley. Tracers zipped by and rounds shredded the ground in front of us as we scurried clumsily toward cover. I could hear the sharp whir of shrapnel flying through the air and the scuttle of debris hitting the ground. Flashes of RPG's and laser grenades erupted everywhere on the street and the world lit up and shook with the roar of their concussion. My body was jarred from the infinite sound waves of high explosives leveling the boulevard like a giant hand sweeping over us. The smell of gunpowder filled my lungs as I ran in the downpour screaming in pain and fright.

"Almost there Frye!" Doc yelled through the pandemonium as he spun around and fired a series of short bursts across the street. Warped shadows cast by steel girders leaped out of the darkness and seemed to grab at my legs as I stumbled forward and almost fell into a crater. I heard the bark of dogs drawing closer and thought my imagination had finally got the best of me as I gasped for breath with every labored step.

"Come on Frye!" Satch hollered as he stood up and ran in my direction. I squinted as a brilliant flare of light shot out of his weapon with a mechanical belch that sent a flash of pain shuddering through my body. "GO! GO! GO!" He coaxed as he sidestepped me. We reeled into the alley and Doc and Satch grabbed the wounded man and lifted him off my shoulders as I collapsed face first into a puddle.

"Don't quit on me, Frye!" Satch rasped as he picked me up and leaned me against the pile of rubble. "There's two more out there…"

"Leave 'im be, Satch!" Doc ordered briskly as he unhooked a medi-pack from his belt and tossed it to me.

"Frye, stay here and tend to the men. That pack is full of amorphenacycline. Use it sparingly. There's bandages in there too. Satch, get your shit, you're coming with me this time. Frye's tapped out!"

"Doc I'll be alright!" I protested.

"Bullshit! You're a fuckin' mess! You stay here and keep an eye on these two."

"But Doc…"

"Shut the fuck up, Frye!" Satch grinned. "This is *my* gig now!"

"Satch." Doc said as he slapped him on the back and ran out into the shattered boulevard.

I watched them disappear into the mist into the bluish-black hue that clattered with the sharp pops of machine gun fire mixed with the splatter of rain and thunder. The wind had died down, but a thin ground fog began to build and creep its way down the street and fill the craters and alleys. It would conceal us from the enemy if it got thick enough.

I shivered as I opened the medi-pack and looked at the wounded men lying on the ground. With the dread of inexperienced hands in basic first aid I made my attempt to comfort them.

I found an old plastic tarp balled up next to a trash dumpster and hauled it out. I struggled for a few minutes to stretch it out over the two soldiers and built a makeshift lean-to over them with some scrap lumber. Not much cover, but enough to keep the rain off them.

"Doc," one of the men said weakly, "what else ya got for the pain?"

I couched next to him, cracked a vile open, and jabbed it in his left arm. We looked at each other grimly as we listened to the firefights raging on the other side of the barrier. I took out a couple of cigarettes, put them in the soldiers' mouths, and sheltered them from the wind as I lit them. They looked at me gratefully as they exhaled. They were both from Alpha Company. Part of the Recon team that was ambushed by snipers that afternoon.

"Shit doc," the soldier with the broken legs said in a drug-induced daze, "it's getting close. The goddamned 15th should be planetside in a couple of hours."

"Yeah, The Clover's gonna be a hot LZ." The other trooper nodded. "It's gonna take a miracle to push the Terekians back."

"How long do you think it's gonna be before we're medevac'ed outta here, Doc?"

"Couldn't tell you. Everything's a clusterfuck right now." I muttered.

"That ain't no shit."

I bit my lower lip in anticipation and grabbed my Bolter as I stood up and scooted to the entrance of the alley with my back against a wall.

"Hey doc, where ya goin'?" One of them asked wide-eyed and concerned.

"Back out to help the others..."

"But Doc..."

"I'm not a medic, son, I'm a journalist..."

II

Isa moved silently on a wide shoulder of the H-12 Clover overpass that towered ten stories above south Volengrad's inner-city housing complex. There was a twenty-eight knot wind from the east that wailed through the skeletons of the smashed Terekian armor littering the lanes of the super highway. The rain soaked the bandaging on her face as she kneeled behind the steel traffic wall facing the battle going on in the streets below.

The haze made it difficult to see through the scope and identify the soldiers. It was a sniper's nightmare, and she would have to compensate for windage when she fired a shot. Lightning crackled above her with a savage energy that was accompanied by tremendous claps of thunder. She flinched instinctively as she peered through the scope and began scanning the mayhem below.

She tapped lightly on a small button on top of the mounting bracket of the scope to enable night vision; every image in the crosshairs was instantly lit in an eerie off-green light. It took her a few seconds to get her eyes adjusted to the change, and then she saw every detail on the terrain below. Isa ran her thumb and index finger over the magnification ring and zoomed her sight in to 300x with five tiny clicks, and locked it into position. She panned over pocked-faced buildings and scanned rooftops for signs of enemy snipers as a stiff gust of wind howled and sheets of freezing rain flogged her relentlessly.

Isa squinted through the scope as she wrapped her index finger around the trigger and brought her breathing under control. She noted the digital read-out displayed below the crosshairs that gave her the distance to where she aimed in meters as well as wind speed and direction. Nothing else existed for her now except for what was in the scope, and the world around her fell away.

Then she saw them. Six Terekians moving cautiously through an alley single file. They had roughly fifteen feet between each man, and each of them carried an automatic weapon. Their point swept his machine gun from left to right with a smooth motion as he walked through the shadows, and Isa could see the wet gleam of the weapon's barrel in the dark and the faint colors of his unit patch on his right shoulder. Definitely Terekian Special Forces. It was a fire team moving into position, and they all held their weapons in the ready for contact.

Isa looked them over for indication of rank. She planned on taking the officers out first then hit the others, but typical of all S.F. units, they only had their unit patches on their uniforms for identification. She decided to target the two men in the middle to cut their team in half, then pick off the rest when they scattered for cover. She hoped to do them in with a single shot per man before having to displace completely; although she was over four hundred meters away and they will probably never see her muzzle flash, there might be a sniper somewhere that might. A gamble that Isa wasn't willing to take with her own life.

She put the crosshairs just left of the forth soldier in line and led him as he walked forward. Isa exhaled silently and squeezed the trigger...

She watched the first soldier clutch his throat with both hands as he fell to his knees with an expression of surprise. Blood flowed through his fingers with every pulse and she could see him gasping for air before his eyes rolled white and he fell backwards into a pile of trash.

Isa drew a bead and fired another shot at the man behind him...

The second Terekian's body stood motionless for a few seconds, perfectly balanced considering his head had been blown off in mid-stride. Blood spouted out of his neck in a red geyser and splattered on the walls before the body fell to the ground and continued to twitch involuntarily.

Three Terekians dove to the sides of the alley for cover while the pointman ran straight ahead clearing his weapon into the dark street. Isa's third shot rang in the distance with a sharp pop, but by the time the soldier heard it, the bullet had made an exit wound six inches in diameter in his upper back between his shoulder blades. She watched him take several more steps before he collapsed into a rain-filled crater on the boulevard. The remaining soldiers hid behind building debris at the entrance of the alley next to a storefront. She could see the flicker of their machine guns lighting up the alley as they fired down the street at a burnt husk of a truck, but she didn't have a clear shot of them.

Then she noticed a large shape moving quickly through the shadows behind the Terekians. She couldn't make it out at first as it slinked forward, but it was huge, nimble, and stealthy. It broke into a dead run and charged the Terekian's position. It looked like a large dog clad in body armor, and Isa watched it bolt through the darkness bearing it's fangs. She had never seen a dog that big before, and it frightened and fascinated her to watch this monster moving in for the kill.

The Terekians jumped up and spilled into the street in sheer panic to escape this creature. Isa was about to fire another round when two of them were mowed down instantly from gunfire coming from the smashed truck down the avenue. She had just drawn a bead on the last soldier when he was tackled by the great canine. Isa watched in awe and horror as the beast tossed the Terekian through the air effortlessly like a toy. Snapping his arms and legs like dried twigs and tearing through his Kevlar body armor. She gasped as the monster tore into his abdominal area and took hunks of flesh off before finally putting him out of his misery. The dog loomed over the unconscious soldier and clamped its massive jaws around his throat and gave him a quick violent shake. Isa grimaced at the sight. Tight-lipped and captivated by the menacing creature, she wondered where it had come from when an Alliance soldier emerged from the shadows, walked up to the dog, put his arm around it, and began to stroke its fur.

She glanced at her watch. It was now 2216 hours on Christmas night...

•••

Turk led a small group of Freemen through a maze of abandoned warehouses in an industrial park five blocks west of where he first encountered Stilman and Sukie. They could see flashes of machine gun fire erupting through the streets ahead and the strobe of grenades outlining the serrated silhouettes of rubble and steel against the black sky. Tracers slashed gracefully through the air in a beautiful and deadly light show that was breathtaking and hypnotic. Fires blazed everywhere throughout Emerald City in spite of the heavy rain. Orange flames leaped uncontrollably a hundred feet high in some areas, and a thick chemical odor mixed with the tang of gunpowder.

They did another weapons check then jogged toward the back entrance of a building that faced the boulevard where there was a skirmish going on.

"Let's get to the forth floor," Turk said uneasily, "and take a look around."

"Shit." One of the Freemen cussed under his breath. "Sounds like all hell's breaking loose over here!"

"It is." Turk grumbled as he kicked the door of the building open and rushed in.

"I ain't never been so scared in my life." The man said desperately.

"Me neither." Another Freeman volunteered.

"I'm scared too." Turk frowned. "Hey there's the stairs. Let's go!"

The small group stumbled up the flights noisily in darkness until they reached a locked door on a landing. Turk put his shoulder into it stiffly and popped it off the hinges as he burst onto the roof of the structure. They ran hunched-over to a parapet wall that overlooked the avenue and peered over the top.

The city was in shambles. Crushed under the treads of war, it smoked and burned under the shroud of night. It's pulse weakened like a dying man; only a shell of what it once was. A slow, painful demise under the cold shadow of extinction. Even its color had paled into a fish belly blue in the layers of ash and dust, grime that no amount of rain could cleanse.

The group of Freemen gasped at the extent of the destruction. They cringed at the sharp echoes of automatic fire that poured from the streets as tracers streaked across the darkness like thousands of tiny comets. Explosions flashed in unison with the lightning from the raging storm. The ground rumbled, and one of them turned to his side and vomited.

"We don't stand a chance, Turk."

"I say we stay here. There's no way I'm going down to that street!" Another Freeman hissed.

"Like I said," Turk coughed as he scanned the buildings around them, "no turnin' back now."

"This is crazy, Turk! We're all gonna get killed!"

"Look!" Turk pointed at a building across the street, "Over there on that roof."

They peeked over the partition and watched four Terekians crouched behind a low wall of a structure that overlooked the next block.

"Hand me the R.P.G.." Turk ordered. "We've got a clear shot at 'em!" he blurted as he snapped up the sights and took aim.

"Turk, no!" one of the Freemen coughed apprehensively, "If you miss they'll see us!"

Turk fixed the crosshairs on the roof as two Terekians hopped to their feet and fired into the next avenue, they were spun around as ground fire chewed up the wall and knocked them off their feet. Turk pulled the trigger and almost lost his balance as the recoil slammed the launcher into his shoulder. He traced the path of the rocket through the darkness. It seemed to float in slow motion with smoke trailing in a thin stream. There was a brief flash of light as the roof was engulfed in a blast of orange flames and the windows of the building were blown out. The soldiers were flipped lifelessly into the air from the concussion and disappeared behind the structure.

"Damn! What a shot!" One of the Freemen shouted as he slapped Turk on the back.

"I need three guys to come with me," Turk gestured as he checked the clip of his Terekian SDX assault rifle, "I wanna go down there."

"Jammer, Hal, Slim, go with Turk! The rest of ya come with me!" A large blonde-headed Freeman with scraggly hair named Swede growled.

"How many nades ya got, Slim?" Turk asked a dark-haired Freeman with a bandana wrapped around his head.

"Six delayed frags, two pyro's."

"That'll work."

"I got some "Black Swan", probably enough to light up at least ten blocks." Jammer grinned and winked.

"Where'd ya get that from?"

"Stole it from that depot we raided two weeks ago on the north side," Jammer chuckled, "hell, I thought it was a case of bourbon 'till I opened it. Came with imploders, det-transmitters, and everything."

"No kiddin'?"

"Yeah! Jinx armed it for me. All's I gotta do is slap the Swan on something with the imploders, press the det-button, and heaven's gates!"

"I don't want you walkin' next to me." Slim grimaced.

"Oh you're all heart, ain't cha?" Jammer smiled. "Besides, you got no room to talk with all them nades hangin' off your belt."

"Come on, men!" Turk waved as he ran to the stairwell. "Let's get down to the street. It's gonna be a long night..."

•••

The atmosphere in the crowded launch bays of the F.S. Normandy was thick with tension as thousands of soldiers stood in formation beside troop carriers and prepared for planetfall. On the lower decks, last minute checks were being run on the anchor points of the armor loaded inside the cargo holds of seventeen Alpha Class Dropships. The 32nd Armored Division had over forty Centurions with reactive armor ready for deployment along with sixteen heavy assault hovercrafts.

Flight crews had begun their final visual walk-around their ships with the Chief Techs and reviewed their flight plans and launch sequencing with the Air Bosses. It would be a tight launch followed by an accelerated entry into 781's stratosphere. What pilots called "burning the pipe" since they would be in full afterburner for the entire decent, a very unpleasant and uncomfortable ride for everyone; especially through stormy conditions that promised severe C.A.T.'s (Clear Air Turbulence) and micro-bursts on their final approach.

The Centurion crews would have it bad. They would be strapped into their tanks for the rapid insertion. Sitting in total darkness in the hulls, feeling every bump and bash on the way down, and having the whine of the ships engines completely engulf their senses with their tremendous drone. Until then, they sat quietly in their squad bays and wrote letters home or chain smoked while they checked over their gear and reviewed street maps of Emerald City.

Statistically, because of their massive size when hitting a hot LZ, dropships were supposed to be off-loaded within forty-five to sixty seconds before their odds of a successful lift-off were drastically reduced to less than a thirty percent chance of survival. Rumor among the flight crews now was that they were at less than fifty percent on initial touch down, and that losses were expected to be extremely high among the flights of the first wave bringing in the armor to the Clover. Either way one tried to reason it out, if you were a crewman on one of those ships, you couldn't help but develop a quiet disdain for the high command ("Those rotten bastards!") that was sending you to what was surely your death.

It was far worse for the Centurion crews; the Terekians considered armor prime targets of opportunity, and every effort to disable and destroy tanks would always be their first objective. Tankers knew this and learned to live with it with an almost casual attitude, but what it came down to was that it was something they would rather not think about. Off-loading in an LZ was when they were the most vulnerable...

"Fucking sitting ducks." Is what one of them said to me as he leaned on the turret of the rumbling monster. "Nothing you can do but pucker-up and submit until you're out of that tin coffin. Ya put the hammer down and wish the motherfucker in front of you would drive faster. Other than that, who gives a rat's asshole about the Coalition's light anti-tank weapons? It's their artillery that scares the shit out of me."

It was now 2230 hours and boarding had begun. Shouted commands of platoon leaders echoed through the bays in the upper decks as three brigades of the 175th Infantry filed into the troop carriers. Of the 15th Division, the 444th Ranger Battalion, the 528th Demolitions Engineers, the 117th Recon, and the entire 53rd Light Infantry were going in as the first wave. The second wave consisted of two brigades of the 42nd Planetary Strike Group, followed by the "Red Brigade"—the 5th Infantry. Over seventeen thousand men and women of the 15th Division were going to be making planetfall at midnight and push to the center of Volengrad along with the 32nd Armored Division.

In Ft. Defiance, eight squadrons of Razorback gunships had already taken off and were in route to Volengrad. The 9th and 64th Armored Wings were on stand by for a scramble, and the 16th was already in the stratosphere in a holding pattern two thousand kilometers north of Emerald City where the dropships of the 15th Division would be making their entry into 781.

The K.I.A. and W.I.A. lists during the siege of Volengrad were already beyond the estimated levels of acceptable loss by Command, and the city still had not fallen. Back in New Sierra, the media was going ape shit over the casualty reports, and anti-war rallies were beginning to erupt into small riots. It was getting ugly. Public opinion was demanding an end to the war and the fear of the Terekians using tactical nukes on Emerald City was spreading—that the Coalition would rather vaporize it than hand it over to the Alliance. All rumor of course.

The Terekian government was on the verge of collapse, and they were desperate. But not desperate enough to surrender yet or go to the bargaining table to strike a treaty with the Alliance. Their military had rapidly disintegrated in the last six months, and key leaders had slipped out the back door as they lost one campaign after another. Volengrad was all that was left. The industrial stronghold of the Q. Their last stand in Bakkus.

Admiral Jonas was right with his statement: it was a knife fight, and both sides were getting bloody. The main player for the Terekians in Emerald City was the shrewdest soldier in their ground force: General Rachel Oss. A soldier feared by the Alliance high command for her cutthroat tactics. Just to mention her name at an M.P.A.A.C. conference was enough to draw icy stares and create an awkward silence from military officials.

She was well versed in Alliance strategy and spoke sixteen languages fluently. Including Terran. An aristocrat from the Terekian New Order, Oss was the one who orchestrated the fall of Trouvaughn and rattled the confidence of Alliance military officials in the early years of the war. She was also the one behind the siege of the Pegasus Bridge and the mastermind of Volengrad's invasion. Since then, every bounty hunter and merc in the region has been after her (including Alliance Special Forces operatives), but all have failed in their assassination attempts. Their capture and executions made public by Oss herself through the use of media hype.

Scuttlebutt had it that she was in the city calling the shots from an underground bunker, but nobody has been able to verify this rumor. It seemed only fitting that Oss would be in Volengrad, she was, after all, the one who lead the invasion force that took it five years ago. It only made sense that she would be there to defend their occupation of the city down to the last man standing.

•••

I squinted through the downpour as I hopped over small craters and weaved through piles of concrete and asphalt. Rounds snapped by me as I dove behind the twisted wreckage of an overturned van and huddled against the cold steel. Hundreds of muzzle flashes blinked from windows and doorways and were punctuated with the sharp bark of machine guns. In the distance, the faint clack of sniper fire rang out along with the werewolf-like baying of dogs approaching our position.

Soldiers darted in and out of the shadowy mist in a deadly game of hide-n-seek as firefights worked through the boulevard with the tat-tat-tat of Bolters and SDX rifles. The ground trembled with explosions and the sting of cement fragments pelted me from every direction. I flinched as stray rounds sparked off the steel husk of the vehicle and splintered on impact with dry metallic pings, and puddles around me hissed as bullets chewed the street and ricocheted off the asphalt.

Bright petals of white phosphorus lit up the boulevard with their brilliance as they bloomed like deadly flowers. Acrid smoke filled my lungs and burned with every breath, and with every explosion came anguish as men caught in their sizzling glow writhed in pain. Grenades. White Phosphorus grenades, laser nades, delayed frags, pyrogen frags, finger charges, toe poppers, Black Swan, satchels, claymores, anti-personnel, anti-armor, shape charges, CVC's, detcords, powder burn, cordite, Bloopers, Boobies, laz and motion detectors. Spinning Jennies, Bouncing Betties, Crazy Eights, and Hornet Nests. Eventually one could distinguish their sound as they detonated; their orange, white, blue, or red flames and particle-lite daggers filling the darkness as they pitted buildings and streets with shrapnel and left the air electrified with the gritty coppery aroma of blood and charred flesh.

The world was blackened by concussion, and I floated in adrenaline as chaos consumed my senses and drove me forward. I leapt to my feet and charged. Screaming to the top of my lungs in total fear as I danced madly through the avenue firing at the shadows that moved against the buildings. Watching men around me jerk back and fall from the impact of rounds. A surreal blur in slow motion as I slipped over fresh entrails and stumbled over severed limbs and torn bodies. I pushed into the downpour searching for Satch and Doc Powers.

"Frye! Frye over here!" a voice called out frantically as he crouched in the darkness.

It was Satch. I turned and sprinted to where he and Doc huddled behind a mound of bricks and splintered wood beams. Doc Powers was frantically bandaging up an unconscious trooper's legs as Satch popped his head up and fired short bursts down the street.

"Keep your head down Frye!" Satch yelled through the din of gunfire. "I think we're in seriously deep shit!"

"Well I kinda figured that out on my own, Satch!" I yelled back.

"About two blocks north of us between those two apartment buildings...Terekian Rattleback!"

Up the avenue concealed in an alley, a Terekian Bopper belched a steady orange flame from the shadows as it poured thousands of rounds into the street with a raking fire that swept low over the asphalt and sent chunks of blacktop flying high in the air. The Bopper was huge and mowed everything down in front of it as it slowly grinded down the avenue on its treads firing at any movement it detected.

...BBBRRRAAAAAAPPPPP!

It was the very distinct growl of a .30 caliber mini-gun pivoting on its tracks and putting out over twenty thousand rounds per minute. I could see the silhouettes of men dashing for cover and getting plowed down in their mad run for life. I shivered at the sight of the orange comet flaring in the gloom as it began to work toward our position.

"It's just a matter of time before it hits us and this pile of shit we're behind is smoked! We need to get the outta here, and I mean now!" Satch scowled.

"Frye, I need your help carrying him!" Doc said breathlessly as he began bandaging his own left arm.

"Jesus Doc you're hit!" I shouted in surprise. "How bad?"

"I think its shrapnel from a frag." He grimaced. "Finish tying this off for me will ya Frye?" Doc gasped.

I dropped my Bolter and wrapped the bandaging around Doc's bicep several more times and tried to tie it off. He was bleeding badly and the dressing was already soaked with blood.

"Gimme a break, Doc!" I bellowed. "Sit still, damn it!"

"Well it hurts you asshole!" He hissed and jabbed my nose with his right fist and knocked me on my ass.

"You ungrateful piece of shit!" I spit as I wiped blood off my face and tugged at the dressing.

"AAAAAHHH! YOU FUCKER!" Doc cringed as he held his left arm.

"You two make a charming couple you know it?" Satch said sarcastically.

"FUCK YOU!" Doc and I snapped simultaneously.

At that moment, a tremendous explosion lit up the night with a blinding light, and the three of us were thrown flat to the ground by the sound wave as the enemy Bopper was buried in rubble when the buildings that surrounded it collapsed into a thick cloud of dust and smoke. Bricks and large chunks of cement skittered down the street and it rained steel splinters and asphalt...

...

Turk led the three Freemen through the shadows in an almost childlike fashion; skittish, and leap-frogging for cover as they stayed close to the buildings. They were a comical sight. Four men in ragged clothes slipping in and out of the darkness hunched over awkwardly as they held their weapons and scurried up the boulevard like street rats.

In spite of their worn appearance, they were rather resourceful in their use of darkness for cover and they moved quickly over the smashed terrain. They trekked three blocks without drawing fire from Alliance or Coalition soldiers. Navigating behind firefights, sidestepping the craters and bodies that littered the sidewalk, and vanishing into the shadows of storefronts in the brief violent flickers of explosions.

Suddenly Slim was knocked forward and fell face-first onto the pavement and the weapon he was carrying slid across the ground.

"Turk!" One of the Freemen shouted as he turned to look at his friend.

"Slim!" Turk cried in surprise as he ran to his fallen comrad. "He's been shot!"

A bullet sparked off the asphalt with a sharp snap. No gunfire was heard.

"Sniper!" Turk screamed. "Run!"

"What about Slim?"

"He's dead!" Turk barked as he jumped up and started running. Let's get out of here!"

They ran for three blocks before taking cover in a narrow alleyway to catch their breath. The Freemen stood silently in the rain for a moment as the word sacrifice took new meaning for them. They adjusted their packs and began jogging at a slow pace, holding their weapons at port as they vanished into the light mist deep into enemy territory. Around them the city erupted and the sky crackled with lightning, giving the air a heavy feeling that weighed into their emotions. It tasted bitter with every breath.

Blast waves rippled with a deep resonance off the walls of the buildings and rattled loose glass and unhinged doors. Most of the smaller buildings didn't survive the air strikes or the artillery barrage and had completely collapsed—reduced to their basic elements of wood, rebar, and bricks. Larger structures still towered over the streets of Volengrad, but they were slowly being stripped down to bare steel as they were pounded by ordnance.

The sound of debris tumbling across the asphalt surrounded them, craters filled with rain, machine gun fire chattered, and fires raged. Shadows quivered over jagged piles of concrete as thunder rolled threateningly overhead. Volengrad was falling apart.

The Freemen rounded a corner and climbed over a pile of bricks and splintered wood. Turk huffed for breath as he fought to keep up with the two younger men. The pile of rubble was only eight feet high, but he could feel fatigue starting to set into his muscles. The rain cut into them, soaking through their layers of clothes as they reached the top and jumped off onto the sidewalk and found themselves in the middle of five Terekian soldiers sitting in a loose circle eating.

For a second everybody just gawked at each other with their mouths open in surprise. Stunned and unable to move. Not knowing what to do. The Coalition troopers' automatic weapons lay beside them within reach, but they made no motion to grab them in the presence of their uninvited dinner guests. One Terekian with a mouth full of food looked over the Freemen and began to laugh at the sight of the ragged trio...

"Lanka hat vera parshat! Sens Alliance tophat jenelco arla mirlat?"

("You've got to be shitting me! The Alliance sent swamp apes to fight us?")

The soldier chuckled as he spit out his food and pulled out a sixteen inch survival knife...

"EAT THIS!" Jammer screamed as he opened fire and killed him and the two next to him at point blank. Blood splattered across the ground as he pivoted to shoot the others when a glancing blow to the head by a rifle butt knocked him down.

The Terekian raised his rifle to shoot Jammer when Turk blindsided him with a tackle and jarred the weapon out of his hands. They savagely exchanged punches and Turk could see sparks of light dancing around him as he took one in the jaw and spit out a tooth. Bloody saliva dripped thickly out of the corner of his mouth as he screamed and dove at the enemy trooper. They ended up with their hands around each other's throats and began to roll on the pavement. Turk found himself pinned to the ground and could feel his life being squeezed out and falling away. He wanted desperately to cough and fill his lungs with air as he tried to pull the Terekian's hands off his throat, but everything around him began to blur and fade to gray. The man was powerful, and hissed at him as he tightened his grip. Turk gasped and strained his arms up and groped at the soldier's face, put his thumbs over the Terekian's eyes and pushed in as hard as he could. The soldier began screaming in agony as he released Turk and stumbled backwards into a puddle with a splash.

"Say goodnight motherfucker!" Jammer growled as he stepped forward, put his boot on the soldier's chest, and fired a round into his forehead, leaving him staring blankly at the sky with his mouth open.

"Where's the other one?" Turk coughed hoarsely as he rubbed his neck and spit out blood.

"Hal's got 'im over there." Jammer pointed.

The other Freeman hunched in the darkness over the Coalition trooper.

"Hal, what the hell're ya doin'?"

"Never you mind, Jam," Hal squinted, "jus' lemme finish dis up and we can go."

The Terekian struggled and tried to cry out, but he was gagged and hog-tied as he lay on his stomach and floundered on the asphalt.

"Alright I'm done wit 'im! I tink dat should 'old 'im for now." Hal scowled as he stood up and kicked the soldier in the ribs several times.

The other two Freemen gathered around the enemy and glowered down at him with contempt.

"Jammer," Turk said quietly as he used his sleeve to wipe blood off his face, "how much Black Swan ya got?"

"More than enough, why?"

"Gimme some."

Jammer pulled a three-inch cube of dark plastik explosive out of a small rucksack slung around his shoulder and handed it to Turk along with a tiny electronic imploder. Turk crouched next to the Terekian as he shoved the imploder's prong into the Black Swan and pressed a red button. The Coalition soldier's eyes went wide with fright as he realized what Turk was about to do to him, and he started to scream in muffled terror.

"Hal," Turk ordered, "turn 'im over and take that gag off 'im!"

Hal reached down and untied the rag that covered the Terekian's mouth as he turned him to his side.

"NO! NO!" The soldier pleaded.

"Shad-dup!" Turk snarled as he lifted the trooper's head up by his hair and crammed the block of plastik into his mouth. The soldier wretched and tried to spit it out, but Turk had pushed it in too far.

"Now gag his ass." Turk said coldly.

"Turk," Jammer said urgently as he put his hand on his friend's shoulder, "that's too much. You don't need that much Swan, you'll take these buildings out around us."

"Eye for an eye, mates, and then some." Turk mumbled grimly as he glared at the enemy. "I hope you enjoyed your stay in Volengrad, you asshole..."

They were eight blocks away when Turk pressed a button on the transmitter that detonated the Black Swan with a purple-white flash that lit up the night with its jagged reach into the heavens. A ripple of violet light in the sky that brought an eerie peacefulness that stretched seconds into eternity as the rattle of automatic fire and secondary explosions from grenades and mortars were engulfed in an unnatural silence as if all the noise from the firefights in the area were pulled into a vacuum and pressed out of existence. Then came a deafening roar as a huge orange flame mushroomed skyward and bloomed into horrific flower of death. The world spun as blast waves surged through the chill and debris pelted the avenues for over five minutes. A dense cloud of smoke and dust rolled through the streets as several buildings were reduced to rubble and twisted steel. Surrounding high-rises groaned from the concussion and swayed heavily as they towered into midnight. The ground rumbled and the streets began to collapse from the epicenter of the explosion— radiating out like a spider's web. Near by boulevards turned into trenches as sidewalks caved in and asphalt sank into the channels. A crater over forty feet deep and eighty feet wide smoldered at ground zero, and busted sewer and storm pipes along with severed electrical cables lay exposed in the mists. It was now Christmas day...

III

The air crackled electrically in the drizzle as a chilling breeze swept through the avenues with a ghostly wail. The chatter of automatic fire filled the darkness and the thump of explosions echoed off the pocked faces of buildings as ordnance punched holes into the ground and pieces of cement whirred into the sky and showered the streets. Shadows pulsed wildly with life against the billows of ash and smoke as lightning flickered across the clouds and highlighted the wraithlike silhouettes of the shattered highrises of Volengrad.

The H-12 Clover towered in the gloom over south Volengrad as the symbol of apocalypse. The last stand in the blue mists of Uluwatu Valley. Three thousand kilometers north of Emerald City sonic booms clapped like thunder through the skies as the first wave of the 15th Division's dropships entered the atmosphere at mach four and began their rapid descent toward the burning skyline. Novas from the 16th Armored Wing flew along side as fighter escort, their sleek profiles a contrast to the bulky shapes of the troopships as they maintained a loose formation.

"Silver-6, Silver-6 actual," a Nova pilot said calmly on the C and C freq to the squadron leader of the dropships, "Angels away."

"Roger Ghostrider, thanks for the company." A voice responded, "We'll see you back on the Normandy."

"10-4 Six, good luck."

"Six clear."

"Ghostrider out." A female voice responded dryly as the Nova-31's broke formation and began their steep climb back into the purple exosphere.

The pilot of the lead ship squinted through his visor as he keyed his mic and struggled to keep the large craft stable through the turbulence of final approach. The orange glow of Volengrad could be seen for miles. "Jesus Christ." He thought to himself as he drew a quite breath and felt the tingle of fear run up his back. He scanned the night as they slowly dropped altitude over the dense forests of Uluwatu Valley.

"Normandy Command, this is Silver-6," he said in a steady voice, "we have a visual of the northern sector of the city and are five-by-five on final. Request sit-rep of LZ, over."

"Roger Silver-6," a voice responded, "ground troops report heavy contact in the gridline and have engaged the enemy. They are on the 3-5 C and C push. Codename Scarecrow. You'll be going in hot. Gunship support from Defiance delayed from the weather ETA fifteen minutes. Over."

"Fifteen minutes!" the pilot exclaimed, "this will be over in five. Do we have gunships anywhere in the area?"

"Affirmative, but they're locked in CAP on the west side with the 5th and 9th Divisions. Over."

"10-4, Normandy, we're dropping to subsonic and going in Lima-Lima. Over."

"Roger Silver-6, drop the armor and get out ASAP."

"Affirmative, Normandy Command. Leaving your push. Silver-6 out."

The Captain raised his visor and turned to the weapons tech sitting behind him with a cold look. "Goddamn it, I hope those fuckers down there can provide us with enough ground fire. Get the smoke ready to deploy. I want it thick when we touch down at the Clover and I want all counter-punch measures ready to engage."

"10-4, Captain." The tech replied as she began to toggle the instrument panel. "We're good to go on smoke and CSF's. Chafe and flare loads are go. EMF, IFF, and ECC jammers are enabled."

"Outstanding, paint the grid. I want to hit our mark and park this beast on a bug's ass."

The pilot dropped his visor and switched the freq on his mic to communicate with the crew in the hull overseeing elements of the 32nd Armor Division.

"Tillie, you copy?" The Captain said sharply.

"Yes sir." A woman responded.

"We're over northern Uluwatu Valley. Three minutes to insertion, Lieutenant. Tell those treadheads to fire-up their Centurions and prepare to roll. We have a hot LZ and I want them moving the moment we touch down."

"Roger that, Captain." The PitBoss snapped back. She turned to her four shipmates as she stood up, "Battle stations!" The lieutenant ordered as she ran to a control panel, grabbed a Bolter off the weapons rack, and pressed an intercom button. "This is it Tankers!" She broadcasted over a sealed channel in a raspy voice. "We are less than three minutes from touch down. Fire-up and brace for insertion. The front office says we have an extremely hot LZ…" the dropship vibrated as the airbrakes opened and the engines went into a high pitch as they decelerated to subsonic speeds.

Tillie pulled down on several levers and the vice-clamps holding down the tanks loosened and released with a hiss and retracted into the steel deck with a clang. The hull of the dropship filled with the earsplitting sound of armor rumbling to life as she jogged down the aisles double-checking the status of her shipmates in their stations and patted her own body armor down to make sure it was buckled tightly before planting herself behind a .30 caliber chaingun mounted on a track at the ramp. The Lieutenant began her final systems check, took a deep breath, and readied herself for the landing.

"Battle stations, report." Tillie said calmly.

"Bay-1 is weapons free." A shipmate answered.

"Bay-3 is hot."

"Bay-2 is weapons hot."

"Bay-4 good to go…"

The ship lurched violently and the bay lights blinked on and off as hundreds of antiaircraft shells detonated in the midnight sky and sent jagged fragments of superheated steel spinning through the formation of dropships.

"Shit!" Tillie cussed as she hooked up her body harness and readjusted her helmet. The hull clanged as groundfire pounded off the armored plating of the transport and reverberated throughout the fuselage.

"Hang on to your asses, damn it, they know we're here!" the Captain squawked on an open channel then toggled into the C and C frequency, "Silver-6 to Normandy Command, be advised, be advised, we are taking heavy anti-aircraft fire from the valley." The Captain reported calmly as he stared hard at the HUD in his visor and listened to hell breaking loose on the main frequency as other pilots screamed…

"…MAYDAY! MAYDAY!" a voice cried hysterically, "Slapshot-9 is hit and losing power! Our vertical stabilizer is wasted! We're going down! WE'RE GOING DOWN! OH SHIT…"

"...Silver-6, Silver-6 actual," another pilot blared, "BlackJack-3 is dropping out. We have a system blackout from the ack-ack. Send SAR. I have no control. Repeat, BlackJack-3 is a dead stick..."

"...Six actual, this is bad, we have heavy damage on Intercoolers. I have three engines blazing and loosing altitude fast. Valkrie 2-2 will not make the LZ!" a pilot shouted frantically, "I'm going to have to set her down in the valley..."

"...OH MY GOD! OH MY GOD! WE'VE LOST OUR WING..."

The Captain glanced out the cockpit and squinted at the churning sky around them. The vessel shook with each explosion as he watched thousands of tracers floating up at them from the dark.

"Fucking steel curtain." He mumbled when the transport flying as his wingman burst into huge ball of flames then disintegrated in mid-air. Their ship rocked violently from the blast wave as the impact of debris slammed into their hull.

"Captain we're being tracked." The weapons tech said grimly as she gazed at a console screen and pressed her hand on her headset, "I'm picking up multiple signals from the valley. I think they've got SAMS down there. I'm getting IFF signature read-outs."

"Fuck it, I'm taking us down lower." The Captain clutched the control yolk and pushed forward as he clenched his teeth and struggled to keep the craft stable in a steep dive. They were less than a hundred and thirty meters above the ground and the trees of the forest clipped the ship's hull as they crossed into city limits.

"This is Silver-6," he bellowed on an open channel to the squadron, "fall-in landing formation and deploy counterpunch measures. Engage retro-jets and follow me in. Watch the buildings. Stay below the rooflines." the Captain ordered as he led the fleet over a blazing industrial district and into the heart of downtown Volengrad. He veered the craft in a hard bank left to avoid a highrise and lowered the landing skids as they thundered over a boulevard that connected to the Clover, "We're almost there."

The armada of dropships flew dangerously low over the streets of Emerald City, cutting through the mists and smoke over the avenues; they weaved between battle-scarred buildings and rattled the structures around them as they closed in on the landing zone.

"This is it! Lieutenant," the Captain's voice sparked over Tillie's headset, "we're over the LZ!" he barked as they went into the transitional flight of hover.

"Good to go, Captain!" Tillie reported, "We are weapons hot and ready to drop the ramp on your mark."

"Roger, L-T." The Captain replied. "Get'em ready, this is going to be tight..." they could hear the muffled "Whump! Whump! Whump!" of the smoke rockets firing down into the streets and detonating.

"...ten seconds to touch down...sixty meters to the deck...drop the ramp!"

Tillie punched a red button that sounded an alarm and the cabin lights dimmed and turned red as the rear bay door of the ship hissed open and exposed them to the chill of the midnight air. The sounds of the battle raging below rang brightly throughout the cargo bay. The staccato of gunfire, the numbing explosions, and the scream of their own engines assaulted their senses as they plummeted to the street.

"...twenty meters..."

Tracers flashed toward them and the hull rang sharply as hundreds of rounds from small arms fire blipped from below...

"...ten meters...nine...eight ..." the Captain's voice growing hoarse as he counted down...

The smell of gunpowder was overpowering, and Tillie could see the outlines of buildings and another dropship through the haze as the smashed ground rose to meet them...

"...seven...six...five..."

The Lieutenant raised her hands to her face instinctively as she watched the dropship behind them vanish in a bright explosion...a fireball of melted steel and fuel flashing brilliantly and illuminating the boulevard as heat from the blast wave rolled over her...

"...four...three...two..."

She could hear the deafening prattle of machine guns as they landed and billows of smoke flooded into the ship...

"We have touchdown!" The pilot hollered. "Get'em outta here!"

"ROLL! ROLL! ROLL!" Tillie shouted into her headset as she poured fire into the night. The Centurions clamored swiftly down the ramp and filed out of the ship in two lines. Bullets buzzed into the hull of the ship and bounced off the titanium alloy walls as they splintered on impact.

"Cover fire!" Tillie shouted as she pivoted the chaingun and fired controlled bursts at the muzzle flashes that blinked at her from the surrounding buildings. "Thirty percent of the Centurions are out, Captain! Cover fire, Bay-4!" The L-T ordered into her headset. "Everything you've got on starboard, Bay-1! Suppressors off!"

"Jesus Christ!" the gunner from Bay-4 screamed as she worked the mini-gun in a sustained burst. "We're fucking surrounded!"

"Getting slammed on this side, L-T!" Another voice cut into the multi-channeled chaos on the inboard radio. "It's too much! It's too much! There's too many of 'em out there!"

The street around the dropship heaved as RPG's worked closer to them and the armored columns exited the belly of the ship. Suddenly, the dropship rocked sideways as it took a direct hit from an armor piercing shell on the starboard side, flames burst through the cargo hold with a roar, and the spray of shrapnel killed the crewmen in gun bays 1 and 3 instantly. Tracers ripped into the thick black smoke and plinked the Centurions as they continued to off load...

"We're taking too much ground fire, Captain!" Tillie coughed as she flipped the fire suppressor off and unleashed a sustained burst on the .30 cal. "We have a breach in the hull. Our reactive armor on starboard is toast. Bay-1 report!"

No response...

"Bay-1 status!" Tillie yelled as she continued to fire. "Talk to me Rosal, goddamnit!"

No response.

"All stations report!" The Lieutenant hollered into her headset. She glanced at the remaining Centurion columns moving behind her, their headlights filtered through the smoke filled cabin as they rumbled past her onto the boulevard.

"Tillie, how we doin'?" The pilot stammered.

"Almost there, Captain..." she could hear the ships engines revving up for lift off, "All stations report!" She continued to yell.

"Rosal and Fish are dead, L-T!" The crewman from Bay-4 coughed.

"Shit!" Tillie cussed.

The ship lurched violently again and Tillie was thrown to the deck hard as RPG's blew the forward cockpit apart and killed the flight crew. The engines burst into flames.

"FUCK!" The Lieutenant screamed as she tore off the headset and scrambled to her feet. The last Centurion rolled out of the ship and came to a stop just outside the ramp. A hatch popped open on the turret and the tank Commander jumped out and ran back into the burning ship...

Tillie shielded her eyes as she groped through the smoke coughing and made her way through flames toward Bay-4. She looked up and could see the street through a gaping rip in the ships hull. She flinched at the heavy thunks of rounds bouncing off the fuselage, hollow punches in the steel that sounded like someone hammering from the outside.

"Tillie..." a voice cried out.

The Lieutenant pressed ahead when she saw her crewmate emerge from the fire. A figure in a tattered uniform matted with blood limped stiffly toward her, both arms torn off and a blackened face beckoned from the smoking wreckage.

"CeeCee!" The Lieutenant screamed as she held out her arms in shocked recognition and ran to meet her comrade. "Oh god, CeeCee! Oh god you're a mess!" She cried as she dropped her Bolter and embraced her friend before they both collapsed to the deck.

"L-T." Her crewmate whispered, "I'm not gonna make it..."

"Nooo!" Tillie frowned as she cradled her friend in her arms. "Hang in there, girl! I'm gonna get'cha outta here, you hear me?"

"Boss..." the soldier said weakly then passed away with her eyes open.

"NOOO! NOOO!" Tillie screamed as she lowered her head and hugged her crewmate tighter...

"L-T!" the tanker shouted above the din of explosions as she waved her arms and covered her face. "Let's get the hell out of here! Silver-6 is a dead stick!"

"WHERE THE HELL IS EVERYBODY? WHO'S LEFT?" Tillie demanded as she wiped blood from her face and grabbed her weapon.

"They're dead! They're all dead! Come on! We gotta go!" the Commander ordered as she grabbed the Lieutenant's arm, lifted her up, and began to hustle her out of the burning transport.

"CeeCee..." Tillie gasped as she glanced back into the burning ship one more time.

"She's wasted, L-T! We gotta get out before the ship blows!"

Bullets popped around them as they staggered down the ramp and through the thick smoke to the waiting Centurion when the tanker was spun sideways as a round tore her leg open.

"AAAHHH! GODDAMN IT!" The tanker hissed as she fell.

Tillie reached over to pick her up when she heard them coming— screaming and howling like animals as they rushed forward with knives drawn...

"KISS MY ASS, YOU RAT-FUCK-SON-OF-A-BITCHES!" Tillie screamed as she pulled her sidearm from its holster and opened fire...

•••

The heavens rumbled as the huge shadows of dropships descended upon Volengrad and the sharp tang of jet exhausts filled the air. Their navigation lights blinked furiously overhead as hundreds of smoke rockets were deployed and detonated on impact with a dull "Whump!" and began to obscure everything in thick clouds of gray. Enemy tracers reached up to them from rooftops and alleys, dotting the gloom with their bright streaks of red and orange. The streets erupted in violence as the piercing shriek of engines melted with the rattle of Terekian ground fire and split the night open with a deafening roar. The first wave of dropships had hit the landing zone in southern Volengrad.

The pavement cracked under the massive landing skids of the vessels as they touched down in the swirling haze. The groan of steel and the hiss of the strut shocks of their landing gear taking on weight. Engines screamed and distorted the air with heat waves. Loose debris tumbled in every direction and smashed asphalt and gravel skittered over the ground.

Gunfire poured from the surrounding buildings at the landing crafts, and the boulevard heaved with the impact of RPG's. Thousands of rounds clanged against their hulls, sparking and splintering against the reactive armor of the dropships.

Ramps down, troops scrambled onto the avenue with clenched teeth, quivering lips, and faces pinched in fear…the city spinning wildly in a blur of tracers and the strobe of explosions. The night air sizzled with rounds, laser fire, and the numbing concussion of grenades. They rushed into black chaos with eyes widened in mortal terror, screaming to release their fear, screaming to release the dark visions of their own demise, to release their lives as they swarmed into the bedlam on the streets of Emerald City.

The gunbays of the dropships threw out an astounding amount of suppressive fire, but many soldiers died on the ramps as the shriek of RPG's ripped through the chill and the vicious bark of automatic fire riddled them upon landing. The mayhem—tracers glowing hot, arms reaching wide to the sky, and laser fire slicing through the night with their vicious blaze. Shrapnel whizzed and snapped, helmets tumbled across the ground as soldiers slipped on the blood-glossed ramps and tripped on the torn bodies of their fallen comrades. The wounded clutched the smashed earth and cried as they were pelted with debris. The ground surged with blast waves as dropships engulfed in flame and smoke exploded and sent steel fragments screaming high into the midnight sky.

"Move forward, get to cover and engage!" A captain from the 444th Ranger Battalion screamed as he stood on the ramp of a transport pushing his men onto the street. "Goddamn Shock Troopers! You stay here, you're a dead man!" He rasped as he jumped off the ramp and squeezed a burst from his Bolter into a building towering over them. "Move out, goddamn it! Get to cover!"

Soldiers ran hunched over as thousands of rounds zipped through the darkness and shredded the streets. Muzzle flashes blinked furiously from windows and rooftops as Terekian troops fired on the landing zone.

"This ain't no good Captain!" A trooper growled as he flinched at the rounds snapping into the ground next to him. "We're getting pinned down!"

"Wadda want me to do, Major, file a complaint with the travel agency?"

"Gee, would you?"

"I'll add it to my to-do list right away, Sir!" The two soldiers ducked behind a smashed automobile as the dropship lifted off the ground with a mechanical groan and floated into the smoke with guns belching in sustained bursts at the buildings around it.

"Listen, Captain, get Delta and Foxtrot Companies to the east end of the boulevard most ricky-tick. One block up and to the right behind those buildings," the Major pointed, "we'll set up a fireline from there. I want Alpha and Hotel Companies three blocks up and to the west."

"Roger that, Sir, sounds like a plan!" the Captain yelled above the din of gunfire.

"Also, I want a sit-rep on friendlies in the area ASAP. I hear 1st Division stepped into the shit days ago and they're in a world of hurt. I need to know how close they are to the rally point. We got elements of the 17th Sniper Battalion and the 249th roaming these streets and I wanna know where the fuck they are! Intel also passed a report that the 249th encountered some kind of local militia in the streets."

"Militia? I thought Volengrad had been evacuated."

"Not according to Commander Noboru. Seems the homeless were left behind and somehow managed to survive the last four years."

"The 117th are already southbound, Sir. They've got heavy contact in streets of the factory district. It ain't lookin' good for them."

"Get the men forward, we need to secure this boulevard and set up a defensive perimeter for the second wave. I'm calling for Centurions on our left and right flanks. I need to get a sit-rep on how many wounded need evac."

"Shit, what a mess." The Captain flinched as a grenade exploded twenty feet from them.

"Yeah, it's a wonderful war!"

Suddenly a group of soldiers appeared from the haze. They fired their weapons at the looming buildings as they dove for cover in craters and behind vehicle wreckage.

"Rangers stay down!" one of the troopers screamed at the as he huddled behind a car, "everyone stay down!"

"Identify!" the Captain yelled over the automatic fire.

"Torres, 22nd Bravo, 1st Division! Listen, on my mark we're gonna throw out cover fire. Get your men up and follow me!"

The Major looked around at his troops scattered throughout the street returning fire into the buildings that surrounded them. "Rangers!" he bellowed into his headset, "prepare to move on this man's signal, follow him on his mark..."

•••

Tremors rattled storefronts as Centurions from the 32nd Armored Division swiftly advanced down the streets in long columns. Their engines rumbled in a unified mechanical roar as gunners propped themselves behind .50 caliber mini-guns on the turrets. Their jaws jutting out of tactical helmets with clenched teeth and maniacal grins as they tracked their weapons back and forth returning fire into the buildings. Barrels spun with bright flares as tracers stitched the chill with destructive velocity. The dark outlines of half-man, half-tank hybrids loomed in the grim shadows like ancient myths come to life in a nightmare of fire as they vanished into the haze.

Turrets pivoted to the sides and the Centurions began shelling the buildings around them as they rolled. Bombarding structures with high explosives from their 104mm Plasma Cannons. The boulevard shook with the salvos as the armored behemoths plowed through piles of rubble and crushed everything that stood in their way. Some MBT's where equipped with plows and cleared a path for lighter vehicles and troops. They pushed aside mounds of smoking debris, torn husks of abandoned cars, and bodies as they pressed toward the Clover.

Explosions flashed in rapid succession sending shrapnel spinning in every direction and plastering the walls. Everywhere the guns barked and the streets turned inside out as fountains of asphalt rose and rained chunks in the darkness. Blaster fire pulsed white with dazzling light as they slashed through the air, slicing through bone and cauterizing flesh.

The dead, the pitiful abandoned dead. With their lifelessness still tell their story as they littered the streets. The tragic expressions of release and pain frozen on their bloody faces; agape with glazed eyes they lay peacefully in the center of chaos by the thousands. Twisted and blown to pieces with the cold unforgiving storm above them, they wait in the gloomy mists for their black rapture.

Dropships lifted off the avenues and buffeted the soldiers in their hot jet-wash as they struggled to gain altitude through the chaos. Smoke swirled in the hot fumes as chainguns from the departing vessels rattled a stream of titanium at the cityscape, shredding everything caught in their raking fire as thousands of empty shell casings sputtered in the rain. Many transports collapsed on the ground, too damaged to fly or just blown to pieces from the barrage. They sat on the boulevards engulfed in flames, their hulls blackened and ripped open from armor piercing shells as their crews jumped out and abandoned them, leaving the twisted steel fuselages to smolder in the downpour...

...

I grabbed my Bolter and crawled over to Doc who lay on the ground with his hands over his head.

"What the fuck was that, a tactical nuke?" I gawked as I tried to regain my senses.

"Oh my aching head."

"Negative, there's no way…" Satch pointed at the cloud of dust up the street that was rolling toward us. "could've been a Gridbuster, but whatever it was took out the Rattleback. Motherfucker…" Satch cussed softly as he shook the soldier we were trying to help.

"Oh damn." Doc cussed as he scurried on his hands and knees to the trooper and examined the shrapnel lacerations and punctures in his chest and stomach. "He's dead. Goddamn this place! This kid had a chance of making it out of here." He frowned as he closed the young man's eyes.

"I think it's time we move." Satch said somberly. "Get the kid's tags."

As we hustled back to the alley, we heard the roar of enormous turbines overhead and saw them coming in loose formation from the north, more dropships than I could count at a glance descending over the city with unearthly wrath. A frightening sight of mechanized shadows that brought thunder to the ground. The earth shook from their sonic booms, and the night strobed from their navigation lights. The 15th Division had finally arrived. The sky filled with tracers as the transports barreled toward the Clover firing smoke rockets into the streets and deploying red flares on their final approach. We were pounded to the ground from the deep rumble of their jets.

We stumbled forward and the city raged in a melee of sounds and clipped visions. The dropships thundered, automatic fire rattled, the thump of explosions; soldiers screamed, rounds snapped by in furious whispers; the ground tremored as the city shook itself to pieces. The air thickened with smoke as time and space compressed into broken glimpses of distorted faces and fragments. Rifles seemed to float in mid-air as grenades detonated. Muzzle flashes blipped around us in unmoving specks of brilliance. Ashes froze in their drift, sprays of blood impossibly suspended in the air. The echo of guns reverberated into forever.

"Jesus Christ! They're fucking here!" Satch shouted as he covered his ears and craned at the incoming fleet of massive crafts. "We need to make our way back to the platoon!"

"Frye," Doc hollered, "we gotta split up! You need to get back to the wounded and stay with them!"

"Where the hell are you two going?" I shouted back as I watched them dodge tracers in an awkward looking dance for life. They dove behind a wrecked automobile and prepared their sprint up the avenue. They huddled behind the twisted husk when RPG's slammed into the blacktop and sent smoking chunks howling in every direction. I instinctively pressed myself to the ground and let the concussion roll over me.

"We gotta hook up with what's left of Bravo and Alpha companies!" Satch yelled through a cupped hand as he sidestepped Doc. "We're gonna need every swingin' dick at the Clover, but I need you to get back to the wounded to watch over 'em, Frye! We'll send back help from the 15th for a dust-off once the LZ is secured! Doc's gonna have his hands full the way the shit's hitting the fan!"

"Goddamn it, Satch, you can't do this to me!" I protested.

"Got no choice newsman. I need you to do this for me!" Satch flinched as bullets sparked off the vehicle's chassis. "Guard the wounded and that's a fuckin' order!"

"You're an asshole, Satch!"

"So are you, Frye. You've been a pain in the ass since I met'cha." He grinned.

I smiled back with a nod and we gave each other the finger. I watched them jump up and run full bore down the boulevard and cut into a side street. For the first time since my arrival to the Q, I felt alone. I was living on the other end of the story now, not as a journalist, but as a shooter. I had sealed myself into the new role and abandoned my job as a noncombatant observer. I grimaced in pain from the blistering rumble of the turbines above. The ships flew so low I could feel the heat from their thrusters washing over my back.

I staggered to my feet and ran toward the alley where we left the wounded soldiers. I strained my eyes and held my Bolter with a death-grip of terror; fighting to keep my balance and sanity as bullets snapped into the street. Hot splinters pelted my legs as puddles hissed and the ground rose in a dark mass of smoke, asphalt, and steel. Muzzle flashes blinked and fires leapt uncontrollably in the background as shadows mixed with the violent flickers of explosions. Tracers slashed through the gloom and I ran ragged painful steps, jumping over wreckage and craters as exhaustion pressed against my body and my muscles throbbed with the concussion of grenades. My lungs felt like they were splitting open and I couldn't get a clean breath of air. I gasped and could hear the beat of my heart in my ears. Every labored thump of fear shrouded my senses and distorted my vision into a warped blur of serenity in the midst of the disorder that whirled like a hurricane.

The moldy dead scattered in the mist emerged with every step I took. Their dull, milky eyes stared with a film of indifference as they stiffly belched in their state of decay. The smell of rot was overpowering and I gagged as I lost my footing and slipped on the slick asphalt. Out of breath and dizzy, I vomited and coughed. I staggered across the pitted ground on all fours and searched frantically for my Bolter. Bullets punched holes into the street and I could feel sting of concrete. An RPG piped overhead and a white flash of light bloomed next to me followed by a numbing roar. I felt weightless as the world spun around and I blacked out...

Floating. A hallucinogenic sensation of dreams. An awareness of suspended time and space and the absence of reality. The cherished moment of embracing your subconsciousness and finding shelter in the warmth of broken memories. Fragments of better times in one's own existence. I could feel the glow of silence. A radiant peace surrounding me and taking me on a journey back to distant a place light years away in mind and body. Home. A vision of tranquility. A morning rain in the soft mists of spring and the cool air filled with the steady chirps of crickets in the woods. The smell of wet grass and the remote howls of timber wolves in the breaking dawn as the sun peeked over the horizon. A catalogue of sounds and feelings opened into a fractured increment of time that pressed itself into the present.

...I could feel myself being dragged over the rough terrain. A tightness around my collar and the steam of breath on the back of my neck. The haze clearing slowly from my mind as the ground shuddered and my senses returned to the horrors of the here and now. A deep growl, thick and guttural, awoke me. It had me, and its drool ran down my back as it drew me across the street in its jaws. A sleek black creature, huge and powerful, pulled me to cover and I began to scream...

...

Turk and the two Freemen covered their heads as they ran down the street and rubble cast high into the sky from the immense blast clattered loudly onto the boulevard.

"Goddamn it Turk," Jammer coughed as a cloud of dust rolled over them, "I told ya that was too much Swan!"

"Over there! Quick!" Hal pointed at a small two-story office building that was blackened over by earlier artillery barrages and air strikes. The plaster facing of the structure was cracked and chipped, and piles of glass from the bay windows of its lobby lay in huge shards around the main entrance. "Hurry!"

They sprinted through the damaged entryway of the ruin and watched larger slabs of concrete falling through the haze and slam into pieces on impact.

"What a fucking mess!"

"Umm...yeah it was a bit excessive wasn't it?" Turk replied as he peered out the doorway.

"I say we hang back in here 'til this shit clears up out there." Hal sighed as he waved his hand in front of his face and coughed.

"I agree." Turk frowned. "We'll never make it to the Interchange. I can't see a damn thing. I'm gonna rummage around and see what I can find in here." Turk peeped despondently as he stepped over some rubbish into a narrow hallway.

Hal gazed at the boulevard through one of the bay windows like a lost child mesmerized in fear. The billows of smoke and ash obscured the surrounding buildings in a fog of grime and dust. He felt helpless and small as he watched his world collapse around him, and he fought to keep the tears from welling up inside.

Jammer set his rifle aside and sat down on a shredded sofa cushion that lay on top of a mound of splintered floor tile. He let out a tired sigh of relief and pulled out a bottle of water to take a sip when a hand reached out from the shadows behind him and cupped his mouth. He froze instantly in fear as a knife pressed heavily against his throat.

"MMMFFPH!" Jammer cried weakly as he dropped his water bottle.

"Slowly..." a voice whispered in his ear, "Keep your hands to your side. Hush. Get on your feet—slow and easy..." the voice threatened.

"Hey Jam, think we'll make it through this alive, bro?" Hal broke his private spell and turned to his friend when he saw the ragged soldier standing behind him with a knife. "Turk! Turk we got company!" he yelped as he raised his rifle.

"DROP YOUR WEAPONS MOTHERFUCKERS! OT SOOK SHEATA!" the soldier piped.

Turk jumped when he heard his name. Instinctively, he flicked the selector switch on his assault rifle to full auto, whipped around, and ran back into the room with his weapon ready to fire. He immediately recognized the Alliance uniform on the trooper holding a big knife to his comrade's throat. Turk could see from the dirty trails of dried blood down the sides of the soldier's face that he was injured badly. At a glance he could tell that the man had been among one of the first of the Alliance's ground forces to arrive in the city. The warrior was filthy, and judging from the condition of his body armor and BDU's, he had seen a lot of action. The stripes on his sleeves indicated that he was also a sergeant.

"Easy big fella." Turk said calmly as he lowered his rifle.

"I SAID DROP YOUR FUCKING WEAPONS OR YOUR FRIEND DIES!"

"Sir," Turk said as smoothly as he could, "we're not Terekian."

"DROP 'EM!" the trooper bellowed as he pressed the blade harder into Jammer's neck and a thin line of blood slowly emerged at the edge of the knife.

Turk nodded at Hal and they dropped their rifles in front of them and held their hands up over their heads.

"Please Sir," Turk pleaded, "you're hurting him..."

"WHO THE HELL ARE YOU PEOPLE?" the soldier demanded.

"Friends—we're citizens of Volengrad..."

"SPEAK UP! I CAN BEARLY HEAR YA!" the soldier yelled as he pulled the Freeman into the shadows.

"I SAID: WE'RE NOT TEREKIANS, WE'RE CITIZENS OF VOLENGRAD CITY!" Turk hollered awkwardly.

"BULLSHIT! VOLENGRAD'S BEEN EVACUATED FOR YEARS!"

"NOT *COMPLETELY* EVACUATED..."

"He's telling the truth mister," Jammer gasped. "Please don't cut me open!" he begged.

"SHUT THE FUCK UP THUMBDICK!" the soldier growled, then the expression on his face softened and his eyes rolled back as he dropped his knife and staggered backwards against a wall. Jammer jumped forward and tripped over a chair as the two other Freemen rushed the soldier and grabbed him before he fell to the floor.

"It's okay! It's okay!" Turk said urgently as he grasped the trooper's left forearm and hooked his own arm under his shoulder. Hal stood to the man's right side to help Turk support the trooper's weight.

"Easy does it, sergeant!" Turk grunted as they leaned him against the wall, "let's sit 'im down, Hal."

"Who—who are you people?" the soldier muttered in a weakened daze.

"Get 'im some water, Hal." Turk ordered, "Sir, you have to believe me, Volengrad was never completely cleared out when the Terekians invaded. A lot of people where left behind, and some of us chose to stay."

"Left behind?"

"Yeah, the homeless. Here, take a swig of this," Turk uncapped a small bottle of water and offered it to the sergeant. Turk took out a clean rag from his pouch, moistened it with water and began to dab the trooper's face clean. "How bad are ya hurt?"

"Grenade. My ears are all fucked up. My equilibrium is fried."

"Ya got a name?"

"Pappy."

"I'm Turk. This over here is Hal…"

"How do." Hal nodded.

"…and that's Jammer."

Jammer stepped closer as he rubbed his neck and looked at the blood on his fingers. "Oh shit, I think I'm gonna faint!"

"It's just a nick, Jam," Hal chided, "quit bein' such a baby."

"Let me see if I understand you right," Pappy grimaced, "you guys got left behind during the evacuation?"

"It's a little more complex than that."

"Tell 'im the truth, Turk," Hal frowned, "we were turned away at the gates because we're homeless, sergeant."

"How did you survive this long? How many of you got left behind? How did you get those weapons?" Pappy fired.

"It's a long story…"

Suddenly, a deep rumble rolled through the dense air. A sustained roar of giant turbo jets putting out stifling decibels reverberated throughout the boulevard as the prelude to a mechanized apocalypse. The building rattled violently and felt like it was going to shake itself apart from the thunder that drowned out the prattle of firefights. The haze in the street swirled wildly from the down blasts of hot exhausts, and loose rubbish tumbled chaotically in every direction. The shriek of hundreds of rockets being deployed from above pierced the darkness with unearthly whistles, and the Freemen dove to the floor as the missiles detonated on the avenues and billowed clouds of gray smoke.

"It's another air strike!" Hal screamed as he curled himself into a ball.

"We're fucked! We're totally fucked!" Jammer cried anxiously.

"Dropships!" Pappy shouted as he got up, staggered to a bay window, and looked up at the smoke churning in the vortexes of the incoming transports, "It's the 15th! They're planetside! They're on their way to the LZ!"

"Stay down, sergeant!" Turk hollered as he grabbed Pappy's sleeve.

"Listen," Pappy snapped, "you gotta help me get to the Volengrad Clover!"

"You're not going anywhere in your condition, sergeant. You can barely stand up." Turk replied as he covered his ears.

"Goddamn it, my unit's over there!"

"Can't let you do it. You're too messed up." Turk insisted, "But I tell ya what, Hal will stay here with you. Me and Jammer will go to the Interchange and send help to come get'cha."

"Don't worry sergeant," Jammer spouted through the calamity, "There's more Freemen out there and they're sure to catch up with us..."

"Freemen?" Pappy gawked.

"Yeah." Hal added sharply.

"...there's a good chance they'll get to ya before the Alliance will. Meanwhile, Hal here's a good man. He'll take care of ya 'til the rest get here."

"What are you, some kind of militia?"

"That's one way of saying it," Turk grinned as he held up his Terekian SDX rifle, "what we are is Volengrad's last citizens."

"We know every square inch of turf here," Jammer glared as he picked up his pack and slung it over his shoulder, "and we ain't givin' up our home. Every Freeman's pledged their life to fight for her."

"Come on, Jam!" Turk yelled as he headed for the doorway, "We need to get goin'..."

"Hal..." Jammer nodded.

"We'll be okay," Hal said with a thumbs up, "Swede and the rest of the guys should be around this area. Now go…"

•••

I flailed my arms over my head for protection as I lay on my back. I looked up into the eyes of the monster looming over me. It barked and lowered its head an inch from my face and growled. I could feel it press its full weight on me as it lay on top and pinned me to the ground.

"Jesus!" I screamed in terror, "Somebody help me! Oh my fucking god—HELP!"

"Stay down, Trooper! Don't move! They've zeroed in on your position!" A voice commanded.

I turned my head to my side and saw a soldier crouched behind a small mound of rubble peering through the scope of his weapon. Rounds ricocheted off the pavement and buzzed around me and the enormous beast. A raking fire swept over the street and clanked loudly into the overturned vehicles on the sidewalks. The soldier stood up, fired his weapon, took three steps and dove into a shallow crater ten feet from where I was about to be devoured by this creature.

"SHOOT IT!" I begged, "THIS MONSTER'S GONNA TEAR ME APART!"

"She's not going to hurt you. She just saved your sorry ass!" the soldier bellowed, "Hey, you wounded? Are you hit?"

"No, I'm alright." I bleated weakly as I tried to catch my breath. The monster licked my face and I shut my eyes tightly waiting for it to bite my face off or tear my throat to ribbons. "I dropped my Bolter."

"Yeah, it's over here in the crater. Can you move?"

"NOT WITH THIS THING ON TOP OF ME!" I coughed.

"She's not going to be able to drag you over here. The fire's too heavy and you'll both get zapped!" the trooper bellowed, "Sukie! Come here girl—JUMP, BABY, JUMP!"

I sighed in relief as the dog got off me, whipped around in a low crouch, and bounded through the hail of bullets into the crater with the soldier.

"Okay then listen," the soldier ordered, "when I get up I'm gonna throw out some cover-fire, when I do, you stay low and get your ass over here!" he yelled back at me.

"OKAY!"

"I'm gonna give you a count. On three, ready?"

"YEAH!" I shouted back hoarsely.

"*One...*"

I took a deep breath and tasted the acrid smell of gunpowder in the air. Fear pulsed through me and my heart felt like it was about to punch through my chest as I exhaled and clenched my jaws together...

"*...Two...*"

...every muscle in my body tensed as I got ready to make my jump through the whir of bullets slicing through the gloom. I felt the surge of adrenaline; a hot flood of energy filled my veins and I mumbled a quick, desperate prayer to myself...

"*...**THREE!**"* the soldier hollered.

...I shot to my feet and dashed toward the crater when I felt a heavy force on my back shove me forward and send me flying into the shallow depression in the road. I splashed into a puddle of grime and coughed as I swallowed the filth.

"Jesus, are you alright?" the soldier hollered as he tossed me my Bolter. "Sukie, stay down!" he said firmly. "Goddamn that was close! That nade blew off half your body armor."

I looked over my shoulder at the largest dog I'd ever seen in my life. The canine was clad in body armor and lying on its belly in the mud with us. Its green eyes gleamed intelligently at me as it kept its massive head just above the puddle.

I'd heard that the military used genetically enhanced canines, but I'd never seen one before. Until now, these dogs were just stories to me. There were rumors that some *actually* lived in households in mainstream society, but I'd never put any thought into it.

"Who are you with?" I asked the trooper.

"I'm with the 249th Devil Dogs. I'm Stilman. That's my teammate Sukie." He nodded affectionately at the canine. I flinched as Sukie barked a response.

"What unit are you with, soldier?" Stilman asked loudly as grenades detonated up the street.

"I'm Jake Frye, a reporter from The Metro. I was attached (had attached myself to them, I thought privately) to 22nd Bravo, 1st Division. Doc, the medic, and the squad leader, Satch, just made their way up the street. They're headed toward the Clover!" I yelled through the din of gunfire.

"You're a fuckin' reporter?" Stilman exclaimed as he gave me that 'What kind of lunatic are you?' look. "What the hell're ya doing out here?"

"Trying not to get killed at the moment. Listen, you gotta help me!" I shouted, "We just busted our asses getting some of our wounded out of the line of fire. We got'em holed-up in this alley. I see that you've got a radio, I need help with them. We need to get'em medevaced. Those boys are pretty fucked up. One of 'em may bleed out if we don't get him the proper attention."

"My headset is on a localized freq. How far up are they?"

"About half a block up the street." I pointed. "We've got to move fast. Looks like the 15th is planetside."

"We gotta big fucking problem, Frye."

"What's that?"

"Take a look around ya, in case you haven't noticed, all hell's breakin' loose."

"Yeah, it's tough to overlook that we've been getting our asses shot off."

"That's because the Company you were with prematurely set off an ambush at the LZ. There's a Terekian Division at the Clover and all up and down these streets throwing everything they've got at our dropships. We think it's the 438th Special Forces."

"The 438th?"

"What I'm trying to say is that the world just turned into liquid shit. You came lookin' for a fuckin' story, newsman?" Stilman ducked as tracers flared over the crater. "I hope you can swim or hold your breath for a long time 'cause we're in the deep end of the pool."

"You gonna help me or not?" I shouted impatiently.

"Yeah, bring us there."

"Okay. We're going to have to make a break for it." I squinted as I peered over the crater's edge and felt the wind of bullets snapping past me, "Shit we must be crazy. Follow me..."

IV

Holly crept through the shadows as he made his way up the street. He needed to put some distance between himself and the Clover. This district was too hot, and instinct told him that any elevated position in that vicinity would make him fair game for enemy snipers, and there was nothing more foolish than ignoring instinct. He needed to get to what he liked to call "the fringe". The area beyond where most snipers considered a comfortable distance for their weapon's range. Holly could push that envelope with his Pershing .50 caliber rifle without compromising accuracy and effectively hunt down Coalition snipers from a further vantage point, but he needed to get to that outer limit first.

He sidestepped corpses that had been hurled around from battle; taking special care not to kick them or look at them for too long, but the dead seemed to be watching him anyway. Their stares following his movement as they lay twisted in the most impossible positions, tracking him indifferently as he wove up the boulevard leap-frogging for cover.

If there was any truth to ancient beliefs about the souls of the dead, then Volengrad would give rise to new tales. People abruptly cut down in their prime, leaving unfinished business and their souls to restlessly wander the planet. Every war gives birth to atrocities, every atrocity has an underlying story that reveals the darkest side of the human psyche, and every dark story contains the rawness of truth; and this is the truth that we can't bear to face for the ugliness that it reflects about ourselves. There were enough dead in the streets to repopulate the city, and enough souls to haunt it for eternity.

Holly frowned at the amount of carnage that littered the avenue and exhaled sadly at the fact that it wasn't even close to being over with yet. He double-checked the sound and flash suppressor on his Kirsten Auto and flicked the selector on semi-automatic. Holly drew a quick breath and continued his journey through the street. He watched tracers zipping through the mist and listened to the distant screams of pain as he dropped behind a pile of rubble and glass next to a dead Coalition trooper.

Suddenly, a hand reached out and grabbed his right ankle and startled him. Holly hissed as he looked down and pointed his weapon at the wounded Terekian he took for dead.

"Arrtow mich..." the Terekian panted softly as he clutched his belly with his other hand, "Arrtow mich delour." He stuttered.

("Kill me."..."Kill me please.")

Holly could see that the man had been suffering for hours. The soldier had a stomach wound and half his intestines were exposed to the night air and covered with grime. Holly pulled out his survival knife and leaned into the Terekian's face knowing what the man wanted him to do.

"Arrtow mich, delour had nasha..." the soldier gasped as blood trickled from the corner of his mouth and tears welled-up in his eyes.

("Kill me, please have mercy...")

Holly nodded as he quietly put his gloved hand over the dying Terekian's mouth and shoved his blade at an angle just below the sternum into the man's heart. He buried his knife to its hilt and gave it a savage twist to the left, then to the right. The trooper twitched and was at peace. Holly pulled out the blade, wiped it off on the soldier's tattered uniform, and sheathed it. He reached up and gently closed the soldier's eyes and moved on.

Holly held his weapon tightly as he sprinted through the debris. Constantly glancing up at the buildings that surrounded him; the broken windows, the rooftops of smaller structures, smashed doorways. To his left, to his right—scanning the street in front of him, sorting through the movements in the shadows, the black outlines dancing in the fires; the smoke, the rattle of machine guns and the thump of explosions. The smoldering craters, the distorted sounds of ordnance whistling, piping, whizzing, and shrieking in the distance. Working its way through the echoes of the wounded. Their tormented voices bouncing off the walls. The faint drizzle of rain gave everything that edge of wintriness, and the sound of his own footsteps on the glossy asphalt, the purple hue of night blending with blue gunpowder mists, and the odor of wet rot put a chill into everything inside him.

Holly ran and could feel the animal fear surging through his blood as he processed everything around him. The claustrophobic feeling of the concrete hell loomed above and to the sides like giants made of stone and iron. Sensory overload, and pure, raw instincts drove him forward through the darkness.

He turned the corner of Tower Three of the Aerodyne/Genesis Corporate buildings when he was spotted by a Terekian patrol. Seven of them were moving cautiously down the sidewalk when he came around the structure and almost froze at the sight of their silhouettes. They were less than fifty meters away when their pointman saw him. One of the soldiers yelled and fired.

Holly went prone as the soldiers unloaded in his direction. Their muzzle flashes lit up the haze as bullets tore into the wall just above his head and sent marble splinters humming. He rolled across the pavement as asphalt popped around him with the sharp ping of rounds sparking off the blacktop. His saving grace was the darkness and an alleyway that he managed to slink into.

He got back on his feet, flipped the selector on his K-Auto to fully automatic, paused a second to catch his breath, then peered around the corner to get a glimpse of where they might be. He could feel the refreshing chill of the jagged shadows cast in long patterns across the smashed terrain. The hypnotic beauty of the night throwing its unholy spell on him. Holly saw the blips of their weapons and jerked his head back and felt the vicious snapping of velocity as rounds whipped by. The Terekians had spread out and taken cover behind the twisted wreckage of an armored column, and he could hear one of them shouting rash commands to the others.

Holly pulled out two pyrogen frags, yanked out the pins, and lobbed them hard at the enemy. He pressed his back against the wall as the grenades detonated and a huge ball of fire illuminated the street with a brilliant orange-white glow of heat. One of the Terekians jumped up and screamed in anguish as he was engulfed in flames.

The explosions were enough to drive the rest into the open when Holly jumped out and fired in a sweeping motion. He clenched his jaws tight as he watched their arms flail in the mists of blood before pulling himself back behind the wall.

He ejected the empty clip from his weapon and slapped in a fresh one as he pressed against the chipped wall and readied himself for another look down the boulevard. Holly caught his breath and steadied his nerves. Slowly, he leaned forward and peered at the street. No movement. The bodies of the Coalition soldiers lay motionless in the puddles.

"Christ." He whispered to himself.

Holly kept close to the side of the building, staying in the shadows as he stepped quickly toward the dead soldiers. He looked over the bodies; taking mental notes of the condition of their uniforms, personal hygiene, the types of weapons they carried as well as the standard gear they were humping.

This was a heavily armed patrol. Each man traveled with extra bandoliers of ammunition, had several containers of water and packets of freeze-dried rations. They were unshaven, dirty, and their BDU's and body armor had signs of heavy wear with the exception of one soldier. Holly raised his eyebrows as he crouched next to the trooper and surveyed his uniform for any indication of rank. This one was a Major, but what got Holly's attention was the trooper's solid black BDU's. They bore patches on the shoulders of a Terekian Special Ops unit that he didn't recognize. Holly examined the gleaming weapon lying next to the body. It was a Baron M249 Assault Rifle. Not exactly standard equipment, even for officers. This guy belonged to something different.

Holly rifled through the man's pockets for information or devices that may be of use and found a small GPS in the Major's Kevlar vest blipping the their current position in the city. He clicked the menu button and got an area map of various caches in the vicinity and a larger highlighted district a few blocks north. Whatever it was, Holly was close to something. Something important.

"Payday." Holly whispered to himself as he slipped the GPS into his pocket.

He took a single IAR and placed it in the dead man's hand (his calling card) and closed the Terekian's fingers around it as he folded the soldier's arms across his chest and closed the his eyes.

Holly glanced at his surroundings to make sure he was unobserved then ducked back into the shadows. He gave the area a visual sweep, scanning back and forth for movement, then darted for cover behind smoldering wreckage. The air was thick with the sharp smell of decomposition and it was difficult to breathe. The trees that lined up and down the boulevard were barren and smashed. What winter hadn't taken, our artillery and air strikes had, and the outlines of their branches in the mists against the flickering background of explosions gave them an eerie quality.

Holly took steady breaths as he moved quickly through the darkness. Tracers streaked everywhere as firefights erupted from building to building and automatic fire prattled from windows and doorways. He avoided contact. Remaining unseen and unheard, he steered himself through burnt-over alleys and blasted-out side streets, stepping over bodies and climbing over piles of rubble. At one point, he saw an Alliance armored column (the markings on the Centurions revealed they were from the 8th Armored Cav) rumbling toward the Clover. The armor platings on the tanks were torn and burnt, fenders were missing, and all of them showed damage from their west-end engagement. Watching the menacing silhouettes of the lead tanks push through the darkness with saber plows was somewhat comforting, but he decided to avoid them fearing the gunners manning the .50 calibers on the turrets would be skittish and might shoot him on sight.

He traveled another three kilometers through the devastation and could feel exhaustion setting into his muscles again, but he pushed himself. "Just a little further," he thought as he pressed deeper into the city. Holly looked at his watch and gasped at how much time had elapsed. It was almost midnight. He had thirty-seven minutes before the 15th made planetfall. This *had* to be it. He had to get off the streets and into position *now*. No working the fringe this time. He was going to be in the middle of it all. He chose a twenty-story apartment building to his right, and broke into a run towards its entrance...

...

"Straight ahead, Doc!" Satch yelled as they dashed through the pandemonium of firefights. RPG's shrieked by and blew holes into the sidewalk across from them, and they dove to the ground and crawled forward as billows of smoke filled the air and bullets snapped by furiously. The two soldiers covered their ears from the scream of turbines as jet wash flattened them with searing heat and a dropship emerged overhead from the haze with its cannons blazing. A technological behemoth that roared and belched thousands of titanium rounds from its mini-guns and plastered the buildings with IAR's. Satch and Doc howled in pain as they were pelted with thousands of spent casings that sizzled as they bounced off the wet street.

"Shit!" Doc shouted, "we'll never find the rest of the company in this mess!"

"They've gotta be up ahead in the LZ rally point somewhere!"

"We're cut-off, Satch! We'll never make it through this barrage!"

The night split open as fountains of asphalt rose to the sky and showered the avenue in jagged chunks. Satch reached for the handset in his pack and readjusted the frequency and volume.

"Red 2-7, Red 2-7, this is Blastgate 1-1, do you copy?" he yelled through the din of explosions.

"Blastgate 1-1, this is 2-7, go!" a voice responded hysterically.

"Reilly, this is Satch, what's your 20, over?"

"Satch, it's me, Torres, we're at 238/153 but moving."

"Torres?"

"Yeah, Reilly's hit bad. Throat wound! I donno if he's gonna make it, where the hell are you guys?"

"We're about two blocks north of you taking fire, over."

"Stay where you are, Satch." the voice crackled, "This grid is hot! We got Trolls all over our asses and the 15th just hit the LZ!"

"Gimme a sit-rep, Torres!" Satch bellowed as rounds tore into the ground in front of him.

"We got wounded everywhere and we can't get to a lot of 'em. Not sure, but I think Alpha's taken about sixty percent casualties. Charlie's about forty percent. We need dust offs ASAP. I think we're up against a brigade and they're throwing everything they've got at us. We just hooked up with some guys from the 444th and we're gonna try to flank 'em and set up a defensive perimeter."

"Roger, Torres, we've got wounded stashed in an alley northwest of us. Frye's back there by himself guarding 'em. We need to fall back and get 'em out! We're coming to you..."

•••

I crouched behind a slab of concrete trying to catch my breath as I peered down the boulevard. I rubbed my eyes and cast a weary glance at Stilman pressing himself against a pile of rubble scanning the terrain as Sukie crouched next to him. The temperature dropped again and I could feel the tingle of midnight brushing against my skin. The overpowering aroma of spent munitions lingered heavily in the mist, and I felt so incredibly alive as I watched the strobe of explosions in the background and listened to the dry barks of automatic fire echo throughout the city.

Explosions lit the gloom with brilliant colors and highlighted the skyscrapers of Volengrad with a peculiar glow that gave their silhouettes a haunting beauty. The ground rumbled deeply as if the earth was about to open up and swallow everything, and the air crackled with a strange energy as thousands of rounds hissed through the darkness and grenades ripped holes into the pavement. Fires raged uncontrollably in the ruins, consuming everything and igniting secondary explosions that sent rubble and steel flying as lightning flickered crooked fingers across the low clouds.

"How far up?" Stilman grimaced through the smoke.

"We're almost there," I pointed down the street, "see that pile of shit over there?"

"Yeah, I see it."

"Behind that is a small alley. They're in there. Some of them are messed up pretty badly. I don't think we'll be able to move 'em again."

"Jesus, Frye, how'd you get yourself into this?"

"Got lucky I guess."

"Okay, check it out," Stilman squinted, "Sukie and I will go first, but we're gonna split up. She's gonna break left and I'll charge forward to the entrance of the alley. You give us cover. Wait a few seconds, then I'll throw out some cover. That's your cue to haul ass, okay?"

"Okay."

Stilman put his arm around Sukie's neck and whispered in her ear. She barked a response as he gave her a pat on the back, checked his Bolter, took a deep breath, and exhaled. "Ready, Frye?"

"Yeah."

"Okay. WE'RE GONE!" Stilman shouted as he leapt to his feet and sprinted down the smashed boulevard. Sukie ran next to him for a few yards then cut sharply to the left onto the sidewalk and disappeared into the shadows. I jumped up and began firing controlled bursts in semi-automatic into the haze in a sweeping motion. Muzzle flashes flared from a second story window and Stilman stumbled as bullets ricocheted off the ground next to him as he scrambled desperately for cover.

I drew a bead on the pane about to pull the trigger when a volley of rounds ripped into the sill and a body slumped half out of the opening. Stilman slid behind a mound of asphalt and opened up in full auto at the window.

"Come on Frye!" he shouted as he tossed a frag and squeezed off a burst.

"Son-of-a-bitch!" I screamed as I ran into the open, jumped over a small crater, and held my hand instinctively in front of my face as shrapnel skittered on the ground. I dropped next to him panting and relieved.

"Good shot!" I stammered as I leaned hard against the wreckage.

"I thought you did that!"

"No, that wasn't me! I..."

"Over here!" a voice bellowed from the ruins of a collapsed storefront next to the alley.

We looked over and could see a heavy-set man with a beard waving us over to the brick building where he and another man took refuge. "Hurry! We got'cha covered!" he shouted raucously.

Stilman and I looked at each other and with a nod we hopped up and dashed hunched-over toward the entrance. Two men stood up from the shadows and began firing over our heads...

"Come on!" one of them screamed as he heaved a grenade across the street and dove for cover, "They're right on your ass!"

I could hear the rounds snap by my head along with the rattle of automatic fire as we sprinted toward them. We just made it to through the doorway when an RPG detonated sharply behind us and sent shrapnel spinning through the air with an evil hiss. I found myself on my hands and knees, jarred into numbness from the concussion. The room spun wildly as rounds poured in from the street and riddled the walls around me.

"GODAMNIT!" I screamed as chunks of plaster flew in every direction and the dim room flickered and quaked from the deafening thud of grenades.

Bright flashes of gunfire blinked rapidly as the Terekians skipped their rounds off the pavement in a raking fire that sizzled through the smoke in blistering fragments of molten steel. Stilman kneeled next to the older man with the beard and fired at the onslaught of Terekian soldiers. They screamed like madmen as tracers zipped through the chill and smacked sharply against the rubble. I noticed the two men were not wearing BDU's but were dressed in layers of filthy clothing.

"Oh shit, here they come!" the younger man yelled as he lobbed another grenade, "We're fucked!"

"Keep throwin' 'em, Jammer!"

"It ain't enough, Turk! There's too many of 'em!"

I crawled next to the bearded man. Took the prone position, and fired in semi-auto at the Coalition troopers advancing through the smoke. Tracers cut through the night like hundreds of tiny comets. Time stretched itself into thin, ragged strands of fear and adrenaline as the seconds imploded into a vacuum where movement became exaggerated and slow. The machine guns sounded muffled in the background. I looked at the bearded man called Turk and watched him screaming maniacally as he pointed across the street and shook his head. My jaws tightened as I aimed at a figure that popped up from behind the twisted husk of an automobile with a mini-gun. A demon in the mist. I pulled the trigger and the soldier dropped his weapon as the round hit the side of his head and sprayed blood and bone onto the building behind him.

"Keep firing!" Stilman shouted, "Sukie, down girl! Stay out of the way..."

• • •

The huge canine growled and barked loudly as she fell back into the shadows of the lobby and paced back and forth with her ears pulled back and fangs bared. She wanted out of the building badly. She usually obeyed orders, but this time Sukie's instinct for danger was too overpowering and she slipped out a side window into the dingy alley where the wounded Alliance troopers hid in the darkness.

In spite of their injuries, the wounded men had crawled forward and positioned themselves on top of the debris to see what was going on. They lay prone and peeked over the rubble at the Terekians taking cover across the avenue and firing at the building next to them.

"Oh shit, they're heading this way." one of the soldiers coughed as he flinched when an RPG slammed into the pavement and sent shrapnel humming overhead.

"Let 'em come." another replied hoarsely as he propped his Bolter on a slab of asphalt, clicked off the safety, and flicked the selector to full auto, " you boys got any frags on you?"

"Six." Another glared through the blood-soaked bandaging on his head and began to unhook them from his vest.

"Three here."

"We'll let 'em in a bit closer, then I'll open up on their point. You think you can throw 'em that far?"

"Yeah, no problem."

"Everyone get your side arms out."

"We ain't got a chance in hell, you know that." The trooper with the injured leg said wryly.

"Yeah, I know," the soldier with the Bolter frowned, "but they're gonna have to work for it when they overrun us, goddamnit."

Sukie crept up on the wounded men from behind and began to howl through the din of gunfire and explosions.

"Fuck!" one of the injured men shrieked as he turned around and saw the great beast in body armor glaring at them, "What the hell it THAT?" he stuttered as he pointed his pistol at the dog.

Sukie wagged her tail and barked loudly as she lowered her head as a gesture of submission and began to whimper.

"DON'T SHOOT IT!" the soldier with the Bolter ordered, "That dog's one of ours, mate!"

"You sure? It looks like it's gonna fuckin' kill us!"

Sukie barked enthusiastically with her ears perked up as she approached the wounded men. The trooper with the injured leg slid down the mound and began to stroke Sukie's fur, "What is it girl? What's wrong?"

Sukie began to howl, grabbed the soldier by the collar, and started to drag him to the back of the alley.

"Easy girl! Jesus my leg!" he grimaced in pain as he clutched his thigh. Sukie kept whimpering as she pulled him backwards through the puddles of water. "Don't just lie there you dumbasses," the trooper gasped, "follow us…"

•••

"Shit, I'm almost out of ammo!" Stilman cussed, "Frye?"

"Three clips." I frowned as I ejected an empty jacket and tossed it down. "Loading!"

"How 'bout you, Turk?"

"Two clips left, four grenades." Turk replied desperately, "Jammer, how much ammo ya got?"

I turned around and the other man had disappeared, his rifle and duffel bag had been set aside into the corner of the room, but he was gone.

"Where'd he go?" I flinched as bullets ripped the header of the doorjamb to pieces.

"Jammer?" Turk turned his head for an acknowledgement from his friend and saw his gear in the corner, "Jammer! Jesus, no!" he cried.

"Turk! Frye!" Stilman bellowed, "keep firing, goddamnit! They're gonna rush us!"

"We need to find a way out of here!" I yelled feverishly as I fired a few rounds then ducked.

"We need to fall back." Stilman spit as he tossed his Bolter down, "Fuck! I'm out of ammo!" and pulled out his side arm and squeezed off a few rounds.

"OH MY GOD! EVERYBODY GET DOWN!" Turk screamed in horror, "IT'S JAMMER!" he pointed across the street at the young man in rags running down the side walk at the Terekians. Jammer weaved down the street with a detonator in his left hand and a knife in his right. He had wrapped a small amount of Black Swan to his belt with an imploder ring and turned himself into a human bomb. It seemed like a crazy notion from a desperate man to make such a sacrifice, but to him it made all the sense in the world.

"If you don't stand for something, you'll go for anything." He thought to himself. And tonight a clear vision guided him. A vision of a journey that took a lifetime to realize; that it was the journey that came first, and then you made your departure. He ran through the darkness and relished the coolness of the midnight air for the first time in his life. He felt a strange serenity as he took deep breaths and embraced the thought that he would find peace on the very streets that he used to aimlessly wander years ago. Peace at last. Shadows reached out their jagged forms and clawed at his feet as he drew closer to the enemy's position. Oblivious to the sounds of automatic fire, he was almost on top of the Terekians when one of the soldiers leapt in front of him and fired his weapon. Jammer staggered with the impact of rounds hitting his stomach at point blank, but he managed to draw his knife across the soldier's throat and sever the trooper's windpipe as he kept running. Blood surged out of his wounds and streamed down his chin with every painful step. His face distorted as a cramping pressure radiated from his guts and he could feel the burn of his intestines beginning to spill out of his torn flesh. He groaned and coughed as he forced himself to keep moving. He was getting dizzy and felt the sting of more bullets entering his frail body. He was so tired, and the pain was so unbearable—it consumed all his senses like fire in his veins. He could just make out the blur of figures around him and he squinted at the flash of guns pumping velocity into his soul as he dropped his knife and took a few more steps into the group of Terekians taking shelter behind the piles of concrete and churned asphalt. By then his entrails were hanging out and some of the soldiers that saw him froze in shock at the sight of this sorrowful man falling apart in their midst. One of the troopers got up to bludgeon him with his rifle-butt, but he wasn't quick enough. Jammer smiled as he pressed down on the detonator with his thumb and lit up the avenue with a blue flash of light that swallowed them with its violent energy...

•••

Isa frowned when she spotted a Coalition sniper team lying prone next to a damaged parapet wall on the roof of a six-story building west of the LZ. She didn't see them the first time that she scanned that structure and it bothered her that she had overlooked the Terekians. Judging from the

323

amount of shell casings that lay between them, they had been half concealed in the shadows for a while. Their brownish-black ghillie suits were sparsely covered with torn rags and newspapers, a very clever disguise for urban warfare with its disruptive appearance, and they blended in perfectly with the bleak environment. Even their rifles were garnished with oily rags and matted in flat black absorption paint that made them almost invisible. This team was good at what they did. Definite pros in their mastery of stealth, but they weren't thorough enough. The shell casings gave them away. That was their first mistake. It was always the neglect of the smallest details that cost the most. They should have displaced after expending ammunition, but they didn't. That was their second mistake. Not following instinct and using common sense, and this lead her to believe that they had a prime vantage point that they weren't willing to give up so quickly, and this error in judgment would prove fatal in the coming seconds...

She scolded herself quietly for not seeing them earlier. The exhaustion of constantly being on edge must be causing her to slip and she couldn't afford to let that happen. Not now, not ever.

She got her breathing down to a slow rhythm and put the crosshairs to the left and just above the lead sniper's head and inhaled softly. In that fraction of time that she exhaled, Isa pulled the trigger back smoothly and felt the recoil of the KC-26 Pulse Rifle bump against her shoulder...

The Terekian was caught completely off guard when the cyrachromium round punched the left side of his cranium and mushroomed into a thick cloud of blood and gray matter as his skull disintegrated from the velocity. The body convulsed violently from the impact, then floundered to a stop as a dark red stream gushed from the lacerated neck into a large puddle.

The spotter jumped to his feet and cast a wild glace of fright at the buildings around him as he grabbed his rifle and began to run across the roof. Isa followed his trek through the scope and lead the crosshairs just in front of the trooper heading for an access door. She held a cold, steady gaze at the target as she exhaled again and squeezed the trigger...

The rifle nudged her again as she watched the soldier spin sideways and drop his weapon. The back of his left shoulder had been torn open and his arm dangled on a few ragged threads of tissue. He staggered forward trying to get to the door when he heard the sharp echo of Isas rifle from somewhere in the darkness. He closed his eyes the moment the bullet entered the back of his head...

Isa crouched behind the barrier and took a deep breath. She adjusted the volume of ear-bud and microphone on her headset, then moved east in a hunched-over run. She made her way through the jagged shapes of wreckage and climbed on top of a burned-out Terekian tank where she discovered the gruesome remains of a Coalition soldier slouched in a hatch. Its head cocked to the side with jaws wide open, and blackened skin from advanced decomposition clung loosely on the skull with the expression of remorse. Isa grimaced as she reached over and shoved the shriveled corpse down the hatch and shut the lid.

She could feel the cold steel against her belly as she went prone in the shadow of the turret and propped her rifle on a stowage rack. A shiver ran up her spine as the wind blew loose trash across the superhighway and the armor creaked loudly in the stiff breeze.

She was startled by a deep, sustained resonance of thunder in the distance as a blast wave rippled across the midnight sky. She pulled out her binoculars and panned across the dark horizon. The city looked dreamlike in the flames as outlines of highrises flickered against the heavens like steel apparitions.

Isa was flattened by the eruption of the tremendous Terekian ground fire filling the sky with thousands of tracers from the city and outlying forests at the incoming invasion of the 15th Division.

"Good god." Isa mumbled to herself as she set the binoculars down and pressed into the turret with her rifle. She squinted through the crosshairs and began tracking movement on the streets that were designated as the landing zones...

•••

"Doc, I think I see 'em comin'!" Satch hollered as he pointed down the dreary boulevard and cued his handset, "Torres! I think I've got a visual on you!"

"Where are you guys?" Torres crackled back, "I'm throwing down a strobe..."

"Negative!" Satch bellowed, "No strobes. Don't mark your position!" he shouted.

"Yeah, roger. Stay where you are. I see you. I see you!" Torres yelled back through the blare of machine guns.

The sharp cracks of sniper fire echoed brightly through the staccato of automatic weapons and Torres was sprayed with blood as one of the Rangers crouching next to him grabbed his throat and collapsed.

"Oh fuck!" Torres cussed as he flattened himself against the wreckage of a Terekian APC. He reached out and grabbed the fallen soldier and pulled him closer and tried to shield him with his own body, "Snipers! Everybody down! Doc! I've got a man down!"

"Goddamnit!" Doc shouted as he crawled behind a small mound of concrete and peered over the top, "Satch, where the fuck are they shooting from?"

"I donno! I didn't see shit!" Satch scowled as bullets tore into the ground in front of him.

"I gotta get over there and help 'im out!"

"Shit!" Satch growled.

"Cover me, asshole!" Doc shouted as he jumped up and sprinted toward Torres.

"Motherfucker!" Satch snapped as he leapt up and fired over Doc's head as he ran forward, "Miserable slag-eating bastards!"

"You kiss your mother with that mouth?" I shouted at Satch as I squeezed-off a burst with a Terekian assault rifle and fell into pace with him.

"She's the one who taught me how to cuss!" Satch screamed as bullets snapped by him.

"Don't worry, it'll be our little secret."

"Move! Move! Move!" Stilman hollered as he shot from the hip and followed behind us, "Come on, Turk, get a move on!"

Stilman was suddenly knocked off his feet and thrown backwards against the pavement as his helmet popped loose and bounced across the wet asphalt.

"Stilman!" I screamed as I turned around and slipped on a pile of entrails.

Bullets splattered across the ground next to me as I got up and staggered into a crater full of rainwater. The ground shook as RPG's whooshed through the mist and pounded holes into the boulevard with deafening thuds. I crawled to the edge of the hole and was relieved to see that Doc made it to Torres' position and Satch and Turk found cover behind the flaming wreckage of a dropship with the rest of Bravo Company and the 444th Rangers.

"Stilman, can you hear me?" I shouted as I looked at his body sprawled on the glossy concrete.

"Frye!" Satch yelled from behind the ruins of a collapsed building, "Goddamn it, keep your head down!"

"I need some help over here!"

"Just sit tight and don't fuckin' move!"

Suddenly, I heard vicious barks from the shadows. I looked up and saw Sukie sailing down the avenue toward her downed handler as grenades detonated and fountains of dirt rose from the heaving ground. Bright daggers of fire sliced through the billows of smoke and ash as muzzle flashes blinked from the surrounding structures and churned up the street around her. Sukie leapt gracefully over craters as the earth surged and automatic fire plowed through the chill.

"Sukie! Come here, girl!" I hollered.

But she ignored me and went straight to Stilman and came to an abrupt stop over him. She nudged him gently with her snout and could see that he was seriously wounded and began to howl desperately. She clamped her jaws down on the crumpled collar of his Kevlar vest and dragged him behind a mound of dirt. I jumped up in a hunched run and slid painfully to his side. Stilman had taken a sniper's round in the chest and his face was covered in blood, he was barely conscious and was trying to speak.

"Jeeesus, Stilman." I frowned as I grabbed his hand and pressed against Sukie as shrapnel whirred around us.

"I'm okay, I just had the wind knocked out of me." He said calmly as he gasped for air.

"Doc!" I shouted, "Doc! Trooper down!"

Sukie crouched over him without putting any of her weight on her companion. She whimpered as she licked the blood from his face and tried to comfort him.

"It's okay, girl," Stilman whispered as he stroked her thick wet fur and looked into her eyes, "It's okay, baby. Frye..."

"Doc help!"

"Frye..."

"Stilman, hang in there, man. We'll get you out of this. DOC!"

"Gimme a minute, Frye!" Doc Powers yelled frantically as he worked on the fallen Ranger.

"Frye, listen to me..." Stilman whispered.

"Stilman, hang on. Doc's on his way..."

"...you've gotta take her in for me..." Stilman grimaced as he hugged Sukie and coughed a thick glut of blood, "Jesus, I'm in a world of hurt." He half-chuckled.

Sukie's whimpering grew louder as she nuzzled her head against Stilman's face. Tears streamed from the corners of his eyes as he looked up at me.

"She's not gonna be any good in the field without me. She'll probably be reassigned as a sentry. I want her to have a home, Frye. Get her out of this fucked-up war. Give her a real life. In my vest pocket," he wheezed as his breathing became labored, "reach in, there's something I want you to have..."

"Stilman..." I whispered.

"Goddamnit, Frye, don't argue with me."

I carefully slid my hand under Sukie and reached into Stilman's torn vest. Sukie looked at me with big wet eyes wanting me to do something to help her friend, and I flinched as the avenue surged with the concussion of explosions. I pulled out a tattered strap of faded pink leather with jewels inlaid in a delicate pattern.

"That's her collar from when she was just a pup."

"Stilman, listen," I blubbered as I held the tiny collar in my shaking hand, "I don't know if I can…"

"Take it!" Stilman rasped weakly, "Promise me you'll take her home with you." his eyes closed from the pain and he was fading fast, "Sukie…" he whispered as he touched her face and pulled her close to his. He mumbled something into her ear that I couldn't hear and she whined softly as she licked his cheek. "Take her with you, Frye. Take her home…" he smiled as he snuggled against Sukie's head and passed away.

Q 6

"This war doesn't need a hero, it needs a savior."

Gen. Rachel Oss (2370-2406), Terekian General

The low clouds of a winter thunderstorm took on an eerie burnt orange color as they swept heavily across the skyline. Illumination rounds went supernova above the city and cast their peculiar white glow over the buildings and jagged shadows danced on the glossy cityscape in the small hours of early morning. The avenues flickered in violent light as brighter daggers streaked through the chill and the dry chatter of machine guns echoed through the torn boulevards. Radios squawked harshly as fire teams coordinated their positions and moved like ghosts cast in the blue mists that enveloped Volengrad with its cruel chill.

The wait. The looming superstructures stood against the backdrop of a troubled sky, towering beyond midnight and defying time. Stretching into the void. Stretching for a dawn where the daylight seemed darker than night.

This was a place where everything spun off its axis and left you off balance for the rest of your life. Shit. It took me years to understand that. It didn't matter if you were religious or how strong your faith was or if you had no faith at all, the only thing worth believing in and hoping for in a place like this was that somehow, some way, you would eventually find your balance. Until then there was just the wait...

I

Holly decided not to take the main entryway and ran to the side of the building to look for another way in. He paused to catch his breath in the purple shadows, adjusted his night vision glasses and equipment, and eyed a shattered window above him. He peeked over the sill and scanned the dark lobby for movement and listened for any sounds that may indicate if it was occupied. All clear. Holly pulled himself over and through and silently lowered himself to the floor.

He crouched and panned his gun sight around the musty reception area as he worked his way through the dark shapes of furniture past the check-in desk. A huge crystal chandelier hung from the cathedral ceilings and tinkled delicately from the vibration of the explosions rocking the streets a block away. He moved quietly through the grand hallway listening to the index of shouts getting closer and braced against a wall and watched shards of glass in a broken window work loose as the building trembled.

He could hear the deep mechanical rumble of an armored column moving in the distance, the sharp booms of their cannons like thunder as they fired salvos of anti-personnel rounds at Terekian gun emplacements that survived the air strikes of Archangel.

The air, cool, thick, and stagnant, had a heavy feel about it as he made his way through the gloom looking for the stairway that would take him to the upper floors. The years had been unkind to the hotel that must have hosted diplomats, high-powered executives, and A-list society members in its heyday when Volengrad shined on the map. Now it hosted a sniper.

He found the fire escape in the elevator atrium and carefully looked over the doorjamb for a trip wire or motion sensor before opening the door and crossing into the stairwell. Even encased in the fire escape he could hear the hollow resonance of explosions and gunfire as he ascended to the fourth floor and slipped into a darkened corridor.

Holly padded quietly through the chilly air as he clenched his Kirsten Auto at shoulder height ready to fire. The carpet was coated in a layer of gray dust and he tracked footprints as he moved along, favoring the wall to his left. No sign of anyone on this floor.

He decided to check out a room and kicked the door open into a well-furnished suite and stumbled through the living room toward the sliding glass doors to the terrace. Holly surveyed the streets and the devastation of the battle began to sink in. He felt his heart ache as he bit his lower lip and pressed his back against the wall and scanned the ghostly mists that blanketed the burning city.

He was in the center of downtown Volengrad and knew that it would be foolish to head down to the streets and expose himself. He tipped a small dining room table on its side and pushed a couch in front of it for a makeshift barricade and began to take inventory of how much ammunition he had left. He noticed a small wine rack over the kitchen counter and silently investigated its contents. His good luck held up and several unopened bottles lay covered in light dust. He reached for a bottle of red wine and smiled as he wiped off the label, took out his knife, and popped the cork off. He closed his eyes as he held the neck to his nose and sniffed the sweet aroma then took a swig. Exhaling selfishly, Holly wiped his lips on his sleeve and belched before taking another gulp. It was good and he relished the flavor as he tipped the bottle gently and took a small sip. It's been a long time since he had indulged in anything so refined and all that was missing now was a good cigar and female company.

Holly set the bottle down and picked up the Pershing .50 caliber rifle to make sure that a round was chambered before leaning it against the barricade. He stepped back out into the corridor with his Kirsten drawn and made his way back to the main entrance where he rigged two pyrogen frags over the doorway then headed back to the suite.

"Home sweet home." He thought bitterly as he set the K-auto aside and propped the barrel of the Pershing on the couch and peered through the scope. He slowly scanned the scape from left to right, checking the windows of the buildings across from him, the streets, and rooftops of mid-rise office structures, and squinting hard at the shadows lurking in the devastation. There was so much movement below and it was difficult to sift through the amount of activity as soldiers of the 15th worked through the streets.

An Angel track flanked by MBT's stood aside a building as medics tended to the wounded lying on the sidewalks. Sniper bait. "Get them inside, damn it!" He thought morbidly, "Get them off the street." Terekian snipers would be targeting this aid station and he would be ready for them. He wrapped his finger around the trigger and scoped the levels of the surrounding structures for movement in the windows. Nothing. He panned the streets again and spotted a firefight two blocks north of his position. Holly could see a trooper crouching behind a pile of rubble and a wounded soldier lying on the ground next to him as others pressed themselves against adjacent buildings for cover, they were all pinned down by what appeared to be an invisible foe.

He turned his attention to the upper floors of the buildings that surrounded them and saw the black matted barrel of a rifle sticking through a broken window. Sniper! A brief muzzle flash, the barrel recoiled followed by a dull pop that reached him a second later. Below, an Alliance

Ranger spun and fell to the pavement. Another trooper grabbed the fallen soldier and pulled him to cover as a medic rushed through the mist to his aid.

Holly didn't have a clean shot at the sniper behind the trigger. He was hidden behind a torn concrete wall. If he fired now the Terekian would displace and vanish. Frustrated, he grabbed his gear and moved out to find a better vantage point. He worked his way down the hall toward the unit at the end of the floor and kicked in the door. Time was running out for the men on the street and he had to act fast before another one of them was picked-off.

Holly slid the glass arcadia door of the terrace open, stepped out onto the balcony in a crouch, and propped the Pershing on the handrail. He panned the scope to the building adjacent from his position and relocated the window where the Terekian sniper still held his ground. Caressing the trigger, he got his breathing under control as he sighted-in the enemy and pulled the trigger.

The rifle bumped his shoulder hard in its recoil as his shot rang through the streets and the soldier's body was thrown back from the impact. Holly chambered another round when the glass door behind him exploded and showered him with thousands of bright bits of glass. He went flat to the floor wondering which direction the shot came from as he crawled backwards into the shadows of the room and rolled behind a counter that separated the formal dining room and a kitchenette.

A shot rang in the distance and a round tore into the cabinets above him, the glass contents inside of them shattered as the splintered doors swung loosely on their hinges. He pressed against the formica garbage module as two more rounds punctured the refrigeration unit next to him with hollow "thunks!" and the assortment of wine glasses that hung on a small carousel was knocked off an overhead cabinet.

Suddenly, the floor shook violently as explosions ripped through the corridor outside. Smoke and flames mixed with screams of pain and wild shrieks of men being burned alive filled the hall. Terekians had tripped the pyrogen frags as they came through the stairwell.

The seconds stretched on uncomfortably as he listened to his enemies perish in the flames. He got on his knees and peeked over the countertop just long enough to see a muzzle flash blip from a shattered window in the upper stories of a highrise a hundred and fifty meters north of his position. A fraction of a second later the round hummed across the counter and blew the faucet off the kitchen sink and sent water spraying into the air with a hiss as it shattered a toaster-oven behind him.

Holly popped up with the Pershing, leaned against the counter as he put the crosshairs on the enemy sniper and pulled the trigger...

...The Terekian cursed loudly as he watched water spray in front of his target. He shouldn't have missed but he did. He squinted through the scope as Holly's bullet smashed through the lens and entered his left eye and took out the back of his skull...

• • •

I reached over Stilman's face and closed his eyes and Sukie began howling loudly with her head raised to the midnight sky in grief. A desperate and beautiful creature lost in sorrow.

"Frye!" Satch bellowed, "Frye! Get your fuckin' head down! Stay put. Both of you! We can't see where the snipers are."

I grabbed a hold of Sukie's collar and strained to keep her flat to the ground. She looked at me sadly and whimpered softly as she glanced at Stilman's body.

"I know, girl, I know." I said reassuringly as I stroked the fur on her neck and pocketed the pink collar. "You're going to be coming home with me. I promise."

The night seemed to close in as I craned at the buildings and wondered which ones housed our assassins. The world a purple hue of shadows, deep and possessed with a lifeless chill that gripped your bones and rattled them harder than any type of ordnance going off next to you could do. It was the kind of shiver that mixed with fear and robbed you of your senses.

Airborne surveillance drones weaved through the skyline and their metallic whines echoed in symphony with gunfire and distant explosions.

"Frye listen up!" Satch yelled, "We've got inbound gunships for air support. E.T.A. is about ten minutes."

"Ten minutes? Shit, I could be dead by then."

"We're gonna get you outta there. Just don't do anything stupid. Don't move."

I pressed myself against Sukie and tried to keep calm and gazed at the superstructures that loomed indifferently around us and listened to the crack of guns in the background. There was a rapid succession of explosions half a block away that shook the ground and dropped fragments of concrete on us and I covered Sukie's head with my helmet as chunks of asphalt hit the street and broke into smaller pieces.

"Okay Frye," Satch yelled, "we're gonna pop some smokes. I want you to wait 'til it gets heavy and when I tell ya to make a break for it you and the dog haul ass this way and make a dive for cover, you hear me?"

"Yeah I hear ya!" I yelled back and flinched as stray rounds ricocheted off the street and hummed by.

Satch and Torres began tossing smoke grenades around us. They detonated with dull pops and hissed as thick gray smoke billowed into the chill of the early morning air. Sukie squirmed beneath me but I held her down as we were engulfed by the cover and could no longer see the buildings around us.

"Frye!" Satch hollered with a rasp, "Make a break for it! Now!"

"Come on girl!" I grabbed Sukie's collar and gave it a hard tug as I leapt to my feet and ran toward Satch. A shrill whistle pierced the darkness above us as we jumped over a crater and dove behind the wreckage where Satch reached out and pushed me to the ground.

"INCOMING!" Torres screamed as the night was split open by mortars. The ground heaved as fountains of concrete rose into the sky with a roar. Everyone ducked as it rained fragments of cement and smoke swirled over us.

"Goddamn it," Doc grimaced, "we need to pull back! We need to get the wounded to an Angel Track ASAP!"

"Torres, where the hell is our air support?" Satch demanded.

"Two minutes out according to Falcon!"

"We ain't got two minutes! It's them fucking snipers, they must've called in our position to flush us out into the open!"

The ground rumbled hard as more rounds piped in and ripped into the boulevard. The smell of gunpower was overpowering as we hunched helplessly against piles of debris in the face of the barrage. Six troopers with KC-26 Pulse Rifles appeared from nowhere and moved forward into the shadows. Snipers. I could see them giving each other hand signals through the haze of dust and smoke. One of the Snipers held up four fingers and pointed at different buildings. Then they scattered and moved through the mounds of twisted steel and asphalt like predators closing in on their prey. One of them crouched and raised his rifle as he leaned against the husk of a car and fired into the upper floor of a structure in an alley east of us. He turned to someone in his fire team and gave him a thumbs up as they got up and repositioned themselves further up the street.

This game of cat and mouse continued for a few minutes until the high-pitched whine of four Razorback gunships filled the night. Their engines screamed as they flew slowly over the boulevard with blinking navigation lights and their hot exhaust washed over us as they passed overhead. We instinctively ducked as their chain-guns barked and peppered the structures; shattering glass and splintering the faces of the buildings as they took turns making their pass. The savage muzzle flashes entranced me as the door gunners opened up with the mini-guns and poured a stream of fire into the upper floors.

The men cheered loudly and raised their fists in the air and Sukie began barking as the ships came to a hover over our position like guardian angels. Their turbo-fans buffeted us and I could see these gunships bore the signs of battle damage from the amount of bullet holes that had riddled their armor plating. Some of their panels were completely missing and one ship had a section of its tail torn open from what must have been a missile hit. They were here, and I was glad. I felt safer knowing that they were around and I felt the sudden urge to want to be in one so that it could take me home.

I couldn't decide if it was better to be on the ground or in the air. Perhaps it was worse being in one of those machines because they went wherever the troops went but they seemed to be more vulnerable to fire. Especially those door gunners. The Crew Chiefs had to be insane to volunteer for that position.

Foot soldiers always looked at these gunship crews with envy because they knew that when they flew back to their base camp after a mission the crew could get a hot meal, shower, and would be sleeping in relative comfort. But when you saw one of those gunships flying fast and low into a curtain of ground fire your heart leapt and would skip a few beats and you always hoped they would make it through. When you saw a gunship get shot down or disintegrate in mid-air into a ball of fire you could feel your stomach twist into a knot and it really brought you to your senses and made you wish you hadn't seen it at all. It must be terrifying flying so fast toward what might be your own death.

"Hey an objective's been added!" Torres spouted as he held a headset tightly to his right ear and covered his left to muffle the sound of incoming rounds. He looked at Satch and frowned as he flinched hard at the sound of a near by explosion. "Defiance picked up some intel on activity going on at a cemetery. Volengrad Shadows. They can't get a satellite image and every aerial drone that's flown over that area's been shot down. They want us to investigate. It's a search and destroy."

"Ah shit!" Satch cussed, "Where the hell's the cemetery at? Someone get me a GPS. What the fuck is it called again?"

"Volengrad Shadows." Turk said solemnly.

"And who the hell are you?" Satch snapped.

"I'm the one that can get you there better than any GPS can."

"Frye, who is this mutt?"

"It's a long story, Satch, quit being such an asshole and listen to him." I demanded. "This man's lived here all his life and he's part of a local militia."

"Militia? Thought everyone was evac'ed from this shithole."

"Not everyone, sir. They call me Turk." The scruffy man replied calmly as he watched the Razorbacks depart and extended his hand with a tattered glove as a gesture that Satch took.

"Satch."

"Hey Satch," Torres interrupted, "I got a location on the cemetery. It's…"

"Fuck the GPS, Torres. Get the men together and get 'em ready to move out."

"Roger that."

" We got ourselves a guide." Satch nodded at Turk. "You look thirsty old man," Satch said with a softer voice as he unhitched his canteen, "here, take this."

"Much obliged, soldier." Turk smiled gratefully.

A brawny Ranger decked-out in black body armor approached Satch and removed his tactical helmet and ran his fingers over his shaved head, "Satch, a word with you?" he sighed as he looked at one of his wounded teammates lying on the ground.

"Yes Captain."

"Listen, that Torres is a damn good man. We owe him and your company our asses back there at the LZ. I've got beau coupe wounded and an Angel Track in route with some tank support."

"Thank god, sir."

"Where you boys headed?"

"We just got word from Command to investigate a cemetery about half a klick west of here. Apparently there's Troll activity in that sector."

"22nd Bravo's been through some shit. We'll take your wounded off your hands 'til the Dust-off's get here. You guys definitely rate some fucking slack."

"Roger that."

"Excuse me gentlemen," Turk said grimly, "pardon the interruption but I couldn't help overhearing your conversation. Satch," Turk pointed, "about three or four blocks that direction there's a group of wounded soldiers in an abandoned department store. At least what's left of one, and a couple of blocks south of them is a trooper that I think belongs to your group. He's with one of my friends hiding in a building. He's a sergeant, I think he said his name is Poppy or something like that..."

"PAPPY!" Satch exclaimed.

"Don't worry troop," the Captain said as he lit a cigarette, "I'll send out a couple of fire teams to get 'em," he said reassuringly as he pulled out a small pad of paper and a pencil and handed it to Turk, "draw me a map of how to get to them, old timer."

"Torres, how we doin'?" Satch bellowed as he checked his weapon and bandoliers.

"Good to go Satch."

"Okay listen up! 1st Platoon on me. 2nd and 3rd Platoons with Torres." Satch ordered. "Watch your spacing, fuckers, I'm taking point. All right Turk, you're with me. Lead the way."

We moved single file over the cast of shadows until Turk took us though a wide alley filled with garbage and decomposed bodies strewn about. The sharp odor of rotting flesh made me wretch and I vomited twice as we jogged through the darkness. The flash of explosions flickered jagged stripes of light against the dingy walls and exposed faded posters of coming movie attractions and painted vandalism of days past: "Terran bastards chew dick", "Chino was here", "It's not gravity, the world just sucks!" and a multitude of other sayings and cryptic tags sprayed with hasty hands that only the street prophets would understand. All symbols that this city once held life instead of the death that now flourished in its streets.

Satch held his fist in the air as a signal to stop and we came to halt at the end of the alley. Everyone stood opposite each other with our backs to the wall and our weapons ready as we tried to see what lay ahead. Word came down the line that we would make a run for it in groups of eight. A boulevard had to be crossed and there was a thick group of trees on the other side.

Turk led the first group through and I could see them sprint into the mist and vanish. Satch leaned against a dumpster and peered around the corner of the building before he let another group of soldiers through and I moved up closer to the outlet into the street. Sukie nestled against me quietly and I looked at the grimy troopers across from me as I waited my turn. I could see that fatigue had worn deep lines into their faces and their eyes were sunken and hollow, and for the first time I wondered if I looked as bad as I felt.

One soldier fidgeted with a photograph and stared at it when the man next to him leaned over and looked at it too.

"That your girl?" He whispered.

"My wife."

"She's pretty."

"More than I deserve." He grinned as he put the photo back into his breast pocket.

We were the next bunch to go. Satch stood next to me and looked at Sukie. "Looks like you've been adopted Frye." He nodded then poked his head out to glance up and down the street. "Okay listen up. See that wasted APC there?" He pointed. "On my mark, haul ass and stop there for cover. Wait for the signal from the guy on the other side of the street to tell ya when it's clear. When you get across, take a position in the treeline. Stay out of sight and keep quiet until everyone gets across. The cemetery's not too far from there. Everyone get that?" We nodded silently and readied ourselves.

"All right men. Go!"

We dashed over the sidewalk and dove behind the torn husk of an APC. The boulevard was glossy like a black mirror and was littered with parts of what used to be a Terekian armored column that was stopped dead in its tracks by an air strike, and the burnt remains of their crews were still trapped inside. I kneeled next to Sukie and scanned the brick structures that lined the avenue. They looked surreal in the haze, pocked with bullet holes, ripped open, and reduced to piles of debris. Illumination rounds diffused their glow and outlined the Clover in the background. A dull gray structure flickering in the night, it looked like a great phantom looming over the city, cold and dead.

My hands ached as I held the rifle close to my chest and kept my head low. The temperature had dropped a few more degrees and a ground fog eddied at the treeline and began to work its way toward us. Turk waved us in and we got up and ran for cover. The muscles in my legs felt baggy and throbbed dully as I ran across the lanes and ducked into some thick shrubs. I felt the warmth of Sukie's body against me and she looked up silently into my eyes. Everyone loses something in this war and it was the cruelest of all to the animals. Her eyes sparkled in the dark, wet and intelligent. She understood that she had no one else and that I was it. I reached over and stroked the thick fur on her neck. I wanted to loosen the buckles of her body armor but knew that would be a mistake, so I unscrewed the cap of my canteen and gave her a drink of water instead.

Volengrad Shadows was a huge cemetery where the most affluent citizens of the city had been buried for generations. Aside from the iron gate on its immediate border, trees grew outside its perimeter and we entered the thickest section called the Groves, which, according to Turk, used to be a haven for the cities homeless population. It was 4am now and a stiff chill clung to us as we moved carefully through the trees. Silhouettes in the haze walking in line like a morbid parade of dirty phantoms. The thin carpet of dead leaves rustled with every step and there was the occasional snap of a twig as the ground fog swirled lifelessly at our feet.

Narrow footpaths spidered in every direction but we stayed off of them fearing the booby traps that could put anyone of us in a world of hurt if one were tripped. I could hear the faint whine of drones circling in the distance as I watched Satch taking the time to watch were he put his foot for his next step. Turk walked next to him as they led us through the gloom. He seemed confident in his knowledge of the area but that wasn't enough to take off the uneasy feeling we all carried inside.

Suddenly an explosion sent leaves and dirt spraying into the overhead foliage shattered the morning. I hit the ground hard and Sukie barked and ran forward as we were showered with dirt and pebbles.

"Goddamn it! Fucking place is booby trapped!" Satch screamed. "MEDIC!"

"There's nothing left of him Satch!" Someone yelled.

"Torres is down!" Another soldier hollered shrilly.

"Davey!" Satch bellowed as he ran toward him.

I got up and ran to where Sukie was dragging a body across the mud...

•••

Holly set the Pershing down for the Kirsten auto and moved toward the door that led to the hallway. Black smoke curled under the crack into the apartment and he could see the faint flicker of a fire on the other side. He wondered how many he'd killed with the Pyrogen frags but it was irrelevant now. He had to get moving and find a new location before more Trolls showed up.

He grabbed his gear and shouldered the Pershing. Holly was about to step out when he turned around and picked up a bottle of wine that survived the duel.

"Hate to see such a good vintage go to fucking waste," he thought as he opened the door, stepped into the hall and came face to face with the largest Terekian soldier he'd ever seen.

Holly instinctively swung the bottle of wine and smashed it against the trooper's head then gouged the side of the Terekian's throat with the jagged edge of the bottleneck. The soldier dropped his rifle and clutched his face as he staggered backwards into the flames before regaining his balance. His face was lacerated and covered with blood and he looked like a demon rising from the fire.

Holly moved in to throw a punch when he caught a blow to his jaw that made lights dance in his eyes and dropped him to the floor on his hands and knees. The Terekian stepped forward to kick him when Holly reached up and sank his fist into the Troll's groin with a quick jab. The Terekian groaned loudly as he doubled over and picked Holly off the floor and threw him into a smoldering wall.

Gasping, with the wind knocked out of him and struggling to keep his focus, Holly blocked a punch with his Kirsten and the Terekian yelped as his fist made contact with the weapon with a dull "tink!" but the soldier managed to grab the gun with his other hand pulled it out of Holly's grip and tossed it aside like a toy. This man was strong and incredibly pissed-off as he glared and wiped the blood from his eyes.

All Holly could do in his daze was back up as the angered troop threw another punch that grazed his face and knocked a hole into the wall beside him.

"SHIT!" Holly exclaimed as he ducked another blow and jabbed at the man's chin with a hard smack that only angered the Terekian more.

"Rasvatz nawer dir shala!" The soldier growled as he pulled out his knife.

(I'm going to skin you alive!)

Holly centered himself in the smoke filled hallway as the trooper stepped forward and began to slash at him wildly. Their shadows danced on the walls as he dodged each swing. The Terekian lunged with a low jab at his gut, but Holly sidestepped the attack and managed to smash the soldier's nose with his elbow.

"FUCK!" The Terekian yelped as blood gushed down his chin.

"Come on motherfucker!" Holly jeered through clenched teeth as he let the Pershing fall from his shoulder and reached for his bowie knife.

They faced each other as the fire around them grew and crackled, knives drawn, stooped over, grimacing, hissing, and lashing out within the confines of the corridor walls. The floor vibrated as the world outside shook from the ongoing battle as armored columns rumbled through the streets and automatic fire echoed between the buildings.

Holly switched the knife to his right hand and slashed up at the Terekian's face but missed as the soldier took a step back then leaned forward and drove his blade halfway into Holly's left shoulder.

"AAHHHH! SHIT!" Holly screamed as he staggered sideways and slammed into a wall. Blood soaked his fatigues heavily and he knew the pain would grow worse as the seconds passed.

The Terekian drove his knife into Holly's left side but he grimaced as Holly sank his blade to the hilt into the soldier's thigh and gave it a savage twist, "Kiss my ass, shit-for-brains!" he coughed.

"YAAAA!" The trooper screamed in agony, "Turn-cilo sea!"

"Fuck you too, buddy!" Holly let his knife go and punched the soldier's nose as hard as he could. Blood erupted from the Terekian's face and gushed down the front of his uniform. Holly gave him a left jab to the throat and could feel the pain from his shoulder shoot up his arm and his guts burning.

They both buckled and fell to the floor as flames danced around them. Holly was exhausted and crawled to his Pershing as he held his wound. He was bleeding badly and getting lightheaded and could see his own blood trailing on the floor. Sweat glistened on his face as he fell and began to pull himself toward the weapon. The heat pressed against him and he groaned when he reached for the rifle.

He was starting to lose consciousness. The room slowly fading into a black spin as his vision began to blur and his punished body throbbed with wicked pulses of pain that consumed his very being. God not here. Not like this. After everything he'd been through, to just bleed out and die on the floor like an animal. He felt so weak. So helpless. His strength ebbing away as he stretched for the Pershing. The pain was tremendous and he labored for every breath as his fingertips touched the steel of his rifle. He felt a great weight on his wrist and looked up to see the Terekian's boot on his arm. The Coalition soldier stood over Holly with his knife and grinned, exposing hideous bloody teeth through his split lips. Behind him the fires flickered and outlined his figure as he grasped the gleaming knife with both hands and raised his arms to deliver the final blow that would end Holly's life. It would be swift and decisive. It would be merciful. Holly squinted at his foe. His face was calm and he was ready.

Suddenly the floor heaved with an earsplitting crash and the plaster ceiling rained on them. The Terekian was knocked backwards and Holly had just enough time to roll over to his side and cover his face as the hallway filled with a cloud of smoke and dust and the entire floor slab beneath them collapsed. They fell through the next two levels and vanished into a huge pile of debris.

Out on the street a column of Centurions whirred and clanked by as Alliance troops flanked them in a leapfrog fashion for cover. The foot soldiers broke into smaller groups and began to storm into the buildings in search of the enemy. The thin red beams of their laser sights cut through the darkness as they moved through the piles of rubble and twisted steel like phantoms. Their dark shapes outlined by the bluish mist from the rain and billows of smoke from smoldering wreckage. The purple sky lit up from illumination flares that floated gracefully above the streets of Volengrad as radios squawked and troops filled the shadows.

...

Torres was on his back and his face was covered with blood and filth. The lower part of his torso had been sheared off from the spinning fragments of the mine when the man next to him stepped on the tripwire and triggered it. The armor on his chest was shredded to ribbons and his intestines were a tangled pink and gray mass beside him. Sukie howled as she stood next to him and began to sniff around the area. Satch kneeled over him as Turk took cover behind a tree and peered down the sight of his rifle as he scanned the woods along with the rest of the company.

"Davey can you hear me?" Satch sobbed as he looked at the broken body of his friend and took his hand. I could see that Torres was still alive as he turned his head to look at Satch and flexed his fingers open and closed in Satch's hand. His lips were moving but nothing came out. "Oh god, look at ya! You're a fuckin' mess!" Satch was shaking when he bent down and hugged his buddy and tried to wipe the blood off of his face. "No. Not you too." He whispered. "Not you too."

Torres looked up with faint recognition, sighed, and passed away as Doc kneeled next to him then reached down to close his eyes. Satch was crying hard and his body convulsed as he put his hands to his face and wept bitterly, "I can't take this shit anymore."

"Satch..." Doc whispered woodenly.

"I can't take anymore of this!"

"Satch, listen to me. Reilly's gone, Torres is wasted, and Pappy and Collins are W.I.A. The company's yours now Satch. You need to get a fucking grip and take us the distance. The men are counting on you."

The words from Doc alone seemed to sober him up a little and he quit shaking.

"Okay, just give me a minute alone with 'im."

"Make it quick, we need you more than ever, man." Doc said gently as he put his hand on Satch's shoulder and got up and left him to say goodbye.

I kept an eye on Satch as he took Torres' dogtags and small personal belongings that he could find. I glanced around to keep track of Sukie's whereabouts as I crouched behind the trunk of an enormous moss covered tree trunk. The ground fog had gotten thicker and visibility was cut down to less than forty meters. I felt the cold drop of dew on the back of my hand and I looked at the black moss that hung above me; thick and moist in the stillness, I swear I could almost hear it breathe. Its wet pulse keeping silent time of genesis and decay.

I rubbed my eyes and stared at the outlines of drooping branches fading into the grayness knowing that somewhere ahead was the cemetery. That thought alone dried my throat with an apprehensiveness that tightened the muscles on my back and made me want to crawl away. There are a few times in my life that I can recall when I was scared, but nothing has come close to the fear I've been subjected to here at the Q. It was a new dimension. Foreign territory that was probably best left unexplored, but I took the voyage anyway, like a moth drawn to light. It was a senseless flight in every direction but took you right to the source in the bitter end. This was the kind of fear that froze you and turned you inside out. You forgot everything, and the seconds stalled as you floated in the moment. The brink, when you could feel your grip on sanity slipping and you couldn't help but wonder what it would be like to let go. To finally let it go.

"PSSST! Frye!" Doc said in a low tone and he moved next to me.

"Yeah what's up?" I whispered.

"Stay here. Whatever's up ahead at the cemetery is waiting on us now. That explosion gave away our approach."

"Yeah, I've got a bad feeling about this but I'm *not* staying behind."

"It's your ass, Frye." Satch said quietly as he crouched next to us. His eyes were puffy and red but he had managed to compose himself. "You've gotta be the most stubborn son-of-a-bitch I've ever met, newsman."

"Hey Satch," I grinned.

"Yeah?"

"Fuck you."

"Thanks." Satch smiled weakly.

"Hey no problem, you know I'm always here for you."

"I feel safer already. When you get home and write your story you better not make me look like a dick."

"How 'bout if I make you look like an asshole?"

"That'll work." Satch shook his head. "Okay, I'm going back on point. Pass the word. Arrow formation by squads and we'll sweep to the boneyard. 1st squad leads. Everyone keeps their eyes open for tripwires and anything that looks fucked up. I want at least eight meters between men. Doc, you and Frye walk tail end Charlie with 4th squad and E.O.D. 1st squad on me and Turk. 2nd and 3rd squads take the flanks one-eighty left and right. I want the FCT's spread out in the middle and tell 'em to get in their coordinates to the Redlegs and have 'em on standby. Moving in three minutes."

"Roger that." Doc nodded.

Satch scooted up to Turk's position where I could see them pointing the direction we were going to take. They stood up and walked forward at a slow pace with their weapons held at the ready and the rest of the company seemed to emerge from the brush and trees like ghosts and spread out around me. Sukie nudged my side and took the lead. We were all in bad shape. Sunken eyes possessed with that stare filled with fear and numbness. Unshaved faces darkened by fatigue, dirt, and sleeplessness. Drooping shoulders that carried the weight of the world and the burden of survival, and torn uniforms and body armor filthy with mud and an indistinguishable mixture of grime and blood. Seventy-three souls moving through the woods. Seventy-three souls hoping to see the dawn...

•••

Isa stayed in the shadows of the smashed armored column as she jogged down the lane of the interchange watching the skies light up from high altitude flares. She saw the dark outlines of drones hovering and weaving between the highrises like nocturnal predators on the hunt. Below, sections of the city flickered bluish-white from muzzle flashes and explosions and the echo of machine guns rattled in her ears. The haze had thickened and she was now too far above the streets to make anything out. Isa had to get back down to street level to be an effective sniper on overwatch.

She pushed her way into a stairwell with her sidearm drawn and began the long descent to the ground. Even in there she could hear the hollow reverberation of explosions bouncing off the walls. The vision of the 15th's planetfall kept playing through her head. She had never seen an invasion and it was paralyzing to witness the power. All those dropships in the dark sky thundering above the streets was a frightening and astounding sight.

Isa swore to herself that she would keep an eye on Bravo Company but she lost track of them in the chaos. She may not be able to find them now but at least she could find another vantage point where she could snipe and provide some protection for the ground forces.

She reached one of the lobbies that led to the street and felt a cool draft coming through the shattered bay windows. Rats scurried across the dusty terrazzo floor in a panic leaving tiny prints in their wake. She took a deep breath and moved slowly through the gloom, keeping close to the scattered ruin of furniture for cover. Isa was startled when she caught a glimpse of a corpse sitting in a chair across from her and grimaced at the cobweb nest filled with tiny spiders in its mouth. The body had been there a while and was basically a skeleton held together by dry tattered skin turned black and stretched tightly across the joints. Its head tilted to the side and the hollow sockets were locked in an empty gaze into eternity. She decided that she had met enough tenants for the night and it was time to get the hell out of here.

Several Centurions rolled by and shook the ground as their treads grinded into the asphalt and left obscene ruts of crushed rubble. Isa put away her pistol and drew the rifle as she stepped outside into the shadows of the foyer. The twisted husk of a dropship smoldered on the boulevard and she could see Alliance Rangers rummaging through the wreckage for survivors.

Suddenly one of the soldiers was jolted hard. He clutched his chest as he was spun off the transport to the ground where he lay motionless. The troopers shouted at each other to take cover as a couple of them retrieved their comrade and dragged him into the fuselage. Isa ducked behind a slab of concrete and panned the crosshairs over the terrain and surrounding buildings. She spotted a Coalition sniper on the third floor of a bombed-out edifice eighty meters away peering through a jagged hole in a wall.

Isa adjusted for the elevation and put the crosshairs on a gray helmet that was partially visible in the haze that hung in a thin layer above the street. She squeezed the trigger and watched blood splatter in a random pattern of red on a grimy wall as the body slumped lifelessly in the broken structure.

•••

Satch signaled everyone to stop and motioned to take cover. In the distance, dogs barked followed by agonizing screams and gunfire as elements of the 249th ferreted and flushed-out Terekians from their positions in the city. The faint squawk of radios carried in the darkness along with the tat-tat-tat of automatic fire and the thump of explosions. I kneeled behind a rotted log tangled in thick vines and squinted to see what Satch and Turk were doing.

Sukie's ears were pulled back and she stood motionless as she stared at something in front of her.

"What is it girl?" I whispered as I clenched my rifle tighter and strained to see what had captured her attention. She bared her fangs with a low growl and I noticed the fur on her neck was standing up. "Shhh, easy girl…" I reached over to grab her collar but Sukie pulled away and began a low crawl through the shrubs. "Sukie, come back here!" I said a little louder and attempted to grab her again but she was out of reach and broke out into a dead run through the woods.

At that moment Satch and Turk stood up and opened fire, "FUCKING CONTACT!" there was a tremendous flash as the earth heaved and fountains of mud sprayed high into the air with the paralyzing roar of explosions. I saw several soldiers engulfed in an orange flame and torn to pieces in the blasts and a wave of heat rolled over us. The concussion

349

shook the ground and bounced me sideways into a puddle of mud. I crawled through a thicket of reeds as the soft earth was churned by a stream of bullets and branches snapped above me.

"Gunners forward!" Someone shouted hoarsely before a bullet punched through his head with a spray of blood and hair that sent him reeling backwards into the bushes. The night filled with the blips of muzzle flashes less than twenty-five feet in front of us. Clouds of gray smoke swirled with the smell of gunpowder when we heard the angry shouts of Terekians. I got up and dove into a fold in the ground next to Satch. Tracers snapped through the chill as leaves showered us and I could hear the enemy screaming as they tried to advance on our position. I could see figures in black uniforms weaving through the woods and ducking for cover.

"Watch the flanks damn it!" Satch bellowed as rounds tore up the tree trunk next to him. "You dirty motherfuckers!" He screamed as he spun around and squeezed off a burst. "Turk keep your ass down! Frye what the fuck are you doing up here! I told you to stay back!" Satch ordered as he fired a burst.

"Kiss my ass, Satch, since when did I ever listen to you?"

I could see the cemetery in the haze. The weathered headstones and mausoleums stood defiantly behind a foreboding veil of time and sorrow. Volengrad Shadows. Even in the midst of the chaos that tore this world apart it stood silently. Separate and dark. Acres of the dead. Once loved but now names carved in stone that outlasted the memories of their owners by generations. For a chilling moment I thought I saw their souls as part of the mist. Expressionless faces by their graves in a wicked and elegant slow dance to faint violins. I blinked and they were gone.

Around me men screamed in terror and pain. The moist earth trembled as explosions thumped like a huge beast plowing its way through the trees, pulling them up by the roots and tossing them aside in its path of destruction. To my right a soldier covered in mud stood motionless in the open; trapped in a gaze as his poor body absorbed the impact of bullets. His eyes dull and a smile on his face as he raised his left arm with a sweeping gesture of graceful death before he fell and vanished into the ivy.

Clumps of dirt flew in every direction as rounds shredded the ground and blaster fire sizzled through the foliage. The air snapped as if charged with savage electricity, it hummed and popped like it was going to burst open and spill itself like a liquid. A trooper blindly ran by me with his hands to his face, his neck lathered with foamy gore. He was lifted into the air as a mine detonated with a flash under him and I was sprayed with torn flesh and blood. I screamed as I wiped my eyes and clawed forward, pulling myself through the grime and mud. I was going to lose my mind.

"Get me an FCT!" Satch shouted back. "I want a fire mission!"

"FCT forward!" was passed back from man to man. I saw Doc running through the shrubs trying to get to a wounded trooper when a mortar whistled in and punched a hole in the ground in front of him. The explosion flipped him sideways in the air and he landed on his feet still in a dead run in our direction. Somehow he was unhurt and the word miracle doesn't even begin to describe what I just witnessed.

A trooper with a radio pack strapped to his back slid in next to us and settled next to Satch. He put his hands over his Tac helmet and his eyes shut tight as another mortar dropped in and shrapnel split a thick tree trunk in half. God he was young. He must have been one of the replacements that joined the company before we entered the city.

Satch looked at the soldier with surprise, grabbed him by the collar, and pulled him into his face, "Do you have the coordinates dialed in for the boneyard?"

"Roger that!" The soldier yelled back.

"Make the call! Tell 'em we're being overrun! I want AP rounds and put 'em thirty meters danger-close in front of us!"

"I'll have to make some adjustments!"

"Do it!"

The radioman looked at a small GPS and flinched every time a bullet snapped by. I could see his hands shaking hard and he grimaced as he punched in the final numbers for a grid. I was startled when Doc scooted to my side and grabbed my arm.

"What the fuck!" Doc gasped through clenched teeth. His hands and face were covered in blood and dirt.

Satch fired the Fulcrum and rolled to his side to reload. "Loading! Goddamnit I'm almost out of ammo and my charger's low!" Doc and I kneeled simultaneously and squeezed off a burst to cover Satch. I saw a Coalition soldier peering from behind a tree through the SDX's sight and pulled the trigger rapidly three times. He dropped his rifle and clutched his neck as he was spun around from the impact.

"Jesus there's too many of them!" I shouted in a panicked tone.

"Keep shooting Frye!" Satch ordered as he jumped up, strafed the treeline and dropped back down, "Fuckin' Trolls!"

"Rover-6, Rover-6 actual! This is Blastgate 1-1 requesting fire mission, over!" The FCT barked into the handset.

"Copy 1-1, Six standing by fire mission, over." A woman's voice answered calm and mechanically.

"AP warheads on my mark, Zulu 5-3-5, X-Ray 2-7-..." the soldier stopped in mid-sentence and floundered in the mud for a second and was still. Doc reached over and turned him over to his side. All that remained of his face was blackened cauterized flesh peeled and melted to the side of his skull. It was completely devoid of features, and the back of his Tac helmet had a smoldering hole in it.

"SHIT!" Doc cussed as glared at the mess that was once a young man.

"Doc?" Satch asked between machine gun bursts.

"He's dead."

"Gimme the radio!"

"It's wasted Satch!" Doc snapped as he fired his rifle and ducked down, "LOADING!"

"Well get another FCT double quick!"

"What do you want me to do, pull one out of my ass?"

"Well goddamnit we're just plain fucked!" Satch flinched as a volley of automatic fire tore up the ground to his left and sprayed dirt at us. "Where's Turk?"

"I don't know!" I yelled back.

Suddenly we heard the familiar and reassuring whine of turbo-fan engines overhead and the treetops swayed from the exhausts of a low flying Razorback. The night was ripped open from the sustained bursts of a chain-gun and a stream of tracers and rockets plowed the earth. The ground fog swirled in huge circles from the gunship's jet wash and leaves fluttered in tornadoes through the chill as Coalition soldiers were blown apart by the steel bird of prey.

"Fuck it!" Satch growled, "1st Platoon move forward!" he screamed hoarsely as he stood up and tossed two grenades then ran forward. The rest of the squad got on their feet and rushed through the woods firing their Bolters and screaming at the top of their lungs. "CHARGE!"

I leaped up and joined the advance, adrenaline pumped through my veins like fire and I screamed. We were on the scent of blood. Faces stretched with rage. Pure instinct and fear drove us through the flickering darkness; wailing and howling like pack animals, without pity or mercy. Primal and savage, we charged baring our werewolf teeth as we drew closer to the retreating Terekians. We were on them. They tried to run but we came as an angry swarm of the bloodletting damned. Killing everything that stood in our way. I stormed through the thick shrubs and vines as a frightened Coalition soldier tried to get away. He turned around and I shoved my barrel to his face and pulled the trigger. His head vanished into a red cloud of gore and I tasted the salt of his blood on my lips. His body convulsed in the mud and I fired more rounds into it and started kicking him, listening to the crack of his ribs as I killed him over and over again. I stomped him until I was drenched in his blood.

A huge shadow floated through the air and I saw Sukie tackle a Terekian. He raised his arms to his face and screamed in terror as she sunk her fangs into his throat and ripped it open. I ran to her side and brought the butt of my rifle down on his head and sprayed us both with black blood as his skull opened up. She stood with her front paws on the dead soldier's chest. Her fur matted with blood and muscles glistening in the dull light.

She raised her head triumphantly and let out an unnerving howl that sent a chill down my spine.

We pushed forward. Stumbling over roots and vines. My head felt like it was full of cobwebs as we reached the cemetery. Suddenly the earth heaved and mud flew in every direction. I threw myself to the ground and crawled behind a small rock formation as the world erupted with automatic fire and clots of dirt flew in the air. Tracers strafed inches above me as rounds chopped and shredded the vegetation. The Razorback banked a hard left over the cemetery when a red streak flashed from the ground leaving a trail of smoke and slammed into the gunship's side with an earsplitting explosion that sent fragments of steel humming through the darkness in flames as the fuselage hurled to the ground and bloomed into an orange and white ball of fire.

"Hydra's!" Someone hollered.

"Everyone down! Stay in the treeline!" Satch bellowed as he squinted at a row of tombstones behind hedgerows that lined the gated perimeter of the burial ground. "Frags out! Everyone get your frags! I need satchel charges, now! We need to take that fuckin' gate out!"

"Give 'em here! Quick!" A wide-eyed reedy kid that looked too small for his BDU's motioned the others as he collected four satchel charges. There was something about his demeanor that reminded me of Scat and I did a double take to make sure I wasn't seeing a ghost. "What's the plan Satch?"

"Okay listen up!" Satch said urgently with a low voice, "On my mark, toss some frags past the hedges. When they blow, give me some cover fire. I'm gonna run out there and drop these satchels next to that section of gate." He pointed, "Pour it on hard, boys, those Trolls are dug-in and I don't want my ass twisting in the wind."

"You're covered, Satch, just give the word."

"All right fuckers..." Satch squinted as he set down the Fulcrum and took hold of the satchels and mouthed, "3...2...1...NOW!"

Five troopers from 1st squad stood up and threw grenades at the first row of stones, they detonated with a flash of white as mud and clots of earth were blown high into the air. We got up and began firing our weapons with sustained bursts as Satch sprinted toward the gate hunched-over. The ground popped around him as the Terekians opened up with a heavy machine gun. He stumbled forward and slid painfully sideways into the hedgerows and set two satchels against the iron gate. He crawled another ten feet and dropped the other two next to an ornamental post that held the sections of wroth iron together. Satch paused for a second before getting back to his feet and making the mad dash back to our position. The mud was kicked high as rounds ripped into the ground behind him as he dove the last few feet next to us.

"Fuck what a rush!" He laughed maniacally as he rolled over and reached for the Fulcrum.

"You're out of your fucking mind Satch!" I yelled through the din of the firefight.

"Bite my ass newsman!"

"What're you threatening me with a good time again?"

"You know the offer always stands, you poge!" Satch spit as he fired in semi-auto. "Down to my last drum."

"You think we got a chance, Satch?" I winced as a bullet ricocheted off the small boulder in front of me.

"At the moment, shit no."

"God I really hate this place!"

"I'm not real fond of it either."

"Hey Satch..."

"Yeah."

"Merry Christmas!"

"Go fuck a reindeer."

The darkness strobed with violent flashes of automatic fire. The constant bark of guns highlighted by grenades blowing the ground open and sending burning fragments spinning through the chill. Men cussed or called the names of their loved ones as they were held by the grip of fear, but they held their ground. This is where they will die. On alien soil with their comrades.

The wounded screamed and clawed at the mud as they frantically pulled themselves across the soft moist earth. There was so much incoming fire the ground looked like it was boiling in some places as thousands of bullets sputtered into the soil and riddled the trees. Mortars shrieked in overhead. That horrible, shrill whistling crashing through the leaves and fracturing the ground with craters. Shadows moved in and out of the dark. Glimpses of phantoms in the flickering woods. Nightmare stalkers in the gloom. The fog heavy upon the soil with a life of its own. A half-life organism consuming the dead with its eerie glow, stealing their last breath and leaving their faces gray.

I saw Doc crawling on all fours trying to get to a wounded soldier as blaster fire hissed around him. The ground rose against the purple sky and he vanished. "DOC!" I screamed as I jumped up and ran to where I just saw him. Out of breath and scared shitless, I felt the hollow pang of loss in my chest growing by the second as I scanned the smoldering terrain. And there he was. Lying on his back in the ivy fifteen feet from the blast. His body armor and Tac helmet had been blown away and his uniform was in blood-covered ribbons hanging off his lacerated body. His legs and left arm were gone and his chest was burnt and smoking.

"OH SHIT! DOC!" I cried as I fell to my knees beside him and felt his neck for a pulse. It was weak but he was still alive. His eyes fluttered open slowly. His face was covered with cuts and black and sticky from grime and blood and he spoke softly, "...water..."

I fumbled for my canteen, put my hand under his head and raised it gently as I pressed it to his lips. "Doc..." I sobbed as he looked at me and sighed.

"I'm not gonna make it am I?" He said tenderly.

"P-Please Doc, just hang in there..."

"No, it's my time."

"Please don't go." I whispered as I reached down and held his hand and pressed my face against his. "Please."

"I think I'm done now, Frye."

"Okay." I trembled uncontrollably. I could feel the sobs tearing out of my body and I thought my heart was going to explode.

"Goodbye, Frye. Another time and another place." He said softly as he squeezed my hand and stared at the dark sky.

"Another time and another place." I closed his eyes and hugged him. A thin violet line appeared on the horizon. A cold and blue light that slowly began to spread in the heavens. Dawn had finally arrived.

There was a thunderous roar of angry voices approaching from behind me. I looked around and was startled to see a huge rabble of men emerge from the haze. They were moving at a jog as they plowed through the undergrowth carrying Terekian rifles, chains, hatchets, machetes, and every imaginable item that could be turn into a weapon. They were scruffy and layered in dark secondhand clothes with red bandanas or rags around their necks. They were Freemen, and they had come in force. Hundreds of them picking up their pace to a run as they drew nearer. Eyes gleamed with determination. Plumes of breath from gritty faces streaked with black and red paint or concealed behind ski masks. The citizens of Volengrad City had come to make their stand.

I grabbed Doc's Bolter and stumbled backwards as they rushed by me when I spotted Turk leading the main group down a muddy path. He raised his rifle grimly above his head; "FREEMEN!" and the sound of hundreds of voices shattered the darkness with a cheer as they charged through the woods to the cemetery. I turned around and I ran with them until we hit the edge of the treeline where the heat came from behind rows of tombstones, sweeping machine-gun and blaster fire that sent men head down into the shrubs. Running on their hands and knees for cover.

"BLOW THE GATE!" Satch bellowed, and the ground shook as it rose into a dark muddy fountain of rocks and flame leaving an enormous gap of twisted iron and burning hedges next to a smoldering crater. We got up and stormed the graveyard through the thick smoke as machine guns rattled and the earth heaved. Everything spun in a blur. The silhouettes of Freemen running in the haze, tracers slicing the air, and the flash of blades being drawn and sunk deep into flesh as the sinister outlines of moss covered stone angels and gargoyles watched indifferently from their monuments through the willows. I tripped on a toppled headstone and ended up on the steps of a mausoleum that had white marble lions posed at the entrance.

I watched the pandemonium in terror as the Terekians and Freemen clashed into fistfights in the mist. Skulls were smashed in with rifle butts, weapons fired at point blank, and knives jammed into ribcages as the battle turned into a savage street brawl. Hallowed ground was churned into a gruesome mixture of blood and mire in the early morning light as bullets shredded the ground and riddled headstones. I tried to get a bead on the Terekian troopers but it was impossible to tell who was who in the calamity.

Satch emptied his magazine into a Coalition soldier's belly and splattered entrails against a small statue of a cherub. He stood up as a Terekian came from behind and stabbed him in the side. He groaned as his flesh was opened wide and doubled-over face first into the mud. The Troll was about to drive his blade into his back when Sukie rushed the soldier and bit his groin. The Terekian shrieked as he dropped his knife and Sukie shook her head violently from side-to-side and tore his genitals off. She knocked him to the ground and snarled viciously as she clamped her jaws around his throat and snapped his neck.

I saw a Terekian on top of Turk with his hands around his throat. Turk struggled wildly tearing at the Troll's face, but the soldier was a lot bigger and overpowered him. The Terekian was cursing as he held Turk down then began slamming his head repeatedly against a fallen headstone. "TURK!" I shouted as I ran over there and rammed the butt of my Bolter into the side of the Troll's face and sent him flying off. The soldier got up and spit blood but I brought my rifle up to waist level, pulled the trigger, and blew his head apart. Turk coughed hard to catch his breath as he crumpled into a ball. I could see that he was seriously wounded. "Hang on Turk, I'm gonna get you out of here!" I reached down and pulled him across the lumpy terrain as tracers slashed overhead and a laser frag detonated a few meters away and sent brilliant daggers blistering through the pale light. A Freeman next to me clutched his face and dropped to his knees when he was hit by blaster fire. I could hear his skin sizzle as he thrashed uncontrollably on the ground trying to scream, and he vomited blood on himself as he clawed at the air. His face was gone. I shot him in the head and began to dry heave as I put my foot into the chest of a dead Terekian that had been blown in half.

I held on tight to Turk and began to scream when a tremendous flash of red blinded me and I felt a searing heat wrap around my body. I felt like I was lifted off my feet by a deafening sound that spun everything around me into a kaleidoscope of intense colors of bright lights. I could feel myself drifting through them; a cold weightless journey like a hallucination of being frozen against an invisible wall. Suspended in time with a thin layer of ice over my eyes; sight and sound blurred and lost. On the ground beneath a shattered sky, broken glimpses of bodies half buried in mud, combat boots running near my face; everything gone black under muffled gunfire, hot breath and steam. The cold smell of rot and moisture, open grave, and darkness again. My broken body being pulled into cold earth. So cold...

"Stat!" Hollow voices echoing and the shadow of an unfamiliar face floating over me. Words filtered thorugh a time warp; Death has come, and she beckoned calmly. A warm sting in my arm. I sighed and I saw nothing...

Q 7

It was a bright Volengrad day. The sky was a crystal blue and the promise of warmth came with the rays of sunshine that blanketed the broken streets and avenues. A feeling of hope welled from deep inside some forgotten place of my subconscious as I looked at the city's skyline towering around me. I could see black smoke from the fires in the distance but the jewel of the Q still stood proudly and had survived the night. The ground vibrated as Alliance armored columns clamored heavily through the boulevards.

My eyes felt grainy from dirt and fatigue as I lay on my back and tried to remember what happened. I turned my head and it came to me slowly as I took in my surroundings that I was still in the cemetery and a dark gray wool blanket was over me. Bodies of the dead and wounded littered the churned terrain as medevacs came and went with a steady whine of turbo-fan engines headed for Defiance. I felt a small tickle on the side of my face and found myself looking into Sukie's eyes. Her body armor was off and she huddled next to me with a bark. I tried to sit up to pet her when a sharp pain shot up my left shoulder and I groaned as I tried to catch my breath.

"Take it easy Frye." A voice said calmly. It was Gerald McMillan.

"What..." I rasped softly.

"You're hit pretty good."

I looked down and noticed my ribs had been bandaged up and my armor was also gone. "How bad? What happened?"

"You got lucky," McMillan grinned, "why don't you ask him?" he nodded his head.

Satch smiled as he sat up and draped a blanket over his shoulders. His head was bandaged along with his abdomen and left leg. "Goddamn this hurts." he grimaced as he put his hand to his side. "Lucky ain't the word. Mortar dropped right next to you, newsman, and blew your ass clean off the ground. Guess you just got scratched up and scorched. Didn't even take a frag." He shook his head then looked at Sukie. "You know, that dog of yours saved us. Pulled you, Turk, and me out of the shit."

"Turk."

"They evac'ed him to Defiance two hours ago. He's gonna be all right but he lost his leg." Satch said solemnly.

"Mac what are you doing here?" I asked as I stroked Sukie's fur.

"I came in with the second wave." McMillan frowned. "Damn, this place is fucked up." He said dryly as he looked around at the carnage. "You know you're the first journalist that's been out in the field in over a year? You've made a name for yourself in our little circle. Ya done good Frye."

Two Medics had worked their way over to us. They looked tired and overworked and their fatigues were stained dark with blood. One of them walked up to Satch and checked on his dressing, "Think you can stand soldier?"

"I can manage." Satch nodded but the Medic helped him to his feet anyway.

"You're on the next dust-off out." The Medic said wearily. "You're going to Charlie-Med at Defiance."

Satch limped stiffly over to me and extended his hand. "Looks like this is where we part ways Frye."

I got up with a bit of effort and shook his hand. "Take care of yourself Satch." I said somberly as I fought back tears welling in my eyes.

"Goodbye newsman."

I watched him limp slowly to the LZ with the Medic to a waiting Osprey. The edge of the landing zone was lined with rows of body bags awaiting transport to New Sierra and an odd feeling of dèjá vu came over me as I gazed across the battered graveyard at the wounded being carried on stretchers or hobbling up to the Medevacs. I sighed with quiet reverence as McMillan gently put his hand on my shoulder, "It's over Frye. It's time to go home."

HOME IS A FOUR LETTER WORD

"The crush of a long time, many years across my back

Blue truth on the airwaves, and living in the matter-of-fact

In a Place where it's said, not a tear's ever shed

I'm goin' home now. Back to my hometown..."

From the song *"Back Home"* by Crimson Reign (© 2405 *Suntek Music*)

I stood elbow-to-elbow in a sea of jungle and tiger stripe fatigues at a departure gate at the New Sierra Gateway Interport waiting to board the dropship that would take us up to the F.S. Cambridge. We were going home. Unshaven and baggy-eyed, I had aged a million years in a matter of weeks. Even the guys in their early twenties looked old. It was all in their eyes as they stood silently watching the runway on the other side of the tempered glass; night after night of minimal or no sleep, freeze-dried rations, long patrols, and constantly being on the edge for over a year had caught up with them and pure exhaustion had set hard and deep in their faces.

I could've taken a civilian flight but I felt comfortable riding with the troops. I wanted to go with them. Needed to. For closure. I traveled so far in so many ways I had to go the distance. A sergeant with the 4th Division adjusted his crutches as he leaned against a wall and wordlessly looked around with an expression of disbelief that he was really here. He had made it through.

Civilians walking through the concourse quietly looked on as they passed and children pointed and stared with eyes of wonder. Some people came to the departure gate to shake a soldier's hand or hug them...bringing embarrassed smiles from the troopers as they blushed at the sentiment. But for the most part it was a very calm and organized affair. The troops stood in faceless masses. Each lost in their thoughts and dreaming of this day. DEROS.

My digital recorder hung loosely around my neck as I tightened my grip on my bag and stared at the gate and blinked heavily. I felt empty and spent.

A surreal feeling hung over us as we listened indifferently to announcements pipe over the P.A. systems and echo arrivals and departures through the concourse, all blurring together and not making any sense. Numb to the environment, but with just enough energy to do that very last thing—go home.

Q 8

January 28, 2407

Before my departure, I spent a couple of months getting my head back on straight at the Weshaur back in New Sierra. Shit, who was I fooling but myself anyway? It will take more than weeks to decompress from something like this. I was in daily contact with my editor John Ryan back at The Metro and he had been gnawing his fingernails since he got word that I made it out of there. I guess McMillan was right, I was the first journalist to go back to the field in over a year and the word made its rounds within the community.

Volengrad was still not secured but the jewel of the Q was definitely in the hands of the Alliance now. There was still savage street-by-street fighting and the rumor was that the remaining Terekian forces there were going to take it to the last man standing. Something that will take months before the end would be resolved. Just one more piece of information that had to be stored away.

I had traveled a long way to find the absolutes in life, and upon reflection I wondered if I had been paying attention. That first day of my arrival at the Pegasus Mountains as I walked through the LZ among the troops should have taught me what to expect; the body bags lined-up and waiting transport back to the world tipped me off but I learned nothing. Otherwise I would have just gotten out. Absolutely out and back to New Sierra. There was a Sergeant Major on the Normandy that tried to talk me out of making planetfall when he found out I was a journalist, "You sure you wanna go? There's some fucked up shit down there." I told him I knew what I was doing, but he knew I didn't, he chuckled and shook his head as he wished me luck when I boarded the dropship.

There was a bar and grill on 34th and Emery called the Renault that drew troopers on leave as well as the press. It was a good source to tap second hand information if you talked to the soldiers that spent their time there. The terrace provided the perfect vantage point that overlooked Emery Avenue and I'd sit there with the others watching the hustle of pimps, pounders, and pushers. The street was always in motion: black-market exchange rates, fevered lust, gangs, red light takedowns, pickpocket jive, students, businessmen, soldiers, undercover ops, sweat and heavy breathers, hawks versus doves, holy men and demons; a schizophrenic circus of cheap neon and carnival barkers advertising the human fetish of life and death.

The Renault itself was a wonder. It was almost like a bunker inside with its dim blue and yellow lighting and smoke-filled air. The music blared with heavy metal and industrial sludge from cheap speakers, and once in a while (the owner said) the touch of psychedelic nostalgia of a long dead velvet voiced swooner backed by a scratched brass section—it was so out of place that it fit. This place was a magnet for the Aggressor Forces and Infantry. A pool stocked with Snipers, Recondo's, and Scouts. Brutal and furious soldiers from the darkest pockets of the war. They all flowed here and disregarded rank and Division.

The stories. God, the stories told. Often with that drunken gleam that only a soldier can have as they looked at your dumb ass and smiled knowing that you would never understand or retell it. Their words would be like machine gun fire sometimes; rapid and sharp like they were running out of time and about to overheat. Sometimes it was understated and they didn't bother with the details, "Ah, you know, we got bushed on the last patrol and gave up ground. Everyone greased and we bugged." A rifleman from the 7th Infantry confided as he raised his shot glass and grinned.

The Scouts were the one group there that always sat at the same tables and eyed people with a deep suspicion. You never wanted to make eye contact with any of them if you could help it. Tribal mercs feared the Alliance forces, but the Scouts and their methods of killing terrified them. They knew that the Scouts spoke their language and studied their culture and religious beliefs. They knew how to live off the land and move through the forests invisibly, and it scared the tribesmen. The local mercs were superstitious and believed that the Scouts were a little more than human. They believed them to be the personification of the evil spirits in the forest sent by an avenging god to prey among men. The Scouts knew this, and capitalized on their beliefs by using the most savage ways of killing. They were a cold group of dread and mystery.

After packing on my last night I stood out on the balcony of my room smoking and wondering how I could possibly write a story that would do justice to the men and women I met here. The whole experience defied standard vocabulary. It was raining again, and in the distance the thunder rumbled in the heavy skies, leaving the glossy streets to reflect the fuzzy glow of streetlamps.

The journey. A new year. My nights were filled with dreamless sleep on the F.S. Cambridge so I made it a habit to explore the ship's levels during those aimless hours. Thinking about the last few weeks was as exhausting as the experience itself. Information overload of the senses. There was far more than I could remember and process and it seemed that my mind had almost shut down. I was tired and my bones ached with a dull throb as I walked back to my quarters and sat on the rack. I yawned as I shut off the light and slowly slipped into darkness wondering how far from home I had strayed in the last hundred days.

Q 9

December 16, 2407

Morning. The rain drizzled through the valley as I stood on the front balcony of my house admiring the scenery while I balanced a cup of coffee in one hand and felt the cold moisture on the stainless steel handrail with the other. Sukie sat regally next to me surveying the dense treeline that stretched for miles before us. Occasionally, rays of sunlight peeked through the cloud cover and added silver highlights to the edges of the incoming cloudbursts as a cool breeze brushed against my face.

We stood quietly together in the pale light. A calm reassuring silence understood between us as we gazed in awe of the sheer beauty of the morning glow.

Overhead I heard the high-pitched cries of a hawk. I looked up and saw the bird of prey floating in the wind; weaving lazy circles over the acres of woodland. Its cries echoing through the valley—so remote, and so alone. I felt a hollowness inside as I thought back to Volengrad and remembered the hawk I saw that afternoon when Willie was killed. Odd, I can't even remember what he looked like now. But my thoughts began to drift back to the people at The Q. The weak images of their faces blurred by time; growing sharper with memories of another life. Another surreal life in some kind of parallel universe of frozen chaos in a world of contradiction and hopelessness.

It's been a year since my return, and I still sleep with the lights on hoping it will keep the shadows in the corners. I also made it a habit to keep a pistol on the nightstand next to my bed—"Lock-n-load, troop, ain't nothing more comforting than hearing one go into the chamber".

I never dreamed when I was at The Q. Maybe it was a way the mind protected itself from everything that happened and everything I saw. But I dream now. Visions of skeletal skyscrapers in half-light blanketed by blue mist and flames. Hazy fragments of conversations with faceless people where we never really talked, but transferred our thoughts in a dark understanding of the unspoken word. Vague blips of laughter and screaming entwined and held together by anxiety and knotted in the storm cloud of memory. It seems my dreams were never really lost, but only misplaced in some dark corner of subconsciousness until they could be dealt with later. But now they have emerged and have found their way back to me across the light years. Bringing their gray fear and the feelings of bleakness and loss along with the faces of Pappy, Scat, Satch, Doc, and Willie. My friends. My dear friends.

I see now that there were really two wars that were fought. The one that brought Terekian aspirations to a stop in their quest for empire, and the one that remains in the hearts and minds of the soldiers that fought it. For those that made it through, there was only one war worth remembering, and that's the one that puts the edge into the night after the lights go out. The one that hibernates but never sleeps. The one that would one day let them come home from that dark frontier. Maybe this time for keeps.

The hawk cried-out again as it looked down upon the lush forest. I looked back up and a flashflood of memories rushed through me, leaving me short of breath and gasping with heartache and sorrow. I felt a hot stream of emotions building-up inside and working their way to the surface; making me dizzy and weak—oh God. Oh dear God, please help me...I remember everything now—"Another time and another place." Their faces are clear. I remember. And I wept.

Epilogue: Crosshairs 12/25/2406

General Oss put on her beret and sunglasses as she contemplated their defeat. It was a long grueling war and she saw the end drawing near. It was just a matter of time before she would be hunted down as a criminal, tried, and imprisoned. She knew the Terekian High Council would topple and their empire would crumble after this campaign. As the Alliance took back Volengrad, all that was left was to escape city limits and vanish into the forests of Uluwatu Valley until the Armada could send a ship to pick her up.

She longed to see the shores where she spent her childhood and could almost feel the sand and cool water washing over her feet, hear the cry of gulls, and smell the brine of the ocean spray in her face. She thought about the good friends she lost under her command as she surveyed the long boulevard that led to the Clover. Sacrifice. There were too many of them. She had not slept in four days and was very tired as she stood in the shade.

The wintry sun shown brightly and cast the long shadows of highrises on the streets. Columns of black smoke bloomed into the atmosphere from the fires that burned through the night, but it was refreshing to feel the warmth of daylight on her clothes. In a strange way she was glad it was almost over. A sense of relief filled her thoughts as she stretched to work the kinks out of her muscles.

She looked at the city's architecture for the last time and found herself still in awe of their designs. Simply the most beautiful skyline she had ever seen and she would miss it greatly. She paused briefly for one last look as she opened the door of the car...and the last thing she heard was a faint pop in the distance that sounded like gunfire...

Isa set down the rifle as blue smoke curled lazily from the end of the barrel. She rubbed her eyes and was glad the night had finally ended.

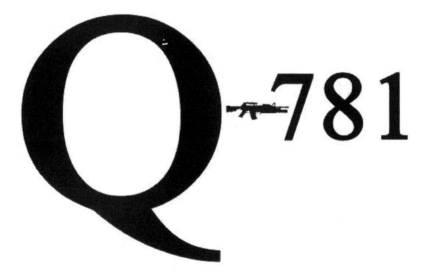

GLOSSARY

Angel Track: Tank converted into a first aid station.

AO: Area of Operations.

APC: Armored Personnel Carrier. An all-terrain vehicle reinforced with reactive armor used to transport ground troops.

AP Warhead: Anti-Personnel explosives contained in ordnance delivered by armored vehicles; three hundred anti-personnel "packs" are contained in one warhead. Each "pack" carries ten thousand steel "darts" that disperse in a 120-degree arc when detonated on impact.

Armored Wing: Designation of a group of Fighter-Interceptor and Fighter-Escort air/spacecrafts. There are eight Squadrons per Armored Wing, and twenty to thirty crafts per Squadron.

Artie: Slang for Artillery.

Aurora: Undulating sheets of light in the sky. They are caused by gases that become excited after being hit by solar particles. Most auroras are 100 to 250 km above the ground.

Bakkus: (pronounced: Back'-us) Sometimes intensionally mispronounced as "Because". Bakkus is a solar system composed of sixteen inhabitable planets with similar atmospheric and gravitational characteristics as Earth. The most heavily populated and primary planet of the Bakkus solar system is Q-781 (also called "The Emerald Planet").

BDU: Battle Dress Uniform/Utilities.

"Boonie Voodoo": Term used by Alliance ground forces—specifically Infantry and Aggressor Force troops in reference to the ancient art of black magic. The superstitious belief developed by soldiers attributing "special powers" to an individual, thereby giving that person control over death, injury, and fate itself.

Bopper: Battlefield Oriented PreProgrammed Robot. Class A unmanned weapons platform usually clad with reactive armor.

"Burning the pipe": Phrase used by pilots meaning to fly with engines in full afterburner to maximize speed in a short period of time and distance.

C and C: Command and Control.

Cell: A group of air/spacecraft flying in formation. There are usually eight to ten crafts that compose a cell.

Cherry: Slang term used to reference an inexperienced soldier. A soldier or unit that has never been in combat.

DEROS: Date Eligible to Return from Outer Space duty. The rotation date of an Alliance soldier (Infantry and Aggressor Forces) that marks the day when their Tour of Duty ends (Forty-eight months) and they are discharged from military obligation.

Drones: Unmanned airborne automaton capable of flying long distances and is usually equipped with cameras, infrared sensors, and EMF jamming devices. Can also be modified as a light weapons platform. Class A drones (military) utilized as weapons platforms are also known as "BOPPeR's" (see Battlefield Oriented PreProgrammed Robots).

Dropship: A large heavily armed VTOL interspacecraft with reactive armor used to transport large amounts of troops and heavy equipment from the outer limits of a planet's atmosphere to the ground in a short period of time.

DSA: Deep Space Assignment. When a soldier is sent to serve on another planet, satellite, or orbiting society in a space station outside of Earth's solar system.

Dust off: Slang for the medical evacuation of wounded soldiers via gunship, medevac, or dropship.

ECM: Electronic Counter Measures.

EMF: Electro-Magnetic Field.

EOD: Explosive Ordinance Disposal. A team of specialists trained in the disarmament of explosive devices.

Exosphere: The outermost layer of Q-781's atmosphere. The exosphere goes from about 400 miles (640 km) high to about 800 miles (1,280 km).

The lower boundary of the exosphere is called the critical level of escape, where atmospheric pressure is very low (the gas atoms are very widely spaced) and the temperature is very low.

"Fangs out": Pilot phrase meaning weapons are ready to fire.

FAV: Fast Attack Vehicle. A two or three man all-terrain vehicle armed with a .50 caliber machine gun.

F.C.T./FCT./S.C.T.: Forward Communications Technician/Forward Comm-Techs/Satellite Comm-Techs. Also referred to as radiomen or "SCaT-men".

FNG: Fucking New Guy.

Frag: Grenade.

"Freq": Frequency.

"Front office": Slang name used to reference the cockpit of any air/spacecraft.

FUBAR: Fucked Up Beyond All Recognition.

Ghost Rider: Slang term used to reference NOVA-31 pilots.

GPS: Global Positioning System. A computer used as a navigational aid.

"Gridbuster": Slang name referencing a high explosive tactical device delivered by air in the form of a missile or smart bomb that can be set to detonate at a certain altitude or on impact. It was given this name by Alliance soldiers for the amount of damage it can do once delivered to the target zone.

Gunship: Heavily armed VTOL (Vertical Take Off and Landing) craft used in close air support missions for ground troops. Also called "Hogs" or "Slicks", they also serve as medevacs and troop carriers.

H/K mission: Hunter/Killer operation. Term exclusive to gunship pilots when they fly sorties into enemy territory in search of targets to destroy.

HALO: High Altitude Low Opening. A tactical parachute jump from a high altitude that requires the use of an oxygen tank to breathe; the parachute is opened at 3,000 feet. This particular type of deployment into an area is used to avoid detection of the soldier's insertion in a hostile environment.

"Hot LZ": Phrase meaning that a landing zone for aircraft is under enemy fire.

HUD: Heads Up Display. A computer targeting and identification system used as a navigational aid.

Hydra: Small surface-to-air guided missile used by Coalition ground forces. Usually carried by Level 3 Engineer soldier class.

IAR: Integrated Aluminum Round. An armor piercing ballistic projectile manufactured by the Hellsing Company that can penetrate most forms of iron, steel, and concrete.

Ionosphere: The ionosphere starts at about 43-50 miles (70-80 km) high and continues for hundreds of miles (about 400 miles = 640 km). It contains many ions and free electrons (plasma). The ions are created when sunlight hits atoms and tears off some electrons. Auroras occur in the ionosphere.

KIA: Killed In Action.

Klick: Kilometer.

LAT's: Light Armored Transports. Fast moving troop carriers. Example: D9R-Armored Hovercraft (Alliance).

"Lima-lima": Pilot term meaning low level flight or "hugging the ground".

LZ: Landing Zone. An area cleared of obstacles to allow for the landing of aircraft.

M.P.A.A.C.: Military Press Advisory and Assistance Committee. Board composed of Alliance military leaders and personnel created to facilitate the proper dissemination of information to the members of the mass media.

MBT: Main Battle Tank. A heavily armed and armored treaded or hovering vehicle. Example: Centurion-1A Tank with reactive armor (Alliance).

Mesosphere: Characterized by temperatures that quickly decrease as height increases. The mesosphere extends from between 31 and 50 miles (17 to 80 kilometers) above Q-781's surface.

"Most ricky-tick": Slang used by ground troops meaning to "hurry up", "make it fast", or "run like hell".

38 MotherFucker: Slang name for the Marlin/Fulcrum-38 Heavy automatic. A .60 caliber mini-gun manufactured by the Marlin & Fulcrum Corporation that utilizes IAR's and has a fire rate of 2,000 rounds-per-minute with the fire suppressors disabled.

M.S.R.: Military Supply Route.

"One digit-midget": A phrase used among Alliance soldiers to describe a trooper who is down to less than ten days before being discharged from military duty and rotation home (see **SHORTTIMER**).

"Paint the grid": Phrase meaning to target an object or an area with a laser designator for an air or artillery strike.

Peepers: Slang name given to Terekian observation drones. These drones are small remote controlled camera platforms equipped with infrared sensors and are capable of flying long distances. The Coalition used these devices to locate Alliance ground forces and to observe their movements.

Playbook: Code Book.

Pyrogen frag: An incendiary grenade that emits extremely high temperatures when detonated.

Rapiers: NOVA-31 Interceptor. A single seat high-speed air/spacecraft designed by the Aerodyne/Genesis Corporation for the Alliance Planetary Strike Force. Its specifications and top speed are still classified by the military.

Rattleback: .30 caliber Terekian BOPPeR. Mobile mini-guns constructed with eight barrels that spin at over four thousand rpm's and capable of expending over 20,000 rounds per minute.

"Redlegs": Term used by Alliance soldiers that refers to artillery crews.

RPG: Rocket Propelled Grenade.

S&D: Search and Destroy.

Satchel charge: A high-explosive contained in a small pack that is detonated by remote control transmitter.

SAM: Surface to Air Missile.

SAR: Search And Rescue.

SAS: Surgical Air Strike.

Shock Trooper: Term used to reference Terekian and Alliance Special Forces soldiers.

Short Timer: A soldier in the Alliance whose tour (military service) is close to completion.

"Sin City": Nickname given by Alliance soldiers to the red light district of Emery Avenue in the city of New Sierra.

"Sit-Rep": Situation Report.

"Slick": Gunship adopted as a troop carrier for its capability to land on uneven terrain. Usually armed with a 7.62mm mini-gun and can be fitted with a Serpent RFCF90 Grenade Launching system.

Stratosphere: Characterized by a slight temperature increase with altitude and the absence of clouds. The stratosphere extends between 11 and 31 miles (17 to 50 kilometers) above Q-781's surface. Q-781's ozone layer is located in the stratosphere. Ozone, a form of oxygen, is crucial to survival; this layer absorbs a lot of ultraviolet solar energy. Only the highest clouds (cirrus, cirrostratus, and cirrocumulus) are in the lower stratosphere.

Syterra: Third largest planet in the Bakkus solar system. Most noted for it's agricultural contibution for this star system. The largest colony on the planet is SC-A-12 (known as Syterra-12).

"Take their legs out": Phrase meaning to weaken the enemy's infantry or ground forces by diminishing their numbers.

Thermosphere: The thermosphere is a thermal classification of the atmosphere. In the thermosphere, temperature increases with altitude. The thermosphere includes the exosphere and part of the ionosphere.

Tour of Duty: The Alliance required forty-eight months of service from an individual when joining any branch of the military.

"Toe popper": An anti-personnel mine concealed in the ground. When detonated by pressure or motion sensor, its explosion sends over 15,000 steel darts flying in a 360-degree radius.

Treadhead: Slang term used to reference tank crews.

Tropopause: The boundary zone (or transition layer) between the troposphere and the stratosphere. The tropopause is characterized by little or no change in temperature altitude increases.

Troposphere: The lowest region in Q-781's (or any planet's) atmosphere. The troposphere goes from ground (or water) level up to about 11 miles (17 kilometers) high. The weather and clouds occur in the troposphere. In the troposphere, the temperature generally decreases as altitude increases.

Troll: Derogatory term used by Alliance troops to reference Terekian soldiers.

Viperhead: Slang term used to reference NOVA-31 pilots (see **GHOST RIDERS**).

Werewolf/Werewolves: Slang term used to reference Alliance Aggressor Force soldiers based on the ancient lore of lycanthrope. Since the training of Special Forces troops is so rigorous, these soldiers were given the characteristics by the other branches of service of the mythical beast to describe their skills as "predatory animals with supernatural powers".

WIA: Wounded In Action.

MILITARY PHONETIC ALPHABET
Reprinted from BULLSHEETS Issue 23441 Revised 3/28/2277

A: Alpha

B: Bravo

C: Charlie

D: Delta

E: Echo

F: Foxtrot

G: Gamma

H: Hotel

I: India

J: January

K: Kilo

L: Lima

M: Monsoon

N: November

O: Oscar

P: Pogo

Q: Quebec

R: Romeo

S: Sierra

T: Tango

U: Ulysses

V: Victor

W: Whiskey

X: X-Ray

Y: Yankee

Z: Zulu

Made in the USA
Lexington, KY
29 August 2011